Diamond Dust

Peter Lovesey

# Diamond Dust

SOHO
CRIME

First published in Great Britain in 2002 by Little, Brown and Company

Copyright © by Peter Lovesey, 2002

First published in the United States in 2002 by
Soho Press, Inc.
853 Broadway
New York, NY 10003

Library of Congress Cataloging-in-Publication Data
Lovesey, Peter.
Diamond dust / Peter Lovesey
p. cm.
ISBN 978-1-56947-322-1
eISBN 978-1-56947-798-4
1. Diamond, Peter (Fictitious character)—Fiction.
2. Police—England—Bath—Fiction.
3. Bath (England)—Fiction. I. Title.
PR6062.O86 D49   2002
823.'914—dc21    2002017567

Printed in the United States of America

10  9  8  7  6

# 1

THE PRISONER STARED at the jury as they filed in. Every one of them avoided eye contact.

The foreman was asked for the verdict and gave it.

A few stifled cries were heard.

Peter Diamond of Bath CID, watching from the back of the court, displayed no emotion, though he felt plenty. Unseen by anyone, his fists tightened, his pulses quickened and his throat warmed as if he'd taken a sip of brandy. This was a moment to savour.

"And is that the verdict of you all?"

"It is."

"But I'm innocent!" the man guilty of murder shouted, his hands outstretched in appeal. "I didn't do it. I was stitched up."

Yes, stitched up well and truly, Diamond thought, in a Pink Brothers shirt and a fine Italian suit that didn't fool the jury, thank God. Any minute now the lowlife inside those clothes will say something nakedly uncouth.

"Stitch-up!" a woman supporter screamed from the public gallery, and more voices took up the cry. The people up there began chanting and stamping their feet as if this was a wrestling match.

The judge slammed down his gavel and ordered the court to be cleared.

\* \* \*

Almost an hour after, the prisoner was back for sentencing, a short, swarthy man with eyes like burn holes in a bedsheet.

"Jacob Barry Carpenter, you have been found guilty of murder, a murder as callous as any it has been my misfortune to come across. If there was the slightest uncertainty in the minds of the jury, it will have been removed upon hearing your criminal record. You are a man of habitual violence, and you have acted in character once again, and this time you will not escape with a light sentence."

"You got the wrong man, for Jesus' sake."

"Be quiet. As you well know, the mandatory sentence for murder is life imprisonment, and that is the sentence of this court. As you are also aware, a life sentence has a discretionary element. It need not mean life in the literal sense. In your case—are you listening?—I recommend that it should. You are such a danger to the public that I cannot foresee a time when it will be safe to release you."

The man reverted to basics. "Arsehole! I was fitted up!"

"Take him down."

Shouting more abuse, Carpenter was bundled from view by the prison guards.

The judge thanked the jury and discharged them. The court rose.

Peter Diamond turned to leave. His pudgy face revealed no joy in the verdict, nor concern at the prisoner's outburst. A mature detective learns to conceal his feelings when a verdict is announced. But when his deputy, DI Keith Halliwell, said, "Are we going for a bevvy?" the suspicion of a smile appeared at the edge of his mouth.

"You bet."

The pub was just across the street from the Bristol Crown Court and some of the team would already be there, celebrating.

Daniel Houldsworth, the QC who had led for the Crown,

put a hand on Diamond's shoulder. "Pleased with the outcome, Superintendent?"

"It's the right one."

The lawyer made it clear he wanted to say more, so Diamond told Halliwell to go ahead. He would join the team shortly.

"I expected the abuse at the end and so did the judge," Houldsworth commented, as if he felt some of the gloss had been taken off the triumph. "They're a cancer, the Carpenters. They've run Bristol for too long." He went on in this vein for some time, until it became obvious he was fishing for larger compliments.

"Top result, anyway," Diamond said, and that seemed to do the trick. He shook hands with Houldsworth and a couple of junior lawyers and left the court. Funny how everyone wanted credit: barristers, solicitor, jury, and, no doubt, judge—when it was obvious the murder squad had done the job. With a shake of the head unseen by anyone else he made for the exit across the flagstoned corridor where the principals in another case waited nervously. He'd missed one round of drinks, and maybe another.

Thinking only how much he would savour that first cool gulp of bitter, he came down the Court steps into Small Street on a beeline for the Bar Oz. Stared up at the sallow February sun, the promise of brighter times ahead. Didn't glance at the small group in conversation on the pavement. Didn't even react when a woman's voice shrilled, "There he is, the shitbag." Simply reached the bottom step and started forward.

His sleeve was tugged from behind. He swung around and got a gob of spit full between the eyes. There was a blur of blond hair, a shout of "Sodding pig!" and the woman clawed her fingernails down the right side of his face from eye to neck. The nails ripped the skin, a searing, sudden pain. She was screaming, "Stinking filth. He done nothing. My Jake done nothing, and you know it."

The next strike would have got his eye if he hadn't grabbed the woman's wrist and swung her out of range. In this frenzied state she was a match for any middle-aged man and she lunged at him again, aiming a kick at his crotch. He jackknifed to save himself, caught his heel against the steps and tripped, falling heavily. He lay there trying to protect his groin, and instead got a vicious kicking in the kidneys.

No one stopped it. People outside the Guildhall stared across Small Street with glazed expressions and pretended they hadn't noticed. What do you do when a woman is assaulting a man twice her size?

What do you do if you're that man? Diamond struggled upright and tried to hobble away. Where were the police? Someone should have seen this coming after the rumpus inside the court.

Still she vented her hate on him, pummelling his back and screaming abuse. If he turned and swung a punch at her it was sod's law someone would get a photo and sell it to the papers. So he moved on stoically. Then, thank God, spotted a taxi and waved to the driver.

The cabbie stared at this man with a bleeding face and a screaming woman raining punches on his back and, not unreasonably, didn't want them in his vehicle. He shook his head and drove off.

Further up the street, a second taxi had been hailed by one of the junior barristers on the case.

Diamond charged towards it and shoved the lawyer aside. "Emergency," he said with as much authority as he had left.

His attacker had come after him and still had a hold on his coat. He elbowed her off and slammed the door. "Police. Foot down," he told the driver.

"Where to?"

"Out of here."

The woman and her friends were running beside the cab beating the windows.

The cabbie drove off fast towards Colston Avenue. "Friends of yours?"

"Leave it." He ran a finger over his smarting face and looked at the blood.

"Top cop, are you?"

"Not really."

"Got to be Jake Carpenter's bird, hasn't she, the blonde? Wasn't he on trial?"

He confirmed it with a murmur.

"Guilty, then?"

"As hell."

"She's marked you. You could do her for assault."

"No chance." He'd been onto a loser the moment she attacked. Really, he had only himself to blame, leaving the court unaccompanied like that. If he nicked her, she'd use it as a publicity stunt, a chance to go over the trial again. And her counsel would plead extenuating circumstances and she'd get off with a caution.

"So where shall I put you down?"

They were heading south, towards the river. He was in no shape now to join the celebration in the pub.

"Bath. I'm going home."

## 2

"YOU'LL TELL ME if it hurts, won't you?" Stephanie Diamond was dabbing her husband's scratched face with TCP. "Is that painful?"

Without thinking, he started to shake his head, and felt the full pressure of the swab. "Jee-eez!"

She drew it away. "Sorry, love."

"My fault." Mortified for being such a wimp, he said, "Iodine's the stuff that hurts. They always used that when I was a kid. Wicked. Why, I couldn't tell you."

Steph waited, swab in hand. She was still in her work clothes, a white jumper with a magnolia design on the front and a close-fitting black skirt. She moved closer again and rested her free hand on his shoulder. "These are deep. She must be a vicious woman."

"Just angry."

"She's marked you with all four fingernails. Do you think I should take a photo?"

"Whatever for?"

"Evidence."

He grinned. "Like when someone runs into the car, you mean?" Patiently, he explained that he wouldn't be charging the woman, and why.

Steph, with her strong sense of right and wrong, didn't appreciate the explanation. "She shouldn't get away with it."

He was basking in her concern, even though it had to be cooled. "She believed he was innocent. I expect he told her he was fitted up and she believed him."

"That doesn't excuse it."

"It means she acted out of genuine outrage, not just spite."

Steph sighed. "Well, the scratches are genuine enough. They're going to be on your face for some time. What are you going to tell people—that I did it?"

He smiled at the idea, and felt his cheek sting when the muscles stretched. "Would you rather I said it was one of my many mistresses?"

"Do you want a scar on the other cheek? I could match them up, no problem."

"Okay. I'll think of something better."

"I could mask it with a concealer stick if you like."

"A what?"

"Make-up."

"I don't think make-up would play too well at the nick."

Later the same evening, after supper, the rich aroma of beef casserole lingered. Diamond, in his favourite armchair, warmed by the cat at full stretch across his lap, was thinking life was improving. Then Steph asked, "What exactly did he do?"

"Who?"

"Jake Carpenter. All you've told me is that he's a well-known criminal."

"And he is."

"But you haven't said anything about the case."

"True." He made it obvious he didn't intend saying much.

"Is it as bad as that? You don't usually shield me from the facts."

"I'm not shielding you, Steph. I wouldn't do that."

"The well-bred English gent sparing his delicate wife the gory details?"

"Cobblers. I just didn't think you wanted to know."

"I do now." Her eyes were on the scratches again.

He yawned, and stroked Raffles under the chin while considering where to begin. "They're Bristol's Mafia—the Carpenters, Jake and his brothers Des and Danny. They live in luxury and make their money out of protection and pimping. They've all got form—done time inside. They're feared. Anyone standing up to them is dealt with, usually by one of their gorillas. But when we succeed in pinning things on any of the brothers they mysteriously get light sentences."

"You mean the law is bought off?"

"So it appears. It may not be cash passing hands, but it happens. This time was different. A mandatory life sentence if he was convicted."

"He'd murdered someone?"

"A call girl by the name of Maeve Smith. Irish. Seventeen years old. Pretty, dark-haired, and a big earner. Unwisely, young Maeve tried to transfer to another pimp, so Jake made an example of her. Two of his thugs took her to a tattooist and had her breasts and buttocks personalised with his initials."

"Beast."

"That's tame for the Carpenters. Girls who step out of line sometimes have acid thrown in their faces. This one was still a top earner, so they left her face alone. After the tattooing he slept with her several times. I suppose he found it a turn on seeing his initials on her."

"How could she, after what he'd done?"

"I didn't say she agreed to it."

Steph took in a sharp breath.

"In court, he claimed she was his girlfriend to support his case that he wouldn't want to hurt her. He failed to see that it gave him a stronger motive when she slipped the leash again."

"Was that why she was killed?"

"Yes, he considered her his property. Her naked body was

found in the Avon below the Suspension Bridge, but she was dead before she was thrown in the water. She'd been beaten about the face and head. Really beaten, I mean. The face was pulp, unrecognisable. The tattooed initials helped us link her to Carpenter, so the rat did himself no service when he ordered that punishment. And this time the forensic stuff led us straight to him. Traces of her blood and DNA material in his car boot and on one of his shoes."

"No doubt about it, then?"

"Not a jot."

Steph looked away, her face creased in sympathy for the young victim, and then her eyes turned back to Diamond. "This other woman—the one who scratched you—must be deluding herself. If she was at the trial and heard the evidence, she knows he slept with the girl. And she knows he's a sadist. How can she defend a brute like that?"

"You tell me."

"I'm saying, Peter—she's deluded. She's trying to convince herself you faked the evidence. She turned her anger on you."

He spread his hands, and the cat jumped off his lap, surprised by the movement. "Steph, I've no interest in what her motives are."

"Do you know who she is?"

"A minor player." He stretched and stood up, wanting to talk of other things. "Hasn't been around long."

"I still think she shouldn't get away with this."

He went over to her and touched her hair, letting a strand rest between finger and thumb. "Leave it, eh?"

"Now you've told me about it—"

Gently but with decision he interrupted. "There are more important things."

"Like?"

"Like let's have an early night."

She hesitated, needing first to shut out the horrors of his

work, then laughed and flicked her hair free. "Fancy your chances, Scarface?"

The taunt brought back the bittersweet agonies of nearly twenty years ago, being in love without being sure of her. They'd met in Hammersmith, when he was in uniform, doing a stint as community involvement officer, which meant lecturing groups on road safety and crime prevention. Much of it was with the very old or the very young. At that time Steph was not long out of her divorce and trying to forget it by being Brown Owl to a troop, or pack, or whatever it was called, of Brownies. Diamond turned up to do his talk and made a total balls of it because he couldn't take his eyes off Brown Owl. At the end he asked her out and she declined. Wouldn't even give him a phone number. So he put in an appearance next week with some leaflets he said he'd forgotten to hand out to the girls. Then made himself useful changing a fuse when the lights failed. Week after week, using flimsy excuses for being there, he let her know how committed he was. These days it might well be called harassment. By degrees, she softened. It was a curious, chaste courtship, with each move witnessed by small giggling girls in brown uniforms. The turning point was the summer camp, when he breezed in unexpectedly with Bradford and Bingley, two donkeys he'd borrowed from the Hammersmith desk sergeant, who'd set up a donkey sanctuary as a retirement venture. Bradford and Bingley gave rides for the next two days. From that moment the girls called Diamond the Donkey Man and convinced Steph he deserved to be an honorary member of the Brownies.

Brown Owl married the Donkey Man the following spring, and it was a strong, loving relationship still, thanks in no small part to Steph's calmness under stress. There had been desperately bad moments, like her miscarriage (she'd suffered three already with her first husband) and the hysterectomy that had followed. There were the plunges in Diamond's rollercoaster career: the board of inquiry, the resignation, the move to the poky basement flat in London, being sacked from Harrods, and the spell of unemployment. Steph had kept them going by being positive and finding a funny side to every experience.

But rollercoasters have their upsides, and the police had needed him back. He returned to his old job as murder man in Bath CID. Since then, life had been kinder—their own house in Weston, a playful cat called Raffles, good neighbours and a Chinese takeaway at the end of the street.

Upstairs, he poured two glasses of Rioja before getting into bed. Steph had been to Spain twenty-five years ago as a student and always remembered the wine. She would cheerfully have migrated to Spain or France. No chance hitched to a man like Diamond, with GB plates welded to his soul.

"When did you get this?" she asked. The Diamonds didn't have wine in store. When they bought a bottle, it was for immediate consumption.

"On the way back from Bristol."

"Nice surprise."

"Mm."

"There's the difference between you and me," she said. "I don't mind surprises."

"You're saying I do?"

"You hate them. That's why you're such a good detective. You take out the surprise element by thinking ahead, every angle."

"I wish it were true."

"Of course it's true."

"Yeah? How many times have I needed your help to second-guess a suspect? More than I can count." He held up his glass.

"Is this to anything special? Another villain off the streets?"

"No, this is to my pretty, wise and understanding wife. Cheers, Steph."

Accepting a compliment is one of the hardest things to

handle. She could have made some flippant response, but she didn't. Coming from her Peter, the awkward little speech was as near as he got to a love poem. She felt for his hand and held it, and they sipped their wine.

"Speaking of surprises," she said presently, "certain of your old colleagues know you're reaching a landmark this year."

"My fiftieth?" He stared at her in alarm. "How the hell did they find out?"

"You had your picture in the papers last summer when there was all the hoo-ha about the body in the vault."

"Oh, and the bloody press always give your age. 'Peter Diamond, forty-nine.' It doesn't take a genius to work out I'll be half a hundred this year." His eyes read her face. "They're not planning anything?"

"It was being whispered about. They asked me, and I did my best to cool it. I said you wouldn't appreciate a surprise party one bit."

"Dead right. Who was this?"

"I'm not at liberty to say."

"They've dropped the idea, I hope."

"I think so, but we may need to think of something ourselves."

"Like being away for the week?"

"Good thinking. I like it." Steph smiled. "You're way ahead of me. What do you have in mind—a cruise?"

He vibrated his lips. "I can't think of anything worse."

"A surprise party is worse."

"Christ, yes."

"Oh, come on. They only thought of it because they're fond of you, in spite of the hard times you gave them. They want to show you some affection."

"Who *are* these misguided people?"

"I promised not to say."

"They should know I get all the affection I want from you."

"Hint, hint?" She put aside her wineglass and turned to kiss him.

Still troubled by the thought of opening a door on a roomful of smiling faces, he curled his arm around her and returned the kiss in a perfunctory way. She wriggled closer and the second kiss was warmer and they got horizontal in the same movement.

"Well, now," Steph said as he pressed against her. "You're quite a surprise party yourself."

# 3

By morning the scratches on his face had darkened and were more obvious. He checked them in the car mirror on the way to work, in a line of traffic on the Upper Bristol Road. No sense in kidding himself people wouldn't notice. Nobody at the nick would be bold enough to ask how they'd got there, but he was damned sure the place would hum with gossip. His team would have noticed he hadn't turned up at the pub, of course. "I had to go to another scene," he'd tell them without saying that the other scene was his home.

He had this bullish reputation that shielded him from comments on his appearance, but inwardly he was more self-conscious than anyone realised. So he entered the nick by the back door, went straight upstairs to his office and closed the door. No one came in.

Just after eleven he was summoned upstairs to Georgina's lair. Georgina Dallymore, the Assistant Chief Constable, gave the scratches a look and may even have winced a little, but made no reference to them when she gestured to him to sit down. "So one of the Carpenters is off the streets now. Nice work, Peter."

"Don't know how long for."

"Yes, he's going to appeal. His solicitor said so on TV."

"Did he? I didn't watch the box last night."

"His friends outside the court made a lot of noise."

"Rentamob, ma'am."

Georgina picked up a pen and scrutinised it as if the writing on the side held some important message. "They're a dangerous family, Peter. I wish we had something major on the other two."

"Des and Danny? No chance," Diamond said. "They don't soil their hands."

"It's all contracted out, you mean?"

He nodded. "The only reason we got Jake was that he let this girl become a personal issue."

"He's not the smartest of the brothers, then?"

"Smart enough to live in a swish pad in its own grounds in Clifton—until yesterday."

She examined the pen again. "What will they do now? Regroup?"

"I expect so. Vice, or Drugs, have better tabs on the empire than I do." He sensed, as he spoke, that he was walking into something, and Georgina's eyes confirmed it.

"Right on," she said. "It's organised crime." She leaned forward a little and her eyes had a missionary gleam. "You'd be good at that—detecting it, I mean."

He reminded her guardedly, "I'm your murder man, ma'am."

"And a very effective one. But there are times, like now, when all we have on the books are the tough cases from years back that nobody ever got near to solving."

"Doesn't mean we give up on them." He didn't like the drift of this one bit.

"I'm thinking your skills might be better employed elsewhere, particularly as you know a lot more about the Carpenter family now."

Elsewhere? He looked away, out of the window, across the grey tiled roofs towards Lansdown. There was an awkward silence.

"You might need to work out of Bristol Central, but it's not like moving house. What is it—under an hour's drive from where you live?"

He waited a long time before saying, "Is this an order, ma'am?"

"It's about being flexible."

'Well, you're talking to the wrong man. I'm not flexible. Never have been. I'm focused."

Georgina's voice took on a harder note. "Focus on the Carpenters, then. Yes, it is an order—while nothing new comes up on the murder front. Liaise with Mike Solly and George Eldon. Get an oversight of the entire operation—drugs, prostitution, protection. Put a surveillance team together if you want. This is the time to strike, Peter. They've lost Jake, so they have to put their heads above ground."

"Have you finished?"

"Careful what you say," Georgina warned him.

"That's someone else's empire. Not mine."

"I've issued an order."

"You want me out of Bath—is that it?" The old demons raged in his head, savaging any good intentions that might have lingered there. He hadn't felt so angry since the day he'd faced another Assistant Chief Constable in this room and resigned from the Force.

"It's not personal. It's about effective management."

"Effective?" He threw the word back at her.

"I think you'd better get out."

"Piss off."

"How dare you!"

"I'm just summing up what you said to me. You've got no use for me here, so you want me to piss off to Bristol." He turned and walked.

Down in his own office, he stood shaking his head, getting a grip on his emotions. Organised crime had nothing to do with this, he believed. Georgina wanted him out. While he'd been tied up with the court case she'd been plotting his removal. Wrongly, she thought he couldn't take orders from a woman. She didn't understand that he didn't let *anybody* push him around. No doubt she planned to put some pussycat in his place. John Wigfull was out of hospital and supposed to be returning to work any time. Bloody Wigfull would fit in beautifully: the Open University graduate who did everything by the book, never raised his voice and kept his desk as tidy as a church altar. Yes, she'd love to upgrade Wigfull to head of the murder squad.

He spent the next hour with his door closed, looking at the paper mountain on his desk, the filing cabinets that wouldn't close and the stacks of paper on the floor. Was it admitting defeat to tidy up? Wasn't it better to leave everything as it was, just to demonstrate that he'd be back?

He didn't go to the canteen for his usual coffee. And they had the sense not to disturb him.

At lunchtime he got out of the place for a walk, not towards the Abbey Churchyard, where he sometimes went when life had dealt him a wicked hand, but round the back of the railway station, across Widcombe Bridge and along the bank of the Avon as far as Pulteney Bridge—as dull a stretch of river as any he knew. Whenever he told people where he lived, they said how lucky he was, but in truth he wasn't attracted to the postcard scenes of Bath. The stately buildings, the rich history, the setting among green hills didn't excite him. He would have been just as content to work in Bristol if he'd been posted there six years ago. But he hadn't. Stuffy old Bath was his patch. He was in tune with it now. That was why he resented Georgina's attempt to move him.

He picked up a "ploughman's" baguette—a contradiction, in his opinion—and a can of beer and sat on a bench in Parade Gardens. By now his rebellious thoughts were being toned down. He was starting to accept the inevitability of obeying orders. Georgina hadn't proposed a permanent move to Bristol Central. The best tactic was to let everyone know this was a short-term investigation. He'd make a point of calling in most days at Manvers Street and keeping track of what was going on there.

Still far from satisfied, he ambled back to the nick without any urgency. After all, nobody could expect him to drop everything and beetle off to Bristol the same day.

There was a sense of important things going on when he walked through the door.

"Mr. Diamond, there you are," the desk sergeant called across the room.

"Something up?"

"A shooting in Victoria Park. A woman is dead."

His spirits soared. Bad news for someone could be a lifeline for him. "Suicide?"

"Apparently not."

"So who's dealing with it?"

"DI Halliwell."

Keith Halliwell was his deputy, and well capable of sussing out the scene. "Even so, I think I'll take a look," he said as calmly as if a rainbow had appeared over the city. "Which part of the park?"

"Crescent Gardens. Down at the bottom, back of the Charlotte Street Car Park."

On his way through the building he thought about leaving a message for Georgina—just to rub in the fact that sudden deaths did occur in Bath—and then decided against it. First, he'd find out for himself what this shooting amounted to. It could be one of those incidents that get cleared up the same day.

Please God, no.

The Royal Victoria Park, on sloping ground to the west of the city, is in effect two parks, one rather gracious, with lawns descending to a wooded area providing the Royal Crescent with its leafy view; and the other, larger and containing the Botanic

Gardens, a fishpond and a children's playground overlooking the gasworks. They are bisected by Marlborough Buildings and its long gardens. The shooting had happened in the gracious part, near the bandstand on the south fringe of the park below the Crescent.

They had sealed off the scene with police tape. The inevitable gawpers had gathered at the margin, but helpfully the trees screened the place from the car park.

The scene-of-crime lads—with at least one lass—in their white zipper overalls were already at work. Halliwell was standing with the constable guarding the access path. Spotting Diamond, he came over to meet him, rubbing his hands.

"We're back in business, guv."

"What do we know?"

"Middle-aged woman, shot twice in the head at close range. No sign of the weapon."

"Apart from two holes in her head."

Halliwell grinned. "Well, I guess that counts as a sign."

"Let's have a look, then."

Halliwell led the way to where the SOCOs were combing the ground for traces of the crime. The corpse was covered with a white plastic sheet.

"Who found her?" Diamond asked.

"A Mr. Warburton, walking his dog. About ten twenty this morning he heard the shots and came over."

"Did he see the killer?"

"No. Too far away. He was up the hill, not far from the Crescent. When he got here, there was just the woman lying dead."

"Other people must have heard it. Well into the morning. People are about. The car park would have been filling up."

"Yes, but he was the only one who bothered to check."

Diamond didn't question this. The common reaction to the sound of shooting isn't to go and investigate. Most people dismiss it as a car backfiring. If they know it's a gun they head in the opposite direction. He stood over the covered corpse. "What am I waiting for—someone to introduce us?"

Halliwell stooped and lifted the sheet from the head.

Diamond ran an experienced glance over the blanched face, one blood-red hole almost exactly in the centre of the forehead and another in front of the left ear. Then he stared. His skin prickled and his muscles went rigid as if volts were passing through them.

From deep in his throat came a sound more like a vomit than distress. He sank to his knees and snatched back the plastic sheet and looked at the woman's clothes. No question: she was wearing the black Burberry raincoat she'd bought from Jolly's last summer and the blue silk square he'd given her on her last birthday. He fingered a strand of her hair and it felt like straw. "It's Steph," he said, gagging on the words. "The bastards have shot my wife."

# 4

HALLIWELL WAS SPEAKING into his mobile. "We have a positive ID on the body in Crescent Gardens. Confirmed as Mrs. Stephanie Diamond, wife of Detective Superintendent Diamond. I repeat . . ."

Diamond remained on his knees beside his dead wife, registering nothing of what was going on around him. This was not self-pity. The focus of his grief was entirely on Steph, and her life so abruptly ended. Dry-eyed and blank-faced, he was weeping inwardly for her, for her compassion, her wisdom, her sense of humour, her integrity, her serenity, her mental strength, her brilliant insights. It had been almost a psychic gift, that ability of hers to draw his attention to hidden truths. With uncanny timing, she had reminded him only the night before how he hated surprises. Here was the worst surprise ever. He hadn't remotely imagined it could happen. Had she? Without the faintest idea of why she had come to this place, he wasn't going to make sense of it now, or in the next hour, or the next day. He knew only that Steph had been the one love of his life and she had been shot through the head at point-blank range. Too dreadful.

Halliwell put a hand on his shoulder and suggested he sat in the car for a bit.

He said from the depths of his grief, "Back off."

Wisely, Halliwell did.

The SOCOs continued their fingertip search of the area, less talkative now. Professionals working at murder scenes often insulate themselves from the horror with black humour that might offend anyone unused to what goes on. Diamond was quite a joker himself. *No sign of the weapon—apart from two holes in the head.* Trust him to make a crass remark like that. Since word had passed round that she was his own wife, the jesting had stopped.

The police photographers (a civilian couple) arrived and Halliwell explained the situation. "Hang on a minute, and I think he'll move away."

They waited five minutes.

"Can't you tell him we're here?" the woman said. "He knows the routine as well as anyone."

"He's not functioning as a cop at the moment."

"Who's in charge, then? You?"

"Technically, Mr. Diamond is, but . . ."

They looked across. Still the big man knelt, hunched beside his dead wife. "How long has he been there?"

"Ten, fifteen minutes. It's one hell of a shock."

"Was he the first officer on the scene, then?"

"No, I was."

"Didn't you warn him?"

Halliwell reddened. "I didn't recognise her. I should have, because I've met her a couple of times. I didn't look at her as you would a living person. Saw the injuries and shut myself off from the victim. Your mind is on what happened and what has to be done. Didn't dream it's someone I know."

"He's got to move away if we're going to get our pictures."

"All right, all right."

Halliwell went back to his boss and explained about the photographers. Diamond didn't take in one word of it. He was holding his dead wife's hand, cradling it between both of his.

Halliwell tried again. "They've got to get their pictures, guv."

Nothing.

"The photos of the scene."

He wasn't listening. The police and their procedures were part of another existence.

Halliwell turned away and went back to the photographers. "I can't shift him."

"Someone's going to have to."

"You can wait, can't you?"

The woman made a performance of looking at her watch. "We're self-employed, you know."

"Bollocks." Halliwell stepped away from them and took a call on his mobile.

It was Georgina, the ACC. "Is this true—about Mr. Diamond's wife?"

"I'm afraid so, ma'am. He's here at the scene."

"Dear God. I'd better come and speak to him."

"With respect, ma'am, I don't think he's fit to speak to anyone just now."

"Where is he exactly?"

"Kneeling beside his wife."

"Poor man . . . I don't think he has any other family, does he?"

"None that I've heard of."

"Close friends?"

"Outside the police? I wouldn't know."

"It's up to us to help him through, then."

Difficult. Halliwell doubted very much if Diamond wanted the ACC to help him through, but he'd told her already to stay away and he couldn't keep repeating it. He looked towards Diamond and saw him reach for the plastic covering and replace it over his wife's face. "I'm going over to him now, ma'am. He may be ready to leave."

Diamond stood up, paused for a moment more beside the body and then walked across to Halliwell. His eyes had the unfocused stare of the freshly bereaved, but he was able to find words now, and he made it clear that he wasn't thinking of leaving. "What have we found, then?" he asked in a flat voice.

"Not much so far, sir. It looks professional."

"You're searching for the bullets?"

"Of course."

"And the cases? If they used an automatic . . ." He lost track of the sentence for a moment, his voice breaking up. Then he managed to control it. "The weapon could still be around. Get some back-up. All this area has to be combed. Every yard of it."

"Right, sir. Can the photographers get their pictures now?"

"I'm not stopping them."

The hiatus was over. He was making a huge effort to show he was capable of carrying out the familiar routines. He checked that the police surgeon had been by to certify death, and Halliwell confirmed it.

"And the pathologist?"

"On his way, sir."

"Middleton, I suppose?"

"Sir." Halliwell found himself slipping in that "sir" far more than usual. Normally he was more relaxed with his old boss. "I'd just like to say—"

"No need," Diamond cut him short. "We understand each other. Take it as said."

The cover was removed entirely from the body for the photographs and video record. More sightseers had gathered behind the police tapes to watch. A violent death in broad daylight was a rare event in Bath. Stephanie Diamond was fully clothed, yet it still seemed offensive that she should be an object of ghoulish interest. Her husband knew if he told them to move on, more would take their places.

So the painstaking process continued. The body was on the grass to the rear of the old bandstand, obscured from Royal Avenue, the road that crossed the lawns below the Crescent. The Victorian shrubbery nearby fringed the car park and trapped the litter that blew across the open lawns. The search for traces of the killer would be a long job.

The forensic team arrived in their vans. While they were putting on their sterile overalls, Halliwell hurried across to warn them who the victim was. Diamond didn't want sympathy from anyone, but he could be spared the backchat that went with the job.

The next twenty minutes passed slowly and mostly in silence, with the white-suited figures clustered around the body.

Someone must have tipped off that old motormouth, Jim Middleton, the forensic pathologist, before he arrived—a merciful act. He said nothing. Just put out a hand and rested it briefly on Diamond's shoulder in a gesture of support. Then took the taped route to the corpse and studied the scene. Diamond followed.

"Has anyone touched her?" Middleton asked.

"The police surgeon," Diamond said. "And forensics. And me. She hasn't been moved."

Middleton crouched for a closer inspection. "Bullet wound to the frontal, almost dead centre. Very close range. You shouldn't be here, you know. You're too involved."

"I can handle it."

"I don't doubt you, old friend, but that isn't the point."

"This is the work of a hitman," Diamond said, ignoring the criticism.

"Do you know something?"

"I'm talking about the bullet wounds."

"Two, to be sure, you mean? I wouldn't read too much into that. They look very deliberate, measured almost, but that's speculation. Could equally be some crazy with a gun who happened to point the muzzle towards her and pull the trigger twice." Middleton crouched and peered closely at the powder burns around the neat hole the bullet had made in her forehead. "Are you sure you want to be here?"

Diamond didn't answer, but remained where he was.

Middleton took a small tape recorder from his briefcase and started describing the wounds. He lifted each eyelid, the beginning of a slow, methodical examination. He inserted a thermometer into a nostril and noted the temperature. Felt the arms and tested for rigor by moving one. Looked at the hands and fingernails. Loosened the clothes around the neck and searched for other signs of injury. Turned the body and studied one of the blood-encrusted exit wounds at the back of the head.

"Have they picked up the bullets?"

"Not yet."

"Buried in the ground, I dare say."

"We can use a metal detector."

The pathologist remained for over an hour before signalling to the waiting funeral director that he was ready to have the body removed to the hospital mortuary. Diamond stood back and watched his dead wife being lifted into a plastic zipper-case, and then into a plain fiberglass coffin, which was carried up the slope, through the crowd, loaded into a van and driven away.

With self-disgust he thought back to his first reaction to this, how he had been elated at the news of a shooting. And later joked about waiting to be introduced to the victim.

"Big shock," Middleton said to Diamond. "You want to go home now, take a Valium."

"There's work to do. You know as well as I do—the first twenty-four hours are crucial."

"Yes, but it shouldn't be you."

He didn't dignify the suggestion with a response. Instead, he walked over to Halliwell. "The bloke who found her—where is he?"

"Went off home, guv. He had the dog with him."

"That's no reason to leave."

"We took a short statement."

"A dog doesn't need to go home. Dog would stay in the park all day if it got the chance. Does he live nearby?"

"The Upper Bristol Road."

"Which end?"

"This end, I think."

"Get him here fast. I want to speak to him."

He escorted Middleton to his car. "Anything else you noticed?"

The pathologist said, "What you don't find can be just as informative as what you do. Did you look at her hands?"

"I held them."

"No damage. No sign that she put up a fight. When someone holds a gun to your head, you try and push it away. You fight for your life. This was quick, Peter. She didn't know much about it." He opened the car door and got in. "I wouldn't expect too much from the post mortem."

Diamond watched him drive off.

Some time after, a constable approached him with a tall, thin man in tow. "Sir, this is Mr. Warburton, the gentleman who found the, em . . ." His voice trailed off.

Warburton, in his thirties, had a down-at-heel look, lank, dishevelled hair, his hands deep in the pockets of a black over-coat that was coming apart at the shoulder seam. The shock of the morning's discovery may have left him looking troubled, or it may have been his stock expression. He swayed a little.

"You've been drinking?" Diamond said.

"A wee drop," Warburton answered. "It helps me some-times. I got the shakes."

"You found the body, I believe?"

"Heard the shots, didn't I?" He flapped his hand in the general direction of the Royal Crescent. "I was right up there with my dog, causing no trouble, and I heard it go off and came down here."

"What time?"

"Couldn't tell you."

"We logged the call at ten twenty or thereabouts. See anything?"

"No."

"Are you sure? How long after the shots did you get here?"

"Dunno."

"Two minutes? Five? Ten?" As he said it, he knew he wouldn't get a precise estimate. The man was three-quarters slewed.

"Thought it was someone taking a pot at a rabbit."

"Here?"

"I've seen them."

"Why bother at all, then, if you thought it was someone after rabbits?"

"Followed my dog, didn't I?"

"Was nobody else about?"

"Not that I saw."

"Had you been drinking?"

"Might have. Don't remember." Pure bad luck that the only witness happened to be a wino.

"So what happened?"

"Like I said, I followed my dog. He found her first. He's a lurcher. Kind of stood over her waiting for me to get there. I thought it might be one of my mates, fallen asleep. Then I see the bullet holes."

"What then?"

"Scared me, it did. I looked around for help and there wasn't none."

"Did you hear anything? Movements in the bushes? The sound of anyone running off?"

Warburton shook his head. "I belted down to the car park and there was a geezer just drove in. He had a mobile and I asked him to call the Old Bill."

"Was anyone else in the car park? Anyone leaving?"

"Give us a break, mate. I was so shit-scared I wouldn't have noticed me own mother walk by."

"And I suppose they told you to wait here and not touch anything."

"If you know it all, why ask me?"

"And pretty soon the first police car drove up?"

"And found little old me holding the fort."

"You didn't find anything near the body?"

"Like what?"

"Like money, for instance? A handbag?"

"Here, what do you take me for? That's a fucking insult considering I did my public duty."

"If anyone did take anything from the scene, they're in trouble. It's a serious offence."

"Don't look at me. I did nothing wrong."

Diamond was inclined to believe him. "Don't drink any more. That's an order. I may want to speak to you again."

He found Keith Halliwell and told him to remain at the scene. "I'm leaving you in charge. I want to check on certain pieces of lowlife and their movements earlier today."

"Shall I do that?" Halliwell offered.

"You find the bloody bullets. And look for spent cartridges as well."

He made the mistake of returning to Bath Police Station to begin his check on the Carpenters. Georgina walked into his office before he'd picked up a phone. She must have asked the desk to alert her the moment he returned.

"Peter, we're all devastated. I can't begin . . ."

He nodded. "I'll cope . . . thanks."

"We'll get them—whoever did this. I promise you that. I've put Curtis McGarvie in charge."

His tone changed sharply. "You what?"

"DCI McGarvie, from Headquarters. A good man."

"It's my case."

Georgina hesitated. "Peter, there's no way—"

"My wife. My case."

"That's the point. You're personally involved. If you took this on—as I'm sure you could—we'd lay ourselves open to prejudice, a personal vendetta. If it came to court, prosecuting counsel would cut us to ribbons."

Diamond shook his head. "I have the right—"

This time Georgina interrupted him. "You don't. I'm sorry. This is hard for you to take, but you don't have the right. You know perfectly well that someone else has to handle this. Curtis is already on his way to Victoria Park."

"He's too bloody late."

"What?"

"She's been moved." His brain churned out a compromise. "Look, I don't mind working with McGarvie, if that's what you want. A joint investigation. As far as the CPS is concerned, it can be his case."

"Absolutely not. You're staying right out of it. You're a witness."

"To what? I saw nothing."

"Be serious, Peter. This looks like a contract killing. The first line of enquiry has to be your enemies in the criminal world. He's going to want a list of everyone you put away, every villain you crossed since you came here."

Your evidence is going to lead us to the killer, and the people behind the killer if—as I suspect—they hired a hitman. You can't be the investigating officer and chief prosecution witness as well."

The truth of that got through to him, but it still denied him what every sinew in his body was straining to begin: the pursuit of Steph's killers. "What am I supposed to do? Take a holiday?"

"You'll be involved, providing information. Oh, of course you should take time off to get over the shock."

"What—sit at home with my feet up, surrounded by memories of Steph? That isn't any use to you or me. I want a part of the action."

"If you'd like counselling . . ."

"Don't push me, ma'am."

"I mean it. You've got to rebuild your life. We have trained people we can call on. Why refuse?"

"Because I sort out my own sodding problems, thanks very much. I don't want time off and I don't want to see a counsellor."

"When you have a chance to reflect, you may see the sense of it."

"I think not."

"Well, I'm going to insist you take a couple of days at least. You can forget our conversation this morning."

He had forgotten it already.

"About organised crime," she reminded him, "and going to Bristol. You'll need to be here when Curtis wants you for interviews. And, anyway, you can't investigate the Carpenters."

"Why not? Have they become a protected species?"

"It would prejudice the case—if they're behind this ghastly crime."

"So I'm sidelined."

"I wouldn't put it that way. Take it day by day. I've asked you to take some time off. You'll need it, believe me. And in the meantime, let's hope for quick results from Curtis McGarvie."

"That's it, then?"

Georgina nodded.

When he'd almost left the room, Georgina said, "Peter."

He swung around. "Mm?"

"Don't defy me."

# 5

PEOPLE IN SHOCK are liable to come out with extreme statements. Steph's sister, when Diamond phoned her with the news, said, "I knew something like this would happen. I told her she was making the biggest mistake of her life marrying a policeman. She wouldn't listen."

"Are you saying it's my fault she was killed?"

"Well, it wouldn't have happened if you'd been a schoolteacher."

With an effort he restricted himself to, "Maybe we should talk again when you're over the shock."

"She was my sister and I'd say it again." Then she softened enough to ask, "How will you manage? Do you want us to come down?"

Like the plague. "No need."

"We'll have to come anyway for the funeral. When is it?"

"She only died this morning."

"So you don't have it arranged?"

"No."

"You'll tell us the minute it's fixed?"

"I'll be in touch."

The prospect of a funeral hadn't fully entered his mind until now. Steph's *funeral,* for pity's sake.

Unreal.

He spent the next hour making more calls to family and friends, and there were repeated offers of help.

Genuine offers, too. Steph had been held in high regard—no, *loved* was the word. Her friends wanted to rally round for her sake. He was under no illusion that they had any strong affection for him. Politely he turned down all the offers, saying he would cope.

Then he called the nick and asked Halliwell what had been happening.

"We found two bullets, guv. Used a metal detector, like you said. They've been taken away by forensics. One of them is in fair shape. The other was a bit flattened, as if something drove over it."

"Christ. How about cartridges?"

"No. I suppose a revolver was used."

"We shouldn't suppose anything yet. You probably heard I'm off the case."

A tactful pause. "Yes, guv. DCI McGarvie has taken over."

"He knows about the Carpenters, I hope?"

"Everything. I'm sure of that."

"Not quite everything. After the case ended, I had some aggro from a woman outside the law courts. She was screaming about me sending down her Jake, so I guess she was the girl-friend."

"You think she could have done this?"

"I don't know, but McGarvie ought to be told. She was hyper."

"I'll tell him."

"And make sure he checks the Carpenter brothers—where they were this morning."

"That's in hand, guv."

"Right. You'll keep me in the picture, Keith." It was more of an order than a request.

He put down the phone, and this time left it down. The urge to keep talking to people, shutting out the silence in the house, was strong. But the pain had to be faced. A number of times in his career he'd knocked on someone's door to tell them a loved one had been killed—the duty every cop dreads. He thought he'd understood something of the way those people had felt. How wide of the mark he was. You lose your grip on reality.

He was an alien in a spacesuit exploring Planet Earth. All his senses were blunted. He looked out through a glass visor. He heard things only when he made huge efforts to listen.

Georgina had been right to take him off the case. He admitted it now. He was in no state to investigate anything. The incentive was there, but he wasn't capable of making himself a cup of tea, let alone running a murder inquiry.

He sat at the kitchen table with his hands propping up his chin, and stared at the chair where Steph sat in the mornings. The *Guardian* was still there, folded to the crossword page, most of the squares completed in her neat lettering. Beside it, the mail she'd received that morning, a couple of junk items she hadn't bothered to open and a postcard from one of her ex-Brownies, on holiday abroad. She'd kept in touch with many of those little girls of years ago, encouraging them, taking real pride in their successes at school and university. He'd been to more weddings and christenings with Steph than he could remember now.

Those ex-Brownies would see on the TV news that she'd been murdered. For Steph's sake, he thought suddenly, he ought to warn them all. They were family to her. Her kids—and his. Somewhere she kept her own address book. He got up and started opening drawers. She had always kept her things organised, and he soon found it with the stationery. What a task, though. The A's alone ran to three pages.

This was what she would have wanted, so he made a start. Even if he didn't get through, he'd give it his best shot.

It was hard, hearing the shock in their voices, and harder listening to the loving things they said about her. Some were former Brownies, some friends she'd made through her work in the charity shops, others she'd kept up with since long before he knew her. So many—and so much love. After some time, he poured himself a brandy, then started another page.

Almost hidden among the "D's he found the number for Steph's first husband, Edward Dixon-Bligh. Was it worth calling that tosspot? he wondered. He doubted if Dixon-Bligh and Steph had spoken since the divorce. The man had been an officer in the RAF Catering Branch (Diamond had dubbed him the Frying Officer) who had let her down badly at the time when she'd most needed help, after three miscarriages. The last they'd heard, he had swapped his commission for a Michelin star and was managing a restaurant in Guildford, Surrey, with a partner almost half his age. Still, he had a right to be told.

Waiting with the phone pressed to his ear, he recalled something Steph had once told him about her ex-husband that seemed to sum the man up. They had once rented a beach hut on the south coast and after the rental expired he'd kept a key. He'd go down to the beach for years after and if no one was using the hut he'd open it and brew some tea and sit there all afternoon, an overgrown cuckoo in the nest.

It turned out that he was no longer at the private number they had in the book. He'd moved into central London. That seemed a good enough excuse to forget him, but out of loyalty to Steph he tried directory enquiries. He was glad of the chance to leave an answer-phone message.

He abandoned this phone marathon when the people he called started telling him they'd heard already on the evening news. Outside, it was dark and he was only up to the "G's. He drew the curtains.

What would Steph have wanted next? It was weird, but he almost heard her say in her calm voice, "Tidy my things, Pete." She would hate to leave disorder. Against all logic he went upstairs and emptied the basket where she put her clothes for washing. Picked her nightdress off the pillow and for a moment held it against his face and got a faint smell of her and said, "Oh, Steph." Brought the clothes down and loaded the machine. Went back upstairs and stripped the bed. Tightened the lid on a pot of foundation cream she'd left on her dressing table.

He said in a whisper, "Is that better?" and then shook his head at his own stupidity.

He heard a car draw up outside and someone coming to the door, so he went downstairs and opened it.

A camera flashed.

The press.

He said to the woman on his doorstep, "Shove off, will you. Leave me alone. There's no comment. There won't be any comment." And slammed the door.

The phone rang.

He snatched it up, ready to give them a blasting.

"Curtis McGarvie here."

"Oh."

"First, I want to tell you how sorry I am."

"Thanks."

"And any number of people asked me to pass on their sympathy and support. Everyone is gutted. You can be sure we won't rest until we've caught this jerk. Do you mind if I talk about it?"

"Feel free."

"The bullets are with forensics. They'll check them against their database and tell us the class of weapon. I've asked them to give it top priority. Some kind of handgun was used, obviously, and I'm assuming it was a revolver."

"Why?"

"There'd have been cartridges lying around if a self-loading pistol was used."

"Not if the killer was careful."

"Picked up the cartridges, you mean?" McGarvie was silent, absorbing the point. "Well, there weren't any, I promise you."

"The striker pin marks the cartridge differently with each gun," Diamond said with the confidence of the weapons training he did in his time with the Met. "Important to ballistics. A professional would know that. He might well decide not to leave them there to be found. I think we should keep an open mind about the weapon."

"I intend to," McGarvie said, stressing the first word. "Otherwise not much came up in the search. Do you know if your wife normally carried a bag of some kind?"

A bag? He meant a handbag. Of course she carried a handbag. "Black leather, quite large, with a shoulder strap and zip. Didn't you find it?"

"Nothing so far. Maybe you could look around the house and see if it's gone for certain."

"I'll do it now."

"No rush."

"I said I'll do it now."

"Okay. And I'd like to come to your place tomorrow and talk to you."

"I'll come to the nick."

"No, I'd prefer to visit your home, if you don't mind. That way, I'll get a better sense of your wife."

He would have done the same. "All right."

"Is nine too early? If you can find a recent photo, we'll need to appeal for witnesses. Have you been bothered by the press at all?"

"Told them to bugger off."

"If it happens again, tell them we're calling a press conference for midday tomorrow. Should get them off your back."

"Thanks. Do you want me there?"

"No need at this stage. Is anyone with you? Friends or family?"

"I'm alone."

"Would you like——?"

"It's my choice."

He searched for that handbag without any confidence that it would turn up. Steph always took it with her if she went out. Just as he expected, it wasn't in the house, which raised a question. If the killer had picked it up, what was his reason?

Would a hitman walk off with his victim's handbag after firing the fatal shot? Unlikely.

It raised the possibility that the hitman theory was wrong and that Steph had been shot by a thief.

He stood in the living room with head bowed, hands pressed to his face, pondering that one. Had she been killed for a few pounds and some credit cards? That would be even more cruel.

He called the nick and left a message for McGarvie that the bag was not in the house.

During the evening he answered the door twice more to reporters, and told them about McGarvie's press conference. And the phone rang intermittently. The word "condolences" kept coming up. And "tragic." And "bereavement." Death has its own jargon.

But he was pleased to get a call from Julie Hargreaves, his former deputy in the Bath murder team—the best he'd ever had. Julie always knew exactly what was going through his mind.

When she'd expressed her sympathy Julie said, "Let Curtis McGarvie take this on, whatever your heart tells you. He's well up to the job."

"Have you worked with him?"

"Yes, and he's good without making a big deal out of it."

"Better than me?"

"For this case—yes. You want a result. If you handled it yourself, you'd get one, I'm sure—only for the CPS to throw it out because you're too involved."

"I've been told that already."

"But your heart won't accept what your head tells you. You

can still play an active part by telling Curtis everything you know."

"It isn't the same, Julie. I want to roll up my sleeves, make decisions."

"Why don't you put your energy into giving Steph the kind of send-off she deserves? A lot of people will expect it, you know. She had so many friends."

"That's for sure." He paused, letting her comment sink in. 'What exactly are you suggesting?"

"Would she have wanted a church funeral?"

"She was a believer."

"Then I really think you should arrange it at the Abbey."

"The *Abbey*?"

"Do your public servant number on the Dean, or whoever decides these things. But insist on having the service the way Steph would have wished."

"Which is . . . ?"

She caught her breath, as if surprised she had to spell it out. "The music she liked. Whoever takes the service should be someone who knew her personally. One or two of her family or closest friends should do readings. You, if you can face it."

"I'd feel a hypocrite. I'm an agnostic if I'm anything, Julie."

"It doesn't have to be out of the Bible. Well, to be honest, I wasn't thinking of you. But you could speak about her if you felt up to it."

"I don't think so."

"You're confident in front of people."

"Barking out orders to a bunch of coppers, maybe, but not this."

"Okay, if you want, you could write something about her life and include it with the Order of Service. Then when it's over, you invite people to lunch, or tea, or whatever, at some local hostelry."

He took all this in before saying, "You're right, Julie. This is what I should be doing. I'll see to it as soon as the coroner releases..." He didn't complete the sentence.

"One more thing, if I can be really personal," Julie said.

"What's that?"

"I can only say this because we worked together so long. You're tougher with people than anyone I know, but not so tough as you are on yourself. It wouldn't be the end of civilisation as we know it if, when you're alone, you shed a few tears—for Steph, and for yourself."

At the low point of the night, before dawn, he remembered, and wept for the first time in over forty years.

# 6

HE NICKED ONE of the scratches shaving and it bled on his shirt—too little concentration after too little sleep. He'd finally flopped onto the sofa and drifted off for about two hours—only to be roused by the *Guardian* being shoved through the door. Then he was forced to accept the unthinkable over again.

"You look rough," McGarvie told him unnecessarily.

"So do you."

Actually McGarvie was one of those people who always look rough—no bad thing in CID work. Still in his early forties, he was marked by too many late nights and too many whiskies. Undernourished, pock-marked, with bags under his eyes, he had a voice like the third day of a Godawful cold.

He'd brought Mike James with him, a newish, far-from-comfortable DC, whom Diamond himself had plucked from the uniformed ranks.

Diamond offered coffee and admitted, when asked, that he hadn't eaten breakfast. He chose not to reveal that he hadn't been able to face food since yesterday.

"So where are we on this?" he asked while they stood in the kitchen watching the kettle. "What have we got?"

McGarvie hesitated. That "we" obviously troubled him. "I've got a hundred and twenty officers on this. Fingertip search. Door-to-door in all the streets nearby. Incident room up and running."

"What I meant is what have we learned?"

"Forensics take their time. You appreciate that."

"But you do know certain things—what time she was shot. Ten twenty."

"If we're to believe the guy who found her."

"She was at home in Lower Weston when I left at eight fifteen."

"That was one thing I was going to ask."

"And the Carpenters?" Diamond pressed him.

"Des and Danny appear to be watertight for yesterday morning."

He shook his head. "Surprise me."

"Des was motoring back from Essex and has a credit card voucher for fuel placing him on the M4 at Reading Services at ten thirty."

"I'd check the forecourt video if I were you."

"It's in hand."

After spooning instant coffee into two mugs Diamond moistened the granules with a dash of milk from a bottle that must have been on the table since yesterday. "You like it white?"

McGarvie frowned at the lumpen mess. "Sure."

Mike James just nodded. He was so ill at ease in the home of his bereaved boss he would have drunk the cat's water if it were handed to him.

"And the other one? Danny?"

"At the gym in Bristol for an hour until ten, signed in, signed out, and vouched for by the staff there, and afterwards went to his solicitor in Clifton."

"Who of course recorded precisely when he arrived and left? They really wrapped this up."

"You think they used a hitman?"

"Don't you?"

McGarvie left the question hanging. Diamond poured hot water into the mugs and handed them over.

Curds and black granules rose to the surface. McGarvie picked up the spoon and stirred his. They carried them through to the living room. The curtains hadn't been pulled.

"DI Halliwell was telling me about this woman who attacked you after the trial," McGarvie said. "Had you seen her before?"

"Just a faint memory of her sitting in the public gallery. She must have been one of the crowd who screamed at the judge."

"But you didn't come across her when you worked on the case?"

"No. It's possible some of the team did. I didn't do all the legwork myself. Do we know who she is?"

"Not yet."

"Blonde, shoulder-length hair. Tallish. Five-seven, five-eight. Probably under thirty. Long fingernails."

"I can see."

Diamond put his hand to his face. The scratches were still there, though the incident seemed like a century ago. "She was in some kind of trouser suit. Black or dark blue."

"Did you see who she was with?"

He shook his head. "Some of the Carpenter mob. Heard them shouting. I was avoiding eye contact at the time."

"I wonder if anyone got it on video. There must have been camera crews around."

"Didn't notice any."

"Let's get back to your wife."

"Wish I could."

McGarvie glanced at Diamond, who gave a sharp sigh, more angry than self-pitying.

"Sorry. Go on."

"This has to be asked. Can you think of anyone with a grudge against her?"

He shook his head. "Steph didn't make enemies. I never knew anyone who disliked her."

"The opposite, then. Someone who fancied her?"

The idea caught him off-balance. "A stalker?"

"It happens. Had she mentioned anyone giving her the eye in recent weeks?"

"No." This line of enquiry was a waste of time in his opinion. "I've got to face it—she was murdered for no better reason than being married to me."

"I'm trying to keep an open mind. How did she spend her time?"

"She's always done charity work, serving in the Oxfam shop and Save the Children at one time, organising the rota, running the stall at this or that event."

"Was that where she was going yesterday?"

"What day was it? I have to think. I've lost track."

"Tuesday."

He shut his eyes to get his brain working. "Tuesday was the morning she kept clear for shopping and so on."

"She didn't tell you what she was planning?"

"She would if it was out of the ordinary. I guess it was going to be the same as any other Tuesday."

"If she'd arranged to meet someone, she'd tell you?"

"Always."

"Did she write it down anywhere? A calendar? An appointments book?"

"Diary."

McGarvie's eyebrows arched hopefully.

"In her handbag," Diamond added. "Did you find it?"

"No."

"It's not here. I can tell you that. She always had it with her if she went out. I was thinking last night it's strange the bag was taken—unless someone else came along after she was . . ."

"Possible," McGarvie agreed.

They both reflected on that for a moment before Diamond said, "I don't think a hitman would take it."

"Probably not."

"And I can't believe she was mugged."

"Why not?"

"Shot dead—for a handbag?"

"You don't want to believe it," said McGarvie, "and I can understand why. But there are yobbos out there who hold life as cheaply as that. We can't discount it. Why was she in the park? Was it a place where she liked to walk?"

"No."

"You mean not at all?"

"That's what I said."

"Never went there?"

"Hardly ever. And she didn't go for walks on Tuesdays. She was always too busy catching up with herself. It was her day for jobs, shopping, some cooking sometimes, housework."

"Was there a phone call?"

"Before I left, you mean? No."

"Could she have made one?"

"Not to my knowledge. You'd better check with BT."

"It's in hand," McGarvie said. He seemed to be doing the right things. "Did she carry a mobile?"

"Do we strike you as the sort of couple who carry mobiles?"

"In other words, no."

"Are you thinking she was lured to the park?" Diamond said.

"Possibly. Or driven there. Met the killer somewhere else." He glanced around the room. "He could have come here."

"I don't think so."

"We can't be sure."

"She's not going to invite a stranger in. She knew better than that. And you're wrong about being driven there. Steph wouldn't get into a car."

"Unless she was forced."

"She'd have put up a fight."

"There are no signs of it."

This was true, he knew. He remembered holding her cold,

limp hands. And the pathologists's remark about the state of them. "Is Middleton doing the PM?"

"Eleven thirty."

He closed his eyes and was silent for a moment. "Who's going to be there?"

McGarvie steered the conversation away. "You said she had no enemies, so let's talk about yours."

"Waste of time."

"Why?"

"Come on. This has the Carpenters written all over it."

"In my shoes, you wouldn't say that. You know the danger of going for the obvious. No disrespect, Peter, but you've roughed up more villains than just the Carpenters."

"Ancient history."

McGarvie drew a long breath to contain his patience. "Don't you think you owe it to her to help me?"

The tactic worked. Diamond dropped his opposition. "Villains with old scores to settle? Here, you mean? In Bath?"

"Let's start here, any road. I remember the case that made your name here, the body in Chew Valley Lake, but that wasn't your first."

He nodded. "There were five before that, three domestic, the others drugs-related. Far as I know, all of the killers are banged up."

"The kid who murdered Mrs. Jackman?"

"Bore me no grudge."

"The con who escaped from Albany?"

"Back inside."

McGarvie displayed a more than superficial knowledge of Diamond's career as he went through the principal investigations of recent years. He must have studied the files overnight. You couldn't fault the man's thoroughness. But as Diamond had warned at the outset, nothing useful came out of it. The killers he'd put away had been mainly loners, not one of them connected with organised crime in the way the Carpenters were.

"What about your private life?"

"My what?"

"People you know outside the job."

"You're thinking I pick fights with the neighbours? I haven't got the energy. I pay my bills on time—well, Steph does. Call at the pub for a quiet pint once in a while, and I mean quiet. They don't know who I am. Come home, feed the cat, mow the lawn—the daily grind."

On cue, Raffles came around the door, sized up the visitors, decided DC James was the softer touch and began pressing his side against the young man's shins. James tried to ignore it.

"Forgive me—I have to ask this," McGarvie said. "Your marriage. Was it going well?"

Diamond said with a slight break in his voice, "It was all right."

"No possibility that she—"

"None."

For a while the only sound was the cat's purring as it continued to lean against James's trousers.

Finally McGarvie said, "I have this major problem with the Carpenter theory. If it's a contract killing, as we suppose, why did they target your wife? *You* should have been the mark. You, or some witness, or the lawyers, or the judge. Not your wife. You and I know what these scum are like. If they take revenge it's not at one remove."

Diamond shrugged. He couldn't understand it either, and he had nothing to contribute.

"Can I feed him?" DC James asked.

"What?"

"The cat. He's hungry."

Diamond hadn't even noticed. "If you like. The tins are in the kitchen. Shelf over the cupboard."

When the two older men were alone, McGarvie once again

raised the possibility that Steph had a secret life Diamond had not been aware of. "We work long hours, get home tired. It's not surprising if our women don't always tell us everything that happened." Seeing Diamond's expression, he spread his hand and held it up. "Don't get me wrong. I'm not suggesting she had a relationship. Just the possibility that she got into something she didn't want you to know about, something slightly dodgy that got out of control."

Diamond glared. "Such as?"

"I don't know. I'm guessing. What do middle-aged women get up to? Gambling?"

"Not Steph."

"She didn't owe money to anyone?"

"Forget it. She wouldn't borrow a penny."

"I suppose she didn't do drugs?"

"This is bloody offensive."

"Would you mind if we searched her bedroom?"

"Christ—what for?"

"Peter, I haven't the faintest idea what might turn up, but it needs to be done."

"Now?"

"It's as good a time as any."

He stared out of the window. "I'd tell you if there was anything."

"But have you been through her things?"

Of course he hadn't. That would be a breach of trust. They'd always respected each other's privacy. He was damned sure Steph had nothing to hide from him.

Being brutally honest with himself, if he were investigating some other woman's murder, he'd insist on a proper search, just as McGarvie was doing. You don't rely on the husband to tell you everything.

"Come on, then."

He led McGarvie upstairs.

Their bedroom was ready for inspection, the bed made,

clothes put away, though that hadn't been his purpose when he tidied up the day before.

McGarvie started with the dressing table, removing the two drawers entirely and placing them on the bed. Steph's make-up, combs and brushes were in one, her bits of jewellery in the other. Apart from her wedding ring, which was on her finger when she died, she hadn't the desire to deck herself in what she called spangles and fandangles. Much of the stuff never saw the daylight and had been inherited from aunts and grandmothers. McGarvie opened every one of the little boxes and looked into the velvet bag containing the single string of pearls Diamond had bought her on their wedding day.

He asked which of the two chests was Steph's, and Diamond pointed to it. With the same thoroughness he pulled the top drawer completely out and felt among her underclothes, watched sullenly by Diamond. At the back of the second drawer was a shoebox full of letters. "Do you know what these are?"

Diamond went over to look. When he saw his own handwriting on one of the envelopes he grabbed the box with both hands. "You won't want this."

"How do you know?"

"They're from me, ages ago."

McGarvie held out his hands. "Sorry, but there may be other letters, more recent ones. I've got to go through the box."

"It's too bloody personal." He didn't hand it back.

Wisely McGarvie chose to let him mull that over, and continued with the search. That second drawer had evidently been Steph's storage place for photos, invoices, vouchers, visiting cards and newspaper cuttings. It would take a team of detectives to follow up every lead. "I'll have to take all this away . . . as well," McGarvie said.

Diamond didn't commit himself. He doubted if there was a clue to the killer in there, but he didn't want to impede the investigation. "Why don't you look in the wardrobe?"

McGarvie was thorough. Every pocket of each coat, each pair of slacks, was searched, but he found no more than a few pence and some tissues. He looked on top of the wardrobe and beneath it and pulled the bed across the floor to see if anything was underneath.

"Bathroom?"

The search moved on. Mike James joined in and they went through each of the rooms.

On the landing, McGarvie glanced upwards. "What do you keep in the loft?"

"She never goes up there. Can't stand spiders."

They took his word for it, which was something. He had some police property up there, including a gun and ammunition. In his present state he didn't care a toss about being compromised. He just didn't want anything to deflect from the hunt for Steph's killer.

They took the search downstairs and still found nothing of interest. McGarvie looked at his watch. He didn't need to say he was thinking about getting to the postmortem. "Did she keep an address book?"

"Yes, but you can't take that away. I'm phoning people all the time."

"I'll have it photocopied. You'll get it back inside two hours, I guarantee."

Her whole life laid out, as if for inspection. With a sigh, he picked the book off the table by the phone.

McGarvie handed it to Mike James. "That's your job. Get it copied and back to Mr. Diamond directly." To Diamond he said, "Is it okay if I take that drawer from the bedroom?"

With reluctance, he gave in.

"And the box of letters? Trust me. I'll examine everything myself. Nothing will be passed around."

It was the best offer he would get. He knew the way things were done.

# 7

HE DESCENDED INTO limbo—or grief—drifting through the days without any sense of what else was happening in the world. He kept strange hours, often sleeping in snatches through the day and sitting up most of the night. Nothing seemed to matter. When friends called he told them he was all right and didn't want help. He rarely answered the phone and didn't open letters or look at the newspaper or listen to music or the radio.

It was a call from the coroner's office that ended this hiatus. All the forensic tests had been completed and the coroner was ready to release Steph's body for disposal. They needed to know which undertaker was in charge of the funeral arrangements.

Shocked out of his zombie state, he remembered his conversation with Julie Hargreaves about putting his energy into giving Steph the sort of send-off she would have wanted.

"What day is it?"

"Wednesday."

"The date, I mean."

"March the tenth."

*March?* More than two weeks had drifted by and he'd done nothing about it.

"I'll get back to you shortly."

He snatched up the Yellow Pages and looked under Funeral Directors. The process took over. The same afternoon,

clean-shaven and showered, wearing a suit, he went into
Bath, from the undertaker's to the Abbey to the Francis Hotel,
making decisions about black Daimlers and brass handles and
orders of service and bridge rolls and chicken wings. He was
functioning again.

# 8

AWKWARD AND TOTALLY out of his element he followed the coffin into Bath Abbey and up the main aisle. An
early plan to use one of the apsidal chapels had been abandoned
when it became clear how many wished to attend the service.
Three to four hundred were seated in the main Abbey Church.
The story of the shooting had featured for days in the national
press and on television and people who had known Steph from
years back had made the journey. The police alone numbered
over sixty, among them the Chief Constable and three of ACC
rank, as well as most of Bath CID and about twenty old colleagues from his years in the Met. The biggest contingent was
of friends Steph had made through her work in the charity
shops, customers as well as staff. There was her "family" of
Brownies grown into adult women. Then there were former
neighbours from the series of places he and Steph had occupied
in London and Bath.

The small family group of Steph's sister, Angela with her
husband, Mervyn, and Peter Diamond's own sister, Jean,
and her eccentric partner, Reggie, looked and felt humbled
by the scale of the affection represented here. None of them
had known of Steph's gift for making lasting friends of almost
everyone she met. Diamond knew of it, but even he hadn't
expected them to come in such numbers.

One of the few who hadn't bothered to respond was Edward

Dixon-Bligh, Steph's first husband. If he *was* in the congrega-
tion, Diamond wouldn't know. He'd seen photos, but never
met the man. In view of the unhappiness of that first marriage,
his absence would trouble nobody.

Julie's advice to make a fitting occasion of this had been
spot on, though in his heart of hearts Diamond wanted it over.
He'd taken leave of Steph already in those wrenching minutes
kneeling beside her damaged body in the park. The service in
the Abbey was for her because she had been a believer and for
everyone else who loved her and had faith that she was going
to a better place.

At odds with his agnostic leanings, he joined in the hymns
as well as he could and heard the address, the readings and the
prayers and wished peace and rest for her. And then followed
the coffin out again and was driven to the crematorium at
Haycombe for what the undertakers had termed the committal.

There, not for the first time in recent days, he had the
strange sensation that he was detached from what was going
on, with the power to switch off as if it were a TV programme.
Some roguish part of his brain was telling him it was all a
nightmare and he would go home and find her there. He had
to make an effort to concentrate.

All the illusions came to a stop when the curtains slid across.

Back to the Francis for the "light refreshments." The pitying
looks and well-meant words of consolation from her friends—
and his—rammed home the certainty that she had gone and
his life had altered immeasurably.

A few went so far as to ask what was happening about
catching the person responsible. He answered that he didn't
know. The case was out of his hands.

In truth, he did know. Things were happening, for sure.
There was an incident room. Appeals to the public. Over a
hundred officers at work. They knew what time the murder

had taken place and where, what calibre of gun had been used, what bullets. McGarvie's first reaction had been correct. The murder weapon was a revolver, a .38. But as for the killer, they were still at a loss.

"Are you back to work yet?"

"Tomorrow."

"Best thing, old man."

Next morning everyone at the nick went out of their way to be sympathetic. He had to run the gauntlet of goodwill before he could close his office door. He didn't count the number of times he was told it was nice to have him back. On his desk were bundles of letters that could only be messages of condolence. He shoved them to one side and leafed through the internal memos instead.

About ten thirty came a call from McGarvie, who had the sense to treat him like a fellow professional. "If you can spare a few minutes, I need your help."

"On the case?" He couldn't disguise his eagerness.

"Yes—but don't get me wrong. This doesn't put you on the team. I want your services as a witness, to take a look at a suspect."

"A line-up?"

"No. We've brought in a woman we think may be the one who scratched your face outside the law courts. You can look at her on camera, tell us if we're right."

"You think she could be the killer?"

"Did I say that?"

"You said she was a suspect."

"For the assault on you."

"That? I don't want anyone done for that," Diamond said at once. "I haven't laid a complaint."

"Hold on, hold on. It gave me a reason to pull her in," McGarvie explained. "I've no plan to press a charge."

"Ah." His brain wasn't sharp at all.

"We'll see what else comes out. If she's so passionate about the Carpenter verdict, she might say something helpful."

"I'm with you now."

"Say twenty minutes?"

His confidence in McGarvie was growing in spite of the lack of any obvious progress. He fetched a coffee from the machine at the cost of another "nice to see you back" from one of the civilian staff and took it to the observation room, where you could monitor interviews.

The woman was being questioned by McGarvie and a female detective in Interview Room C. Diamond had to watch the screen for a while before making up his mind. The last time he'd seen this woman she was practically foaming at the mouth. Now there was no discernible aggression. She was in control of herself, if not entirely at ease.

But definitely his attacker.

McGarvie was saying to her, "You don't deny you were in court?"

"That's no crime."

"What was your interest in the case?"

No response.

"You're a friend of Jake Carpenter's—is that right?"

"If you know it all, buster," she said with a flat, nasal twang more London than Bristol, "I don't know why you bother to ask me."

"I'm giving you the chance to explain what happened."

"Oh, sure."

"You were also seen outside the court demonstrating—if that's the word—about the verdict."

"It's a free country."

"So you don't deny you were one of the people shouting?"

She showed more interest. McGarvie was making headway, even if she insisted on ducking the last question. She flicked some blonde hair from her face and tilted her chin to a more challenging angle. Defiant, but sexy. Meticulously groomed and fashionably dressed in a black suit and wine-red polo. It was easy to see why Jake Carpenter had been attracted.

"Did you follow all of the trial?" McGarvie asked. "Did you hear all the evidence?"

"Evidence? I call it a stitch-up."

"So I'm told. Were you there right through?"

"Not every day. I couldn't stomach it: watching a fine man brought down."

In the observation room, Diamond said, "I feel like throwing up."

McGarvie pressed on. "What's the truth of it, then, in your opinion? The poor woman was violently murdered. Her face was raw meat when they took her out of the river. You wouldn't argue with that?"

"Jake ain't a violent man. He may have his faults, but he don't treat women like that."

"The blood in his car matched hers."

"Piss-easy to arrange, innit?"

"Watch it, Janie."

"Some nutter killed her," she said. "She was on the game. It's a risk they take."

"Jake was her pimp," McGarvie told her. "She flew the coop and paid the price with her life."

"Your lot were out to get him, and this gave you the excuse."

"Her blood was on his shoe as well."

"Of course it was. A few spots in his car wouldn't do the trick. It stands out a mile what you did. You wrap it up as science and the stupid jury swallows it."

They could have gone on like this indefinitely. McGarvie had the sense to change the script.

"How long have you known the Carpenters?"

"Seven months."

"You're not local, are you, Janie? Where are you from?"

"Dagenham."

"But you don't know Bristol very well, or you wouldn't be holding a torch for the Carpenter brothers. Where did you meet Jake?"

"Nightclub."

"Local?"

"London."

"And he brought you here and set you up in a nice apartment in Clifton? Did you stop to think what the price tag is?"

Her eyes blazed. "Sod off, will you?"

"So it was pure romance," McGarvie said with heavy irony.

"I'm not on the game. Never have been."

"Nor was Maeve Smith before she met Jake. Get real, Janie. He's evil."

"Take a running jump."

McGarvie paused before shifting to another line of questioning. "Who were the people you were with outside the court?"

"His mates."

"Family?"

"Don't ask me. We just stood together to make ourselves heard."

"You didn't know them by name? They were mainly women."

"I told you."

"One of the women attacked Superintendent Diamond, the senior detective on the case."

She said vaguely, "Oh, yeah?"

"Scratched his face and kicked him when he fell. That's assault on a police officer."

"Serve him right."

"What?"

The temper ignited. "He framed my boyfriend, got him sent down for life. What do you think I'm going to do? Cook him a fucking fruitcake?"

"Are you admitting to the assault?"

"Bollocks."

"You know his wife has been murdered?"

She switched to defence. "Oh, come on—you can't pin that on me just because . . ." In time, she managed to stop herself saying any more.

"You appreciate how serious this is?"

"I never . . . It's a load of crap. Is that why you pulled me in? I wouldn't do a thing like that to my worst enemy. I didn't even know the woman. I don't have a shooter. I never handled one in my life."

"Don't get hysterical," McGarvie said. "Listen, Janie. No one is pinning anything on you. I may even take a lenient view of the assault on DS Diamond if you can put me on the trail of the killer. What have you heard?"

"Now he wants to do a deal," she said as if to the unseen gallery. "I keep telling you, I know sod all about the murder of this lady."

"Was it a contract job? You could tell me that."

"Go to hell."

McGarvie tried different tacks, but either she was too afraid to speak, or she knew nothing. Presently he broke off the interview and came out, leaving Janie and the woman officer facing each other in silence.

He came to the observation room. "Well?"

"She's the one with the sharp nails," Diamond confirmed. "What's her name?"

"Mary-Jane Forsyth, apparently. Likes to be known as Janie. Twenty-six. No previous. Calls herself a beautician."

"And what's your take on her?"

"She's small change in the Carpenter setup. Doesn't know much. But she's been around enough to know I won't press charges for the assault on you."

"You're going to let her go?"

"When I'm ready."

"If you like, I could try and get a reaction."

"Peter, you're a glutton for punishment. Thanks, but no. I don't want you involved, and you know why."

"Are you going back in?"

"Yes, but you don't have to stay and watch."

"Try and stop me."

When the tape was running again, McGarvie resumed with a fresh approach. "Did you visit Jake while he was on remand?"

"Course I did," Janie said.

"You're still number one in his life?"

"He's always been kind to me."

"Have you been to see him in Horfield Prison since the trial?"

She shook her head. "They don't get many visitors."

"But you're his girl. He'd like to see you more than anyone else."

"I expect I'll get a turn. His brothers want to go first and talk about business things. Family stuff."

"I bet they do. Did they warn you off, then?"

"Celia—that's his brother Danny's wife—said I have to be patient and they'll let me know."

"So you know that side of the family?"

"I met them once. They came round to Jake's place for a barbecue on one of them hot days in the summer."

"Got on all right?"

"All right."

"Was Celia one of the crowd you were with outside the court?"

"No."

"And Des—the other brother?"

"I don't know him."

"What's happening about your flat?"

"It's on a lease until next month. Jake paid six months upfront."

"Generous. What are your plans?"

"I'll have to go back to London, won't I?"

It ended on that downbeat note. McGarvie went through the motions of warning Janie to respect the law in future and told her she wasn't going to be charged this time. If he'd entertained thoughts of using her, they were dashed. It was starkly clear she wouldn't get her turn to visit Jake in prison. She was history so far as the Carpenters were concerned.

Yet she was better off than Maeve Smith.

And Stephanie Diamond.

Diamond was summoned to the ACC's office early in the afternoon. Clearly there had been discussions before he arrived. Georgina was holding court with McGarvie, Halliwell and two others of DCI level in attendance. An empty chair was positioned centrally.

He had a sense straight away that he had walked into a trap. Georgina looked uncomfortable. No one looked at ease. "Peter," she began, meeting his eyes in a way that could only promise conflict, "I don't have to tell you that the investigation into your wife's murder has been running for almost a month. We've put all the resources we can into it. Curtis here has been working long hours, excessive hours, trying for the breakthrough."

"I know," Diamond said with caution. "I've no complaints."

"That's good. Unfortunately, the results are disappointing. The obvious suspects, the Carpenter brothers, have very good alibis."

"Can't fault them," McGarvie chimed in. "Everything checks."

Diamond said, "They hired someone."

Georgina didn't challenge the statement. "The theory of the professional gunman? Obviously that's high on the list."

"Top of it. Must be."

She let that pass. "The most likely way we'll get a line on a hitman is through informants. We're asking all the sources we know, and the Met are making soundings as well because it's more than likely, if it happened, someone was brought in from London. But so far, nothing has come up. Meanwhile, we must explore every other possibility."

He shrugged. Couldn't argue with that.

Georgina looked to McGarvie to pick up the baton.

"Can't ignore the stalker theory either," McGarvie said.

"She wasn't a pop star."

"Come on, Peter. Ordinary people get stalked. If you're unlucky enough to grab the attention of some crazy, you get stalked, whoever you are."

"No one was stalking Steph."

"She may not have mentioned it."

"She'd have told me. I don't buy this at all."

"But you'll agree as a detective it has to be given an airing?"

He leaned back in the chair. They seemed to want his endorsement. "Air it, then."

"All right. She worked in the charity shop. Any woman—anyone at all—who works in a shop is on display. A stalker knows where he can see her and when. It's the kind of shop anyone can step into and browse around without being asked what he wants. Sometimes he can walk by and just look in the window. He fantasises that she'll take an interest in him. Maybe he asks a question or buys something. She was an outgoing woman, good at her job, pleasant to the customers. He takes it as a come-on."

"You don't have to labour it," Diamond interrupted. "Why does he turn nasty?"

"When this obsession is at its height, he finds out she's happily married to you. In his eyes, that's disloyalty. The love turns to hate. If he can't have her, neither will you."

Diamond rolled his eyes upwards and let out a long sigh.

McGarvie was right. It couldn't be discounted. "Any other scenarios?"

McGarvie nodded and said, "The mugging that goes wrong. Some drug user, desperate for cash, points a gun at the first woman he sees in the park. She tells him to get lost and he pulls the trigger."

"If someone pointed a gun at Steph and asked for money, she'd have the sense to hand it over."

"Her bag was missing."

"Anyone could have picked that up, including the wino who found her."

"I know, I know."

There was an awkward silence while McGarvie exchanged a look with Georgina. Neither seemed ready to go on. Finally Georgina cleared her throat.

"We have to explore every avenue. Do we agree on that?"

"Doesn't need saying."

Still she hesitated over the real purpose of this meeting. "Well, in a straightforward case of murder, there are procedures we use almost without thinking." Another pause. "You don't have to take this personally, Peter. The first person questioned is the spouse."

He gripped the arms of the chair and looked at each of the embarrassed faces. Now he knew what this pantomime had been about: easing him into the frame. "Isn't that what's going on now?"

"I'm speaking of something more formal."

"You're serious?"

"We can't make any assumptions," Georgina went on. "Of course it's an imposition. You're a trusted colleague. None of us seriously believes . . . In short, I've asked Curtis to conduct an interview with you."

"What do you think I'm hiding, for Christ's sake?" he demanded. "He's been to my house, been over every room, taken things away. I've told you all I can."

"You're one of us," McGarvie said without any conviction at all, fingering the knot of his tie, "and that's the problem. I can't put certain questions to you without giving offence."

"Such as?"

"I don't propose to start here. This should be done in a structured way, in an interview room, on the record."

"An *interview room?* Give me strength."

"It may seem over-formal, but . . ."

"You really do have your suspicions."

"An open mind."

To think he'd been impressed by McGarvie.

Georgina tried her best to give it an ethical spin. "We owe this to Stephanie, you know, leaving absolutely nothing to chance. You wouldn't want us to skimp. Why don't I send for some coffee before we do anything else?"

"I'd rather get on with it," Diamond muttered from deep in his gut.

# 9

In Interview Room C, in the same chair his attacker, Janie Forsyth, had occupied only an hour ago, Diamond listened in a dazed, disbelieving way to the familiar preamble to a taped interview with a suspect. Was told the identity of his interrogators, McGarvie and Georgina Dallymore, as though he had never met them. Was advised that he was attending voluntarily and was entitled to leave at will unless informed that he was under arrest.

The world had gone mad.

"For the record," McGarvie was saying, "I'd like to clarify your movements on the morning your wife was shot. You were at home first thing, I gather?"

"Mm?" He stared blankly.

"What time did you leave the house?"

"The day it happened? I told you already. Eight fifteen."

"Can anyone confirm the time? Did you see a neighbour? The postman?"

He shrugged. "I got into my car and backed it out and drove off."

"Leaving your wife at the house?"

"You don't have to make it sound like a crime."

"Do you sometimes give her a lift into town?"

"Only if she wants one." With each response he was stifling the urge to tell them it was no business of theirs. Until now he hadn't ever considered how closely he guarded his private life.

"She didn't want the lift on this occasion because it was her morning off. Right?"

"Correct."

"How was she dressed at the time you left?"

"Is that important?"

"Night things? Day clothes?"

"I see. The things she was found in, apart from the raincoat and scarf."

"So you drove here, to work?"

"Yes."

"Arriving at what time?"

"Must have been before nine. I didn't check exactly. Ten to?"

"It takes you that long?"

"The traffic is heavy that time of day."

"Which way did you enter the building?"

"From the car park."

"Using the back stairs?"

"Does it matter which stairs I used?"

"Anyone see you arrive?"

"I've no idea."

"You didn't pass the time of day with anyone, in the car park, or coming upstairs?"

"Don't remember."

"Okay. Where did you go?"

"My office."

"Without speaking to anyone at all?"

"You asked that already."

"And then?"

"Took off all my clothes, stood on my head and recited *The Charge of the Light Brigade*. For the love of God. What does anyone do when he comes into his office in the morning? Opens the window, looks at the stuff on the desk, kicks the wastepaper basket. One day is like another, and I can't tell you what I did."

"Perhaps you used the phone?"

"First thing? I doubt it." Eyes closed, he made an effort to think back. "At some point I was called by Helen, the ACC's PA, and asked upstairs."

"We know that."

"Then you don't need to ask. And you know what time it was."

"Shortly after eleven. Were there any callers prior to that?"

"Not that I remember."

"In short, you can't name anyone who can place you at work in your office between nine and eleven o'clock."

"Someone could have come in. I don't recall." He was in difficulty with this line of questioning. Everything prior to Steph's murder was very hazy indeed. It was almost like the after effect of concussion, with the trauma blocking out everything. He hadn't expected to be questioned about it, and until now hadn't given a thought to what he had been doing.

"Two hours, alone in your office?"

"Things were quiet in CID. I was keeping my head down. If you show you're at a loose end in this place you get dumped on." Having said this, he knew it wouldn't win any sympathy from Georgina, but it was the truth and he was too far gone to care. Georgina was tight-lipped.

McGarvie drew his right hand slowly across the table as though testing for dust and pressed his palms together, rubbing them lightly. He was ill at ease, and his next question showed why. "Forgive me. I have to ask this. Was your marriage in good shape?"

Diamond heard the words, played them over in his head, and had an impulse to grab the man by the shirt and headbutt him. He'd asked the same insulting question when he came to the house. This was bloody incitement.

Then Georgina chose to come in with her smooth talk, learned in all those management courses for high-ranking officers. "You appreciate that we need to know for sure. It is a legitimate question, Peter."

Legitimate? It was a bastard question, and they knew it. "I didn't have any reason to shoot my wife, if that's what you're asking."

"No," McGarvie said, "that isn't what I asked."

He pressed down on his legs to stop them shaking. The stress had to break out some way. "Steph and I were happy together, happy as any couple can be. Is that what you want to hear?"

"Do you own a gun?"

Another crass question. He hesitated before answering, "No." It was the truth . . . just about. The Smith & Wesson revolver in his loft at home was police property, acquired years ago when he worked in London.

"In the Met, you were listed as an authorised shot."

"I let it lapse some years back."

"The .38 that was used to shoot your wife could well have been a police weapon."

He took a sharp, deep breath. "What are you on about? I don't believe this."

Sensing that it was time to draw back a little, McGarvie said, "In the days leading up to the incident, did your wife mention any concerns, anything that might have suggested she was under stress?"

He'd been over this in his own mind many times. "No. Nothing at all."

"Was she at all secretive?"

"If you'd known her, you wouldn't ask that question."

"Had there been any change in her routine?"

"Not that I noticed."

"Had she received any threatening phone calls or letters?"

His patience was draining fast.

"For the tape," McGarvie said, "the subject just shook his head." Then he tossed in another grenade. "Did she have links with the criminal world?"

"What? Steph? Are you completely out of your mind?"

It wasn't the kind of response McGarvie wanted for his precious tape, but the gist was clear. He sniffed and moved on. "Did she have a car of her own?"

"No. We shared it."

"She could drive, then?"

"Oh, yes. But I was using it."

"We need to establish how she travelled to the park. Would she have walked?"

"Could have, quite easily. It's scarcely a mile from where we live, but not too nice when the traffic is heavy on the Upper Bristol Road. It's more likely she caught a minibus. They pass the end of the street every fifteen minutes, so she generally took one if she was going into town."

"She'd be at the park in a very short time."

"Depending on the traffic."

"We reckon she'd have got off at the Marlborough Lane stop to make her way up to the park."

"If she took the bus, yes."

"We've questioned each of the drivers on that route. Not one remembers a passenger of your wife's description. Of course they don't necessarily take note of every middle-aged woman who boards their bus."

"You could ask the passengers."

"The regulars? It's being tried. Nothing so far."

Diamond remarked, "All this presupposes she went to the park of her own free will."

"You think otherwise?"

"I don't know any reason she would go there."

"By arrangement?"

"Then she would have told me."

McGarvie commented tardy, "If she told you everything."

He leaned forward, showing more of his bloodshot eyes than Diamond cared to see. "Before you take offence again, consider this. The whole thing is strange, you've got to admit. You tell us she was acting normally that morning, had no secrets from you, had no reason to visit the park, yet that's where she was shot within two hours of your leaving for work."

"If I knew why, I'd have told you."

"At what stage were you told she'd been shot?"

"Nobody told me. I found out for myself."

There was a pause while the horror of that moment was relived, and when McGarvie resumed again, there was less overt hostility. "Okay, to be accurate, you heard that a woman had been shot and you went to the park and recognised the victim as your wife?"

"You know this. Do we have to go over it?"

"DI Halliwell was competent to deal with the incident. What prompted you to go there?"

Amazing. Even his attendance at the scene was viewed as suspicious. This experience on the receiving end, having to account for everything he had done, would change forever his attitude to interviewing a suspect.

"I said we hadn't seen much action."

"Point taken. Spurred on by the prospect of something happening, you went to the scene. You saw who it was, and you ignored procedure at the scene of a crime and handled the victim—"

"She was my wife, for pity's sake."

"We're going to find blood on your clothes."

"How inconvenient." He'd taken enough. "You know what really pisses me off about this farce? It's not the personal smear, the assumption that I might have murdered her. It's knowing the real killer is out there, and every minute that goes by his chance improves of getting away with this."

"This isn't our only line of enquiry," McGarvie said. "I've got over a hundred men on the case."

"For how much longer? What happens when Headquarters

ask for your budget report? They'll cut the overtime. The whole thing will be scaled down."

Georgina said with determination, "I'll deal with Headquarters." She asked McGarvie if he had any more questions and he said he was through and they stopped the tapes.

"I've had it up to here with you lot," Diamond said. "I'm going home."

But he didn't. Instead, he drove out to the crime scene, now abandoned by everyone, and restored to normal except for the wear on the turf of hundreds of police boots. The one place where the ground had not been trampled was a small oval of fresh grass where Steph's body had lain. Someone had placed a bunch of flowers there. No message. He could have brought some himself, but he knew Steph would have been troubled by the idea of cut flowers without water. She wouldn't willingly deprive anything of life.

If he'd written a message, it would have been the one hackneyed word people always attach to flowers they leave at murder scenes. "Why?"

He looked around him, taking in the setting. Previously he'd been aware of nothing except Steph lying dead on the ground. Now he saw a curved path lined with benches about every thirty yards. In spring, he remembered, the daffodils sprouted here and made a glorious display. The shoots were already visible. Lower down, the remains of the Victorian shrubbery, a long line of trees and bushes, hid the Charlotte Street Car Park from view. You wouldn't believe all those cars were actually only a few paces away.

Higher up the slope was the unprepossessing rear of the old bandstand with its domed roof. He walked up to it and around to the front.

The facade was much more elegant than the back, being visible from the Crescent. He could imagine an audience seated here listening to one of the German bands that were so popular around the turn of the century. The shell-shaped design was more modern in concept than the weathered stonework suggested.

At either side, separate from the bandstand, two large stone vases with handles, chipped and stained, but evidently marble, were raised on plinths. Each was protected by a flat stone canopy mounted on pillars and surrounded by a low railing. Along the top of the stonework was an inscription stating that the vases were the gift of Napoleon to the Empress Josephine in 1805, something Diamond had never noticed until now. They were spoils of the Peninsular War, presented to the city by some Bath worthy. The overgrown bushes almost hid them from view, but he could make out the letter "J" in an Imperial circlet of leaves. It was the kind of detail that fascinated Steph, and forgetting everything for a second, he looked forward to telling her what he had found and bringing her here to see it.

Caught again. This wasn't the first time. He supposed it was what psychologists referred to as denial.

He moved back to the spot where Steph had been found. Why had the murderer chosen this location? For one thing, the park was reasonably quiet, even now, in the afternoon, and fairly well screened by trees. If it was right that she had been lured here, her killer could have remained hidden among the bushes, or behind the bandstand, until the last minute, and then approached her, keeping the gun concealed. Since there had been no evidence of a struggle, it was reasonable to assume the weapon had been held to her face and fired twice in a swift, professional action. Most gunmen knew you couldn't be certain a single shot would kill, even at point-blank range. Apparently he (or she, though it was difficult to visualise a female assassin) had quit the scene by the short route to the car park, which was huge, with more than one exit. So that was the special appeal of this location: the certainty of getting away fast. All in all, a well-chosen place.

The biggest problem must have been persuading Steph to come here.

For the first time since the murder, he was functioning as a detective. Until now he had been too devastated to think straight. For that reason alone it was right that someone other than he should head the team. Moreover, the official line made sense: having the victim's husband in charge would undermine any prosecution. Fine—so long as McGarvie was a competent, energetic stand-in. But after that farcical interrogation, Diamond's confidence in the man was in tatters. The competence was flawed, the energy misdirected. There was a sense of desperation in what was going on.

A single crow stalked the lawn, foraging for worms. The bleak look of this scene reinforced the lost opportunities.

Steph deserved a good investigation.

No sense in offering advice. Georgina and McGarvie wouldn't listen to a man they were treating as a suspect. No, the only way to get results was to go solo. Throughout their marriage Steph had put up with his cack-handed attempts at all things practical: shelves that fell off the wall, doors that stuck in the winter and let in draughts in the summer, electrical wiring that blew the fuses. She had never directly benefited from the one skill he had: sleuthing. She was entitled to it now. He would find her killer, and to hell with the problems it raised.

His spirits improved. He was putting his career on the line and maybe his life. Bugger that, he thought. This is the right decision. I refuse to be sidelined. She's my wife and no one can make me walk away from her.

At home that evening he opened a can of lager and dug about in the freezer and cooked himself a satisfying meal of one of Steph's beef casseroles with fresh potatoes and carrots. He watched a repeat *of Fawlty Towers* on TV and smiled for the first time in weeks.

Towards midnight, he woke in the armchair and realised he'd dozed off. He'd been dreaming, an anxious, vivid dream of being shot in the leg by an invisible man with a gun. Of limping away and feeling more shots, and dripping blood. The shots fitted the film that was running on the box, some spaghetti western with Clint Eastwood. Clint looked in fine shape still. The film bullets had obviously missed.

Diamond fingered his own leg.

"Daft."

But it had gotten to him, that dream. He decided to fetch his handgun from the loft. In the coming days he might need to defend himself. He had no plans to use it, except as a deterrent. So he went upstairs, opened the hatch and let down the folding ladder. Switched on the loft light and of course the sodding thing flickered and went out.

No matter. He knew where the shoebox was that contained the gun wrapped in a cloth with two rounds of ammunition. At the top of the steps he put his head and shoulders through the hatch, reached and found what he wanted at once.

But there was no weight to the box. Nothing was inside. He took off the lid. Not even the cloth was in there.

Impossible.

He groped around the plasterboard where the box had been. Dust and cobwebs. Nothing else. No other box, no Smith & Wesson .38 wrapped in cloth.

Deeply worried, he collected a torch from downstairs and replaced the light bulb. Spent the next hour searching the whole of the loft, struggling with old suitcases among unwanted rolls of wallpaper and discarded carpets. He tried to remember if anyone except himself had been up there. A plumber, to look at the cold storage tank? Electrician? TV aerial man?

Not to his knowledge.

What in Christ's name was going on?

# 10

THE TWO MEN talking in a London taxi knew only as much as the media had told them about the shooting of Stephanie Diamond, but after the shock wave of a killing there are ripples washing up on some unlikely shores.

"It's beautiful, Harry."

"It always is at the beginning," the voice of experience spoke. "I hate to disillusion you, old friend, but the beauty soon wears off. By the end it's revoltingly ugly."

"Not this time, I promise you."

"Would you care to take a bet on that?" Harry Tattersall gazed out of the window at the traffic in Piccadilly. At forty-two, he'd seen many a pretty plan turn to dross. "Who else is in?"

"That's the beauty," Rhadi said. "We are a small, talented team. Five only."

"Who?"

"Wait and see."

"I don't work with failures."

"These are pros. You're going to be impressed."

"Where's the meeting?"

"This is a top job, Harry. Top job needs a top meeting place."

The cab wound its way around Trafalgar Square, under Admiralty Arch and up the Mall towards the Victoria Memorial. Tourists stood snapping the sentry at the gates of Buckingham Palace.

"Not there?" Harry said, only half joking. This was such a weird setup, he was ready to believe anything.

"No, not there."

They were driven up Constitution Hill to Hyde Park Corner and came to a halt outside one of the more exclusive hotels. A white-gloved hand opened the door.

"Didn't I tell you?" Rhadi said.

"It takes more than one flunkey to impress me," Harry said. He had been to a good public school and liked everyone to know it.

A doorman ushered them in and a black-suited young man wished them good afternoon in a way that asked to know their business.

"We're expected," Rhadi said with a princely air. "The Napoleon Suite."

"Very good, sir."

In the lift, Rhadi said, "What do you think? An improvement on the Scrubs?"

"So long as it isn't a short cut back to the Scrubs," Harry said. He'd done one six-month stretch in an otherwise unblemished fifteen-year career of confidence trickery, and he hadn't cared for it one bit. "I'd better warn you, I'm not going to be bounced into anything."

"Lighten up, old friend."

Rhadi knocked and the door was opened by a Middle Eastern man.

"What's this—Ali Baba and the Forty Thieves?" Harry said.

He'd known Rhadi so many years that he never thought of him as an immigrant. Wasn't even sure where he came from originally. Confronted now by two more Arabs in expensive suits, he felt outnumbered. Rhadi hadn't said a word about the nationality of the personnel involved.

"Is there a problem, Mr. Tattersall?" one of them asked, a

near-midget with a set of teeth that wouldn't have disgraced a camel.

"I didn't expect . . ." Harry started to say, and let his voice trail away when he saw the second Arab's hand slip inside his jacket.

"This is Ibrahim," the teeth said, "and I am Zahir. You were not expecting to be involved in an international enterprise, I dare say."

"If it's terrorism, I'm leaving."

Rhadi gave him a gentle push in the back. "Go in, Harry. Forget about terrorism. This is big time."

"It had better be," he muttered. "Where are you all from, anyway?"

Zahir ignored the question. "You want a drink? It's against our religion, but there's plenty here if you want something."

"I think I will." It wasn't a mini-bar, either. This was a drinks cabinet, courtesy of the hotel. He poured himself a large single malt while he pondered that remark about religion. He didn't think he'd been invited to a prayer meeting.

Ibrahim had closed the door. Harry took stock. Zahir, the spokesman with the teeth, had to be Mr. Big, though not in stature. Ibrahim, silent, built like a water buffalo, was the muscle. The fifth man apparently hadn't turned up yet.

"You were at King's, Canterbury, I believe?" Zahir said out of nowhere.

"Is my old school important?"

"That's true, then? Straight up, as they say?"

"Anyone can check the register."

"Did you row?"

"No. I was a cricketer. Opened the batting." Harry refrained from revealing that he opened for the third eleven and ended the season with an average of nine.

"In that case," Zahir said, "we wouldn't have met. I coxed the first eight. Eton."

With the pecking order established, Zahir invited Harry

to take a seat. "Rhadi tells us you're the smoothest con artist in London."

"Rhadi isn't bad at it himself," Harry commented.

"You once took one of the big merchant banks for a cool fifty thousand?"

"Three banks together," Harry said. "It was a matter of persuading them it was a notional adjustment."

"And none of them understood what was going on?"

"They still don't."

"Rhadi also tells us you might not be averse to another payday."

"That depends."

"Naturally. Have you ever dealt in diamonds?"

"Diamonds?" He twitched and frowned. "I'm not a diamond man."

"Don't look so alarmed," Zahir said. "No one is asking you to do anything outside your experience."

"So what's the scam?"

Zahir hesitated. "This is more than a scam. We're not talking thousands, Mr. Tattersall, but hundreds of thousands. We can all retire on the proceeds. But you'll understand that I need your total commitment before I unfold the plan."

"Before? That's asking a lot. I don't know you. Rhadi is an old friend, but the rest of you . . ."

"Well, it's a good thing some of us aren't familiar to you. You wouldn't want to be getting into bed with a bunch of well-known criminals, would you?" He flashed the enormous teeth.

"You've got a point there."

"Let's see if we can resolve this. What if you were guaranteed a hundred thousand pounds?"

"A hundred grand? What are you snatching—the Crown Jewels?"

"Better. These are uncut stones. Some of the finest gem crystals in the world."

Harry was silent for a while, still cautious. "It sounds wonderful, but why have you come to me? What am I supposed to do?"

"What you're best at doing, Mr. Tattersall. Conning people."

"Ah, but I know damn all about the diamond industry. I need to understand what I'm talking about."

"No you don't."

"Sorry, my friend," Harry insisted. "That isn't the way I work. I absolutely refuse to wing it."

"You're not listening, Mr. Tattersall. Your part in this project doesn't involve the diamonds. You don't need to talk about them. In fact, you are expressly forbidden to mention them. You will be a go-between. We require someone who is English, not Arabian, a true-blue English gentleman."

"That I can do."

"So you're on the team?"

"Hold on," Harry said. "First I want to know the job and who else you've signed up for this."

"You know Rhadi, and you've just met Ibrahim and me."

"I was told there are five."

"Who told you?" Zahir's eyes flicked to Rhadi. "The fifth man must remain anonymous for the time being."

"Why?"

"He's the key to everything."

"The peterman?"

"The what?"

"Safe-breaker. The fellow who liberates the rocks."

Zahir's face was a study in distaste. "We're not proposing to break into a safe, Mr. Tattersall."

"How else are you going to lay hands on them?"

Rhadi broke into the dialogue in some excitement. "This is the beauty, Harry."

Zahir said, "We're having the diamonds delivered to us."

"*Delivered?* Who by?"

"The owners. The top dealer in Hatton Garden, the home of the London diamond trade."

"How do you arrange that?"

Zahir exchanged more looks with Rhadi and Ibrahim. "This is what will happen. Rhadi will go to Hatton Garden and inform the dealer that a prince of the Kuwaiti Royal Family has come to London to buy rough diamonds and is staying at the Dorchester Hotel. In Hatton Garden they know that the Kuwaitis are rich beyond dreams. They will arrange to take their best stones to his suite for inspection."

"Before you go on," Harry said, "these Hatton Garden people aren't fools. They'll check with the hotel."

"And when they check, they'll find that it's true. There will be a Kuwaiti prince on the hotel guest list."

"You, I suppose," Harry said, not over impressed.

"No. A true member of the blood royal. The Kuwaitis visit London frequently and stay at the Dorchester. They have a financial stake in the City. Anyone checking will find this is totally on the level."

"Get away. The fifth man is a Kuwaiti prince?"

"No, no. You're still not listening. The prince isn't in the plot. We time our heist to coincide with the visit."

Harry still needed convincing. "How will you know when one of the princes is over here? Private visits by royalty are arranged in secret. They're very aware of security."

"Rightly so," Zahir said, unfazed. "We'll know because we have a man inside the Dorchester."

Harry digested this.

"Clever," he said, after a pause. "The fifth man?"

"Yes. He's on the staff, on the catering side. When royalty are coming, they have to order food supplies specially, so he's one of the few to be entrusted with advance information about VIP guests. He will advise us—through you—when one of the princes has a booking. We will then book one of the best suites for you under the name of Lord this or the Earl of that. Your job. You can impersonate one of the aristocracy, I hope?"

"With ease."

"Good. I suggest you are disguised. Dyed hair, glasses, moustache. You will check in, and occupy the suite. Presently I will arrive with Ibrahim. Within a short time you will remove your disguise and leave by the back stairs. Your job will be over. It's as simple as that. Shortly after you depart, the Hatton Garden dealer will arrive and be met in the foyer by Rhadi, posing as the emissary of the Kuwaitis."

"He may have security with him," Harry warned.

"We're prepared for that. Rhadi will escort him to the suite where I will be waiting with Ibrahim, both dressed in the *jubbah*. If they bring a security officer, he will be ordered by Rhadi to remain outside the door. You don't bring functionaries such as that into the presence of the blood royal. The dealer takes out his parcel of diamonds and we relieve him of them. As smoothly as possible. Minimum violence. He is tied up and gagged. We leave by another door."

"Isn't that the neatest scam you ever heard?" Rhadi said.

"Sounds all right," Harry grudgingly admitted. "But why do you need me?"

"For your special talent and our protection. You have two functions. First, you are the go-between, as I mentioned. Our man on the Dorchester staff will communicate with you, not with Arabs, which might arouse suspicion. There is sure to be a security enquiry after the heist. He will, of course, deny having given information to anybody."

"And secondly?"

"You are the decoy—the peer who booked the suite. It will take some time for them to realise how it was done. For all they know, you may have been a genuine peer abducted by the gang."

Harry was silent for several seconds as he reviewed the plan. Certainly it had attractions. No safe-breaking, fiddling with security systems, no guns, no excessive violence. The concept of the dealer being conned into bringing the rocks to the hotel was neat, as was the idea of timing the scam to coincide with a genuine royal visit. Yes, it appealed. His own part didn't sound too demanding. He'd taken bigger risks in the past.

"And if it all goes to plan," he said, "how will you fence the diamonds? If they're tiptop items, they'll be well known in the trade."

"These are uncut stones, Mr. Tattersall," Zahir reminded him. "The industry is worldwide now. Huge. There are factories in Bombay, Tel Aviv, Smolensk. Every damned place. There is no difficulty in unloading top quality roughs for a decent price, believe me. They will be out of Britain within hours and cut and polished within days. And once a stone has been cleaved, it changes personality, just as you do for a living, or so I'm told. Are you in?"

"For a hundred K guaranteed?"

"Guaranteed."

"I'll incur some expenses."

"We can take care of that."

"Over and above my hundred grand?"

"Expenses—yes. What do you have in mind? The disguise?"

"A suit. I can't walk into the Dorchester in what I'm wearing." It was worth the try, Harry thought, and he was mightily impressed when it got a result.

"I was thinking the same," Zahir said, looking him up and down. "Fifteen hundred in expenses, then."

"Upfront?"

"Rhadi will see to it."

They shook hands.

"What next?" Harry asked, trying not to show his awe at the deal.

"You buy some decent clothes and then you wait. We all wait."

"For the word from your fellow in the Dorchester?"

"Which he will give to you."

"Is this hotel man reliable? One hundred per cent?"

"Be assured of that. He held the Queen's commission. He was an officer in the Royal Air Force Catering Branch."

"How did you . . . ?"

"Your door was open."

"Bloody liar. You put your boot against it."

"So it was open," Diamond said.

He didn't usually force an entry when calling on a witness, but the rules change for winos. Warburton clearly wasn't in any shape to get up and greet a visitor. He was on the floor, his back propped against a greasy leather armchair on which the lurcher was curled up asleep, oblivious of Diamond's arrival. Maybe it, too, was pie-eyed. Empty cider bottles were scattered about the floor.

"You're that copper," Warburton said through his alcoholic haze as if Diamond needed reminding.

There was another chair, an upright one, with a plate on it with the dried remains of a meal of baked beans. Diamond chose to remain standing. He was trying to decide if the man was capable of coherent answers. *In vino veritas* is a maxim reliable only up to a certain intake of the vino.

"What you want?" Warburton asked.

Diamond ignored him and walked through to the second room of this foul-smelling basement.

A mattress on the floor and an ex-army greatcoat slung across it, presumably for bedding. More empty bottles.

He stooped and looked under one side of the mattress. And

then the other. Nothing except some dog-eared pages from a girlie magazine. He brushed his clothes in case of lice.

Back in the main room, watched by the still-supine tenant, he sifted through the few possessions. From a carton containing cans of dog food, baked beans and a stale loaf, he picked out a supermarket receipt.

"What's this? Thirty-eight pounds fifty-three? You had a good splurge on the twenty-third. In the money, were you?"

"Me social, wasn't it?"

"On a Tuesday? Come off it, Jimmy. This was the day you found the woman in the park. You nicked the cash from her bag, didn't you?"

"I never."

"So what did you do with the bag?"

No answer.

"Where is it, Jimmy? No messing. This is a murder inquiry."

Warburton blurted out in a panicky voice, "I never killed her. I reported it, didn't I?"

"You did the right thing there. And I've been asking myself why you bothered, Jimmy. So public-spirited that you felt compelled to raise the alarm? I don't see it."

"'S a fact."

"Now that I have this . . ." Diamond held up the till receipt ". . . I'm starting to get the picture. You're not such a hero. I was asking myself how a down-and-out like you reacts when he comes across a body in a park. Does he get to a phone immediately and report it? Does he? Hell! He's on the lookout for goodies. You found the handbag."

Warburton shook his head.

"It won't do, Jimmy," Diamond told him. "The date matches. You raised the alarm, yes, but there can only be one reason. Someone came along when you had your thieving hands in the bag. They saw you right beside the body, maybe even thought you'd fired the shots. You were forced to play the innocent, pretend you were just about to call the police. You stuffed the handbag under your coat and hightailed it to the car park and did the decent thing because they were breathing down your neck. Am I right?"

"Has she been onto you?"

Diamond pounced. "She? It was a woman, then? Better unload, Jimmy."

The man looked so sick that Diamond wasn't sure what he would unload.

"Tell me about her, this woman who spotted you."

"Nothing to tell."

"What was she like? Where did she come from? What did she say? Come on, man. Do I have to shake it out of you?"

"Dunno," Warburton said. "Came from nowhere. I looked up and she was there."

"What age?"

He shrugged. "Thirty. Thirty-five."

"Wearing what?"

"Tracksuit. Blue. Dark blue."

"A jogger?"

"Yeah. Could be."

"So what colour was her hair?"

"Christ knows. She had one of them woolly hats."

"Wearing trainers?"

"Didn't see."

"How tall?"

"Average."

"Brilliant. What happened?"

Warburton dragged his hand down the length of his face, pressing the pale flesh as if to squeeze out some memory. "Asked what I was doing and I told her I found the stiff on the ground, which was true. She said we ought to tell someone, so I got up and legged it to the car park—"

"With the handbag under your clothes?"

"Don't want to talk about that."

"Spill it out, Sonny Jim, or I'll have you for obstructing the police as well as withholding evidence and theft. Have you done any time?"

He didn't answer.

Diamond took a step closer. No one could look more threatening. "What happened to that handbag? Is it here?"

"Chucked it, didn't I?" Warburton said.

At least he hadn't pinned the blame on the jogger.

"Where?"

"Dunno."

Diamond took a handhold on Warburton's T-shirt just below the throat and screwed it into a knot.

"I could have stuffed it out of sight," Warburton piped up.

"We know that. Where? The car park?" There were big collection bins at one end for newspapers, bottles and cans. Maybe he'd got rid of it there.

"Can't say."

"Get up."

"What?"

Warburton found himself hauled off the floor. "You're going to have your memory jogged."

The lurcher woke up and wagged its tail, uninterested that its master was being forced outside against his will. The chance of a walk was not to be missed. Except that it wasn't going to be a walk simply because Warburton wasn't capable of staying upright that long.

In the car, the dog stood with its front paws on the back of Diamond's seat, licking him behind the ear. Warburton immediately fell asleep.

They drove up Charlotte Street and took the car park turn. Diamond stopped beside the bins. "Recognise them?"

No answer.

He rammed an elbow into Warburton's ribs. "Is that where you got rid of the handbag?"

"No."

"You're certain?"

Charlotte Street Car Park is vast, the largest in Bath, with tiers of parking space separated by hedges. A hedge wasn't a bad place to get rid of an unwanted bag, but these had already been combed by McGarvie's search squad. Whilst Warburton lolled against the headrest with his eyes closed, Diamond toured the car park trying to picture the scene. He drove to one of the higher tiers nearest to the old shrubbery. Every parking slot was taken, so he just stopped between the rows, got out and dragged Warburton from the car. The dog jumped out as well.

"Now. Where exactly did you find the guy with the mobile phone?"

Warburton looked vaguely about him. He flapped a limp hand that seemed to take in the whole of the car park.

"Do you know who I'm talking about? You asked him to dial nine-nine-nine."

"Could have been right here . . . Or over there . . . Or there."

"Did you have the handbag with you?"

"What?"

"Under your coat—did you have the woman's bag under your coat?"

No response.

"Listen. I'm trying to get this straight. The jogger came along while you were beside the body going through the bag. She told you to get to a phone, and you made a show of looking for help. You came here, to the car park, and I think you had the bag with you."

"I did—'s a fact."

"Good. And we know you found the guy with the mobile

and he got the number and you spoke to the operator and she put you through to the police and they asked for your name and told you to wait at the scene. Right?"

"Mm."

"This was seen by the man who owned the mobile. Must have been. So I don't think you dumped the handbag here with him watching. I think you took it back to the park."

"Yeah."

"So what did you do with it there?"

"Dunno."

Diamond clenched his fist. The urge was strong. Somehow he suppressed it. Warburton was barely capable of standing upright without support. The fresh air seemed to be sobering him up a little. A poke in the guts wouldn't help. "Okay. We're going to reconstruct the scene, do the walk, just like you did." He opened the car and took out the pack containing the vehicle service record and documents. "This will do for the handbag. Where did you have it? In your shirt? Under your arm?"

Warburton took the pack in his hands, eyed it in a puzzled way, and then looked to Diamond for guidance.

"We're pretending this is the handbag."

"Ah."

With an effort at co-operation, Warburton lifted the flap of his jacket and shoved the documents out of sight in the front of his jeans.

"Good. What next? You've called nine-nine-nine. Do you go back directly to the scene?"

"Yeah."

"The guy with the mobile—what did he do?"

"Got in his motor and pissed off quick."

So much for the great British public. In all probability Warburton would have quit the scene as well if he hadn't stupidly given his name to the operator.

"So you went back to wait by the body?"

"Yeah."

"Still carrying the handbag?"

"Yeah."

"Let's walk it through, then."

The lurcher led the way up the path. After stumbling a little and being steadied, Warburton began to move rather better. Diamond was trying to think himself into this man's befuddled brain on the day of the shooting. There was this short period before the patrol car responded to the call. The jogger had moved on and the man with the mobile hadn't wanted to get involved. This, surely, was the opportunity to see what was in the handbag, remove any money, and then get rid of the bag before the police arrived. But where?

In the open area beside the bandstand a man was helping a child fly a kite, obviously unaware that someone had been murdered in this place. Victoria Park was back to normal. Life had moved on. Diamond had seen it happen before when murder scenes were reclaimed for everyday use, watched the families of victims unable to understand how the rest of the world could be so unfeeling.

They reached the spot where Steph had fallen. That sad bunch of flowers was still in place, yellow tulips spread wide, roses dropping their petals.

"Right. You came back here. You had a few minutes in hand. Was this when you helped yourself to the money?"

Warburton didn't answer.

"I'm giving you a chance. Tell me what you did with the bag and I may not charge you with theft."

The last word sank in. Warburton looked about him as if coming out of a trance and then started walking to the left side of the bandstand where one of the Empress Josephine's vases stood. He reached under his shirt and tugged out the document wallet. "Want me to chuck it in there?"

"In the vase?" The great stone amphora was large enough to

take a dozen handbags. Surely the searchers had looked inside. Or was it possible they'd been so absorbed in their fingertip search of the shrubbery, lawns and car park that they'd omitted something so screamingly obvious?

"If you're wasting my time—"

"Not."

Diamond stepped over the railing, pushed aside an overgrown rose bush and climbed on the plinth. Put an arm into the huge vase and groped around. Dead leaves, for sure. He felt for something more solid and brought out a rust-covered lager can and chucked it angrily aside. The lurcher chased it.

"There's no bag here, you berk."

"Some bleeder took it, then."

"Bullshit." He climbed down, scratching his hand on the rose. "Where is it, Warburton?"

"It was in there. I swear."

"You don't even remember, you piss artist. Give me that." He grabbed his car documents. "Find your own way home. I've wasted enough time." He turned and marched back to the car, angry and disappointed.

Driving home, he tried telling himself that it hadn't been totally fruitless. He was sure now that Warburton had taken the money. Probably the bag had been slung into the river or a builder's skip. It might yet turn up.

The frustration was that he'd appeared to be succeeding where McGarvie had failed. The bag *could* have been lying inside that pesky vase.

He was halfway to Weston when he thought of the obvious. Talk about Warburton's bosky state—what kind of state was *he* in?

He did a fast, illegal U-turn and drove back to the park.

The handbag was in the second vase.

# 12

Curious as to what this fascinating object might be, Raffles arrived on the table with an agile leap whilst Diamond was performing a delicate operation with salad servers and a chopstick.

"Get out of it." He didn't want paw prints on Steph's handbag.

Raffles jumped down and went to look at the feeding dish instead.

Neither did he want more of his own fingerprints. He must have left some when he picked the bag out of the stone vase. Since then he'd been careful to handle only the strap. Forensics would bellyache about contaminated evidence. So he eased the sides open with the chopstick and started removing the contents with the salad servers.

Plastic rain hat.

Kleenex tissues, soggy and disintegrating. The damp had penetrated the bag.

Compact.

Oxfam ballpoint.

Lipstick (a devil to grip with the servers).

Purse, unzipped and empty except for a few small coins. But the credit cards were still in place in the side pocket. Warburton must have known no one would believe he possessed a credit card. He'd gone for the cash.

Keys.

Aspirin bottle.

Her little book of photos of her parents, a group of her Brownies and Diamond himself, in uniform, the year they'd met. The pictures had suffered in the damp.

But where was the one thing he wanted to find?

He probed with the servers. Held the entire bag upside down on the end of the chopstick. A Malteser fell out and rolled across the floor. He watched Raffles hunt it down and flick it with a paw before discovering it was coated in chocolate. One item forensics would have to manage without.

They would get everything else. Presently he'd go into work and take quiet satisfaction in presenting McGarvie with the handbag and saying he'd found it at the scene. What was the figure they kept quoting—over a hundred officers involved in a fingertip search?

In truth, he knew how easy it was to miss something as obvious as the stone vases. Could have happened to anyone.

He poked with the chopstick at the objects on the table, trying to work out where Steph's diary was. Not in the house. She *always* had it with her. That little book was essential to the way she ran her life. Dates, times, important phone numbers and addresses. She didn't use it as some people use a diary to write up a daily record of their lives. Recording the past was alien to her outlook. She was forward-looking. She scribbled in appointments, names, birthdays.

That diary was of no conceivable interest to anyone else.

So where was it?

He said, "Stupid arse."

The answer was as obvious as the stone vase in the park. In the lining inside the bag was a zip. She kept the diary in an inner pocket. Impatient now, he dropped the chopstick and used his finger and thumb to open the zip and feel inside.

Result.

The diary was dry and in near perfect condition. He turned

to the date of the murder: Tuesday, February the twenty-third, and found an entry. Steph had written in her blue ballpoint:

*T. 10 A.M. Vict. Pk, opp. bandstand*

He frowned at the page, baffled, disbelieving, shocked. He'd been telling everyone it was most unlikely Steph had arranged to visit the park—because she hadn't said a word to him. But why hadn't she mentioned it? She was so open about her life. Always told him everything.

Didn't she?

All at once his hands shook.

He hesitated to check the rest of the diary. It would be an invasion of her privacy. Already he felt shabby for opening it. Then an inner voice told him the murder squad would pore over every page after he handed it in, and he was more entitled than they to know what was in the damned thing.

He had this gut-wrenching fear that his trust in Steph was about to unravel. Up to now he'd never had a doubt about her loyalty. Theirs had been an honest, blissful marriage. That had been one of the few certainties in his case-hardened life. Was it possible he'd been mistaken, that she had secrets she'd never discussed with him?

This looked horribly like one, this appointment in the park. Did "T" stand for a name, someone she'd met, or—please, please—something totally different and innocent that happened in parks like . . . like what, for Christ's sake?

Tennis?

Outdoors, in February? Ridiculous.

T'ai Chi, then?

Why not? Steph was forever trying therapies, holistic this and alternative that. Didn't always speak of them because she knew he dismissed all of it as baloney. It was not impossible she'd joined a group who exercised in the park.

Somehow, he couldn't picture it.

Briefly he was tempted to destroy the diary without looking at any more of it. If he'd been living an illusion, wasn't it preferable to hold onto precious memories even though they might turn out to have been unfounded?

He dismissed that. The diary was pivotal evidence, whatever else was in it. The killer had to be caught, and this proved Steph had made an appointment to go to her place of execution. The chance that some casual mugger had killed her was now so unlikely that it could be discounted. She'd obviously been lured to her death. The murder squad had to be told.

So he started leafing through. It was a small diary with seven days spread over two pages, and Steph's entries were short. They took some interpreting. "Ox" meant her stints at the Oxfam shop. They varied a bit from one week to the next, so she had to keep a record of them. She'd also scribbled in appointments with the doctor and dentist, family birthdays, dinner invitations and theatre bookings. He was looking for other things.

Disturbingly, he found them.

*Monday 15 February Ox 2-5 P out. Must call T.*

With that, the T'ai Chi theory went down in flames.

*Wednesday 17 February Ox 10-1. Hair (Jan) 1:30. Friday 19 February P out. Call T tonight.*

On the following Tuesday—Shrove Tuesday, the diary reminded him—she'd had her fatal meeting in the park with the person she called "T." These were crucial entries and he copied them into a notebook of his own.

It was deeply worrying, not to say hurtful. The first mention of "T," on Monday the fifteenth, seemed to be linked with the note that he, "P," was out. He remembered. It had been one of his regular, mind-numbing PCCG meetings with local residents' groups. Evidently on the Wednesday she'd had her hair done, which was usually a sure sign of some important occasion ahead. Another call to "T" on Friday. And she'd said not a word about all this.

Hold on, he told himself, this is your wife Steph. Don't read too much into it. But the suspicion of a secret affair was planted. How could he interpret it as anything else?

*For crying out loud, be realistic! Steph wasn't two-timing me. I'd have picked up some signals. She was as loving as ever in those last few days of her life, on our last night together. There's another explanation. Has to be.*

He went methodically through the eight weeks up to the date of her death and found no other mention of this "T." It was no use looking for last year's diary because she always threw them away at the end of the year. His hands still shook as he replaced this one in its pocket of the handbag and closed the zip.

There was no sense of triumph in handing the bag to McGarvie. He simply walked into the incident room, passed it over and said where he'd found it.

"I thought those bloody great things were solid stone," McGarvie said as if Diamond himself had conned him. I suppose you looked inside?"

He nodded. "You'll find some of my prints on it. And Warburton's, no doubt. The purse is in there, minus the money. And her diary."

"The diary." The tired eyes widened.

"She had an appointment in the park the day she died."

"Who with?"

"Someone she called 'T.'"

McGarvie looked around the incident room. "Did you hear that, everyone? This is the breakthrough." He looked animated for the first time in a month. "Any thoughts?"

Diamond shook his head. "Like I said, she hadn't mentioned a thing."

"Boyfriend?"

"Some boyfriend, if he put a bullet through her head."

"Sorry. I've got to cover every angle. And you think Warburton took the cash?"

"I'm sure of it."

"And tossed the bag in the vase?"

"He told me he did. Took me to the place. There was only forty quid. If you're thinking of charging him, don't. He gave me his co-operation."

"I'll handle this my way. I still want to speak to him. Look, I'm grateful you found this."

"But . . ." Diamond said.

"You know what I'm going to say?"

"Save it. I'm not trying to take over. I'll keep my distance."

"That's not good enough, Peter."

"It's the best you'll get."

Specially, he thought, when I'm ahead of you.

He turned right outside the police station and walked the length of Manvers Street and beyond, where it became Pierrepont Street. At the far end he turned left into North Parade Passage and straight to Steph's hairdresser called What a Snip.

He asked for Jan. She was with a client.

"If it's about an appointment," the receptionist said with a dubious look at Diamond's bald patch, "I can do it from the book."

"You can show me the book. And you can tell Jan to break off and speak to the police."

She went at once.

Steph's name was in the book for one thirty on Wednesday, February the seventeenth.

"Does this tick beside her name mean she definitely came in?" he asked Jan when she appeared.

"She did. Mr. Diamond, I can't tell you how shocked I was when I heard what happened," Jan said. She was the senior stylist and manager, meaning she was all of twenty-one with the confidence of twice that, blonde, elfin, with eyes that had seen everything and dealt with every kind of client. You wouldn't mess with Jan. Steph must have liked her.

"I want you to cast your mind back to that Wednesday. I'm sure she chatted as you were doing her hair."

"A bit, yes."

"Can you remember any of what was said?"

"That's asking. The weather, naturally. My holiday in Tenerife. The night before's television, I expect. And the kind of cut she wanted."

"Did she say anything about the reason for the hairdo?"

"Not that I remember."

"Try, please. She wasn't one for regular appointments, as you know. She only booked you when she had something coming up. Did she mention what it was?"

She shook her head. "I would have remembered if she'd said anything. People often do and I like to know about their lives. But I never ask if they don't want to say. I don't believe in being nosy."

"Are you sure she didn't tell you something and ask you to keep it to yourself?—because if she did, it's got to come out now. You don't have to spare my feelings, Jan. I need to find her killer before someone else is murdered."

"And I'd tell you if there was anything to tell, but there isn't."

He believed her.

The phone was beeping and the cat mewing when he came through his front door. He ignored the phone but Raffles got fed. Then he heated some baked beans, cut the stale end off a loaf and made toast topped with tinned tomatoes and a fried egg that smelt fishy. Looked at the post without troubling to open anything. The solicitor, the bank, the funeral director. They could wait. In less than twenty minutes he was out again, driving to Bristol.

He called at two pubs in the old market area and asked for John Seville, an informer he'd known and used a few times. No snout is totally reliable, but Seville was better than most. The problem was that nobody had seen him since the Carpenter trial. Bernie Hescott, hunched over a Guinness in the Rummer, was definitely second best.

"Haven't clapped eyes on him in weeks. I wouldn't like to think what happened. He was too yappy for his own good, I reckon."

"Maybe you can help." Diamond showed the top edge of a twenty-pound note, and then let it slide back into his top pocket. "You heard what happened to my wife?"

"It was in all the papers, wasn't it?" said Bernie, a twitchy, undernourished ex-con in a Bristol Rovers shirt. "Wouldn't wish that on anyone."

"It was done by a pro."

"You think so?"

"I was going to ask John Seville if he'd heard a whisper about a hitman."

"Was you? Well, he's not around."

Diamond fingered the note in his pocket. "I could ask you, couldn't I?"

Bernie shrugged and took a sip.

"Who do the Carpenters use—their own men, or someone down from London?"

"What—for a contract?"

"Yes."

"Job like that—I'm talking theory now—she was gunned down in broad daylight, I heard—job like that doesn't look like a local lad. There's no one I can think of in Bristol."

Diamond took the folded banknote from his pocket and placed it on the table with his hand over it. "I could show appreciation, Bernie, if you put out some feelers."

"Bloody dangerous."

"You can't help me, then?"

"It'll cost you."

"This is personal. It's worth it" He took his hand off the banknote and revealed a crisp new fifty. He lifted it and the twenty was underneath. He returned the fifty to his pocket and slid the twenty across the table. "I'll be in again Friday or Saturday."

He drove up College Road to Clifton, looking for the house where Danny Carpenter lived. Back in the early nineteenth century when the city had been infested with cholera, the affluent Clifton residents instructed their servants to leave blankets and clothes halfway down the hill for the poor wretches in Bristol, and the place still has a determination not to be contaminated by the noxious life below Whiteladies Road. Danny's residence was on the Down in one of the best positions in the city, with views along the Gorge to the Suspension Bridge. Old stone pillars at the entrance with griffins aloft gave promise of a gracious house. In fact, the original building at the end of the curved drive had been demolished at the time when architects went starry-eyed over steel and concrete. To Diamond's eye the replacement was an ugly pile of lemon-coloured, flat-roofed blocks. Even so, its location and scale represented money.

Before he got out, the security lights came on. A dog barked. A large bark. No need, really, to touch the bell push, but he did and was rewarded with the first bars of *Danny Boy*.

The door opened a fraction and a snarling muzzle was thrust through.

Diamond took a step back. Someone swore and hauled the dog inside. A man's face appeared, without doubt the face of a minder. "Yeah?"

"Danny at home?"

"Yeah."

"I'd like to see him, then."

"Yeah?"

"The name's Diamond. He's heard of it."

"Yeah?"

This might have continued for some time if a woman's voice had not said from the inner depths, "Who is it, Gary?"

Silence. Gary had forgotten already.

Diamond called out his own name and presently Gary's ravaged head was replaced by one easier on the eye, one Diamond knew, red-blonde and green-eyed. She had been in court for much of the Jake Carpenter trial.

"Evening, Celia."

She said, "You've got a bloody nerve."

"I'm here to see Danny."

"Not by invitation, you're not."

"About the murder of my wife."

"We don't know nothing about that. He spoke to your people and he's in the clear."

"Then he hasn't got a problem. He can see me."

"Aren't you forgetting you banged up his brother for a life term? Why don't you go forth and multiply, Mr. Diamond? Danny's busy." She turned her head and shouted, "Gary, we may need that dog again. The visitor is leaving."

"I've got some questions for you," Diamond said.

"*Me?* What have I got to do with it?"

"Do you want to come down to Bath, or shall we talk inside?"

"Hang about," Celia said. "What's this about?"

"I don't conduct interviews on doorsteps, Celia."

"I've done nothing wrong."

"So it's a trip to the nick, is it?"

She opened the door wider. "You'd better come in, you sly bastard."

The entrance hall was virtually a foyer, circular, with doors off, a grand staircase and a marble fountain. A life-size statue of a nude woman held up a shallow bowl from which the water cascaded.

Celia showed him into a reception room that seemed to have been removed from a safari lodge, with zebra skin hangings, Zulu shields, crossed spears and huge wooden carvings of animals.

She told him, "I'm not saying a word without Danny here."

That suited Diamond. "Good thinking. You'd better fetch him right away."

She was so flustered at being fingered as a possible suspect that she didn't realise Diamond had gotten his way.

He stood at the window taking in the view and musing on these villains' overview of all the little mortgaged houses like his own.

He heard someone behind him say, "You've been upsetting my wife."

"Someone murdered mine."

He turned. Danny Carpenter, the best looking of the brothers, still dark-haired at forty-five or so, stood in a red polo shirt and black jeans in front of a mural of a stalking lion. Celia wasn't even in the room. No matter, now Danny had been flushed out. His short, bare arms had the muscle tone of a regular weight lifter.

Diamond added, "I'm trying to find the reason."

"What reason?"

"Why she was murdered."

"Not here, you won't," Danny said. "We're clean. Your people spoke to me already."

"You've got nothing to hide, then."

"I was at the gym."

"And afterwards with your solicitor. I heard. A five-star alibi."

Danny displayed his gold fillings in a slow, wide grin.

This stung Diamond into commenting, "It's almost as if you knew something was going to happen."

"Watch it."

"Your brother Des is watertight, too."

"This is going nowhere, squire," Danny said.

"Don't tell me the Carpenter family draw the line at killing women. You could have used one of your heavies. Or hired someone."

"You've got to be joking," Danny said. "Who do you think we are—Fred Karno's Army? Listen, if we wanted to get at you, we wouldn't top your wife."

Put like that, it chimed with Diamond's own assessment, the main objection to the Carpenters as the killers: their uncomplicated notion of revenge would have resulted in his own death, not Steph's.

"If you want us off your back," he said as if he was speaking for the entire police operation, "you could tell me what the latest whisper is. Have you heard anything?"

"About the shooting?" Danny shook his head. "What sort of piece was used?"

"Point three-eight revolver."

"Doesn't say much."

"It will when we find the weapon."

"He'll have got rid of it, won't he?"

"Not necessarily," Diamond said. "This was a professional job, and professionals get attached to their pieces—don't they, Danny?"

"Let's leave it there before you say something that really gets up my nose."

Not yet, he thought. Up to now, he'd got no signal that Danny knew more about Steph's murder than he wanted to admit. The purpose of this call was to assess the man, tease out the guilt if possible.

He tried another approach. "You think your brother Jake's conviction was down to me, don't you?"

"You were on the case, sunshine."

"He wasn't fitted up, you know. The girl's blood was on his shoes, in his car. This was no contract job. He flipped when she tried to sling her hook. You didn't see what he did to her face. I did. Seventeen, she was."

Danny stared out of the window, unmoved.

Diamond said, "There was never any doubt. The jury took under an hour."

Still the brother was silent.

"PC Plod could have handled the case," Diamond pressed on recklessly. "Okay, Celia and the other women stood outside the court giving me lip and one of them clawed my face, but they know it wasn't down to me. Your brother Jake is a stupid, sadistic killer."

"Still family," Danny said in a low voice, without challenging the statement.

"What's happening to Janie, then?"

"Who?"

"His girlfriend. The woman who marked me."

Danny shrugged. He appeared to have no interest in Janie. Or what she had done to Diamond.

Diamond reminded him, "She was wanting to visit Jake. She said you and Des monopolised all the visits."

"She'd better piss off back to London," Danny said. "She's nothing to Jake."

"You haven't spoken to her since the trial?"

Danny shook his head.

"Is it possible Janie felt so strongly about the case that she fired the shots?"

"Don't ask me."

"I'm trying to get your opinion, Danny. You said if the family was out for revenge you wouldn't target my wife. You'd go for me. Well, Janie isn't family. Is this a woman's way of settling the score? Does she have a gun?"

Danny turned to face him. "You're boring me. Why don't you leave?"

"Maybe I should."

He'd got as much or as little from this member of the Carpenter family as he was likely to. The trick in making home visits to known criminals is judging when to leave.

# 13

TEN DAYS WENT by.

Ten more days in the process of grieving, this grudging acceptance of the stark reality. One day he decided he would take all Steph's clothes to a charity shop because that was what she would have wished (so long as it was not the one where she worked). He carried the dresses downstairs and draped them across the back seat of the car so as not to crease them. If the helpers in the shop decided to throw them in a corner in the back room or stuff them into plastic sacks, so be it. He wouldn't do it himself. Then, in a fit of sentiment he picked out one of her favourites, the fuchsia-coloured silk one she'd worn to the theatre last time they'd gone, carried it upstairs again and returned it to the wardrobe. It should have gone with the rest. There was no logical reason to keep it. He simply couldn't part with it yet. And when he looked at the other clothes, he couldn't be separated from them either. He drove around with those dresses on the back seat for days, reaching back to touch them at moments when he felt really down. You're a pathetic old idiot, he told himself when he finally removed them from the car and put them back on their hangers.

Of course he tried immersing himself in work, but that was fraught with problems he hadn't experienced before. The danger of working in isolation, he learned the hard way, is that you are forced to rely on hunches and theories. In a CID team, you have information coming in all the time, ninety-five per cent of it useless, but at least your brain is occupied reading reports and statements and checking the records. In the Yorkshire Ripper inquiry they had so many statements on file that the floor of the incident room started to cave in. The storage problem is less in this computer age, more a matter of pressing the right keys. McGarvie could cross-reference all known cases of murder using .38 revolvers: shootings in public parks, suspicious deaths of police and their families. He could analyse statements, classify the long list of objects found in Victoria Park and Charlotte Street Car Park, go through years of Peter Diamond's case notes looking for people with grudges. Bloody McGarvie had plenty to occupy him.

This parallel investigation of Diamond's had to be run on a wing and a prayer. A certain amount leaked out of the incident room, of course, through old colleagues, and he barged in there repeatedly on the flimsiest of pretexts, but it was obvious the team were under instructions not to tell him things.

One afternoon, in a quiet corner of the canteen, Keith Halliwell confided to him, "The lads are on your side, guv, even if it doesn't look like it. There's a lot of anger about the way you're being treated."

"I'm not looking for sympathy, Keith. A result is all I want."

"It isn't sympathy. Well, you know what I mean. We do feel for you. Of course we do. This is something else. Personality."

"The Big Mac?"

"He doesn't speak for the rest of us. We want you to know that."

"He's doing the same as I would. I'm a hard-nosed git when I'm on a case, as you well know."

In truth, he wasn't impervious to sympathy or support from his colleagues. However, he would trade it for hard facts on where the investigation was leading—if anywhere. Too many theories are a pain. They keep you awake at night. They're difficult to disprove without the backup of the murder squad.

His only backup was the snout, Bernie Hescott, and he hadn't anything to offer when Diamond drove to Bristol for the fourth time and looked him up in the Rummer. "I'm working on it, Mr. D. Got more feelers out than a family of bugs. I'm not sleeping at nights."

"Join the club."

"Give me another week and I might have something for you."

"This isn't what I came to hear, Bernie."

"It's all the people I have to see."

"You wouldn't be stringing me along?"

"No way. Wednesday, then. And Mr. D . . ."

"Yep?"

"I've run through my expenses."

He got twenty more.

Next morning, appallingly early, Peter Diamond's lie-in after a night of little sleep was disturbed by a heavy vehicle drawing up outside the house, followed by a voice issuing orders. He would have sworn and turned over in bed if the voice had not been pitched so low that it was obvious something underhand was going on. He groaned, sat up, shuffled to the bedroom window and was amazed to see men in police-issue Kevlar body armour scrambling out of the back of a van. Two of them carried an enforcer, the "fifty pound key" used by rapid entry teams as a battering ram. Curtis McGarvie got out of a separate car and marched up the short path to the front door.

Diamond belted downstairs in the T-shirt and shorts he slept in and flung open the door. "What the fuck is going on?"

McGarvie raised his palms in a pacifying way. "Stay cool, Peter. We need to make a further search."

"Go to hell."

"Can we speak inside?"

"You're out of your mind."

"I'd rather not have this conversation on your doorstep."

"What are you looking for?"

"The firearm used in the murder of your wife."

"For crying out loud."

"So I'm formally requesting permission to search your house and garden."

"You can piss off, McGarvie."

"I thought that would be your response." He handed over a sheet of paper. "This is your copy of a warrant issued by a magistrate last night."

"A *search warrant?* This isn't happening."

But it was. And you don't argue with a warrant unless you want your door smashed in. Diamond stepped aside, and three of the ninjas moved in. "Why wasn't I told? You can pick up a phone."

"Do you want it straight? I had reason to think you might dispose of the evidence."

He was speechless.

McGarvie admitted more men, and every one avoided eye contact with Diamond. They obviously had their orders. They must have been briefed before dawn. Some went straight upstairs, others through to the kitchen.

Diamond slumped into a chair in the front room.

McGarvie told him, "You know you have the right to ask a friend or neighbour to witness the search?"

"I don't need lecturing on my rights."

"Don't you want to see what's going on?"

"No. This whole charade is a waste of time."

"In that case why don't you get dressed? I'm going to take you in whether we find anything or not."

"You'll find sod all. You're out of order. I'll hang you out to dry for this."

"It's all according to the book."

"I opened the place to you before. You've been through here already."

"That wasn't a full search."

"God help us." Diamond trudged upstairs and saw what he meant. Three men in the bedroom were ripping the fitted carpet from its stays. His entire wardrobe had been emptied and the clothes were on the bed. All the drawers had been removed from the chests and sideboard.

He looked out of the window. Two officers with metal detectors were at work in the garden.

He grabbed a pair of trousers and got into them.

At the nick—his own nick—they offered to call his solicitor. He said he'd done nothing wrong, so he didn't need one.

They kept him waiting over three hours.

His anger hadn't subsided. In the interview room with the tapes running he stared McGarvie out like a boxer at the weigh-in. A sergeant he'd never seen before was in the other chair. He was damned sure Georgina and most of the senior detectives were watching on video monitors.

McGarvie said in that voice like a rusty lawn mower, "At the previous interview, you stated that you didn't possess a gun. Is that still your position?"

His thoughts flew to the empty shoebox in the loft.

They couldn't have found anything. He'd gone through the place. "Yes, it is."

"When you served in the Met, you were an authorised shot—right?"

"We've been over this."

"For the tape, would you confirm it?"

"I was trained to use firearms, yes."

"Were there occasions when you were issued a handgun?"

"Yes."

"A Smith & Wesson revolver?"

He said with mounting unease, "That was the standard sidearm before they switched to automatics."

"Point three-eight?"

"You know as well as I do."

"At Fulham, where you served, guns were issued and returned according to procedure, were they?"

"To my knowledge, yes."

"You always returned the guns you carried?"

"Of course." This could only be leading one way, he thought with disaster bearing down on him. How could McGarvie have learned that he acquired that gun back in the nineteen eighties? It had been signed out and signed in again.

"Before we go on," McGarvie said with obvious relish in prolonging this, "I'd better give you some background. We've been in contact with the Met."

"The Met—what for?"

"A certain Smith & Wesson revolver at Fulham—where you served—went missing in nineteen eighty-six, about the time the change to automatics took place. It hasn't been traced since."

"Nothing to do with me."

"You were the last to be issued with it."

"And I bet I returned it. Always did."

"Yes, the paperwork was in order. But after that, there's no record of the gun with that serial number."

"Not my fault. You can't stick that on me."

McGarvie smiled with the confidence of a player with trumps in hand. "Procedures at Fulham in the eighties were somewhat relaxed—shall we say? It's not impossible the issuing officer made a mistake."

"Not in my case, he didn't. You just agreed it was returned and signed in."

"The officer in question later appeared before a disciplinary board charged with negligence. A number of weapons couldn't be accounted for. Clearly the rules were breached in some way."

"Am I missing something here? What has this got to do with my wife's murder?"

"She was shot with a point three-eight revolver. When I questioned you before, you denied owning one. You just repeated that denial." McGarvie's brown eyes glittered. Reaching under the desk he took out a sealed evidence bag and passed it across. "For the purposes of the tape, I am now showing the witness exhibit D03, a police-issue point three-eight Smith & Wesson revolver recovered this morning from the garden of his house in Lower Weston."

Diamond's voice shrilled in disbelief. "What are you saying? You found this in my garden?"

"With some ammunition. Wrapped in a cloth in a biscuit tin buried in the vegetable patch."

Vegetable patch? This had to mean the little plot where Steph grew tomatoes last summer. He was silent while his brain raced, trying to make sense of it.

McGarvie added, "The serial number confirms this gun as one missing from Fulham since nineteen eighty-six. You were issued it and apparently returned it. Do you have any explanation?"

He was up to his eyeballs now. A horrible hissing started in his ears—the old blood pressure problem threatening. After a long pause he said, "I wasn't strictly straight with you just now. This gun has been in my possession ever since I was in the Met."

McGarvie gave a grunt of satisfaction. "So you lied."

"Well—"

"You lied."

"They were dangerous times. We had some hard men on our patch."

"Face it, Peter."

"You asked if I *owned* a gun. I don't. It's still police property."

"Now you're playing with words."

"Okay. I should have come clean when you asked me."

"What stopped you?"

"Didn't want to draw you up a blind alley. All this horse shit about the gun has nothing to do with my wife's murder."

"Ho." McGarvie turned to exchange a look with the sergeant beside him. "And if it turns out to be the murder weapon . . . ?"

"No chance. It was in the loft of my house, in a shoebox."

"Until when?"

Another crushing uncertainty hit him.

"Don't know," he was forced to admit. "After you interviewed me last time, I went up to the loft to look for it, and the box was empty."

"Is this another half-truth?"

"No."

"Why did you need the gun?"

"For protection. If you want it straight, I was losing confidence in your investigation. I thought I might need to open up some fresh lines of inquiry."

"With a gun in your hand? Going it alone, eh—contrary to the ACC's instructions?"

Diamond shrugged. There were more important issues now than defying Georgina.

"If the gun wasn't in the loft, who could have moved it except you or your wife?"

"I've tried to think ever since I noticed it was gone. I don't have an answer."

"You don't have answers to much. Sure you didn't panic after we visited the house? Sure you didn't take the gun from the loft and bury it in the garden?"

"I didn't bury it."

"You didn't?"

He sighed heavily.

"Then who did? Someone trying to fit you up, I suppose?" McGarvie said with sarcasm.

"I've no idea. This is a total shock to me. Listen, if I wanted to get rid of the thing, why would I bury it in my own garden?"

"No one suggested you wanted to get rid of it. Far from it. You thought you might need it again."

"This is unreal."

"It isn't looking good, Peter. There's a time period on the morning of the murder when you have no alibi. You say you came into work, but no one here saw you before eleven."

"I was in my office."

"Keeping your head down—to quote you. Then, ten days ago, you brought in your wife's handbag."

Incensed at the way things were being twisted, he blurted out, "That was a responsible act."

"In the bag was her diary with certain entries suggesting she'd been in contact with someone referred to as 'T,' and who—apparently—she'd arranged to meet in Victoria Park on the morning of her death."

"Well?"

"We can't say for sure if those entries were written by your wife."

"Jesus! Of course they were."

"We've checked the record of phone calls made from your number. There's nothing on the fifteenth or the nineteenth. Both days are blank. There were no calls to 'T.'"

"Doesn't mean they didn't happen." He cast about for an explanation. "Maybe she used the phone at work or went out to the callbox up the street."

"Why?"

"For privacy. Or maybe she intended to call, but 'T' called her first. There won't be any record of incoming calls."

"I think it's more likely the diary entries are forgeries. Manufactured evidence."

"Oh, come on."

"An attempt to deflect attention."

"It's Steph's handwriting, for Christ's sake."

"I wouldn't call it handwriting. Most of the entries are printed."

"Her printing, then."

"Easy to fake."

Diamond gave an exasperated sigh.

McGarvie added, "You had plenty of time to work on it."

"The diary was in the bloody handbag in the stone vase in the park."

"That's open to question. Our search team didn't find it."

"Because they didn't look in the right place."

"They tell me they did."

"They're covering their arses. Ask Warburton. He slung the bag in there."

"He's a dipso. His memory isn't reliable."

"He remembered enough to tell me."

"So you say. You didn't pass the information on to us. That bag was potentially crucial evidence and you recovered it yourself, if your account is true, with no witness. Hours later, you handed it in."

"I told you at the time, I looked at what was inside."

"Did you write anything in the diary?"

"Did I *what?*"

"You heard me."

"Oh, get away! You're losing it, McGarvie."

McGarvie reached for the package containing the gun and drew it back across the table like a gambler who has scooped the pool. "The next step is to have this test fired and see if the rifling matches the bullets found at the scene."

"You really want to stick this on me, don't you?" Diamond said. "Have you given any thought at all as to *why* I would murder my wife?"

McGarvie was unfazed. "Why would anyone murder her? She appears to have been a popular, charming, inoffensive woman. If anyone has a reason, it's you, and it's well hidden. I don't know what happened in your marriage, but it'll come out—unless you want to open up now."

"You disgust me."

"In my shoes, you'd think the same, Peter. The husband has to be the number-one suspect, and when he brings suspicion on himself, you act."

A telling comment.

Diamond said bleakly, without conceding anything, "What happens now?"

"I'll get you to write a statement about the gun. When ballistics have checked it, we can talk again. I'm not going to hold you here."

"Am I supposed to be grateful? In the meantime, the real killer is laughing up his sleeve."

"We're pursuing every possible lead."

"Oh, sure."

"Interview terminated at four twenty-six."

# 14

THE PHONE WAS going when he finally got home after six. He'd had all the hassle he could take for one day, so he didn't pick it up. They'd give up presently. He and Steph had experimented with an answerphone for a time. It hadn't survived long. It was faulty (or, more likely, his attempt to install it was faulty) and kept running the messages into each other. You'd get a "Hi, Diamonds" from Steph's sister and then a male voice would come in selling double glazing, followed by the tail end of a message about a parcel some unknown firm had been trying to deliver for days. He'd ripped out the contraption in a fury and plugged in the simple phone they'd used before.

He took a brief look around. A search team executing a warrant was supposed to do its work with "minimum disruption." The door of the living room wouldn't open over the rucked-up carpet, the pictures were still off the walls and the drawers in the wall unit wouldn't close and were in the wrong places. Steph would have spent the evening straightening up. He ignored the mess. Out in the garden, he stood looking balefully at the place where the tin box containing the gun was supposed to have been found. No use denying there was a hole in the ground. One more weird twist to this nightmare. He had no explanation. His world had gone so crazy that he actually asked himself whether he could have buried the gun himself and wiped the episode from his memory. So much had been squeezed into the five weeks since Steph's death that certain things already seemed remote, if not unreal. Why would he have wanted to hide the gun—unless his brain had flipped and he'd done the unimaginable thing he'd been denying?

"Christ, no," he said aloud. "You may be so dumb you couldn't find your arse with two hands at high noon, but you would never hurt Steph."

He returned indoors and the phone started again, so he lifted the receiver and clicked it dead. Made himself tea and tried to decide if he could stomach beans on toast again.

The cat wanted to eat, for sure. It pressed against his leg, making piteous sounds. He opened a tin and put down some food.

Then the damned phone went again. "You're bloody persistent, whoever you are," he said before finally putting it to his ear. "Yes?"

"Where have you been?" a familiar voice asked. "I've been trying to reach you for days."

"Julie. If I'd known it was you . . ."

"Great! You just let it ring, do you? What if it was a real emergency instead of an old oppo wanting to know how you're coping?"

"What do you mean—'a real emergency'? Don't you think I'm in a real emergency already?"

"Still getting to you, is it?" Julie's voice sounded more concerned. As his deputy until a couple of years ago, she knew all about his mood swings. They'd led in the end to her request for a transfer to Headquarters.

"I'm up shit creek, Julie. The prime suspect. They searched my house this morning, with a warrant—would you believe?— drove me to the station and put me through the grinder. McGarvie thinks I'm Dr. Crippen."

"How ridiculous. Whatever for?"

He told Julie about the gun.

"That *is* a facer," she agreed. "Whatever possessed you to keep a gun? Oh, don't bother. What are they doing? Testing it?"

"Yes, and when it turns out to be the murder weapon, I'm screwed."

"How could it be?"

"You tell me. I didn't expect it to turn up in a tin box in my garden."

"You think someone is trying to frame you?"

"Trying? It's done and dusted."

"McGarvie wouldn't stoop to that. You may not like him, and I understand why, but he's honest."

"And so wide of the mark, Julie. He should be out there catching the real killer instead of breathing down my neck."

"Yes," she admitted. "I thought he was going to make a fist of this. I misjudged him."

"You're not alone."

"But I told you he was good. I'm sorry." She tried sounding a brighter note. "What about you? I bet you haven't been sitting on the sidelines these last weeks. What have you dug up?"

"Sweet f.a., apart from Steph's diary." He told her how he'd tracked it down with the help of the wino, Warburton, and how McGarvie was alleging that the entries relating to "T" were faked.

"That man has certainly got it in for you. How did you get up his nose?"

"You know me, Julie. A touch hot-headed."

"Only a touch?"

He sensed that she was smiling.

She asked, "What else have you been up to?"

"I'm still convinced this was a contract killing. I called on one of the Carpenter brothers—Danny. I can hear you saying, 'That wasn't wise,' and you're right. He'd think nothing of topping me. He's bitter about Jake, never mind that the toerag got what he deserved. But Danny Carpenter wouldn't see the point in having Steph killed. That's too devious for him."

"You count him out?"

"Unless there was some motive I'm not aware of."

"But who else would hire a gunman?"

"I've been over that many times, Julie. McGarvie took me through all the cases I've had anything to do with in Bath and Bristol. Most were domestic. No one fits the frame."

"How about earlier—when you were in the Met?"

"Bloody long time to harbour a grudge. More than ten years. It's true I came up against professional criminals more often in those days. But, Julie, the hard men think like Danny Carpenter. If they wanted to hit me, I'm a big enough target."

Julie asked suddenly, "In your time with the Met, did you ever rub shoulders with a DCI Weather?"

"Say that again."

"Weather."

Anything outside the focus of his attention was an effort to take in. "In the Met, you said? There was a copper of that name at Fulham. We called him Stormy, of course. He could be the same guy. Chief Inspector now, is he? Why—have you met him?"

"No. His wife is missing. She's ex-police. A sergeant at Shepherd's Bush until a year or so ago. Pat Weather. I read about her in one of those Scotland Yard bulletins that get sent out—the ones you never bother with."

"How long has she been gone?"

"More than a week."

"Problem in the marriage, I expect."

"I just thought I'd mention it. If some evil-minded crook was looking for a way to settle old scores, he might be targeting detectives' wives."

He weighed the suggestion. "You think this missing woman is dead?"

"I just wonder."

"It's a big assumption, Julie."

"At this point, yes. But if anything *has* happened to her . . ."

"Let's hope not, for both their sakes. But thanks. I'll keep tabs on this one. Stormy Weather. Right now I don't remember anything about the guy except his nickname, but he could have been involved in cases I was on. Let's see how it plays. Can't call him with the news that my wife was murdered when he's hoping his is still alive."

"So what are your theories about the diary?" she asked him.

"This 'T'? I'm foxed. Can't link it to anyone. And not for want of trying. I've been through our address book as well as Steph's."

"If it's the killer, you can bet you won't find the name in your address book."

"Right. The odds are on a new contact."

"Does McGarvie have any leads?"

"I told you. McGarvie has convinced himself I forged the diary entries as some kind of red herring. Working out who 'T' might be is not high priority."

"Are you certain it's Steph's writing?"

"No question. It's printing, actually, but she often wrote things like that."

"You made a copy?"

"Yes."

"Then I think you should put all your efforts into cracking this one."

"Tell me about it!"

"Maybe the people in the charity shop heard her mention something."

"I'll give it a go. I drew a blank at the hairdressers."

"You'll crack it, I'm confident of that. Could 'T' stand for a surname?"

"If you ask me, Julie, it's invented. The killer isn't going to give his real name, is he?"

"Depends. If it was someone she knew already, they wouldn't use a false name."

"Good point. Actually, I can't see it being a surname. Steph liked to be on first-name terms with everyone. I reckon if she met the Queen, she'd be calling her Liz in a matter of minutes. I tried going through all the Christian names from Tabitha to Tyrone, but I'm convinced this is someone I haven't heard of."

"Nicknames? Taffy? Tich? Tubby?"

"Those, too. I won't give up. I just have to cast the net wider."

She asked how he was coping with living alone and he told her everything was under control, at the same time eyeing the curtain the search team had tugged off the rail. Why burden Julie with his problems? She didn't want to know that he hadn't slept properly since it happened, that he still reached across the bed for Steph, expecting the warmth of her smooth skin, and still ached for her wise advice, her marvellous gift of defusing the troubles he faced.

"Raffles has taken it harder than I have."

"Poor old Raffles."

"Cats aren't so forgiving as humans. He didn't like his litter box being searched."

"That's a liberty."

"Hasn't used it all day."

"Where does he go?"

"Outside when I open the door—at the double."

She laughed. "At least they dug a hole for him."

"You haven't seen the size of the hole. For a cat it would be like squatting over Beachy Head."

"And you still can't think how the gun got from the loft to the garden?"

"No idea. That's something else I need to find out."

"You ought to get the locks changed."

"I should. There's plenty to keep me busy."

"You're going to need some domestic help. A cleaner."

"I'll cope, thanks. Life is complicated enough."

"A cleaner would simplify it."

"I can manage without."

"You were always too stubborn for your own good."

"Thanks, Julie. I'll have that on my tombstone."

"No, there's a better epitaph than that," she said. "'*Stuff 'em all.*' Good luck to you, guv."

He was starting to speak his thoughts aloud. A bad sign, so he'd always heard. Worse, he was speaking to Steph as if she were there in the room.

"You've got some explaining to do, my love. Either you buried that shooter yourself, or you know who did. I don't see a sign of anyone breaking in. It happened while you were here, didn't it? But why, Steph?"

He'd never told her he'd kept the revolver all those years. She didn't know the threats he was under when he left the Met. That was why he'd hidden it in the loft where she hardly ever went because of her fear of spiders.

"Well, now," he continued, as if she were standing in the room. "Just suppose you *did* go up there for some reason and found the damned thing. You must have been deeply shocked. You hated guns and weapons of all kinds. It would get to you, having a handgun in the house. So I guess you may have decided you couldn't live with it. I can understand that. I can even understand you thinking of burying it. What I just can't fathom, Steph, is why you didn't mention it to me. I was secretive, yes, and I'm sorry for that, more sorry than I can say. But you were always open about everything. You would have told me, wouldn't you?"

He filled the silence with a sigh.

There was something else she hadn't told him. She hadn't mentioned a word about "T"—whoever that was. There were three references in the diary to this "T." Two phone calls, and the meeting in the park, all in the two weeks prior to her death. And she'd had her hair done specially. All this cloak-and-dagger stuff was so unlike Steph. Maybe she didn't think it was important enough to mention. Was that a reasonable assumption? If "T" was a woman friend, for instance, someone Steph knew well, and not a man, as the demons in his head kept whispering, might she have made these diary entries without saying a word about it?

Unlikely. She *always* told him things.

At best, she had acted out of character. At worst, there was a secret liaison with someone who turned out to be a killer.

And now, instead of talking to Steph, he turned on himself. "You're a flake, Diamond. You're starting to mistrust her. While she was alive, she never gave you a moment's uncertainty. She was loyal right to the end. How can you think this way?"

## 15

THIS WAS A sharp suit, a two-piece by Zegna, in a pale grey woollen cloth with a faint blue thread. Harry Tattersall bought it for nine hundred pounds, off the peg at Selfridges. With his slim build the only tailoring he ever needed was to the leg length. The silver-tongued West Indian salesman told him he looked as smooth as a dolphin, which was meant as a compliment. Harry would have preferred to look like a lord—the object of this exercise—but he guessed he would also need a good white shirt and an old boy's tie to get the aristocratic effect.

The Arab way of doing things appealed to Harry. Who else paid cash upfront to kit out their team? These fellows had style. And the good thing was that his part in the scam would be over before the punch-up began. He'd be out of the Dorchester and hightailing it to a safe distance. Even if the others were all nicked, he'd still be sitting pretty in his dolphin-smooth Zegna suit with six hundred in the back pocket.

Rhadi called him at the weekend and asked if he was ready.

"Is this the lift-off, old chum?"

"No, no," Rhadi said. "I'm just checking that you'll be prepared when the time comes."

"At concert pitch. I've bought the suit."

"You had enough dosh to cover it?"

"Enough for a shirt and shoes as well."

"And the disguise?"

"All under control."

"Don't go downmarket for the hair colouring, will you?" Rhadi cautioned. "Nothing looks worse than badly dyed hair."

"A cheap wig."

"You're wearing a *wig* for this?"

"No. You said nothing looks worse. I'm telling you a cheap wig does. Don't fret. I'll look the part."

"Have you picked a name yet?"

"How does Lord Muck strike you?"

"For the love of Allah take this seriously, Harry. I told Zahir you're totally dependable. If you mess up, if he even *thinks you* might mess up, we're both dead meat."

"He's as dangerous as that?"

"He's all right if you do the job. Now what are you calling yourself?"

"Sir John Mason. There are several in *Who's Who*. A computer-hacking friend of mine has found me the credit card details of one of them, and I've had my own card made by someone in the business. Satisfied?"

"It will do, I guess." Rhadi cleared his throat nervously. "Now, these are your instructions. Listen carefully. When the time is right—and we don't know when that will be—you'll get a call from someone who won't give his name."

"This ex-RAF type?"

"He'll simply tell you that the goods you ordered are coming in on . . . and he'll name a date."

"The payday?"

"Yes. Thank him and put the phone down. Don't say any more. Then it *will* be all systems go. First, you pass on the info to me."

"This will be the date the Prince has booked at the hotel?"

"Right. Then you go to a payphone at some suitable place— let's say the Festival Hall—and call the Dorchester as—who was it?"

"Sir John Mason."

". . . and reserve one of the roof garden suites. Say you want it for a week."

"A week from when?"

"The day following the date you have just been given. The Prince will be well installed by then."

"I give them the credit card details. If they check, they'll find it's all kosher."

"All right. You still have some money left, I hope?"

"A little. Good suits don't come cheap."

"You will also need some new luggage. A case, of superior quality. Fill it with bulky objects unconnected with yourself. Cushions, newspapers—something like that. Be careful not to leave fingerprints."

"I wasn't born yesterday."

Rhadi said primly, "I'm telling you all this because we won't be in contact again—not until after it's over. On the day, you must arrive in disguise by a taxi hired outside one of the main railway stations. You will be carrying the suitcase. You check in to the Dorchester at two in the afternoon. No earlier, no later."

"How do I let you know which suite I've been given?"

"Do you have a mobile?"

"Of course."

"Get a new one. New number. Use it only for this. Once you're alone in the suite, call Zahir and tell him where you are. This is his number. Got a pen?"

"Go ahead." Harry noted it. "Do I call you as well?"

"No need. Shortly after, Zahir will knock. You will admit him and Ibrahim, and your job will be over, apart from leaving discreetly."

"I think I can manage that."

"Where will you go?"

"Straight to Ireland. I have a cottage there."

"Good man."

"But I'll be back for the payout. A hundred grand, we agreed. I have to say this, Rhadi. Perish the thought, but if your friends should be so unwise as to change their minds about my share, I know enough to put you all away, and I can arrange it at no risk to myself."

"Harry, that won't happen. These are men of honour. When they give their word, they keep to it."

"They'd better."

Georgina looked into Diamond's office on the Thursday, two days after the search of his house. "Don't get up."

Unusually he was at the computer, checking the Scotland Yard site for the latest on the missing wife of DCI Weather, the old colleague Julie had mentioned. There was nothing new.

"You look busy," she told him.

"Raking through the embers, that's all." He looked at her over the screen fearing the worst. "Have you heard from forensics?"

"About the gun? No. You know what they're like. It could take another week." She remained standing with her hands on the back of the chair in front of his desk. "Peter, I'm sorry the search had to be done the way it was, without even telling you in advance. I sanctioned the application for the warrant after Curtis McGarvie convinced me you probably had the gun in your possession. It wasn't just a hunch. He looked at your service record, found you were an authorised shot."

"He told me."

"The point is that the fatal bullets could have been fired from a police handgun. The calibre—"

"I know this, ma'am."

"And when he learned there were problems over the firearms issued from Fulham in your time there, and asked to see the records and found you were the last to use that particular gun, it couldn't be shirked. You'd already denied owning a weapon. You weren't going to put your hand up unless we produced it."

"Which you have."

"We're not being po-faced about this. You wouldn't be the first officer, or the last, to acquire a gun for his own protection. Because you denied it, we don't automatically disbelieve everything else you said."

He listened in silence, thinking this wasn't the heart-to-heart it was meant to appear. She was doing her best to soften him up. When this didn't work, McGarvie would put the boot in.

"There's tremendous sympathy for you in CID—as there is throughout the station," Georgina went on. "You're under huge stress even without the extra pressure of the investigation. I have to say that Curtis has risked a lot of unpopularity from the ranks."

"My heart bleeds."

"He knew what the job implied when he took it on. He'll get to the truth."

"He's taking his time."

"That isn't fair, Peter. He's working flat out and so are the team. If you'd been frank about the gun, you'd have saved him many hours of work."

That angered him. "If you really want to know, I didn't own up to the gun because I knew it would distract them. Yes, I'm out of order to have kept the thing, but everyone's wasting their time on it. It's six weeks since the murder and the trail's gone cold."

"We don't know that. Other lines of enquiry are being followed."

"Give it another two weeks and you'll be standing people down. We both know the score."

"We're giving this top priority."

"Next you'll be telling me budgets don't exist, Headquarters aren't already breathing down your neck for a budget report."

"Peter, people are working overtime for nothing because of their loyalty to you. They want this killer caught."

He nodded. "So why are you talking to me, ma'am? What's behind this?"

Sounding almost maternal in her concern to keep him sweet, she said, "Is there anything else you haven't mentioned? Anything we should know?"

She was fishing for the motive. The confession that his marriage was in trouble.

The devil in him made him lead her on a bit. "Off the record?"

"There are only the two of us here."

He could almost feel the heat of her charm.

"I'll come clean, then." Leaning forward, he said, "I loved my wife. Still do. Long after McGarvie has folded his tent and crept away I'll be on the case. It may never come to court, but it'll be solved, I promise you."

Georgina's voice altered. He'd touched a raw nerve. She told him, "How do I get through to you, Peter? We can't allow you to get involved. It would sabotage everything. You know that."

"But I *am* involved. I'm your number-one suspect."

"Now, come on. That's a bit much."

"So who's in the frame apart from me?"

She was unprepared for that one. She could only counter it with an impatient sigh.

He said, "If I don't point you in the right direction, I'm hung, drawn and quartered."

"Oh, be reasonable."

"Be reasonable? My place was searched twice. You authorised a warrant. You've taken away my wife's private letters, interviewed me on tape, looked for dirt in my career record, accused me of forging the things in her diary. Is it any wonder I'm starting to sound paranoid?"

She said, "I've told you I'm sorry about the way some of this has been handled. You and Curtis are totally opposite in most ways, but you share one thing. You don't believe in sugaring the pill. I should have seen there would be personality problems when I asked for him. He's still the best detective I could get. He has my confidence—I want to make that clear."

"You have, ma'am."

"And in case you're wondering whose idea this conversation was, it was mine. I haven't known you as long as most of the people in this place, but I share their respect for you and their concern. I want to see you come through this."

"I will," he told her. "I will."

On Monday morning he attended the inquest. It was mercifully straightforward, since the salient facts of Steph's identity and where, when and how she came to be dead were manifestly clear. As the coroner explained, apportioning blame was outside his jurisdiction. The jury might decide murder was done, but the process of identifying who was responsible would be up to the criminal court. Diamond listened to the two main witnesses, Warburton, passably sober this morning and wearing a suit, and Jim Middleton, the pathologist. The facts of the case were so firmly lodged in Diamond's own mind that he could listen impassively even when the phrase "an execution-style shooting" was used. His own testimony was limited to stating when he had last seen Steph alive and explaining that he couldn't account for her being found in the park.

The police were represented by McGarvie, who gave evidence about the recovery of the bullets and the finding of the handbag and the diary entry. He said nothing about the discovery of the handgun in Diamond's garden, merely informing the court that enquiries were continuing.

The coroner adjourned the inquest, pending further investigations.

Outside, Diamond declined to make any kind of comment when the press converged. They took their photos on the move while he marched briskly to the car park.

And then stopped.

McGarvie was beside his car. "I know you've been waiting

on the ballistics tests, as we all have," he said. "I called them first thing this morning."

"And . . . ?"

"The results are inconclusive."

"You mean the bullets weren't fired from the gun?"

"No. They can't say either way, so they're test-firing again."

"At your request, I suppose."

"Yours also, I expect," McGarvie said with a faint smirk. "It's in everyone's interest to have the truth, I would have thought."

"Did they find any prints on the gun?"

"Wiped. It was wrapped in a cloth."

Diamond got into his car and drove back to Bath.

"Inconclusive" meant that the rifling on the test round was not identical with the bullets they'd found but close enough for suspicion. One bullet had been crushed by some emergency vehicle and was probably unsuitable for ballistic analysis. The other had passed through bone and possibly struck stone when hitting the ground, and the match was likely to be less than perfect. Like fingerprinting, ballistic proof depends on sufficient points of similarity.

So he still faced the sickening possibility that Steph had been murdered with the gun he had stupidly kept all those years. How the killer had found it, he could only guess. He had two hypotheses, equally painful to accept. Firstly, it was possible Steph had discovered the gun herself and instead of asking him what the hell he was doing with it, she had confided in someone she mistakenly believed she could trust—this "T." Theory number two: she had trusted someone, some Trojan Horse, so well that he was given the run of the house and went up into the loft and found the gun. It seemed fantastic, but a fantastic crime required a fantastic explanation.

He bought a burger and a beer and sat in his usual seat below the west front of the Abbey where the mediaeval stone angels, scarred and mutilated by five hundred years of weather, clung resolutely to their ladders. Watching them at the edge of his vision he sometimes caught them on the move. He'd fix his gaze on the left side, and the angels on the right would climb up a rung or two, always upwards. He knew it was impossible and an optical illusion, but it lifted his own spirits when it happened.

The events of the last twenty-four hours were being manipulated by the police to make him break faith with Steph. Uncomfortable facts had to be faced. What other construction was there to put on the entries she'd made in the diary than that she was meeting somebody she'd never mentioned to him? None he could think of. Fair enough, she was his wife, not his ten-year-old daughter, and she had a perfect right to meet people without telling him every detail. She didn't demand to know how he spent every hour of each day. Yet it wasn't in Steph's nature to have secrets from him. She was open about everything. She would enjoy telling him how she'd spent each day and he'd looked forward every evening to hearing her lively slant on the things she'd done and the contacts she'd made. This had been one of the strengths of their marriage. Nothing had been off-limits.

Nothing except . . .

He sat forward and his hand went to his face. There *was* a part of her life they scarcely ever mentioned. Her first marriage, a time of such unhappiness that it never lost the power to hurt.

Her dipstick ex-husband, who hadn't bothered to turn up to the funeral, nor even leave a message that he regretted her cruel death, had been called Edward. That was the name she'd used on the rare occasions she spoke of him. Edward. The formality distanced him from her.

Edward Dixon-Bligh.

What a mouthful.

Surely when she lived with him she would have called him Ted.

His eyes travelled up the Abbey front. One of those angels had just moved.

# 16

THAT EVENING HE repeatedly tried the London number he believed was Dixon-Bligh's and kept getting the same answerphone message: a plummy voice asking the caller to leave a name and number and "I'll get back to you toot-sweet." It grated after the third or fourth try, especially as the message didn't supply a name. Never having met the man, he couldn't tell for certain if the voice belonged to Steph's ex.

He left a message saying it was extremely important that they spoke, however late.

But in this case, "toot-sweet" meant "not tonight."

Lying awake waiting for the call that didn't come, he tried to think of a reason why that pig of a husband might have resurfaced in Steph's life. The most plausible was that he'd run through his money and appealed to her for funds. She'd always been a soft touch, helping scatty friends who couldn't pay the phone bill and were threatened with disconnection. She sometimes bought the same *Big Issue* three times over to help homeless people. It wouldn't have required much of a sob story from Dixon-Bligh to have her reaching for her chequebook. She hadn't forgotten the misery of life with him, but she'd still fork out.

Even Steph, generous as she was, must have sensed that it wasn't a good idea to meet her ex-husband. She would have preferred dealing with him by phone and post. Most likely he concocted some reason for meeting her in the park. It had been written in her diary, so it was fixed ahead of time. Maybe he'd offered to hand over something that belonged to her.

Surely he wasn't blackmailing her?

*Blackmail?*

At night, a tired brain can dredge up dark thoughts, and Diamond's years in the police had given him plenty of practice. Was it possible Dixon-Bligh had evidence—letters, photos, press clippings—touching on some part of Steph's early life she had wanted to forget? Some youthful indiscretion? A drugs episode? Drunk driving? A relationship with some notorious character? No, it wasn't about covering up old scars. It had to be more damaging. Could she have committed some criminal act that had gone undetected?

Come off it, he told himself. This isn't Steph you're thinking about. She was no more of a saint than any other spirited woman, but she wasn't into crime.

He turned over and looked at the clock. One fifteen.

Then he sat up and switched on the light. This had to be thought through. If he was dealing with anyone else but Steph, he'd put blackmail top of the list. It was a classic setup: the no-good ex-husband worming back into her life and threatening to tell all. He'd offer to hand over the evidence in return for cash. She'd agree to meet him on neutral ground. The diary appeared to confirm it.

Then what?

My God, he thought as the scenario flashed up in his brain. She had armed herself. She must have gone up to the loft one ill-starred day and found that sodding gun. When Dixon-Bligh resurfaced in her life making threats and demanding money, she'd taken it with her to meet him in the park. Most likely she had no thought of killing him. She'd meant to produce the gun and demand the return of whatever he was using as the basis of blackmail. That much was consistent with Steph's character. She had a streak of defiance and was as fearless as a tigress.

She had taken the gun with her, but she had no experience of handling it. Dixon-Bligh had grabbed it and shot her. If charged, he would offer that well-tried defence: there was a struggle and the gun went off.

But right now, he'd be thinking he'd got away with it. He'd have judged correctly that Steph wouldn't have mentioned the blackmail to anyone else. He wouldn't know about the diary entries.

Certain he wouldn't get to sleep for hours now, Diamond got up and pulled on the clothes he'd dropped in a heap in the corner a couple of hours before. He needed physical activity. Fresh air.

Fresh it was. A sharp east wind was blowing up Weston High Street, shifting the discarded packs and paper cups outside the takeaway. He pulled up the collar of his overcoat and jammed his old trilby more tightly over his bald patch. The occasional car passed him, but no one else was desperate enough to be walking the streets.

It was painful, this process of speculating on the bits of Steph's life she may have wanted to keep from him. It was alien to their relationship. She had known the worst about him and taken him on with all his faults, and he'd always told her everything. No, he thought, that isn't true. Who am I kidding? I kept things back. I didn't tell her I kept the gun all those years, mainly because I knew she'd hate to have such a thing in the house. And if I wasn't open with Steph, and she found out, she was entitled to feel let down. Was it any wonder she kept quiet about what happened after she found it?

Those diary entries hurt him just as she must have been hurt when she found the gun. You work at your marriage, trusting, believing, and the more honest the relationship is, the more devastating is any deceit. The people we love the most are capable of inflicting the greatest pain.

Still, if there were ugly things in her past, he couldn't

ignore them. He might feel guilty probing, but he'd sworn over her dead body he would find her killer. That outweighed everything.

His thoughts were interrupted. A car had crept up and was cruising beside him at walking pace. He'd got to the top of the High Street and was approaching the Crown. They came so close that he heard the nearside window slide down. Someone who'd lost his way, he thought, and turned to see.

It was a police car with two young officers inside.

"Do you mind telling us where you're going?"

"Home, eventually," he answered.

"And where's that?"

"Just up there, off Trafalgar Road."

"Out for a walk, are you?"

"That's the idea."

"At this time of night?"

"There's no law against it."

"Most lawful people are in bed and asleep. Don't I know you, chummy?"

"You should . . . constable."

There was a murmured consultation inside the car, followed by, "Christ!" Then a pause and, "Sorry to have troubled you, sir. There was a break-in higher up on Lansdown Lane, and we—"

The voice of the driver said, "Leave it, Jock."

"Night, sir." The car drew off at speed.

He shook his head and walked on.

In the morning he called the nick and told the switchboard he'd be late in. These days nobody objected. They were relieved when he was out of the place. He was an unwelcome presence, reminding everyone of the poor progress so far. He had the files of unsolved crimes to keep him occupied, supposedly, but he was forever finding reasons to look into the incident room.

He took an early train to London and was in Kensington

by ten. The last address he had for Dixon-Bligh was in Blyth
Road behind the exhibition halls at Olympia, not far from his
old patch. He wasn't in a nostalgic mood.

The tall Victorian terraced house was split into flats
and the motley collection of name cards stuffed into slots
beside the doorbells didn't include a Dixon-Bligh. He
stepped back to check the house number again. Definitely
the one he had.

He rang the ground-floor bell. This was not the kind of
establishment that operated with internal phones. After several
tries no one came, so he pressed the next bell up and got a
response. Above him a sash window was pulled up and a spiky
hairdo appeared. Male, he thought.

"Yeah?"

He said he was looking for Dixon-Bligh and didn't know
which flat he was in.

"Dick who?" the punk said.

"No, Edward. Edward Dixon-Bligh. Man in his forties.
Ex-Air Force. Used to own a restaurant in Guildford. May be
sharing with a younger woman."

"Never heard of him." The head disappeared and the window
slammed shut.

It wasn't unusual for people in London flats to know nothing
of their neighbours. Diamond studied the names beside the
remaining doorbells and wasn't encouraged. Both looked
foreign.

He pressed the first and got no response. The second was
answered eventually by a woman in a sari who came down two
flights of stairs with a baby in her arms.

He stated his question again.

She shook her head.

"You don't know, or you think he's moved?"

She took a step back and smiled and shrugged. She didn't
understand a word he was saying.

But at least he got inside the building. Picked up weeks of junk mail heaped on the floor to his right and eureka!—found a seed catalogue addressed to E. Dixon-Bligh. Without a date stamp, unfortunately. Showed it to the woman, pointing to the name, but she didn't understand.

He moved past her to the door of the ground-floor flat. There was a note pinned to it: *Sally and Mandy are at the shop all day.* Didn't sound like Dixon-Bligh. He went upstairs past the punk's door to the second floor. The woman in the sari followed. No one answered when he knocked at the door of the second-floor flat. According to the bells downstairs the occupier was a V. Kazantsev. He was probably at work spying on the Foreign Office.

The woman joined him on the second-floor landing. The child was asleep.

He tried once more. "Edward Dixon-Bligh?" Used his fingers to mime an RAF moustache, though he had no idea if Dixon-Bligh had one. This was desperation time.

She shook her head.

He returned downstairs, frustrated, and sorted through the junk mail and found a couple more addressed to Dixon-Bligh. No clue as to how long they'd been there. It was unhelpful that the Post Office didn't frank mass mailings.

What next?

He wouldn't leave this building without a result. Up he went to the punk's level. The door was vibrating to enormous decibels from inside. Pity the people upstairs and down. He hammered on it with both fists. At the third attempt he was heard. The punk looked out and said, "Piss off, mate. You're wasting my time."

Diamond's foot was against the door and he grabbed the man by his T-shirt. "Who's the landlord?"

"Get off, will you?"

"The landlord."

"How would I know? I pay my rent to the agent."

"Which one?"

"Pickett. North End Road."

The woman in Pickett's was guarded. "We never give information about clients."

"This one seems to be an ex-client."

Her eyes widened. "Who's that?"

"A Mr. Dixon-Bligh."

Client confidentiality no longer applied. "Certainly we know a Mr. Dixon-Bligh. He was a tenant in one of our Blyth Road properties for three years, but he moved out at the end of February."

"Where to? Do you know?"

She gave a bittersweet smile. "I was hoping you would tell me. He left no forwarding address. We'd like to trace him ourselves. He owes two months' rent."

"You didn't give him notice?"

"He did a flit. The first we knew of it was when Mr. Kazantsev came in and said he'd heard there was an empty flat."

"Kazantsev? So Dixon-Bligh had the second-floor flat?"

She checked the card index. "Second floor. Yes."

"Do you think Kazantsev knew him?"

"No. He heard from one of the other tenants. Blyth Road is a desirable address. Places there are snapped up fast."

"Do you know what line of work Dixon-Bligh was in?"

"We never ask."

"References?"

"Not these days. If they can put down the deposit—and he did—we take them on."

In case the agency traced their runaway tenant, he left his phone number, but he rated the chance no better than a meeting with Lord Lucan.

He sat in a North End Road cafe eating a double egg and

chips and pondering the significance of what he had learned. Dixon-Bligh had upped sticks at the end of February, just about the time of the shooting. He may well have returned from the murder scene in a panic, determined to vanish without trace. He was top of the list of suspects now.

But the trail stopped here.

He had no idea where to go looking for Dixon-Bligh. He doubted if it could be done without help.

Well, he'd served in the Met. That was the obvious place to start. He'd look up his old nick in Fulham. See if any of the team had survived into the new century.

The sight of the tarted-up new building was not encouraging and neither was the face across the desk. They were getting younger all the time. This one probably had to shave once a week.

"Afternoon, sir."

"Is it already?" Diamond said. He introduced himself and asked if anyone was there who had served in the mid-eighties and almost added, "Before you were born."

"I doubt it, sir. Do you know about tenure?"

He'd heard of it, and very unpopular it was in the Met, the system of moving officers between squads and stations. Nobody was allowed to dig in forever. "Maybe somebody I knew—somebody really ancient like me—has done the rounds and returned to base. Is there anyone fitting that description?"

He was invited to the canteen to find out, and there he was recognised at once by the manageress, a big Trinidadian called Jessie. Her smile made his day. She wanted to feed him—even though he insisted he'd just eaten—so he settled for rhubarb crumble, Jessie's speciality.

"Have you seen Mr. Voss yet?"

"Louis?" he said, his spirits rising. "Louis Voss is still here?"

"He come back January. Civilian now. They make him computer king. On first floor with all the pretty chicks in tight skirts."

That rhubarb crumble disappeared in a dangerously short time.

Louis (spoken the French way) had been a detective sergeant, a good ally through some hair-raising jobs at a stage when each of them had more hair to raise. They'd lost touch when Diamond had moved to Bath.

He'd altered little. The slow smile was still there and the irreverent gleam in the eyes. He'd kept slim, too. "Amazing," he said, and Diamond guessed it was a comment on his own disintegration.

Louis must have read in the papers about Steph's murder because he spoke of it at once, probably to save Diamond from bringing it up. He didn't ladle out the sympathy but just said he was more stunned by the news than words could express. He remembered Steph from before they were married. "Let's get out of this place and have a drink," he suggested. "If there's a problem, they can call me on the mobile."

In the saloon at the Fox and Pheasant, a Victorian pub just off the Fulham Road, Diamond gave his version of the past five weeks, the full account, including the finding of the handgun.

Louis listened philosophically. He wasn't surprised that the Met had passed on information to the Bath police about the lax firearms procedure back in the eighties. "There's been such a stink over corruption in the past few years that this is small beer, the odd gun going astray. Old Robbo faced a disciplinary board and was retired early, as you know, but he still got his pension."

"Is he still about?"

"Died some years ago. I'm surprised you kept the gun."

"Forgot about it for years. It was up in my loft—or was until someone decided to bury it. You don't expect to have your own house searched."

"Did Steph know you had it?"

He smiled and shook his head.

"She wouldn't have approved?"

"That's putting it mildly. I ought to have had more sense. But it's a side issue, this gun."

"Unless they prove it was the murder weapon. You say they've done tests?"

"Inconclusive so far. The killer used a point three-eight revolver, same as mine, but there are thousands in circulation."

"Looking on the black side, what if they prove it was your gun that was used?"

Louis had always been a dogged interviewer. Diamond took a long sip of beer and outlined his theory about Dixon-Bligh attempting blackmail and Steph taking the gun to the park to demand the evidence.

"Wouldn't she have talked to you before doing something as drastic as that?"

"Normally, yes."

"But blackmail isn't normal?"

"Right. And I guess she felt she could deal with Dixon-Bligh herself. I can't think what he had on her. I suppose we all have things in our lives we're not particularly proud of."

"How long was he married to her?"

"Just a few years. Four or five."

"And she didn't stay in touch with him?"

"No, it ended in bitterness."

"Enough for murder?"

"I never thought so. He was the problem, not Steph."

"If he did fire the shots, how would the gun have ended up buried in your garden?"

"Big question, Louis."

"You must have thought about it. Wouldn't he have got rid of the thing some other way?"

"I can only guess he wanted to incriminate me."

"But he wouldn't have known it was a police-issue weapon.

It's a big risk, when he knows he's killed her, visiting your place." Louis glanced at his watch. "Would you like another?"

"Just a half, then."

Louis had made a sound point. Reflecting on it, Diamond was less confident about his theory. But *someone* had taken the risk of burying the thing.

They were drinking Black Baron, a speciality here. When Louis returned, Diamond asked him, "Did you hear about that woman going missing, the wife of Stormy Weather, one of the Fulham crowd from the old days, though I can't recall him too well?"

"Saw something about it on my screen. Marriage tiff, I reckon."

"That's what I thought."

"Changed your mind?"

"Obviously, I hope she's okay, but . . ."

"Hope you're wrong," Louis said. "I've known her for years. You'd remember her yourself, I reckon. She was around in your time here. Fresh face, bright blue eyes, dark hair. Bit of an organiser. We called her Mary, after Mary Poppins."

"It rings a bell, but faintly."

"Nice woman, anyway, and good at her job. She got to be a sergeant at Shepherd's Bush. Then she changed careers. Went into business on her own running some kind of temping agency."

"Where do they live?"

"In the suburbs. Raynes Park, somewhere like that. Stormy is still in the Met, I think."

"Just hope his wife is all right." Diamond returned to the main purpose of his visit. "So how am I going to find Steph's ex-husband?"

"He was local, you say?"

"Blyth Road—until the end of February."

"Has he got form?"

Diamond shrugged. "I wouldn't know. Owes a couple of months' rent."

"Then it's going to be difficult, Peter. I can put out some feelers. Dixon-Bligh is an unusual name, and that may help. If you did this through official channels you might get a quicker result."

"Can't do that," Diamond said. "It's only supposition up to now. A few entries in her diary that could—or could not— refer to him. Some things are starting to link up, but not enough for a general alert."

They walked back together. The chance to air his thoughts to an old colleague had given him a lift. But the parting hand-shake they exchanged outside the entrance to Fulham nick was a reminder that he was going to have to battle on alone.

## 17

TWO MONTHS HAD gone by since Harry Tattersall had bought the suit. He'd worn it a few times around the house so that it would feel comfortable and hang well on his trim physique. Two months. He was beginning to wonder if the diamond heist had been cancelled. Nobody had been in touch even though his answerphone was always switched on. Arabs, of course, are well known for taking the long view, hardly ever giving way to impatience—something to do with riding camels vast distances across the desert. Or drilling for oil. He had to take the long view himself. A hundred grand would be worth the wait.

Finally the call came one Sunday evening about eight thirty, and he was at home to take it in person, watching *The Sting* on TV.

"Yes?"

"Mr. Tattersall?"

"Speaking."

"The goods are coming in on the tenth of next month." An accent redolent of blue-grey serge and brass buttons and high tea in the officers' mess, well up to Dorchester Hotel standards.

The phone clicked, and that was it. Harry thought: I wonder if he gets a hundred K just for that?

Slightly under two weeks, then. He poured himself a large Courvoisier.

He was relaxing with the drink, spending the money in his imagination, with the movie still running on the box, when a troublesome thought popped into his head. Suppose this entire operation was a clever sting. There was a way of checking if the call came from the Dorchester. He got up and dialled 1471. The caller had withheld his number.

No sweat, he told himself. Any professional would do the same.

Next morning, positive again, he took the tube to Waterloo, came up the escalator to the mainline station and strolled in sunshine along the South Bank walkways to the Royal Festival Hall where he used one of the public phones in the foyer.

He called the Dorchester and reserved one of the roof garden suites in the name of Sir John Mason for a week from the tenth.

Simple.

He called Rhadi and told him the booking was made for the tenth. They kept the conversation short.

Then it all went quiet again. He swanned around London enjoying the good weather, the parks and the pubs. Two days before the heist was due, he went into Boots in Oxford Street and picked some hair colouring to go nicely with the moustache he'd already bought. He spent a long time choosing. Sir John Mason, he decided finally, would favour Rich Chestnut. Personally he favoured rich anything.

# 18

McGARVIE WAS SUSPICIOUS when Diamond asked for the return of Steph's letters and papers. "Why do you need them?"

"They were my wife's property and they belong to me. You've had them nearly two months."

"You won't let go, will you? You won't leave this to us?"

"It's a simple request."

"You can have them at the end of the week." From McGarvie's tone it was clear he'd be going through every scrap of paper again in case there was something incriminating he had missed.

Diamond asked, "What's the latest on the gun?"

"Still with forensics."

"They're taking their time."

"Does that bother you?" McGarvie said, his eyebrows arching. "If you know you're in the clear, why do you keep asking?"

"Because all this concentration on me is bogging down the whole inquiry. You have a budget for overtime now, and it's being wasted. They'll scale you down soon."

"You're not the only line of enquiry, Peter. The hitman theory is still a strong runner."

"Well, obviously."

"I'm glad we agree on something. The shooting looked professional. Two shots to the head."

The image darted into Diamond's brain once more—and it hurt. He was getting better at hiding his grief. "Who would have put out a contract?"

"Someone you sent down for a long stretch. It's not impossible to organise a murder from behind bars."

"Like Jake Carpenter?"

"Or some other villain."

"Apart from Carpenter, it's a long time since I tangled with a big-time crook."

"We know that."

"You'd have to go back to my service in the Met. The eighties."

"Which we are doing."

"Are you? I thought about this myself."

McGarvie was quick to say, "Would you care to share your thoughts?"

"Don't mind." He knew they must have trawled through his career already. "There was the Missendale case that got me into so much trouble."

"The black boy?"

"Yes. Murder in the course of an armed robbery. A building society job. One of the customers tried to tackle the gunman and was shot in the head. Hedley Missendale was a known robber, and we pulled him in and he confessed. I wasn't the SIO—that was Jacob Blaize—but I did the main interview. Missendale was sent down for life, and then after two years someone else put up his hand and said he'd found Jesus and the murder was down to him."

"Jesus?"

Diamond glared. "No, this born-again Christian. He produced the gun to prove it. Missendale was pardoned and Blaize took early retirement and I was up before a board of inquiry. Well, you know. It's on my file."

"You were cleared."

"Officially, but there was stuff in the report about my methods. *'His physical presence and forceful demeanour were bound to intimidate.'* What was I supposed to do? Buy him a box of chocolates?"

McGarvie wisely passed up the chance to comment on Diamond's demeanour. "So do you think it could be Missendale getting back at you?"

He shook his head. "Hedley had a few dodgy friends, but I don't see him or his chums harbouring a grudge all those years. They lived for the moment."

"He's in Maidstone Prison," McGarvie said. "Been there two years for RWV."

"Is that so? He seems to be in the clear, then."

McGarvie turned to another of Diamond's cases. "You were on the Brook Green shooting."

"Headed it. That night was just like the OK Corral, except they were using Kalashnikovs. Three men died. Basically it was a skirmish in a drugs war. Two barons claiming the same patch. We collared Kenny Calhoun and two of his heavies. They all got life. Calhoun was in Brixton, the last I heard."

"He died last year," McGarvie said.

"Did he? Can't honestly say I'm sorry."

"The other two?"

"Logan and Crampton. Thickos. Guys who wouldn't remember their own names, let alone mine."

"This isn't much help. Can you think of any other villain you crossed?"

"I'm doing my best. There was a mean character called Joe Florida we nailed for a protection racket. He was American, I think. Scared the shit out of Asian shopkeepers. He got a twelve stretch, which means he could be out now and back to his bad old ways. Yes. Joe Florida."

"Was it personal between you and him?"

"It seemed so at the time. I haven't heard of him for years."

"Was he the sort who'd gun down your wife?"

"Hard to say. He'd have gunned me down, that's for certain."

"Was he organised?"

"You mean did he run a gang? Sure."

"Joe Florida. I'll see what the Met knows. Are you sure there's nobody closer to home apart from the Carpenter family?"

There was—but for the present, Diamond preferred to deal with Edward Dixon-Bligh himself. The case against Steph's no-good ex-husband was tenuous, and he didn't want McGarvie rooting around for the evidence of blackmail. So he shook his head. "I've been over and over."

And on Wednesday evening at home, he had a call from Louis Voss. "I think we've traced your man. One of the two women in the ground-floor flat did some detective work of her own. She has a business in Walham Green selling weavings—wall hangings, curtains, throws, that kind of thing—and she lent him a few items to brighten up his flat. She does that, apparently, and it helps to get her work known. When he did his flit, he took off with all the choice items she'd lent him, and she went berserk."

"She found him?"

"She told everyone who came into the shop. That's the way to get the word around. One of her customers saw him walking out of Paddington Station last Sunday afternoon and followed him. He's living in some crummy street at the back of the station, right under the Westway flyover. Seventeen Westway Terrace. You'll be glad to hear Sally has recovered all her wall hangings."

"I'll be overjoyed if she left him in one piece."

"Will you come up again?"

"Tomorrow. And thanks, Louis."

Seedy as Blyth Road had looked with its peeling stucco, it was state of the art compared to Westway Terrace. A hundred years of coal dust from the trains was sealed with the mud and oil sprayed from the flyover. A sane person would not have ventured there without a protective suit.

The first mystery: how did the place come to be named after a flyover when it obviously predated it by half a century or more? He could only assume it had been called something else in Victorian times and was given a change of name during the twentieth century. One possible explanation for a change of street name was that the address had become notorious because a murder had been committed there. He was willing to believe it.

No doorbells here. He knocked at number seventeen and got no answer. These were labourers' dwellings of the two-up, two-down sort. He tried peering through the window and made out a square table with a newspaper on it. Some cardboard boxes stacked against a wall. He felt certain Dixon-Bligh was not at home. What mattered was whether he had left altogether after being tracked there by Sally—or was it Mandy?—the angry weaver.

He tried the houses on either side and still failed to rouse anyone. He thought he heard a faint sound from within the second place, but they weren't answering for sure. It was the kind of temporary home illegal immigrants are dumped in after a long, expensive journey in a container. They'd hardly want to come to the door.

A forced entry was an option he preferred not to take. Better, surely, not to alert the suspect. Within walking distance was the Grand Union Canal and the upmarket area of Little Venice with its trees, pubs and cafés. Maybe Dixon-Bligh had found work there. He'd been in the catering trade. For Diamond, it was a good enough incentive to leave this depressing street and go looking.

He had not gone far when a cyclist turned the corner and pedalled towards him: the first sign of life. A man of around his own age, dressed in a blue suit and flat cap, riding along in that focused way cyclists have. Diamond didn't hail him, as he might have done. Westway Terrace was a cul-de-sac, so it was certain that the cyclist would stop at one of the houses and there was just a chance . . .

His hunch was right. The man came to a halt outside number seventeen and felt in his pocket for keys.

A change of luck was overdue.

"Mr. Dixon-Bligh?"

The cyclist turned and stared. There was panic, or guilt, or both, in the look. His hands gripped the bike as if he was considering escape. He didn't say a word.

Diamond stepped purposefully towards him. "I'm Peter Diamond, Steph's second husband."

He watched it register. *Diamond the policeman.* Saw the eyes widen, the jaw gape. Any jury would have convicted on that reaction.

"Mind if I come in?" Diamond asked with a huge effort to sound friendly and disarming. "I'm up from Bath to see you."

"What on earth for?"

"It'll be easier inside."

Dixon-Bligh unlocked and wheeled the bike in first, leaning it against the wall just inside. Diamond stepped in after him and closed the door. The place smelt damp and the wallpaper was coated with mould.

"I tried to reach you on the phone. The number I had was obviously out of date. Are you on a mobile these days?"

Dixon-Bligh was not saying.

"You did know she was killed?"

He nodded. It had been in all the papers and on radio and television, so he could hardly have failed to find out.

Diamond added, "I tried to let you know about the funeral. She had a good one, in the Abbey. Lots of people came."

The funeral didn't interest Dixon-Bligh. "What do you

want from me?" he succeeded in saying. He still hadn't taken off the hat.

"A cup of coffee wouldn't come amiss. Didn't get one on the train. Can't stand those paper cups."

Glad, it seemed, of any opportunity to mark time while he marshalled his thoughts, Dixon-Bligh stepped through to the kitchen, and Diamond made sure he was close behind. There wasn't much in there, considering this was a professional caterer's kitchen. A packet of cornflakes and a cut loaf. One mug. Dixon-Bligh looked around for another and took one out of a box, still wrapped in newspaper from the house move.

"You don't have many visitors, then?" Diamond remarked. "I'm having to get used to being a loner myself. Can't say I'm much good at it."

No matey response to that.

"Is this where you keep the milk?" He opened the small fridge to the right of the door and took out a packet of semi-skimmed and checked the sell-by date. It was just about drinkable. "I expect you get a main meal at work, like me. You *do* work?"

Dixon-Bligh nodded and picked up the kettle and filled it. The old-fashioned gas ring had to be lit with a match. Then he took off his cap and hung it on the door, accepting the obligation to say something. Now that the words came, they were fluent and articulate. "I'm sorry about the way she died, truly sorry. Thought about coming to the funeral and decided against it. The point is, there was a residue of bitterness after we parted. The marriage had been a mistake. I'm sure Stephanie must have told you. Harsh things were said, deeply wounding on both sides. I'm ashamed, looking back. I gather she was happier with you."

"It worked," Diamond said, not trusting himself to say more.

The man was pouring on the oil now he was over the first shock. I decided turning up at the funeral would have been hypocritical. I should have let you know, written a note or sent a card at the very least. I have this tendency to turn my back on things I can't handle." He took a packet of teabags from an otherwise empty cupboard. "I expect her family came to the funeral. Her sister . . . the name has gone."

"Angela. Yes, she was there."

"Didn't approve of me."

"Me, neither," Diamond said to encourage confidences. "She thinks my job contributed in some way to Steph's murder. She could be right."

"Really? I hadn't thought of that."

"Do you have any idea who would have wanted her killed?"

"None whatsoever. She didn't have enemies. She wasn't that kind of person, as you know."

This comparing of notes by the two men Steph had married was taking out some of the tension. Dixon-Bligh may not have dropped his guard yet, but he was willing to respond to questions.

Diamond said, "I was going to ask if you remember anyone who took against her with or without cause."

"From that far back, you mean? It's a long shot, isn't it?"

"You were in the Air Force when she met you, I believe."

"True, and there were some weird characters around then, but Steph didn't come across them. We weren't housed in married quarters. We had a flat in the city, and she didn't see much of the other officers. Even on mess nights, when some of the wives attended, Steph stayed at home because I was always on duty supervising the catering staff. Wouldn't have been much of a night out for her."

"Where was this?"

"Hereford. Not a bad posting."

"Hereford, right," Diamond said placidly, making immense efforts to suppress his gut feeling that the man had murdered Steph. "She spoke of it quite often, and I didn't link it up with the RAF. I thought she'd lived there at some earlier stage of her life. She liked it there. She more than once mentioned the view of the Black Mountains from the kitchen window."

"Typical."

"What's that?"

"Steph remembering the view. You could see it on a fine day, but most of the time it rained."

"She was an optimist. And how about you? Did you like Hereford?"

"Unreservedly. Great pubs, good cider, terrific steaks."

Diamond's eyes widened. "Was Steph eating steak in those days?"

Dixon-Bligh grinned faintly. "No, that was a personal memory." The water had come to the boil, and he tossed a teabag into each cup and poured some in.

Judging that the preliminaries were at an end, Diamond sat at the table and asked, "Do you mind talking about what went wrong in your marriage?"

"I don't mind," he answered evenly. "We went into it blindly, that was what was wrong. We were attracted to each other, very considerate when we were going out together, full of plans. After we married, after the nuptial bliss, I relaxed—or relapsed—and became the selfish bastard I am. To Stephanie, this came as a shock. Service life makes heavy demands anyway. A career officer is expected to spend time in the mess and she couldn't understand why I was out so often." With a sigh, he said, "If you want the absolute truth, I had affairs. My duties in the catering branch meant I had more women around me than men, and—well, you know how it is—there are always those who are game for some fun."

"Did she find out?"

"Not for a while. She had her suspicions, I'm certain. Even so, our sex life was normal. I'm a twice-a-day man, or was, given the opportunity. I think if we'd had the child she wanted, we might still be married, regardless of my playing around. She was so keen to get pregnant."

"I know."

"The miscarriages did for us. She was weak and weepy and I couldn't handle that at all. I played away more blatantly than before. She found out and angry things were said and we split. Simple as that."

"Had you spoken since the divorce?"

"Only when necessary. Some couples stay friendly, I know. In our case, it was impossible."

"You say 'when necessary.' Did you get in touch in the weeks before her death?"

"No." A fiat denial without a glimmer of guilt. This was not what Diamond had come to hear.

"You're certain? Her diary mentions phone calls and meetings with someone."

"Not me, old chum."

The cockiness of that "old chum" got to Diamond. He went for the kill.

"She called you Ted, I expect?"

"Hardly ever. I was Ed to her."

"Easy to say now."

"But true." Dixon-Bligh widened his eyes. "Why? Is this important?"

"The diary entries speak of somebody called 'T.'"

"And you thought . . ." He flushed deeply. "Christ, I nearly walked into that, didn't I? No, she didn't call me Ted. Ever. You ought to know that. She must have spoken about me. Did she ever refer to me as anything but Ed?"

"She rarely mentioned you, and then it was always Edward. Never Ed."

"Never Ted either, I'll bet."

"I've been looking at witness statements. Various men were seen in the vicinity."

"Matching me? I don't think so."

The frontal attack hadn't succeeded. He made a tactical switch. "Any idea who this 'T' could be?"

"I'd have to think. It's not going to be someone from our Air Force days, surely. No, I'm at a loss."

"When were you last in touch with her?"

"Must be at least two years ago, some photos of her parents I found among my things. I was running a restaurant then, living in Guildford. I phoned Stephanie to ask if she wanted them sent on."

"And that was the last time?"

"Absolutely."

"Sure you didn't ask her for money?"

Dixon-Bligh shot him a hostile look. "That's insulting."

"True. Answer the question."

"I didn't ask her for anything."

"Maybe you demanded it."

"Get lost."

"You're skint. This place is a comedown from Blyth Road and you owe two months' rent there."

"They'll get their money. That was a flat, and bloody noisy. This is a house."

"It's a tip."

"It's temporary—until I find something better."

"Not the sort of place I'd expect to find an ex-RAF officer living in. What's the attraction? Are you working now? Something just a bike ride away?"

Dixon-Bligh said, "What does this have to do with Stephanie's death?"

"Everything. If you're on the skids and don't like to admit it, you could be lying about not asking her for cash. It's more than likely she was being blackmailed."

"Blackmailed? What about?"

"Something in her past. Something you're well placed to know about."

Dixon-Bligh sneered. "You must have a lower opinion of her than I thought, you filthy-minded git."

Weeks of bottled-up anger went into the punch Diamond swung at the man. The table tipped up and the chair crashed over. His fist struck the side of Dixon-Bligh's jaw and keeled him against his cardboard boxes with a crunch that must have shattered any breakable contents.

He was out cold, blood oozing from one side of his mouth.

Satisfying as it was, the blow had solved nothing. The encounter was over. Nothing useful had come of it.

Diamond walked out and slammed the door.

## 19

AT THE END of the week, he went to see McGarvie again.

"My wife's letters."

"Ah."

"You said you'd return them."

"I did. And they're here." McGarvie took some keys from his pocket.

What kind of man keeps his desk locked all day? Diamond thought. It doesn't demonstrate much trust in the rest of the team.

Steph's shoebox of old letters was pushed across the desk to him together with a polythene bag filled with the invoices and assorted papers the search party had taken from her drawer.

"I expect you want me to sign for these."

"If you please." The sarcasm fell flat. McGarvie actually had a chitty ready. "And there's something else." He delved into the drawer again.

"What's that?"

Diamond was handed another polythene bag containing a single brown envelope. He was amazed to see his name on it, just the word *Peter*—amazed because it was written in Steph's hand.

"You can open it."

"Seeing that it's addressed to me, I should think so."

"I mean it's safe to handle."

What did McGarvie think it was, then—a letter bomb? Steph taking revenge on her killer husband from beyond the grave?

"We've carried out the necessary tests."

"Tests? What for?"

"Prints. Handwriting."

"I mean why?"

"You haven't seen this letter before?"

Diamond frowned. "Is that a trick question? No, I haven't. Was it with the others?"

"We found it in the biscuit tin."

His heart pumped faster. "What—the one the gun was buried in?"

"That's the only biscuit tin we've got."

So Steph *had* written him a message. "You didn't tell me," he said, outraged. "Why wasn't I told?"

"You'd better read it."

Diamond unzipped the wrapper, took out the envelope and found a single sheet inside. In Steph's tidy handwriting was written:

*My dear Peter,*

*Just in case you find this before I have the pluck to tell you, I had to brave it out with the spiders in the loft to look for my old violin, which I'd promised to give to the shop since I haven't played it for years—and I found the gun. It was a great shock, Pete. You know my feelings about guns. I left it there for a week, telling myself I would talk to you about it, and I kept putting it off not wanting to cause an upset while you were so stretched on this dreadful Carpenter case.*

*I know you'll insist the gun was there for some good reason, but the knowledge that a weapon that could kill someone is in our home has been preying on my nerves.*

*Please try to understand. Rather than creating a scene and
making us both feel guilty I decided to bury it and tell you
when you're not under so much strain.*

*Your loving,*
*Steph*

He read it twice before asking McGarvie, "Why wasn't I
told about this?"

"My decision."

"I know that."

"It could have been a forgery."

"Who would have forged a letter like this?" His stomach
lurched as the realisation struck him. "Me? You think I might
have written it?"

McGarvie gave a prim tug at his tie. "Quite possibly, as a
diversionary tactic. I decided to have it tested for prints. And
have a graphologist look at it. You'll be relieved to know it's
genuine. And we found no trace of your prints."

"What do you mean I'll be '*relieved to know*'? I've never seen
this before in my life."

"Noted."

"You could still have informed me when you found it."

"Yes."

"But you chose not to. Why?"

"If you *had* forged the note, you'd be puzzled as to why we
hadn't produced it."

"Nice," he said as the deviousness struck home. "You thought
you could trap me into saying something about it when I wasn't
supposed to know it existed. Well, thanks for the vote of
confidence."

"My priority is to get to the truth, Peter, not pander to your
feelings. You know as well as I do that in major crimes it's
standard practice to keep back certain information."

He took a long, deep breath, trying to tell himself to stay cool this time. In McGarvie's shoes, would he have played it the same way? He couldn't be certain. The one sure thing was that the suspicion was real. It riled him that his so-called colleagues treated him as the major suspect. By now he should expect nothing else. He needed to put aside his anger and deal with the new evidence. And it was good news. It put him back on side, didn't it?

"If the note is genuine, then you know I didn't use the gun."

"How do you work that out?"

He spread his hands to emphasise the obvious. "Well, if Steph buried the gun herself, I couldn't have shot her with it."

McGarvie shook his head. "It's not so simple. She could have told you she'd buried it. She had every intention of telling you, just as she says in the note. It's possible she told you on the day the Carpenter trial ended."

"Well, she didn't."

"Then I ask myself how you reacted," McGarvie ploughed on, ignoring Diamond's denial. "You'd certainly have dug the gun up. You may have had a blazing row about it, just as she feared. It could have been the reason she was murdered. No, hear me out. If you shot her yourself, you had a neat get-out. Bury the gun again with the note as your alibi."

The blood pressure rocketed. "You don't give up, do you?"

"Would you?"

He ignored that question and asked one of his own. "If we had a blazing row and I shot her in the heat of the moment, how is it she was killed in Royal Victoria Park?"

"I didn't say anything about the heat of the moment. This was a planned murder."

"What—to punish her for burying my gun?"

"The motive has never been established."

Conversations with McGarvie were an incitement to violence. He bit back his resentment and tried all over again. "Have you heard any more from ballistics? It's beginning to look as if mine wasn't the murder weapon."

"They say they can't prove the bullets were fired from that gun."

He held out his hands in appeal. "So?"

"There's still a good chance they were."

"What do you mean?"

"There are points of similarity, but insufficient for legal proof. As you know, the bullets weren't in the best condition. They may have been tampered with, prior to firing, to hamper the investigation."

"How?"

"By scratching the jacket, or scoring it with a file to distort the rifling. It suggests a professional gunman—or someone with a knowledge of weapons."

"Like an authorised shot?"

The drooping lids of McGarvie's eyes lifted a little, but he said nothing.

"Is that their last word on the subject?"

"Apparently."

"Trust the men in white coats to foul up. So it's back to the drawing board, is it?"

McGarvie said with an air of self-congratulation, "We're going on *Crimewatch*."

"So you admit you've run into the sand?"

"Not at all. It's the right move at this stage. There must be more witnesses out there. After all, this happened in daylight, in the open, close to an enormous car park. We still haven't traced that jogger."

Diamond had dismissed the jogger from his thoughts.

This was the woman Warburton had claimed he spoke to at the scene.

McGarvie added, as if Diamond had never seen *Crimewatch*, "They'll do a reconstruction with actors. It's worked in the past."

"And the best of British."

"And what about you?" McGarvie said. "What have you learned?"

"I'm not on the case."

"Get real, Peter. We know you've been out and about talking to snouts—or is that just a blind?"

He wasn't being provoked into passing on information until he judged the moment right. He'd handle Dixon-Bligh himself.

"If I hear anything, you'll be told." He almost said, *You'll be the first to know.* There were limits.

# 20

No question. Harry looked every inch the aristocrat when, precisely at two, he strode up to the desk at the Dorchester with a porter in tow wheeling in his smart suitcase filled with telephone directories.

"Sir John Mason. I made a reservation. You have my details."

"Yes, Sir John. One moment."

Harry glanced through his horn-rimmed frames at the staff behind the desk busy issuing keys and taking phone calls and printing out accounts. No chance of spotting the stoolie who had tipped him off. He'd be somewhere behind the scenes preparing medallions of venison with chestnuts.

"We've got you down for one of the roof garden suites, Sir John."

"That's what I asked for."

"Would you care to make a reservation for dinner?"

"Tonight I shall dine out, thank you." True. Instead of sampling the *haute cuisine* of his fellow conspirator he'd be grabbing a bacon sandwich at the airport cafe while he waited for his flight to Cork.

"Very good, sir. And would you care to order a newspaper for tomorrow morning?"

"*The Times.*" An uncollected paper outside the door was better than a "do not disturb" sign at keeping the staff away.

"Jules will take you to your suite and show you how the key works. Enjoy your stay with us."

"I intend to."

He followed Jules to the lift and up to the roof garden level.

"Are you staying long, sir?" Jules asked.

Under an hour, if the Arabs are up to the job, he thought privately. "Just the week."

"London has so much to offer this time of year."

"Let's hope so. Is the hotel busy?"

"Very."

"Full of wealthy foreigners, I expect."

"Quite a few visitors, yes."

He hoped Jules might throw in a mention of the Kuwaiti Royal Family, but you don't get everything you wish for. And they didn't pass any white-robed gentlemen in the walk from the lift to the door of the suite.

He was shown how to use the plastic key and they entered a light, luxurious sitting room with original paintings on the walls. Jules hoisted the suitcase onto a stand and switched on the TV. A message flashed up saying "Welcome to the Dorchester, Sir John Mason," and giving a rundown of the facilities. Jules showed how the curtains worked and opened the doors to the bedroom and bathroom. Harry tipped him two pounds.

Alone in the suite, he took out his mobile and called Zahir. "Yes?"

"Yes." He gave the name of the suite.

So professional. Nothing more was said. He switched off and put on a pair of polythene gloves he'd thoughtfully brought with him, collected some tissues from the bathroom and busied himself wiping the suitcase to remove any prints of his own. His part in the scam was nearly over, thanks be to Allah. He looked at the time.

The doorbell buzzed. He opened it.

A woman in hotel uniform carrying a bunch of flowers. "I'm Mary the housekeeper, just checking you have everything you require, Sir John."

Everything except my dusky friends, he thought. "I'm quite content, thank you."

"May I change your flowers?"

He hadn't even noticed the lilies on the coffee table. "If you're quick. I'm expecting visitors."

She fussed with the vase and left with yesterday's blooms. Harry looked at his watch again.

Ten more minutes passed. *"Shortly after, Zahir will knock. You will admit him and Ibrahim, and your job will be over."*

Bloody long "shortly after."

He stood by the sliding windows and looked across the roof garden and noticed a movement behind one of the taller shrubs. First he thought it must be a bird or a cat. Then another movement showed it was larger.

Someone was out there.

The hairs straightened on the back of his neck. He backed away from the window, waited a few seconds and then took another look. The same figure ducked out of sight behind a bush, but not before Harry noticed he was cradling something that looked horribly like a submachine gun. There was another movement at the edge of Harry's vision. Two of them at least. He had an impression of black uniforms.

Police marksmen.

Jesus.

He swung away from the window, back out of sight against the wall. It didn't take rocket science to work out that it was an ambush and he was cornered. They'd have men in the corridor as well, waiting to pick up the others if they hadn't nicked them already.

Hold on, he thought. They won't bust us until after the crime is committed. They'll let Rhadi bring the Hatton Garden man in here and they'll delay until the moment the diamonds are snatched.

They'll need to time it right.

The place must be bugged.

A listening device is so small you can hide it anywhere. There wasn't time for him to make a proper search.

His eyes darted left and right and lighted on the flowers the woman had brought in. Was she really a hotel employee? He stepped closer. Those enormous lilies could hide a microtransmitter with ease. The police couldn't have known in advance which suite would be used, so it was a cool move. He bent closer and examined the flower arrangement without touching anything.

The bug was there all right, lodged in the side of one of the spike-shaped buds.

He picked up the entire arrangement in its vase and carried it to the bedroom, placed it on the floor of the wardrobe and gently slid the door across. Then he returned to the main room, shutting the bedroom door after him.

He took out his mobile and called Zahir again.

An agonising pause followed. Then Zahir's terse voice asking, "What is it?"

"Pull the plug."

"What?"

"It's off. Cancelled. We've been shopped. Tell Rhadi, will you?"

"We can't do that."

"Why?"

"He doesn't have a phone."

"Christ."

Harry switched off. Then he collected the flowers from the bedroom and replaced them on the table.

His old friend Rhadi was going to walk into the trap. Surely those bastards could stop him.

No, he thought. They'll save their own skins and to hell with everyone else. Thick as thieves, the saying went. Thick as thieves, my arse.

Think of a way out of this, Harry, he told himself. You're a con man, the very best. You can save Rhadi and yourself.

But it wouldn't be easy up here on the top floor with armed men outside and every exit covered.

He made a rapid check of the rooms, looking for the ventilation shaft or the loft space he could use as an escape route. No such luck.

Determined not to be downed, he told himself he wasn't a goddamn escapologist anyway. He was a con artist. He'd do this his way. Sweet talk his way to freedom.

He sat on the sofa, removed his gloves and gave the matter some thought.

Rhadi was going to arrive any minute with a Hatton Garden diamond merchant expecting to do business with a Kuwaiti prince. Or—far more likely—with a policeman posing as a Hatton Garden diamond merchant. The fuzz had obviously got advance information, so they would have planned this. They would send in one of their SO19 people, armed and ready for combat. At a signal from him, police gunmen would burst in from all sides.

Harry let out a long, nervous breath. He'd only agreed to do this because it didn't involve violence.

Every instinct urged him to get out now and plead ignorance and hope for leniency. Only his brain told him there was a better way.

The buzzer on the door sounded.

He got up and looked through the little spyhole and saw Rhadi in the corridor with two men, one carrying a briefcase.

He opened the door a fraction and peered out. Rhadi saw him and looked horrified. It should have been Ibrahim or Zahir who opened the door. Harry should have been out of the hotel and on his way to the airport.

Harry said in the elegant accent he'd used when he was

registering, "A slight hitch in the arrangement, gentlemen. The Prince isn't here."

"Not here?" Rhadi said in disbelief.

"We had an appointment for three o'clock," the man with the briefcase said.

"Yes. His Royal Highness went for a massage and isn't back yet. You're welcome to come in and wait."

"Who are you?" the man with the briefcase asked.

"Er—his secretary," Harry said. "Smith—Henry Smith. He's only at the fitness centre. He shouldn't be long."

Rhadi stared at him. This wasn't in the script.

"Won't you all come in?"

The man with the briefcase exchanged a glance with his bodyguard companion who gave the matter some thought and then nodded. The bodyguard stepped ahead and did a rapid check of the other rooms.

"Care for a drink?" Harry offered.

They shook their heads.

"Why don't we all sit down?"

Harry's mind was racing. He was certain these were policemen, and he was pretty sure the briefcase contained a video camera. There was an eyelet at one end that could easily be a hidden lens, and it was pointing at him. He said to Rhadi, "We'd better remind the Prince about this. He's due at the Embassy at four. Why don't you go to the fitness centre and speak to him?"

"Can't you phone?" the bodyguard said.

"You don't phone a member of the royal family," Harry said with scorn. "Not when he's in the same building."

"I'll go and speak to him," Rhadi said, catching on at last.

The police were as undecided as anyone. Their game plan was in disarray and they had no way of getting fresh instructions without blowing their cover.

Rhadi was allowed to leave. If he had his wits about him,

he'd bluff his way past the waiting policemen and go straight to the fitness centre and make his escape from there by a back exit. He was off Harry's conscience.

Alone with the heavy mob, Harry marked time for a bit. He noticed how twitchy they appeared. It made him feel more confident. He crossed the room to the drinks cabinet and was amused to see the briefcase being turned to follow his movement.

"Whisky, anyone? No? I think I will."

He poured himself a generous measure. The next few minutes were to be a formidable test of the con man's art.

"How long have you worked for the Prince?" the cop with the briefcase asked.

Harry smiled, took a deep breath and answered in a West Coast American accent that amazed everyone. "Matter of fact, my friends, I don't work for him at all. I'm on your side. I'm Roscoe Hammerstein, CIA."

"Say that again."

"CIA." Harry put out his hand. "Put it there, officer."

The officer just gaped. His companion was frowning.

"Face it, guys," Harry said, twisting the hand outwards and upwards in a gesture of candour. "This is one gigantic cock-up. Don't know if my people are responsible, or yours. I spend fifteen months tracking these jerks, getting their confidence. Finally I make it. I'm on the team, and what happens? You guys pull the plug."

"Are you saying you infiltrated the gang?"

"*Saying?* Why do you think I'm here? It sure isn't for my health."

"You work for the CIA?"

"Didn't I say that?"

"What's the CIA's interest in these men?"

"Come on," Harry said, almost convincing himself, it sounded so plausible. "You know where they come from."

"The Middle East."

"Right on—and where do the world's most dangerous terrorists have their base?" He spread his hands. "How do they finance their operations? From heists like this. A multi-million-dollar diamond job."

"Can you prove any of this?"

"You mean do I have my ID with me? You think I'm crazy? There's no more certain way to guarantee a quick death."

"You must have a control—someone we can call to verify this."

"Sure," he said smoothly. "I can give you a number to call. But shall we decide what happens next? They could be back for a showdown any time now."

"What was your plan, Mr. Hammerstein?"

"To play along with them."

"In robbery with violence?"

"I'm undercover. As an organisation we're not interested in how they raise their funds. We have a greater objective—the defeat of terrorism."

"Are British security aware of your involvement?"

"I couldn't tell you. Listen, pal, I'm just an agent putting my life on the line. The top dogs decide who they tell."

The other man asked exactly the question Harry had been waiting for. "You say these are terrorists. What sort of terrorism are they involved in?"

"Bombings."

He waited for it to sink in.

They weren't as impressed as he'd hoped. It seemed they still needed convincing that he was genuinely CIA. "How did you know we were police?"

"It stands out a mile. There's the bug in the flowers. The marksmen outside. The camera you're pointing at me." He stared into it and said, "Hi, guys."

"Do you think the other man sussed us?"

"Which other . . . ? You mean Abdul, the guy who brought you up here? How would I know if he spotted you?"

"He looked nervous when you opened the door."

"Maybe he smelt a rat."

"He could abort the job."

"Sure." Harry was content to let them find their own rambling route to the point of panic.

"We'll know if they don't come back."

"You bet."

"They've been gone some time already. Which floor is the fitness centre?"

"Couldn't tell you."

The man with the briefcase said, "We could be sitting here like dummies while they make their escape."

"Maybe."

Another minute went by.

One of the cops looked at his watch. "This isn't looking good." He got up and went to the window, returned and sat with the others. "What's in that?"

"In what?"

"The suitcase."

Harry eyed the case he had personally filled with phone directories and lugged here. He frowned. "It's just for show, I guess."

"What's in it?"

"You've got me there."

"You don't know?"

"I told you."

The less talkative of the cops suddenly said, "Jim."

"What?"

"These people are bombers."

"Jesus," Jim said. The penny had finally dropped.

Harry stood up. "You could be right. This damned case could be packed with explosives. They can detonate by remote control. We'd better get outta here."

Jim was first through the door, followed closely by Harry. The corridor looked empty, but this was deceptive. Jim yelled, "There could be a bomb in there. Clear the floor!" And immediately the doors of two other suites opened and men carrying submachine guns came out. "It's off," Jim said. "Everybody out."

Harry had already picked his route. Instead of using the lift, which was open, he turned left and took the stairs. Before he was down the first flight he'd ripped off the moustache and pocketed the horn-rimmed glasses. On the third floor he emerged alone. The alarm system had just been switched on. Walking steadily, but without suspicious haste, he made his way along the corridors to the stairs on the opposite side of the building. He descended to ground level and strolled into the street and down the tube.

## 21

### AND STILL THE KILLER WALKS FREE

*Six months ago this week the wife of a Detective Super-
intendent was gunned down and murdered in Bath's elegant
Royal Victoria Park within view of the world-famous Royal
Crescent. The most intensive investigation ever mounted
in the city has so far failed to find the killer of Stephanie
Diamond. In this special report, we examine the conduct of
the inquiry and get the views of two of the principal men
involved: Detective Chief Inspector Curtis McGarvie, who
leads the investigation, and Detective Superintendent Peter
Diamond, the victim's husband.*

On Shrove Tuesday morning, last February 23rd, at 8:15,
Peter Diamond kissed his wife Stephanie goodbye and drove
to work as usual. It was the day in the week when Mrs. Diamond caught up with household chores and shopping. On
other days she worked as a volunteer in the Oxfam shop.
That morning she was her usual cheerful self and showed no
sign of stress. She didn't mention any arrangement to meet
anyone, or visit the park, although a note was later found
in her diary apparently fixing a meeting with someone she
called "T." About 10:15, two shots were heard close to the
Charlotte Street Car Park. An unemployed man walking
his dog on the far side of the park heard the shots and presently found a woman's body in Crescent Gardens beside the

Victorian bandstand. Two bullets had been fired into her head at point-blank range.

Peter Diamond, the head of Bath's murder squad, arrived at the scene within a short time of the shooting before anyone had identified the victim. One of several distressing features of this case is that he himself recognised the dead woman as his own wife. In spite of repeated appeals for witnesses, nobody appears to have seen the shooting. Police believe the gunman must have escaped through the car park, and video footage from the security cameras has been examined without any helpful result. A number of reports of drivers leaving around the time of the shooting have so far proved unhelpful. Eleven detectives and five civilians are working full-time on the case which is believed to have cost three quarters of a million pounds already.

The SIO (Senior Investigating Officer), DCI McGarvie, has appeared on *Crimewatch* and *Police Five* appealing to the public for assistance. A reconstruction was staged at the scene of the crime with a policewoman dressed in similar clothes to the victim. "There was a huge response from the television audience," the Chief Inspector told our reporter, "and we fed every piece of information into our database, but we still lack the crucial evidence that will identify the killer." McGarvie is convinced there are people who know someone who acted suspiciously at the time of the murder, and he urges them to get in touch as soon as possible.


## THEORIES

Sitting in the incident room surrounded by photos of the victim, in life and in death, and a computer-generated map of the crime scene, DCI McGarvie outlined the main theories his team have so far produced:

    1.   The killer acted under instructions from someone in the

underworld with a grudge against Det. Supt. Diamond. As a murder squad detective in the Metropolitan Police and Bath CID, Peter Diamond has been responsible for many convictions over a twenty-three-year career. The problem with this theory is that a criminal bent on revenge is more likely to attack the officer who put him away than his wife.

2. The killer was hired by the wife or girlfriend of a convicted man. It is felt that an embittered woman might have ordered the killing in revenge for the loss of her own partner.

3. The wife or girlfriend of a convicted man fired the fatal shots herself as an act of revenge. Such a woman with underworld connections might have access to a firearm, though shootings by women are rare.

4. Stephanie Diamond, an attractive woman looking some years younger than her age of 43, was shot by some obsessive person or stalker, a "loner" who believed she stood in the way of their fantasies. Stalkers have been known to "punish" the women they idolise for what they see as infidelity.

5. The "T" mentioned in her diary was trying to blackmail Mrs. Diamond about some secret, or supposed secret, in her past and killed her in frustration when she refused to pay up.

6. The killing was a mugging that went wrong. The killer drew a gun. Mrs. Diamond resisted or even fought back. The first shot was accidental and the second was fired in panic.

The difficulty with theories 4, 5 and 6 is that the shooting has the hallmarks of a contract killing. The murderer timed the shooting at an hour when Victoria Park was quiet. The scene of the crime was close to the Charlotte Street Car Park, enabling the killer to get away rapidly to a vehicle, if the police theories are correct. A .38 revolver was used. "Two shots to the head are characteristic of a professional gunman," says DCI McGarvie. "People have been known to survive a single shot to the head. The second bullet makes certain."

## CONFIDENT

Curtis McGarvie remains confident of an arrest. "This is by far the biggest test of my career in CID," he admits, "and it's taking longer than I expected. I thought there would be more witnesses, considering where the shooting took place. We've been unlucky there, unless someone else can be persuaded to come forward. We've done reconstructions, and we know the killer took at least ten seconds to leave the scene and return to the car park. We are pretty sure they used a car. Somebody, surely, heard the shots and saw the gunman return quickly to the car park and drive off." He is conscious that the costs of this case are mounting and there is already pressure to scale down the investigation. "Up to now, I've had unqualified support from the Police Authority. A long-running case is automatically reviewed by the top brass. We've had two such reviews, and my leadership hasn't been faulted. But I can't expect to carry on indefinitely at this pitch when we're up against manpower shortages and budgets."

Detectives speak of unsolved cases as "stickers" and hate to have them haunting their careers. The murder of a police colleague's wife is particularly hard to consign to a file of unsolved cases. "Peter Diamond is a man highly respected by everyone who knows him," says McGarvie. "No one here is going to give up while there is the faintest chance of progress. He's in a difficult position because even though he is a fine detective with substantial experience it wouldn't be right or proper for him to investigate the murder of his own wife. We owe it to him to slog away as hard as he would to find the killer."

That killer, according to the profilers who these days assist the police on all challenging murder inquiries, is most likely to be male, efficient, unexcitable, with a link to guns, and some knowledge of Bath. He drives a car. His friends or relatives probably have suspicions about him.

## FRUSTRATION

Detective Superintendent Peter Diamond, the victim's husband, is 50 and has an outstanding record in bringing murderers to justice. He admits to frustration at having to stay at arm's length from the investigation. "I know the reasons and I respect them. If I got involved I would be open to charges of bias. But it's hard. My heart wants to do what my head tells me I can't. I'd like to be working round the clock on this for Steph's sake. I'm an experienced investigator, and I have my own ideas on what should be done." But he refuses to be critical of the detectives working on the case. "This is about as tough as they come. You need luck on any case, and they haven't had much up to now." Echoing McGarvie, he adds, "My main worry is that soon the cost of all this will panic the people who hold the purse strings into scaling everything down."

When asked which of the main theories he subscribes to, Peter Diamond is cautious. "They should rule nothing out until evidence justifies it. There are compelling reasons to suppose it was some kind of contract killing for revenge, but it's still possible that the killer was a loner acting for himself—or herself. It's not out of the question that a woman did this. And there may be a motive the murder squad are unaware of."

The shooting of Stephanie Diamond on that February morning put tremendous strains on her husband. "You find out how much you depended on someone when they are taken from you. She was a calmer personality than I could ever be, very positive, with a way of seeing to the heart of a problem. She understood me perfectly. I don't know of anything you could dislike in Steph, which makes her murder so hard to account for. The killer has to be someone who didn't know her at all or some deluded crazy person."

After the shooting there was the added ordeal of being questioned about his own movements. Peter Diamond shrugs and says, "It had to be faced. I'd have pulled in the guy myself, whoever was the husband. You always take a long look at the husband in a case like this." But if he was at work in Bath Police Station, surely he had a perfect alibi? "Actually, no. On that morning I went straight to my office and worked alone. There was no one who could vouch for me." He adds wryly, "I may look big and threatening, but off duty I'm a baa-lamb. I think I convinced them in the end that I wouldn't have dreamed of harming my wife."

Peter Diamond's fiftieth birthday came four weeks ago. "I didn't do anything to mark it—but then I wouldn't have done much in normal circumstances. Oddly enough I discussed the birthday with Steph the night before she was killed and per-suaded her I didn't want a so-called surprise party with old cronies from years back. That's not my style. We would have gone out for a meal together, Steph and I, and had a glass or two." He is in regular contact with Curtis McGarvie and has co-operated fully with the murder squad, even to having his home searched and his wife's private letters and diary taken away for examination. He is as puzzled as the murder squad over the diary entries mentioning somebody called "T." "This must be the killer," he says, "and the odds are strong that the letter 'T' was meant to mislead, but the diary mentions phone calls and an appointment in Royal Victoria Park, which Steph hardly ever visited, so it has to be the best clue we have. What foxes me completely is that she didn't say a word about going to the park that morning. My wife wasn't secretive. She was the most open of people. I find it hard to accept there was something hidden in her life, but what other explanation is there?"

Peter Diamond continues his work at Bath Police Station, busying himself on other cases, trying to block out the knowledge that the incident room for his wife's murder is just along the corridor. Shortly before the shooting he gave evidence in the murder trial of Jake Carpenter, a notorious Bristol gang leader who was given a life sentence for the sadistic killing of a young prostitute. The possibility of some kind of revenge killing by Carpenter's associates was a strong theory early in the case. It has still not been ruled out entirely, but intensive enquiries in Bristol have so far proved negative. Diamond himself agrees that it was probably a mistake to link the killing to the Carpenter conviction. "My own reaction was the same as the squad's," he says, "but with hindsight we may have leapt to a premature conclusion and missed other leads. The first forty-eight hours in any inquiry are crucial."


TENSION


They work in separate offices on the same floor of Bath Police Station in Manvers Street, these two experienced detectives. Curtis McGarvie is the outsider, the man drafted in from headquarters. He is at his desk by 8 A.M. There is an air of tension in the incident room and it isn't just the pressures of the case. For this should be Peter Diamond's domain. He has led the murder squad for eight years. McGarvie refuses to let sentiment trouble him. He is a gritty Glaswegian, thin as a thistle, with deep-set, watchful eyes, a professional to the tips of his toes, focused and unshakeable. "If I were this killer on the run, I'd be sweating. I wouldn't want Curtis on my trail," says a colleague at Avon

& Somerset Headquarters who knows McGarvie well. He has a long string of successful prosecutions to his credit. But his team in Bath are Diamond's men and women, loyal to their chief, wanting passionately to achieve the breakthrough, yet unfamiliar with their temporary boss.

Meanwhile Peter Diamond sits alone in his office up the corridor sifting through other "stickers," trying to give them his full concentration. He is a big, abrasive man who speaks his mind without fear or favour. Few in Bath's CID have escaped the rough edge of his tongue at some point in their careers. But right now there is a strong current of sympathy for this beleaguered man excluded from the action through no fault of his own. If commitment to the cause counts for anything, the killer of Stephanie Diamond will soon be found.

## 22

R E A D I N G   T H E   *C H R O N I C L E*   piece, Diamond was surprised how much the journalist had coaxed from him. He couldn't fault the quotes. She'd done her job well. Deprived of Steph's company for all this time, he'd been a soft touch for a bright woman journalist. The interview, over coffee in Sally Lunn's, hadn't seemed at all intrusive. He'd found her interest agreeable, almost therapeutic, having his brain exercised with a series of unthreatening questions, the sort Steph put to him when he was more under pressure than usual. Thank God he hadn't said what he really thought of McGarvie.

For obvious reasons he'd kept quiet about the cringe-making incident of the revolver the search party had dug up, and he was glad McGarvie had not mentioned it either. His feelings about that gun were complex. There was a basinful of guilt. He deeply regretted being so stupid as to hang on to the damned thing all those years. It pained him that Steph had found it and been so troubled that she buried it. He was sick to the stomach that her last communication to him—a beyond-the-grave message—had to be a kind of rebuke for all its sensitive phrasing. But he had to be grateful she'd written the note and buried it with the gun. One last rescue act. She had removed a great burden of suspicion from his shoulders. Imagine McGarvie's fury, just when he felt he'd got the sensational evidence he needed, at finding the note that put Peter Diamond in the clear. The counter theory about Diamond finding the gun and murdering Steph with it and then reburying it had been the sophistry of a desperate, disappointed man.

Among those theories listed in the newspaper there was no hint of the suspicion about Steph's former husband, Dixon-Bligh. He'd given away nothing on that front because it was a line of enquiry he was pursuing alone. He didn't want Steph's past life dissected by the press or the police unless it proved absolutely unavoidable. If Dixon-Bligh or anyone else had tried to blackmail her, he would root out the dusty old secrets himself—and he didn't expect they amounted to much.

One question the gently probing reporter hadn't put to him: was it bloody-mindedness that set him against McGarvie at every turn? Bloody-mindedness? It's not so simple as that, ma'am. It's force of circumstance. I'm under an embargo, you see, orders from above to leave the detective work to the murder squad. But don't you feel bitter about all the horseshit thrown at you by McGarvie, the false charges, the invasion of your privacy? I've got broad shoulders. I can take it. Or the abysmal lack of progress in the investigation? It's a brute of a case, my dear. But if I'm totally honest, if you were to tease the truth from me, I'd be forced to admit that, yes, there could be a tiny chip on these broad shoulders of mine: I hate the man.

In the next week, doggedly pursuing his own line of enquiry, he took another trip to London and looked up Dixon-Bligh—or tried to. There was a twist in the plot, and not a welcome one. The house in Westway Terrace was empty. The boxes and the few bits of furniture had gone from the front room. A neighbour said she hadn't seen the gent for weeks. The Post Office had no forwarding address. Dixon-Bligh had done another flit.

The trains on the Portsmouth line to Waterloo had run better than usual lately. The winter problems of frozen points and leaves on the line had meant a few delays and cancellations earlier in the year, but compared to previous years the service was improving. Whether the credit went to Mother Nature or the railway companies was much debated by the regular commuters. But as long as the wheels continued to roll along the tracks it was all good-humoured stuff.

Then one September morning when it was still too early for frosts or leaves, an "incident" (unspecified, except it was "up the line') brought everything to a prolonged halt. People don't like sitting in stationary trains for any length of time. For one thing they have places to go to, appointments to keep; and for another they feel unsafe. There's that troublesome suspicion that the longer your train waits the more likely it is that another will come along behind and smash into it. There are signals to prevent such catastrophes, but signals have been known to fail.

In the 7:37 from Portsmouth, some people blocked out their nervous thoughts by turning to newspaper articles they would otherwise have skipped, about travel in the Greek Islands or training for the marathon. Others switched on their mobiles and rescheduled the morning. A few made eye contact with the passengers opposite and gave little tilts of the head that said you couldn't travel anywhere with confidence these days. This being Britain, not many words were exchanged at first, but after twenty minutes voices began to be heard.

"Where are we, exactly?"

"You talking to me?"

"I said where are we?"

"Almost at Woking, I reckon."

"What do they mean—an 'incident'?"

"Could be anything from a suicide to cows on the line."

"I blame privatisation."

"No, it goes back further than that. It all started going wrong about the time British Rail stopped calling us passengers. When I first heard myself being called a customer I knew they'd stopped trying to get us from A to B as their first aim. They were out to sell us things."

"You mean the reason we're all sitting here is so they can empty the refreshment trolley?"

"Dead right."

One man in a pinstripe let down the window and looked out. "There's another train pulled up ahead of us. Must be the 7:07."

"My sainted aunt," a reader of the *Independent* said. "They won't let us move until that one's well clear."

The pinstriped man turned from the window and reached for his hat and umbrella.

"Where the blazes are you going?" the *Independent* reader asked.

"Up the line. I can't afford to sit here all day. I'm going to board the 7:07. It's a more comfortable ride, anyway. Better than this old rolling stock."

"You want to be careful."

"It's safe enough. I know what I'm doing." He opened the door and stepped down onto the gravel at the side of the track and started walking.

"There's always one, isn't there?" a woman in a suit said, looking up from *Pride and Prejudice*. "If he gets knocked down we'll have another hour to wait."

But not two minutes later, pinstripe was back and asking his companions to open up and help him back inside. "You're not going to believe this," he said when the door was closed again. "There's a leg down there."

"What's he beefing about now?" the *Independent* reader asked.

"I said someone's leg is down there, or part of it, from the knee down." Pinstripe put his hand to his spotted silk tie and tightened it. "Horrible."

"Where?"

"Just a short way along, by the side of the track at the bottom of the embankment. You wouldn't spot it unless you were down there."

"It'll be a dummy from a dress shop."

"No, it's real. I could see the raw flesh. It must have been chewed by a fox or something."

"Leave it out, will you?" a *Sun* reader said. "You're making me puke."

"Has anyone got a mobile I can use? We ought to tell the police."

"Do us all a favour, mate," the *Sun* reader said. "Leave it till we get to Waterloo. If you call the Old Bill now, we'll be here till lunchtime."

Not everybody chimed in, but no one objected. Three minutes later, the 7:07 resumed its journey to London, and in another three minutes the 7:37 was in motion, leaving the leg behind.

The senior officers were sitting in armchairs and there was a table in front of them with filter coffee and chocolate digestives, but nobody was comfortable.

"As you know, I managed to get full backing from Headquarters," Georgina was saying. "We're in the seventh month of this inquiry, and they've given it one hundred per cent support."

"So have my team," McGarvie said. "They've put in hundreds of hours of unpaid overtime."

"I know. They've been terrific. We can be proud of them." Diamond said, "But you're going to scale it down."

"The office manager has shown me the costings, Peter. It's impossible to keep it running at this pitch."

"You told me budgets didn't exist in this case. You'd see it through, whatever."

"That was in February."

"And we're no further on. That's the truth."

McGarvie took this as a personal attack. "We're miles further on. We've got statements, forensic reports, video footage, we've recovered her bag, her diary and the bullets, we've interviewed over six hundred people."

"For what? Nobody's in the frame."

"Are you saying I've mishandled it?"

"I'm saying this isn't the time to shut up shop."

"Gentlemen," Georgina called them to order. "I don't want this to get personal. We're all under stress, me included. Headquarters are the paymasters, and I have to listen to them. Curtis, you're going to have to manage with six officers and two civilians."

McGarvie swayed like a boxer riding a punch.

Georgina went on in the sock-it-to-them style she had to use with these obstreperous characters, "You'd better decide who you want to keep. Peter, it's no use looking at me like that. I know how you feel. This is no reflection of how strongly we care about your loss and how keen we are to bring this murderer to justice. The commitment is still there. We have to face realities. Policing is about—"

"With respect, ma'am," Diamond interrupted, "I don't need reminding about priorities and neither does he. We both knew this was on the cards."

"Right, then."

"But why did you call me in?"

"You have a moral right to hear it."

"Thanks." He hesitated. "I thought you might invite me to take a fresh look at the evidence."

Georgina's lips tightened. "That is not my intention, Peter, and you know why."

"Off the record?"

"You're not to get involved. If you have any suggestions, you can pass them on now, and we'll be glad to look at them, but they won't get you on the team."

He gave a slight nod, acknowledging the small, significant shift in Georgina's position. No longer was she treating him with suspicion, whatever the lingering doubts McGarvie harboured. "So what's the focus now? Have we ruled out the Carpenters?"

Georgina looked towards McGarvie who seemed reluctant to divulge the time of day while Diamond listened, but finally conceded, "Our sources in Bristol haven't come up with anything. The word is that if some sort of revenge killing was authorised, Stephanie Diamond wouldn't have been the target."

Georgina said, "You mean they'd have targeted Peter?"

"Or the judge or someone on the jury. Mrs. Diamond would be well down the list."

She said, "That would hold true for any of the criminal fraternity seeking revenge for a conviction."

"Yes," McGarvie said, "unless the killing of Mrs. Diamond was seen as like for like."

"Meaning?"

"Someone who was deprived of their partner—and blamed Peter for it—decided he should suffer the same way."

"This is the theory that a woman is responsible?"

"Or a man whose wife was put away."

Georgina swung towards Diamond. "When did you last arrest a woman for murder?"

He cast his mind back. "Before you took over, ma'am. Ninety-four. But there wasn't a man in her life."

"So for all practical purposes we're looking at vengeful women," Georgina said. "What about the one who scratched Peter's face?"

"Janie Forsyth."

"She was shouting about a stitch-up, wasn't she? And she was Jake Carpenter's girlfriend."

"I've interviewed her twice," McGarvie said. "The big objection to Janie as a suspect is her behaviour after the trial. If you're planning a murder you don't draw attention to yourself by screaming in the street and assaulting a senior detective."

"She was in an emotional state," Georgina said as if that was the prerogative of her sex. "She could have got a gun and shot Stephanie. Let's remember the shooting happened the very next morning."

McGarvie said, "Let's also remember where it happened.

Mrs. Diamond went to the park by arrangement. We're confident of that. The diary shows she was due to meet the person known as 'T' at ten."

"You're right, of course," Georgina admitted at once. "And she'd been in touch with 'T' for some days."

"Just over a week."

"You now believe the diary is reliable evidence?"

McGarvie coloured a little and avoided looking at Diamond. "We were cautious at first, but we now accept that the entries were written by Mrs. Diamond. And if the first contact was at least ten days before the murder—"

"Remind us what it said."

"Must call 'T.' That was on Monday the fifteenth of February. It suggests a prior contact."

"All of which makes it unlikely that the Carpenter verdict was the motive for the shooting."

"That's my interpretation, ma'am."

"Mine, too," Diamond said. "Early on, before the diary was found, I was sure they were behind it. Shows how wrong you can be."

"You have another theory." Georgina spoke this as a statement. Whether she got it from intuition or the nuances of his tone, she spoke from confidence.

He wavered. He hadn't meant to bring Dixon-Bligh into this without more evidence, but the man was so elusive it was becoming clear back-up would be needed to stay on his trail. "I don't know about a theory. Her first husband was called Edward Dixon-Bligh. I'm not certain of this, but she may have called him Ted."

It was as if he'd just said the word "walk" to a pair of dogs. They sat up, ears pricked, eyes agleam, and if they'd hung out their tongues and panted, they could not have looked more eager.

They continued to give him undivided attention while he told them everything—well, *almost* everything—he knew about Dixon-Bligh and Steph's unhappy first marriage. The one thing he did not reveal was the thump he'd given the man the last time they'd met.

This new avenue of enquiry so intrigued them that nothing was said about Diamond defying the injunction to stay off the case. By now, Georgina and McGarvie knew they couldn't stop him doing his solo investigation.

"Did you ask him if he'd been in touch with her?" McGarvie said.

"He denies it, of course. Says the last time they spoke was two years ago when he found a photo of her parents and returned it."

"And you think he's short of cash?"

"Either that or he's on the run. He quit the Blyth Road flat at the end of February for a place no better than a tip."

"The week of the murder?"

"Yes. And Westway Terrace looked a very temporary arrangement to me. He's moved on from there."

"Where to?"

"Don't know. I haven't kept tabs."

"We can ask the Met. Does Dixon-Bligh have form?"

"Not that I've heard of."

"Does he strike you as capable of murder?"

He weighed the question, trying against all the odds to be impartial. "He did the 'I'm a reasonable man' bit. Said he'd put any bitterness behind him. Blamed himself and his affairs for the break-up. Called himself a selfish bastard. Said he was sorry about the way she died, but to turn up at the funeral would have been hypocrisy. I'm not the best person to ask, you understand, but listening to him, I had this feeling he was laying it on."

Georgina said, "He doth protest too much, methinks."

Delving deep into the small cellar of quotes once laid down for his Eng. Lit. exam, Diamond said, "Wasn't it the lady who protested too much?"

"Immaterial. I was making a general point."

McGarvie, floundering, asked, "Which lady?"

"Don't try me," said Georgina sharply. "Was he ever violent to her?"

"She never mentioned violence to me," Diamond had to admit. "She spoke very little about him."

McGarvie, trying to recoup, thought fit to point out, "As an ex-officer in the RAF, he'd have had weapons training."

Georgina pulled a face. "In the *catering* branch?"

"As part of his general training, ma'am. They all go through that. He may also have been issued a handgun at some point in his career. A foreign posting in a war zone. Did he serve in the Gulf?"

"Couldn't tell you," Diamond said.

"He's got to be interviewed as soon as possible," Georgina decided. She asked McGarvie in an accusing tone, "Why hasn't his name come up before this?"

There was some injured virtue in his answer. "I was told he dropped out of her life a long time ago, and when he didn't attend the funeral . . ."

"It should have rung a warning bell, Curtis."

Back in the office, still uncertain if it had been a wise move to put them onto Dixon-Bligh, Diamond listened to his voice-mail. The first voice up belonged to his old oppo, Louis Voss.

"Peter, I may have something for you. Could you call me back pronto?"

He closed the office door first. Then learned the hot news Louis had gotten from his computer about a dismembered body found on the railway embankment near Woking. "That's no big deal on its own," Louis told him equably. "Desperate people sometimes lie on railway tracks to kill themselves, but this doesn't sound like a suicide. This one has two bullet holes in the skull, and first indications are that it's a woman around forty."

# 23

FOR ONCE DIAMOND did the approved thing: phoned the CID Headquarters at Surrey and asked if he might visit the scene. Making his pitch to a cautious-sounding inspector, he explained he was "involved" in a case of fatal shooting that might conceivably be linked to the Woking incident.

Needless to say, his own CID wouldn't have regarded this as the approved thing. For the time being he preferred not to have them involved. McGarvie would be better employed trying to trace Dixon-Bligh.

"You're quick off the mark, sir," the cautious Surrey inspector said.

"It's the computer age, isn't it?" Diamond remarked as if he spent all his time in front of a screen.

After a pause and some murmured consultations at the end of the phone, the decision was made. "If you think it's worth your while, come down. Bowers is our man at the scene. DCI Bobby Bowers. He and his lads will be there the rest of today and most of tomorrow as well."

"Is he extra thorough, then?"

"It's the location."

"By the railway?"

"Horribly overgrown and on a wicked gradient and the body's in several pieces from all I hear. Are you still up for it?"

"Of course."

"I'll tell Bobby to expect you."

He looked at a map of Surrey. Woking is southwest of London, a short way south of the M25 and within five miles of another motorway, the M3. Convenient both for commuting and dumping a body.

It is also a main railway station on the Portsmouth line to Waterloo.

During the drive he prepared himself mentally for his first visit to a murder scene since that February morning that remained as vivid in his memory as anything in his experience. He wasn't sure how he'd react. The sight of the corpse should not trouble him, he thought. He'd seen plenty in his time, and they were all different. This one was in pieces anyway, and while that prospect might turn many people's stomachs, he would find it more acceptable than a recognisable body. The acid test would come when he met the professionals at the scene. He wasn't sure if he was ready yet for black humour. It was going to take an effort to stay calm, let alone join in.

In an effort to loosen up he tried to recall the wording of a press release—probably apocryphal—he'd laughed at many years ago during his training. It was along the lines of: "Portions of the victim's dismembered body were buried in seven different locations. She had not been interfered with." This time, it didn't amuse him.

Driving at his usual sedate pace, he eventually spotted the signs for Woking and by four fifteen was there. It looked no different from any other dormitory town as the rush hour got underway. He crawled the last stretch in the queue along the A324 with the patience of a Buddhist. What's one murdered corpse when twenty thousand of the living have to get home for a meal and *The Bill* on television?

Surrey Police were well organised. Two caravans and several people carriers were lined up in the street nearest to the scene. More promising than that, a mobile canteen was in place with some exhausted coppers in white overalls standing about drinking from cans. He parked as close as he could, introduced himself and accepted tea and a doughnut before moving on to a mobile caravan. He showed his ID to a uniformed sergeant and asked for DCI Bowers. The chief was down by the track.

The access was a short path through a public park where three little boys in the Manchester United strip were kicking a ball around. With just such little boys in mind, the railway embankment had been fenced off from the park, but the wire fence was rusty and holed in places. He could shake his head about young vandals, yet he remembered as a ten-year-old cutting holes in fences to trespass on his local stretch of track. The big dare was to leave pennies on the rails to see how the train wheels crushed them.

This July and August had been wetter than usual, producing a dense ground cover on the fenced-off side. The nettles and ferns were shoulder high in places. From the top of the embankment Diamond parted some bracken and looked down on a sixty-metre stretch cordoned with crime-scene tape. Screens had been erected to shield the scene from passing trains. A team was at work stripping back the growth. Hot, backaching work. He'd done it in his time. You don't picture yourself scything a way through the jungle when you join the police. Sooner or later it happens, and then you have to be grateful you're not excavating the council tip or up to your waist in stagnant water. That, too, can happen if you stay long enough in the lower ranks.

Someone pointed out the recommended way down to the trackside. It was a biggish detour, but the quick route would have been a steep slope straight through the search area. Surrey CID would not appreciate the big man from Bath sledging in on the seat of his pants. He did the right thing.

Which of the search party was DCI Bobby Bowers was not immediately obvious. Three young men were directing operations from a chart of the search area pinned to a trestle table, and to Diamond's eye they looked like schoolkids. He gave his name and had his hand shaken firmly. Close up, Bowers, in a black polo shirt and faded jeans, looked marginally older than the others.

"You're from . . . ?"

"Bath." He explained—with some telescoping of the facts— that he'd learned about the body from the police computer, and it might possibly have links with an unsolved case seven months back in Bath.

"Hope you're right," Bowers said. "We need all the help going."

"What have you got so far?"

"Only what the animals left us. A well-chewed torso and one leg found here." He tapped a finger on the chart. "Skull, with two bullet holes and exit wounds, here, farther down the slope. The other leg—or part of it—on the gravel beside the track. And miscellaneous bits scattered over a wide area. Putrefaction well set in. The lads are calling her Charlie."

"Ah," Diamond said without fully catching on.

"Charlie—cocaine—she gets up your nose," Bowers filled in for him. "The pathologist estimates six months to a year on a first look, but he'll give a better estimate when he's had the maggots analysed."

"Definitely female?"

"Unless it's a bloke in tights and a C-cup."

"Age?"

"Too soon to make an estimate."

"I was told she was about forty."

"That's our impression from the clothes."

"Any possessions? Handbag?"

"Not yet. We're still picking up bits."

"Rings?"

Bowers shook his head.

"How about the bullets?"

"You're joking, I hope."

"I suppose she was shot somewhere else and brought here."

Bowers sniffed and looked away, "Yeah, we worked that out."

"Why wasn't the body noticed before today, with trains going by all day?"

"You didn't see the place before we started to clear it. You could hide the Red Army here and no one would know."

"At this time of year, yes. What about six months ago?"

"The scrub would still have been dense enough to hide a stiff, no problem. There's years of growth. A railway embankment is a clever place to dispose of anything, when you think about it. Nobody much comes down here apart from railway workers."

"So who discovered it?"

Bobby Bowers rolled his eyes. "A prize nutter. All the trains are held up for some reason, stacked up waiting for a signal, so chummy decides to get out and board the one in front, the fast one he missed back at Guildford. He hasn't gone more than a few yards when he sees this half-chewed leg beside the track. Gets the screaming abdabs and climbs back on the train. But—mark this—he doesn't call nine-nine-nine till he gets to work. It's a crowded commuter train. You know what they're like these days with bloody mobiles going off every couple of minutes. Our wiseguy insists that the rest of the good citizens on the train told him not to call the fuzz right away because it was sure to mean another delay. That's your great British public. We finally got the shout at ten twenty."

"You've made some inroads, then." Encouragement is always appreciated and Bobby Bowers sounded as if he needed some.

And sometimes it has to be underlined. "It's no picnic," Bowers said. "My lads have a job to keep their footing. The pathologist said he wanted danger money."

"What did he say about the dismembering?"

"That's down to the foxes. They're rampant around here. There's no sign she was hacked about by the killer." He glanced along the embankment. "Ay-up—somebody's found another bit."

Conversation was suspended while they stepped along the side of the track to where one of the search party was waving. "What have you got for me, Marty?"

"Two fingers, sir."

"I know how you feel, but what have you got for me?"

Marty gave a tired grin. They clambered up the incline to examine his find: the brown bones of the fingers with enough skin still attached to link them at the base. They were well-camouflaged against the dark soil. The searchers had to be eagle-eyed.

"You were asking about rings," Bowers said. "This will be the little finger and the ring finger of the left hand. We already found the right."

"No joy, then."

"None for us, anyway. The killer may have removed it, of course."

"Or she may not have had a ring."

Some sinewy material remained attached to the bones, and there were traces of varnish at the base of a fingernail, but there was no chance of finding the impression of a wedding ring.

Bowers thanked his man and had the find marked and called for a photographer.

Diamond asked about the skull. Was it still where they had found it?

"No, the doc decided to lift it. It's in one of our boxes waiting to be moved to the forensic lab. You can see it if you want."

They trudged back to the centre of operations. He had the box opened and the skull grinned at him, or that was the effect. The bared teeth and the curve of the jawbone, picked clean by the joint efforts of foxes, magpies and larvae, seemed to pass on the message "Don't count on me to give you any help."

Trying to ignore that, he looked at the circular bullet holes on the right side, just above the ear cavity. No exact match with the pattern of Steph's shooting, but the firing of two shots at such close range did suggest a professional killing.

"Lift it out if you want," Bowers offered. "You might like to look at the hair. Some is still attached at the back."

"No need," Diamond told him. "I don't know what I'm looking for. Dark, is it?"

"Tinted brown."

He switched his interest to the teeth. "One or two fillings, anyway. If you can find her dental records, you might get a name."

"A handbag would be quicker," Bowers said. "Did you find one with yours?"

"Mine?"

"Your stiff."

A pause.

Diamond made a huge effort to sound untroubled. "Er—it was hidden, but yes."

"So you knew pretty soon who she was?"

"Right." He put the lid on the smiling skull before it unsettled him more. "What about those clothes you mentioned?"

"We found a few. Want to see?" Bowers turned to a stack of cardboard storage boxes. "These would tell you she's over thirty even if the bones hadn't. More Country Casuals than Top Shop." He opened a box and took out two transparent zip-bags, each containing a shoe that didn't look the latest in snazzy dressing, even to Diamond's untutored eye. "Size seven, squat, narrow heel. No bimbo wears things like this."

Bowers opened another box and lifted out the tattered remains of a green padded coat in some man-made fabric. "Ripped to shreds by the foxes. The fact that she was wearing a thing like this means she was probably shot last winter or the spring."

"It also makes it likely the shooting happened outdoors," Diamond said more for his own benefit than anyone else's.

"Agreed."

"What was she wearing underneath?"

"Woollen stuff for warmth, a thick pink jumper, though not much has survived. Black woollen skirt. Very little left of it. Imitation leather belt. Black tights. And Marks and Spencer underwear, same as yours and mine, I dare say."

"Speak for yourself."

There was a break in the dialogue while Bowers marked his chart with the latest find. The police work all seemed highly efficient except that each time a train went past, one of the screens blew down and several of the search party had to shore it up again.

"What do you think?" Bowers asked when the chart was updated. "Any chance of a link between your stiff and mine?"

The force of that word struck home harder this time and it took some strength of will to let it pass. Bowers had no idea how close he was to being smeared all over his precious chart. "It's a long way from Bath, of course," Diamond succeeded in saying after a pause. "The two shots to the head are the common factor, plus the sex and approximate age of the victims. Middle-aged women aren't killed this way. Mind, there are some differences in the m.o. Yours was hidden from view, mine left on the ground in a public park. She was found very soon after the shots were fired."

"Who was she?"

"My wife, actually."

Bobby Bowers gave a nod, then in a double take, a wide-eyed stare. "Did you say . . . ?"

Diamond answered with formal precision as if giving evidence, "Her name was Stephanie. She went to the park to meet someone known as 'T,' according to her diary. She was gunned down in broad daylight."

"Christ, I read about this." Bowers raked a hand distractedly through his hair. "Bloody hell. Didn't connect you."

"Well, you wouldn't. You'd expect someone else to be on the case, and he is."

This drew a frown from the young DCI. There is only so much you can take in at a time, even when you're a fast-track superintendent in a polo shirt and jeans.

With a candour that actually surprised himself, Diamond explained, "I'm here unofficially, acting on my own. Way out of line, I know, but I mean to find out why my wife was murdered and who did it."

There was a forced interruption as a train went by.

Then, from Bowers, "Have you found out anything of use?"

"Here? Not yet."

"Are you working with the team on your wife's case?"

"Wish I was. Protocol doesn't allow it."

"So you're doing a Charles Bronson?"

Diamond grinned faintly. "Better not put it in those terms."

"I'm glad you told me. I might have said something really tasteless. You don't mind me asking—were you and your wife—?"

"Happily married? Yes."

"But you must have some theories why she was killed."

"How much time have you got?" He was relieved the young DCI had taken it so calmly. That generation was less hung up on protocol, thank God. In the next five minutes he sketched out the main facts of the case pausing only when another train thundered past. At the end of it, he said, "If you hear all this again from a certain DCI McGarvie, do me a favour and try and sound interested."

"McGarvie?"

"He's the SIO."

"I may call him," Bowers said.

"That's up to you."

"Not much point till we know who the, em, victim is."

"Right." Diamond suddenly felt devious again, and he didn't

enjoy it when Bowers had been so obliging. He had a strong theory who the dead woman was, but his maverick status made it necessary for him to keep it to himself. "It shouldn't take long."

Bowers looked less confident.

"So how do you think she was brought here?" Diamond asked.

"By road, almost certainly. As you saw, you can bring a vehicle really close."

"You don't think she was pushed off a train?"

"Unlikely. Too many people travel on them. We're assuming she was driven here by night, already dead, and dumped on the embankment. Most of the torso was found high up the slope. You can park a van up there out of sight of any houses."

"The killer knew the area, then. A local man?"

"I wouldn't bet on it," Bowers said. "The thing about Woking is it's so near the motorways. Driving the M25 is a joy at night. Any street map would show him how close he could get to the trains. He could have scouted out the route one evening and brought the body here the next."

"He'd still need to have decided on that stretch of embankment."

"Thousands of people use the trains. Some guy living as far away as Portsmouth could have planned it. Or equally someone in London."

"Bath is way off the route," Diamond said, as much to himself as Bowers. "It's not too likely he came from Bath. The killer of my wife had local knowledge."

"Doesn't matter where he comes from," Bowers pointed out. "A professional hitman does his homework first. They suss out the spot they want on a couple of visits."

Fair point, Diamond had to admit. This young detective had a good grasp. He'd be an asset in any investigation.

When he drove out of Woking that evening, with the September sun shooting blood-red streaks above Bagshot Heath, he was mentally crossing theories off his list.

# 24

ALL THE WAY back, chugging along in the slow lane of the M4 at a steady fifty (the fastest he drove under any circumstances), he argued with himself over his next move. He was home shortly after nine and went straight to the phone and called Julie Hargreaves, the ex-colleague he could safely confide in. This link with Steph's murder—and he was ninety per cent sure it was a link—had huge possibilities, and no one else was aware of it yet. Ahead of the field now, he knew his dangerous tendency to rush fences, and even he could see that this one had a built-in hazard. Julie's advice was worth seeking.

They got the preliminaries out of the way. Yes, he was coping better than he expected, and yes, he was sorry he hadn't been in touch for months. The subtext, understood by them both, was the awkwardness he felt as a widower calling up a woman friend. You couldn't do it without suggesting you were feeling the strain of living alone. For her part, Julie said she was sorry they hadn't been in touch more. She'd tried phoning any number of times. She asked what had happened to the answerphone he'd once had.

"Binned it," he told her, relieved to have something functional to speak about. "More trouble than it was worth. And don't tell me I'm back in the Stone Age, or I'll come looking for you with my club. I want your advice, Julie, but not about phones." He told her everything he knew about the human remains beside the railway at Woking. "You'll understand what drew me there. Middle-aged woman shot twice through the head, execution-style. That's so rare in this country; I can't recall any other case except—"

"Neither can I," she cut in. She was as keyed up as he was.

"She's been dead six months to a year, they estimate. It's mainly guesswork at this stage based on the clothes she was wearing. The body's terribly chewed up."

"And how long has it been since . . . ?"

"Seven months on Tuesday," he said. "February twenty-third."

"I suppose there could be a connection. On the other hand," she sounded a more cautious note, "there are obvious differences, aren't there?"

This was why he had phoned Julie, for her ability to weigh the facts.

"Such as?"

"You said this woman was shot twice in the side of the head."

"I wouldn't make too much of that. Steph took one to the forehead and one to the side. That could be down to a head movement as the shots were fired."

"All right. There's a bigger difference, isn't there? You say this body at Woking was well hidden?"

"The weeds are shoulder high."

"Well then, the killer went to some trouble to take the body there and hide it. She might not have been found for years. Whereas Steph was shot and left in the open where she was certain to be seen."

"Okay, I'll give you that, Julie. It's not the same m.o. at all."

"And Woking is a long way from Bath."

"That doesn't bother me," he said.

Julie said, "You're keeping something back, aren't you? Is she identified?"

"Not yet."

"But you think you know?"

"An idea—that's all."

She was there. It wasn't intuition or telepathy that made her say, "The missing wife of that DCI? The ex-police sergeant. What was her name—Weather? Wasn't she found?"

Doubt flooded in. "Was she?"

"I'm asking you," Julie said.

He was mightily relieved. He'd built a mental case study of Mrs. Weather's murder already. "If she'd turned up, we'd have heard something, wouldn't we?"

"Maybe."

"I'll check the Missing Persons Index."

"What makes you think it's her?" she asked.

"Hang about, Julie. You put the idea in my head."

She gave a quick, nervous laugh. "Yes, I did."

"And that was before this body turned up. Think about it. We know Mrs. Weather went missing a week or so after Steph was shot. Early March. She'd have been wearing winter things."

"Agreed."

"You saw the computer item about her. Was there a description?"

"Nothing about clothes I can recall. There may have been something on her age and build. Hair colour. We can check again." She paused before asking the key question. "Why would anyone murder the wives of two policemen?"

"The wives of two detectives who worked out of Fulham nick in the early eighties," he stressed.

She digested that for a moment. "If it's true, it's going to transform the case."

"Right—we can ditch all the cock-eyed theories and focus on this."

"Where did Mrs. Weather live?"

"Raynes Park, I was told by Louis Voss."

"That's near Wimbledon, isn't it? How far from Woking?"

"Twenty miles, maximum," Diamond said, sounding like Bobby Bowers. "A hitman plots his route and goes where he needs to." He hesitated. "Julie, is this just one more theory, or have I struck gold?"

"I wouldn't go as far as that," Julie said. "But it deserves an airing. What's your next move?"

"That's my problem. Bowers is quick on the draw. It won't be long before he puts a name to his corpse. If she is Patricia Weather, they'll find out tomorrow, I reckon. All they have to do is check the MPL."

"Against what?" said Julie. "It's not so straightforward. They have some bones of a mature woman and some unremarkable clothes. No handbag, no rings."

"Teeth."

"That only helps if they can match them to a dental record."

"They'll have a record for her."

Still Julie doubted the efficiency of the system. "They won't have her name—unless you suggest it. Remember there are different police services involved. I'll be surprised if anything is confirmed in the next twenty-four hours." She paused. "Is that what you wanted to hear?"

"If it buys me time, yes."

"To outflank Curtis McGarvie?" Julie knew too well how he felt.

He said in his defence, "It isn't personal. OK, I don't get on with the man, but I'm professional enough to put that aside. My confidence was shattered when he turned up on my doorstep with that search warrant. That was overkill, Julie. My worry is that when he gets this information, he'll cock up. The killer will get wise and head for the hills."

"McGarvie is smarter than that."

"I can't take the risk."

She sounded sceptical when she asked, "What can you do on your own?"

"If my gut feeling is right, and this body is Weather's wife, I'll know this goes back fifteen years to my time in the Met. Some psycho out there has a major grudge against Stormy Weather and me. We need to compare notes."

"You'd tell him?" Now there was definite disapproval in her voice.

"That's the size of it, Julie. Poor sod, he's going to be pole-axed when he finds out his wife has been lying dead for six months, half eaten by foxes."

"You can't tell him that. You don't know for sure."

"He'll read about the body in the paper tomorrow. It's going to cross his mind, isn't it?"

"That may be so, Peter, but I think you're making a mistake here. You should let things take their course."

"What? Wait for everyone to find out?"

"Mm."

"For Christ's sake, why?"

Julie said in the firm tone she'd learned to use when this ex-boss of hers was at his most overbearing, "You're asking for my advice, and this is it. Talking to Weather at this stage isn't going to help you. He'll be in no state to think straight."

He was silent, locked into his own thoughts, forced to accept the simple truth of her conclusion. "That's a point. I wasn't."

She waited a moment, making sure it had sunk in. "So you'll stay clear?"

He sighed heavily. "Of Stormy? I guess I'll have to. But I can do some ferreting of my own—with a little help from my old chum Louis Voss—getting up to speed with stuff I thought I'd never need to bother with again."

"Case files from the nineteen eighties?"

"Yes."

"Property of the Met? Dodgy."

"You're not going to give me another no, no?"

"I wouldn't dream of it, guv."

After putting down the phone he fed the cat from one tin and himself from another. The basics of existence. Coping better than I expected, he'd claimed to Julie. True, in a way. He didn't have space in his life for self-pity. The drive to find Steph's killer occupied him totally.

But he would let Stormy Weather have one more night in ignorance.

He put in an early appearance at the nick next morning. Early by his standards. Curtis McGarvie, the focused, committed, hot-shit detective was always in by eight and expected the incident room to be humming when he arrived. An impressive regime—and what results had it achieved?

So Diamond looked in about eight thirty, trying to fix his eyes on people rather than the photos of Steph's body displayed along one wall. There was a school of thought that said a murder squad worked better with visual reminders of the crime all around them. He'd never subscribed to it.

Keith Halliwell came over. "All right, guv?"

"Fair to middling. Is robocop about?"

"Upstairs with the ACC. Something he saw in the papers."

No prize for guessing. He'd catch up with the papers shortly. "Maybe you can tell me, Keith. What's the latest take on Dixon-Bligh, Steph's ex?"

"None that I heard. We asked the Met to trace him if they can. Thought it would be straightforward, but nothing has come through. He's covered his tracks apparently."

"I put the frighteners on him. Between you and me, Keith, he gave me some lip and I stuck one on him. Better not tell your boss."

"I won't. Is he a toerag, then?"

Diamond couldn't let it pass. "Who do you mean?"

Straight-faced, Halliwell said, "Dixon-Bligh." He'd missed the point entirely, which was a good thing.

"Don't ask me," Diamond said. "I'm going to be biased, aren't I? Actually, I shouldn't have hit him. I was needling the bastard, trying to get a response, so it's no wonder he slagged me off. I hardly know the guy. What I heard from Steph didn't impress me much. No doubt you've checked his service record and everything else?"

"School reports, library tickets, vaccinations, birth weight and date of conception," Halliwell said with a slight smile. "We don't do things by half. He was running a restaurant after he left the Air Force."

"Yes, he——" Diamond stopped before the rest came out. "It was in Guildford, Surrey, that restaurant."

"That's right, guv. Is it important?"

Diamond was asking himself the same question. Guildford was only five miles south of Woking, the next stop on the railway. Anyone travelling from Guildford to London would pass the stretch of embankment where yesterday's body had been found. "May be nothing," he told Halliwell. "Just a passing thought. He had a partner in the restaurant. Did you find out her name?"

"Fiona Appleby. They parted, we understand. Then he sold the business and moved to London."

"Blyth Road, Hammersmith, for a bit. Then Westway Terrace, Paddington."

"Right. Then he goes off the screen. Do you really think he hoofed it because you showed up in his life, guv?"

"Could be. But I have to say Westway Terrace is not a place anyone would want to stay in for long. Does he have a job?"

"He isn't on the unemployed register."

"Got on his bike and looked for work, I expect," Diamond murmured. He heard someone enter the room behind him and noticed a change in the posture of the civilian computer operator, a definite bracing of the neck and shoulders.

Without turning, he said, "Morning, Mr. McGarvie."

"Peter. Is this a courtesy call, or have you remembered something?" asked the Senior Investigating Officer with a touch of sarcasm. There was a distinct gleam in the bloodshot eyes this morning.

"Just comparing notes with Keith on Dixon-Bligh," Diamond said. "He's proving elusive."

"Rather." But McGarvie had something more urgent on his mind. "Seen the papers?"

"Not yet."

He had the *Daily Telegraph* folded open at an inner page. "What do you make of that?"

Diamond skimmed through the report of the grisly find by the railway at Woking. "Nasty."

"Is that all you've got to say?"

"Shocking, then."

"This woman was killed by two shots to the head."

"I spotted that."

"And you can't find anything more to say than 'shocking'? Doesn't it strike you as a remarkable coincidence? A middle-aged woman?"

"Actually, no," Diamond said in the bored voice of a man who has heard nothing new. "I don't think it's a coincidence at all. This is another shooting by the same gunman. I'd put money on it."

McGarvie glared. "My point exactly. I've just been with the ACC, and she agrees. We've contacted Surrey Headquarters and I'm going up to the crime scene this afternoon. It could be the breakthrough I've . . ." His voice faltered.

"Been waiting for?"

He'd laid himself wide open, and he knew it. "I'll remind you that this case has twice been reviewed, and each time I've been confirmed as the SIO."

"They must think highly of you. Enjoy your trip to Woking."

He managed to resist adding, "Been there, done that." He'd asked that bright young detective Billy Bowers to play dumb with McGarvie, and he probably would.

About the time McGarvie was motoring along the M4 to Woking, Diamond boarded the train to London. Whoever wrote the slogan about letting the train take the strain could have had the big detective in mind. Travel by motorway was on a par with ordeal by fire. In the comfort of the InterCity Express, he could review a case and decide on the next move. That was the theory, anyway. He read the report in the *Express* of WOMAN ON LINE SHOT "EXECUTION STYLE" and woke up at Paddington unsure when he'd nodded off.

He was fully alert when he entered the Fox and Pheasant in Fulham. Louis Voss came in soon after with a briefcase under his arm.

"I feel like a character in a le Carre novel."

"In your dreams, Louis. Inspector Clouseau, more like. Is it a lager for you?"

"Scotch."

When Diamond returned with the drinks, he came straight to the point. "You've got something in the briefcase?"

"I thought it would be simple accessing the old files through the computer system, but of course you were pre-computer. I had to go downstairs to Records and talk my way in there. Then it was a matter of sorting through any number of dusty old packets tied with string."

"And . . . ?"

"My clothes are filthy. I've a good mind to send you the dry-cleaning bill, but I think I found your main cases—except for Missendale."

"That went to a board of inquiry. It wouldn't be down there. Doesn't matter. It wouldn't have any bearing. You found the protection case, I hope? Joe Florida?"

"That's there. And the Brook Green shooting. Two or three others."

"Great work, Louis."

"What you've got here are photocopies of the main documents. I couldn't copy everything."

"Understood."

Louis eyed him speculatively. "Does a le Carré character ever ask George Smiley what the hell he's up to?"

Diamond shook his head. "They skirt around it. That's why the books are so long."

"Would it have anything to do with the body found at Woking yesterday?"

"You read the papers, too."

"Couldn't miss it. You want to be careful, Peter. There's a professional gunman out there. You may think you're on his tail, but he's on yours."

"Thanks, Louis. I'll sleep better for knowing that."

He left soon after with the files.

# 25

JULIE WAS RIGHT. It took two whole days for anyone else to make the connection with DCI Weather's missing wife. Two days of inertia for Peter Diamond. True, he studied the case files Louis had photocopied. He combed them minutely, regardless that he'd extracted everything of substance inside an hour on his train ride back to Bath. Top of the heap was the protection racketeer, Joe Florida, released from Wandsworth in 1995 after serving seven years of a twelve-stretch. Joe Florida's wish list of slow tortures, emasculations and other cruel fates for police officers who had crossed him was well documented. He told Diamond in one of his interviews prior to being charged that he would "blow you away, you pig" (though Diamond remembered some adjectives the transcription left out) and repeated the threat more graphically in court after sentencing. As he was being taken down he had shouted—and Diamond remembered this clearly—"I've put a notice on you, copper. I'll do the business on you when I come out. You'll wish you'd never heard of me." Such taunts from the dock were not uncommon, and the police and judiciary treated them philosophically in the knowledge that several years behind bars dulled the memory and weakened the intent. But in view of what had happened, Joe Florida had to be taken seriously. The probation service had kept tabs on him for three more years after release. He'd returned to West London to a flat in an upmarket street in Chelsea, so he was obviously not without funds. Under "Current Employment" on his file someone had written *Nothing known,* a succinct summing up. He was a career crook well capable of slipping back into crime without drawing attention to himself.

Tucked away in a section about the surveillance operation on Joe Florida was a name Diamond noted with interest. He circled it with a pen. One of the team assigned to watch the suspect's flat had been DC Weather. A minor role apparently, but it was not impossible Stormy had helped make the arrest and got himself on Florida's wish list.

The Assistant Chief Constable herself, Georgina Dallymore, brought the news late Monday afternoon when things had gone quiet, stepping unannounced into Diamond's cluttered office and exclaiming breathlessly, "Peter, I think we have the breakthrough. Curtis has been talking to the Surrey Police at Woking where the remains of that woman were found at the end of last week. They have an ID now, and she's confirmed as an ex-police officer, the wife of a CID officer *you may well have worked with in the Met.*"

"DCI Weather," he said as if they were discussing nothing more enthralling than last night's television. "Yes, I know the bloke."

"You've heard already?" He'd just shot Georgina's fox, and she was not pleased.

He said in the same flat tone, "Mrs. Patricia Weather, aged thirty-eight, dark-haired, five-six, stocky, dressed in a dark green padded coat, black woollen skirt with an artificial leather belt, pink jumper, Marks and Spencer underwear, tights and low unfashionable black shoes, size seven with a narrow heel."

"How do you know all this?"

This was not the time to mention his trip to Woking. "Most of it is in the papers, apart from her name, ma'am. That's on the PNC under missing persons."

Georgina eyed him warily, suspicious she was being gulled. Nobody associated computer science with Peter Diamond.

As an extra touch, he explained, "And the Yard puts out these bulletins."

"And you put two and two together?"

"It wasn't quite so obvious as that. I couldn't say for sure."

"But you worked it out. Independently of our inquiry, you worked it out."

"I do have an interest in the case, ma'am."

Still huffy, she told him, "I came to put you in the picture, and there's no need, apparently."

"Ah, but it's nice to have it confirmed."

She nodded and said with as much acid as she could convey, "In the unlikely possibility that it *hasn't* reached your ears, I've called a case conference for tomorrow afternoon, and Surrey Police and the Met will be represented. I'd like you to be there as well. Any theories you have about this development will be of interest to us all."

He thanked her, a necessary gesture. Even he recognised the need to kowtow on occasions.

Georgina unfroze a couple of degrees. "Let's hope this brings a result. You're entitled to expect it. A fresh perspective ought to make a difference." It was as near as she would come to saying McGarvie was all at sea.

Still she lingered and Diamond waited. Eventually she said, "I was never in the Met, so I can't speak from first hand about things that happened in the eighties. Everyone knows corruption was endemic then and the official inquiries didn't deal with the problem. Countryman should have made a difference and was wound up far too soon. What was that other inquiry run by Number Five Regional Crime Squad?"

"Operation Carter."

"Yes, they collected some damning evidence and didn't

deliver in the end, or were shut down. You were at Fulham in those days. You must have seen abuses."

"They weren't the norm, ma'am."

"Don't take this personally, Peter."

Whenever he heard those words he knew something personal was about to be slung at him.

"You had to face a board of inquiry over that Missendale case. I know you took it to heart at the time."

"I was angry."

"You were exonerated."

"With a rider about my overbearing manner."

"Which everyone except you has forgotten. Will you hear me out? This changes everything, this identification. Both murders could well have roots in things that happened at the time I'm speaking of, things you'd rather forget. We need to know what they are, Peter. We've all had episodes in our past we gloss over. Speak frankly, and you have my word there will be no witch hunt."

"What about, ma'am?"

"Anything at all. The point is this. We have to stop this killer from murdering anyone else. That's paramount. Your iffy conduct fifteen years ago doesn't matter a jot compared to that."

He was stung into a sharp riposte. "No, ma'am," he told her, feeling the blood rush to his face, "*this* is the point. My wife had two bullets put through her brain. If you think I'd hold back on anything to shore up my dodgy career, you must have a low opinion of me."

"That isn't so," she said through tight lips. She turned and left the room.

He felt a twinge of guilt. Georgina had come in spontaneously, genuinely wanting to share her news with him. So often of late when she'd spoken to him, there had been a hidden agenda. This time she'd dredged up his past—or tried to—and said a couple of tactless things and he'd reacted more tetchily than ever. He needn't have put her down. Too late to mention it.

Another of the case files he'd acquired from Louis featured a white teenager, a crop-headed loner called Wayne Beach who had a liking for guns. As a juvenile, Beach had twice been caught in possession of firearms acquired by his criminal family. For a short time in the early eighties he had made a living robbing and shooting taxi drivers. His method was simple and effective. He'd hail a cab late at night when the driver had stacked up an evening's fares in the West End and ask to be driven to some street where he'd already parked a stolen car. He'd get out and instead of paying the fare, he'd pull out a handgun and shoot the driver, usually in the leg, and demand his takings. The drivers always paid up. He would smash the two-way radio and put another bullet into one of the taxi tyres before walking calmly to the stolen car and escaping. One night in Edith Road an eagle-eyed constable spotted a parked car reported as stolen three hours before. On the off chance that this was the taxi bandit, a team headed by Diamond was issued arms and sent to lie in wait. Beach was ambushed and shot in the hip. It was not stated in the file whether Stormy Weather had been one of the DCs in support.

Beach had been given five years on that occasion and had served several terms since for malicious wounding. The significant feature in his case was the way he felt about guns. He was a trigger-happy hard man with no scruples about inflicting pain on innocent victims. It wasn't enough to use the gun as a threat. He always fired. The case notes said he had an image of himself as a holdup man in the old American West. He put bullets into people without any compunction whatever. Killing hadn't featured among his crimes, it was true, though one of the drivers had almost bled to death. But he had to be taken seriously as a possible killer now.

He'd been released from Wormwood Scrubs last Christmas, in plenty of time to have shot Steph and Patricia Weather.

Georgina said to the room in general, "This is Detective Super-intendent Peter Diamond," and added on a softer, apologetic note, as if suddenly realising she was in the holy of holies, the Chief Constable's suite, "the husband."

"Widower," Diamond corrected her.

"We already met," DCI Bobby Bowers said without elab-orating, and nobody picked up on it.

The case conference was around the oval table where offi-cers' careers were blessed or blown away. Coffee was served in porcelain cups and saucers instead of mugs and there were Jaffa Cakes instead of chocolate digestives. There was little else to report. It was a fact-finding exercise for all concerned, and no facts were found that were new to Diamond.

At one stage someone made the ill-considered remark, "Patsy Weather was a copper, one of our own. This time we'll get this guy, whatever it takes."

Diamond demolished him with a look.

Afterwards he offered to show Bowers the way down to the car park.

"Nothing else at the scene, then?" he asked the young DCI.

"Only bits of bone."

"No bag? No rings?"

"I'd have mentioned it just now, wouldn't I?"

"When's the post mortem?"

"Tomorrow." Bowers glanced at his watch. "Would you have time to show me your crime scene?"

They drove out to Royal Victoria Park in Bowers' white Volvo. This late in the afternoon they found a space easily on Royal Avenue below the Crescent and walked across the turf to the place near the stone bandstand where Steph had fallen. The sympathetic tributes of flowers and wreaths had long since disappeared. No one would have known this was a murder scene. A couple of schoolkids locked in a passionate embrace behind the bandstand had not been put off. The proximity of strangers didn't put them off either.

Bowers stared across the lawns, velvety in low-angled sunlight, to the glittering row of parked cars along the avenue and above them the curve of the most-photographed terraced building in Europe. He took in the great trees to the left and the conifers away to the right. Turning, he noted how close were the tall bushes screening them from Charlotte Street Car Park.

"Hard to equate with my railway embankment."

"You've got a park nearby."

"Yeah, but this is so open." He took out a pack of cigarettes and offered one to Diamond, who shook his head. "And she was just gunned down and left here?"

He nodded, not trusting himself to speak without emotion.

"There was no attempt to move her?"

"Too risky."

"You mean he would have been seen dragging her to his car?" Bowers cupped his hand over his lighter to get a cigarette going and exhaled a long sigh of smoke that seemed to express the difficulty he was having with this crime scene. "Why wasn't he seen shooting her?"

"*He?*"

A pause. Bowers raised an eyebrow. "You don't really suspect this killer is female?"

"I'm keeping an open mind—or trying to. But you asked about the risk of being seen. I've given thought to that," Diamond said, more comfortable talking practicalities. "You'd think a public park in broad daylight would be a stupid place to murder someone, but this was a cold morning in February at a time of day when most people were already at work—and I've checked more than once. It *is* deserted here around that time."

"Do you think he—or she—worked that out?"

"Probably."

"So he *could* have moved the body if he'd wanted to."

"To a car, you mean?"

"The car park is right here behind us."

Diamond was dismissive. "No chance. Its use is totally different. By that time of the morning it's busy, three-quarters full and with cars coming in all the time. The people aren't coming this way. They're going down into town for shopping and looking at the tourist sites. You couldn't carry a body to a car without being seen. Besides, there are cameras and, yes, every tape has been checked."

Bobby Bowers raked a hand through his crop of dark curls. "I seriously wonder if we're right to link these two shootings."

"Tell me why."

"Your wife was certain to be found in a short time. It was a bold, professional hit, as if they didn't care who heard the shots. But my shooting has all the signs of being covert. The killer took pains to move her to a clever hiding place. The body might never have been discovered. If he's so brazen about murder A, why go to all the trouble of concealing murder B?"

Diamond had no explanation. "Have you spoken to DCI Weather?"

"Only to confirm identification. That was enough for starters. He was in shreds, as you must have been."

"God only knows how I would have coped with chewed-up bones. I suppose he identified her from the clothes?"

"Yes. The bones were no help. Her dental records were sent for. They match."

"When will you interview him?"

"It's being done as we speak by the two DIs you met at the scene. I'll know more after I've heard the tape."

"Will you see him yourself?" Diamond asked.

"Sure to." A feral glint invaded Bowers' eyes for an instant.

Diamond's sympathy went out to Weather. "He'll get the third degree like I did, the husband being the first suspect."

Bowers declined to confirm this. He said, "I don't know about the treatment you were given."

Diamond enlightened him and at the end of it said, "I was saying Stormy Weather can expect the same."

"Depends."

"But you don't rule it out."

"Would you, in my position?"

The chill of evening was in the air and the first lights were visible in the Crescent. Without either man suggesting enough had been said, they returned silently across the turf to the car, leaving the scene to darkness and the snogging schoolkids.

At home with a mug of tomato soup in his fist and a chunk of bread on his lap, he watched the nine o'clock news on TV. Nothing. Maybe they had run the Woking story the previous night. He didn't watch much these days. The news seemed as remote from real life as the soaps.

He'd delayed for as long as he could manage. He reached for the phone and pressed out the number he'd obtained that morning from the incident room.

"DCI Weather?"

"Who is this?" The voice was defensive.

All too vividly he remembered being under siege by the press. "Peter Diamond. I don't know if you remember me. We have a couple of things in common. I'm deeply sorry to hear about your wife."

There was no response at all. But what do you say in the circumstances? "*So am* I'? "*No problem*'? "*Thanks*'?

Diamond waited, then said, "We served together, you and I, at Fulham back in the eighties."

"That's right," the voice became a touch less combative, yet still drained of animation. "And your wife has been shot like mine. They told me."

"So I know how you feel. It's hell."

"Worse."

"Look," Diamond said, "may I call you by your first name? It's so long ago I only remember—"

"The nickname." The way Stormy Weather closed him down made the tired old joke seem one more infliction.

"And your real name is . . . ?"

"Dave."

"Dave. Right. A lot of guys came and went," Diamond said to excuse his defective memory.

"And I was just a DC in those days," Dave Weather said.

"I'm Peter."

"You said."

"I'd like to meet up if possible. You're going to be under all sorts of pressure. It may help to talk to someone who knows what it's like."

"I don't feel like talking."

"I know. I didn't. But you want to find the dickhead who killed your wife, right? And the high-ups are telling you to keep away. They don't want the likes of you and me getting involved."

"They've got their reasons."

"Like leave it to us, it's in good hands?"

"Something like that. And as the husband I'm personally involved."

"I heard it all seven months ago. I'm still waiting for some progress, let alone an arrest." Diamond was trying his damnedest, and at the same time sensing he should have waited a couple of days. The man was shell-shocked, just as he had been.

He still refused to give up. "You know they're treating the two killings as connected? There was a case conference here in

Bath today. I was called in to give the dope on operations you and I were both involved in. Hard task, all these years later. When you feel up to it we really should compare notes."

"Is that what they suggested?"

"No. This is my idea."

The response remained lukewarm. "If you think it will make a difference."

"I'm certain," Diamond said, elated at the small concession he'd winkled out. "I'll come to you. You're in Raynes Park, aren't you?"

Dave Weather backtracked. "My place is a tip. I've done sod all to keep it straight in the last six months and now I've had the CID all over it."

Which Diamond treated as an R.S.V.P.

"Likewise. I'm still in chaos here. Dave, I don't give a toss what your place looks like. What's the address?"

## 26

THE MOMENT STORMY Weather opened the door of his mock-Tudor semi in Raynes Park, Diamond remembered him. How could he have forgotten a skin like that, the colour of freshly sliced corned beef? A man could spend his life shovelling coal into a furnace and not end up with so many ruptured blood vessels. You never knew when he was blushing because it was his natural appearance. Happily for Stormy, it wasn't off-putting for long. If anything, it endeared him to people. With a few exceptions, none of us likes our own face much, and it's a relief to be with someone who has more to put up with than we do.

Today the poor bloke was understandably careworn as well as florid. A faded black Adidas T-shirt and dark blue corduroy trousers hung loosely from his tall frame. He took a moment to register who his visitor was (Diamond put this down to his own hair loss) and then invited him inside, through a hallway littered with newspapers still folded as they'd been pushed through the door. "You'll have to make allowances," he said, kicking some aside. "Patsy would go spare if she saw the place in this state. She kept a tidy house."

The sitting room was misnamed now because there wasn't a seat available. The chairs and sofa were all piled high with drawers, books and CDs. It looked like the aftermath of a burglary. "They went through the place a couple of days ago,"

Stormy explained. "I can't pretend it was tidy before, but they didn't help matters."

"They" must have been a police search squad.

"It happened to me." Diamond stooped and picked a framed photo off the floor, a black and white shot of a young woman at the wheel of a police Panda car. "Is this your wife?"

Stormy reached for the photo and practically snatched it from him. "I've been looking all over for that. I thought they must have taken it away." He held it in both hands. "Yes, this is Patsy about the time we met. Well, you must remember her. She was on the relief at Fulham when you were CID."

"So I was told. Can I have another look?" Diamond stood beside Stormy, then drew back to get a clearer view. Soon he'd want glasses. More than once Steph had told him to see an optician. "Of course I knew her. Didn't we call her Mary Poppins?" Instantly regretting he'd come out with anything so crass, he added, "But her real surname—what was that?"

"Jessel."

"Yes. Pat Jessel." Clumsily, he tried to make up for his boorishness. "I can't for the life of me remember how she got that nickname."

Stormy sighed and told the story, and the canteen humour of twenty years ago jarred on the ear like an old LP. "She was the fresh-faced rookie with very good manners who tried too hard to please. She had a perpetual smile and this amazing posh accent like Julie Andrews. One day Jacob Blaize sent down for a coffee and Patsy wanted to know if he liked it black or white and someone said 'White, with just a spoonful of sugar' and the whole room started whistling the tune. She was stuck with it then. No one called her anything but Mary after that."

"Right." Diamond gave an apologetic smile. He now remembered Mary vividly. "We were a cruel bunch."

"It was a bit OTT. She got tired of the whistling and singing.

And of course every time an umbrella was handed in it was hung on her peg. Though I have to say she fitted the role in some ways. She was a born organiser."

"So when did you marry her?"

"November, eighty-six," Stormy said, and for a moment his face creased, but he controlled the emotion and stood the photo on the empty wall unit.

Diamond, too, was thoughtful, marvelling that a young woman as pretty as "Mary" Jessel had fallen for the Bardolph of Fulham nick.

"She was younger than you?"

"Fifteen years."

"And she got to be sergeant."

"At Shepherd's Bush. Served all her time at two stations just down the road from each other. She would have made inspector if she'd stuck with it. She was a fine copper."

"She jacked it in?"

"Only about a year ago. She set up her own secretarial agency from home. It was just starting to build when . . ."

"Was she ever with CID?"

He shook his head. "Uniform for the whole of her career and pleased to do it. Very good with the public, anyone from juveniles to junkies."

"And no one looked better in a white shirt," Diamond reminisced. "So she wouldn't have been on any of the cases you and I got roped into?"

"Not as CID. Do you want tea? Or there's a pub only five minutes away."

"Sounds good to me."

From the way they were greeted by the landlord of the Forester, Diamond guessed Stormy—or Dave, as he was trying hard to think of him—had spent plenty of time here lately. The urge to get out of the house where every picture, every

chair, every cup has the potential to strike at the heart is hard
to resist, as he well knew.

Over a glass of bitter at a corner table in the saloon bar, his
old colleague was more at ease. They had never been close
companions or even said much, but the shared experience drew
them together. Diamond found himself speaking more frankly
about the impact of Steph's murder than at any time up to now.
"There are days . . . The worst part is when you've been relaxing
without knowing it—let's face it, forgetting what happened—
and then something touches you like a finger, forces you back
to reality, and . . . and . . . there's no other way to put it——she
dies all over again."

This drew a nod of recognition from Stormy.

Diamond added, "What keeps me going is the promise I
made to find the scumbag who did it. And I will. They keep
telling me to stand aside and leave it to the murder squad. How
can I? You feel the same, don't you?"

So much intensity from someone he'd known as a senior
officer must have been daunting, but Stormy nodded at
once.

Diamond was well launched. "The murder inquiry is going
nowhere. I've found out more through bloody-minded obsti-
nacy than McGarvie and his television appeals and scores of
men on overtime. It's incentive, Dave. You can't sit back. Even
if they were right on the heels of the killer—which they're
not—I'd still be going it alone. I owe it to Steph."

"I know how you feel."

Diamond took a long sip of beer, willing Stormy to open up
a little, and he did.

"They kept saying she'd come back, hinting all the time
that we'd had a run-in—as if it was something unusual. We
were always having dust-ups. We were one of those couples
who scrap all the time and feel better for it. Doesn't mean we
didn't love each other." He looked down into his drink. "When

a grown woman goes missing, nobody takes it seriously, not for weeks. She's just another name on a list."

"How did it happen?"

"Her leaving? Nothing happened. Everyone was hinting there must have been some great punch-up. There wasn't. I came home from work one evening and she wasn't there."

"When was this?"

"A Monday in March. The twelfth."

"Two weeks and a bit after Steph was killed."

"Right. I actually read about your wife being shot, and I remembered you from the old days, and was really sorry. I didn't send a card or anything because I didn't think you'd remember me, and it's difficult to know what to write."

Diamond gave a nod. "What about when your wife went missing? Did it cross your mind what had happened to Steph?"

"No, I didn't connect them. I didn't think Patsy was dead. You don't. I hoped she'd walk through the door any minute. And I guess I didn't want to face up to the worst possible explanation. You think of everything else, loss of memory, an accident, a coma. Anything that lets you hope."

There are different degrees of torture, Diamond thought. Steph's sudden violent death had seemed like the ultimate. Stormy's months of not knowing was another refinement, and he wasn't sure how he would have coped with it. "It's very isolating. No one knows what to say to you. They shun you if they can."

"Tell me about it."

"And of course they don't want us to investigate. I don't know if you've been told this, but the argument goes that a smart defence lawyer would cry foul if you or I helped to arrest our wives' murderers."

"So get lost. Yes," Stormy said, "I was told that."

Encouraged, Diamond moved a stage on. "Yet if you and I put our heads together we'd be more likely to get to the truth than anyone else. We know who we crossed swords with. They don't."

Stormy's brown eyes met Diamond's, slipped away and then came back. "You're right," he said with sudden fervour. "Together we could nail this jerk."

Warming to the man, Diamond took him into his confidence, telling him about the case files Louis Voss had copied.

Stormy heard all this with awe. He'd only just grasped that unofficial action was possible. Diamond's bull-necked attitude must have come as a shock. But as soon as the Joe Florida inquiry was mentioned, Stormy recalled being on the surveillance team. "He was given a long term."

"Twelve. He was out after seven."

"Out?" Stormy was appalled. "That beats everything. That toerag. Most professional crooks have something to be said for them. Florida was evil."

"You met him personally?"

"Twice. I sat in on interviews."

"Questioned him?"

"No, I was only a DC at the time. Blaizy was in charge. You do remember Jacob Blaize?"

Too well, Diamond thought bitterly. "Retired to Spain, the last I heard."

"For some reason, he wanted me as the back-up in those sessions. I didn't mind. Saw myself as the up-and-coming detective, hand-picked by the guvnor. I didn't know Blaizy couldn't stay in an interview room for more than ten minutes at a time."

Diamond frowned, then grinned as the explanation surfaced. "His prostate problem? I'd forgotten about that."

"It meant I spent more time alone with Joe Florida than anyone would wish to."

"Did he talk?"

"Did he hell. He was after cigarettes. He could see I was a smoker. I may have been wet behind the ears, but I knew you don't dish out fags for nothing. So I took a fair amount of flak from Joe Florida."

"Did he threaten you?"

"Let's say I wouldn't have needed a vasectomy if he'd got to me first."

"He made his living out of threats," Diamond recalled. "I took a few. And in the protection racket you're not a serious player unless you mean what you say."

"Joe did. Two shops torched, was it?"

"And a child almost died. She was in the cot upstairs. They got her out in the nick of time."

"I remember."

"So you spent time alone with him?" Diamond said eagerly. "I didn't know that. Was there anything more serious from him than bumming a fag?"

"Such as?"

"He didn't try and make a deal? What I'm driving at, Dave, is something big enough for him to hold a grudge all the time he was in jail."

"And then murder my wife, just to get back at me? No, there was nothing *that* extreme. I can't think of anyone who would behave like that. Even a shitbag like Florida."

Diamond nodded. "I keep saying the same. It's not just evil. It's twisted. Insane." He paused. "Do you think prison blew his mind?"

"He wouldn't be the first."

"I mean to find out. I'm going to find him. If he murdered Steph, I'll have him."

"I'm with you all the way."

The hackneyed phrase had never meant so much to Diamond.

"Another beer?"

When he returned to the table, he said to Stormy, "I was telling you about those files."

"Files?"

"From Louis Voss at Fulham."

"Right. I'm with you."

"One was the Brook Green shooting."

"I remember that."

"You do?"

"Only I wasn't on the team."

Diamond blew gently at the froth on his beer. "Okay. There are others. Let's shuffle the pack again. How about a teenager by the name of Wayne Beach?"

The name brought a glimmer to Stormy's eye. "Remind me, will you?"

"A loner. Armed robbery. Taxi drivers."

"Ah—that little prick. We ambushed him one night in Edith Road."

This was better than Diamond had hoped. "*We?* You were there? Tell me you were there."

"I was. It was all very sudden. You were in charge, weren't you? You needed licensed shots and I was roped in along with anyone else who happened to be there. I was behind a hedge in the garden opposite."

"You didn't fire the shot?"

"No. That was another guy across the street. A sergeant. The name's gone now. But after Beach threw down his weapon I was one of the first to pin him. And I escorted him to the nick."

"So he knows you?"

"I wouldn't think he remembers now."

Privately, Diamond thought the opposite. Stormy's geranium-coloured skin had instantly triggered his own memory when he called at the house.

"He'd remember you better," Stormy added.

"Maybe. I did the interviews and gave evidence. The thing about Wayne Beach is that he's a gun freak. He's done several stretches."

"He'd be in his thirties now."

"Thirty-four. Released from the Scrubs last December."

"December? Shortly before . . . ?"

"Right."

"So we have an address?"

"Thanks to the Probation Service, yes. Some high-rise in Clapham. Are you game?"

Stormy raised both thumbs.

"He'll be armed," Diamond cautioned. "Do you have a shooter?"

"Sorry. Do you?"

"Not any more." Diamond leaned back and rested his hands on his paunch as if that concealed a secret weapon. "Just have to outsmart him."

"We can do that," Stormy said with confidence, raising his glass. "Here's to us. Whatever it takes."

"Whatever." Diamond clinked his glass and drank deeply. He had an ally now.

The outsmarting of Wayne Beach needed neutral ground and the surprise element, they decided. It would court disaster to visit his flat. They sat in a CID Vauxhall opposite the graffiti-scarred building in Latchmere Road, Clapham, watching the residents come and go. Their man would emerge at some point to buy cigarettes or food, or place a bet, or pick up his social security. It went without saying that he hadn't gone into honest employment.

After a couple of hours with no result they were thinking about food themselves. They'd seen a number of dodgy-looking people enter or leave the building, but that was not remarkable. It was a run-down, fifties-built tower block, a place of last resort that probably housed more lowlife than Wayne Beach.

Towards four, when the butcher up the street started

clearing his window, Diamond left Stormy in the car and went over to see if there was a pork pie left. He was lucky.

"You know, I'm thinking of Plan B," he told Stormy while they ate.

"What's that?"

"Ask the neighbours."

"Risky. He could hear."

"He could be somewhere else."

It was decided Diamond would go alone. After ten flights of stairs breathing heavily and not enjoying what he breathed, he emerged on Beach's landing. He'd passed no one.

According to their information, Wayne Beach occupied the sixth flat along, number fifty-six. There was a reggae beat coming from fifty-five.

"Hain't seen him, man," the tenant said when Diamond asked after his neighbour.

"It's okay, I'm a friend."

"Still hain't seen him in ages. Nobody in there. If you asking me, him Scapa Flow."

Diamond risked a look through the window of fifty-six. The place certainly looked unlived-in. A free paper had been crammed in the letter box. He pulled it out, held the flap open and peered through. A heap of junk mail was inside.

"Man, he won't be back," was the opinion of Diamond's informant, and in the circumstances he was probably right.

"Was he ever here?"

"Place is empty since Christmas. One time I hear someone unlocking, walk in, walk out. Picking up his letters, I guess."

Stormy insisted on driving Diamond across London to Paddington Station. "We won't let it get to us, Peter," he said. "We're still ahead of the game."

"Not for long," Diamond said. "McGarvie's no fool, and neither is Bowers. You can bet they spent today going through those old files, reaching the same conclusions we have. My worry is that they'll go in like the tank corps and the killer will see them coming a mile off."

"Looks as if Wayne Beach already has."

"He's using the place as a cover. As far as the social services are concerned, he's trapped in that slum, living from hand to mouth. No doubt he's got a nice pad somewhere else."

"And a nice income as a hitman."

"Could be."

"So we wasted our bloody time."

Briefly it seemed Stormy might be going cool on cooperation, but this proved false.

"There was something you said earlier about us putting our heads together and finding the truth before anyone else. I was impressed."

"You want to keep trying?"

"Definitely."

If Diamond had believed in fate, he might have been awed by what happened to him that evening. Exhausted after so much waiting with no result, he fell asleep on the seven-thirty from Paddington and was out to the world when it stopped at Bath Spa. He ended up at Bristol Temple Meads Station sometime after nine thirty. Not for the first time. Only now there was no one at home to phone anymore. Rather than cross the bridge and wait for a train, he made the best of his situation and took a taxi to the Rummer.

Bernie Hescott, his well-paid, worse than useless snout, was not in the public bar. "Haven't seen him all week, squire," the barman told Diamond.

"Doesn't surprise me. I'll have a pint just the same."

"Bitter?"

A fair expression of his state of mind. He settled down with the drink and let ten minutes go by. The place was warm and the music just about bearable.

Then fate gave an emphatic pull on the strings, for in walked the informer he should have used in preference to Bernie. John Seville caught Diamond's startled eye, turned and left the bar at once. He went after him.

"Can't help you," Seville said while Diamond tried to keep pace with him, striding through one of the paved alleyways behind the Exchange.

"You don't even know what I want."

"Jesus Christ, the whole world heard what happened, and I know sweet fuck all about it."

Diamond grabbed his arm and shoved him against a shuttered shop front. "John, if this is your way of raising the stakes, save your breath. I'll pay top dollar."

"I'm not haggling, Mr. Diamond. I got nothing for you. Nothing."

"What are you scared of? The Carpenters? Forget them. They're in the clear for once. This wasn't local. This has a London connection. You do know what I'm talking about?"

"Your wife. What can I say? I wouldn't wish that on anyone. But I know nothing."

"Someone, some hitman, gunned her down in a public park in broad daylight. He'd done his homework, John. Picked his spot. Got away fast. Did you hear of anyone—a Londoner, maybe, a professional, who was holed up here six, seven months ago?"

"In Bristol?"

"Bristol or Bath, but he's more likely to have used here as his base. Bristol is bigger, easier to get lost in. What have you got for me, John?"

"I keep telling you—"

Diamond jammed a thumb under Seville's chin, forcing his jaws together with a crunch. "I'm not messing. I want a result. I can pay fifty, or I can beat it out of you, or I can tell my chums at Bristol Central to make your life impossible. Which is it to be?"

"You just cut my tongue."

"Too bad." He relaxed his hold.

Seville wiped blood from the edge of his mouth and stared at his fingers. He darted looks to either side. No one was about. "You said fifty?"

"This had better be kosher."

"Take it or leave it, this is all I have. There's an ex-con living in clover in a smart house on Sion Hill, near the Suspension Bridge. Been around most of this year. Makes trips to London sometimes. The word is that if you want to buy a shooter, that's where you go. But don't bring me into it, for Christ's sake."

"A local?"

"No, not from round here."

"I'll need his name."

"Beach. The name is Beach."

John Seville got his fifty pounds.

## 27

EVER SINCE THE diamond heist went wrong, Harry Tattersall had dreaded hearing from his old friend Rhadi. He expected a witch-hunt. The deviser of the plot, that sinister little man Zahir, wasn't going to let the whole thing rest. Much as Harry hoped that the Arab philosophy might be to offer a thousand blessings to Allah for a lucky escape, he knew in his gut that it was not to be. Zahir would want to know who had shafted them.

Never mind that Harry was blameless, having acted like a hero and saved everyone from arrest. His Houdini stunt at the Dorchester wasn't going to work in his favour. With their devious minds the Arabs would think he'd been *allowed* to walk away. It wasn't true, of course. He'd been as horrified as anyone when things came to grief. He hadn't grassed, and he didn't know who had.

The first days after, he'd stayed out of sight, fearing Special Branch or one of the security services would come in pursuit. He hadn't gone to Ireland as planned, in case that part of the operation had been blabbed. He'd stayed with a friend in Tunbridge Wells. As the weeks passed, he'd returned to London, deciding he was safe from the authorities. The real threat was from his fellow conspirators. He'd heard disturbing stories of Arab retribution: thieves having their hands severed and adulterers being stoned. He didn't care to discover what happened to informers.

The call eventually came one Monday evening.

"I'm so glad you're in," his friend Rhadi said, as if he was selling insurance. "We need to talk."

"Only you and me?" Harry said, more in hope than expectation.

"No. All of us. The team." And it was obvious from Rhadi's voice that he wasn't alone. "We wish to compare notes on our, em, disappointment. A debrief, as they say."

"A debrief," Harry repeated, thinking it sounded like the prelude to castration.

"We'll come to you. Be with you inside an hour. Don't go to any trouble."

It was under the half hour when the knock came. Little Zahir strode in first without even a nod of recognition, followed by Ibrahim and Rhadi. They were in black suits, like a funeral party.

Rhadi said, "Sorry about this, but we need to frisk you."

So much for team spirit. He submitted to Ibrahim's large hands.

"Isn't the other fellow coming?" Harry asked while this was going on. He'd given thought to the way he would handle the workover.

Zahir didn't answer for some time, and the others seemed to feel any response should come from him. He was sitting in Harry's favourite armchair, well forward so that the tips of his shoes kept contact with the carpet. "Which other fellow?"

"The man from the Dorchester."

"No, he can't make it."

"We could be wasting our time, then, trying to work out what went wrong."

"Why? Do you have a theory?" Zahir said, baring the big teeth.

Harry backtracked. "Not as such. I simply thought we should all be in on the discussion."

Zahir gave a shrug. "Our colleague at the Dorchester can't be here tonight. Now, Mr. Tattersall, sit down and let's discuss the fiasco. The first we heard from you, on your mobile from the hotel, was a positive message. You called me with the name of the suite."

"Exactly as arranged," Harry stressed, taking a seat as far from his interrogator as possible.

"You didn't say anything was amiss."

"Nothing was at that stage."

"A few minutes after, you called again and told me to pull the plug or some such phrase."

"Correct."

"So something must have happened between the two calls."

In an effort to react positively, Harry slapped a hand down on the arm of the chair. "Indeed it had. First, a woman who said she was the housekeeper knocked on the door wanting to change the flowers. That made me suspicious."

"So how did you react?"

"I let her in."

"Why?"

"I was trying to act like a normal guest. You don't send the housekeeper away without good reason. It would have drawn attention to us."

"So she came into the room. What then?"

"She put fresh lilies in a vase. As I mentioned, my suspicion was aroused. After she'd left the room, I went to the window and looked out at the roof garden and spotted a movement. I was horrified. There was this fellow hiding behind a bush and holding a submachine gun. And there was another marksman as well. It was obvious we'd been rumbled."

"*Rumbled?*"

Rhadi gave an interpretation in Arabic.

"I immediately checked the flowers and found they contained a bugging device," Harry continued, underlining his efficiency. "I put them—flowers, vase, the lot—in a wardrobe to mask the sound and then called you on the mobile."

"Yes." It was a "yes" pregnant with reservations.

"That's it." Harry waited.

Zahir brought his hands together and cracked the knuckles. "The operation was called off at your suggestion, yet you remained in the room. Why didn't you get out while you had the chance?"

His worst scenario. They suspected he was in collusion with the police. "If you remember," he said, feeling the blood drain from his face, "I asked you to let Rhadi know the problem, and you said you couldn't because he didn't have a phone. It was clear to me he was going to get arrested if I didn't help. He'd walk straight into the trap. He's an old friend." He glanced towards Rhadi, who was clearly uncomfortable and avoiding eye contact. "There's such a thing as loyalty. So I waited until he came to let him know the whole thing had gone pear-shaped."

"Pear-shaped?"

Rhadi interpreted, and there followed an earnest dialogue in Arabic between Zahir and Rhadi.

Finally Zahir said, "Your old friend confirms that you sent him away. He believes you."

Harry gave his old friend a look of gratitude. "He would have done the same for me."

Then the sting. "Yet you remained in the room with the men we now know to have been detectives."

"For a time, yes."

Zahir's tiny feet curled upwards. "Why, Mr. Tattersall? Why?"

He tried to make it sound the most obvious thing in the world. "That was my best chance—to bluff my way out, and that's what I did by letting them think there was a bomb in the suitcase. I told them I was CIA."

"Are you?"

"Good God, no."

"But they believed you?"

Rhadi said in support, "He does a very good American accent."

"It got me out and away. The alarm system went off, there was a hotel evacuation and I stepped out to the street along with everyone else."

"That's all?" The dissatisfaction was all too evident in Zahir's voice.

"What else can I say except I'd like to know who stitched us up and why? It certainly wasn't me. I was going to get a hundred K."

"We were all looking forward to a share," Zahir pointed out. "None of us had any obvious reason to play traitor, yet someone did."

The right moment, Harry decided, to point the finger elsewhere. "We were sold down the river before the scam got under way. Those gunmen were in place when I was shown into the room. The police knew where to lie in wait. They must have been tipped off well ahead."

"Wrong," Zahir said.

"Why?"

"If they'd known in advance they'd have bugged the room already. They wouldn't have needed to send a woman in with flowers."

Clever. This was a point Harry hadn't considered. He frowned in the silence, grasping desperately for an explanation. Finally one came to him. "Well, maybe the police suspected some of the hotel staff were in on the scam. They couldn't risk taking them into their confidence. They played along with the plot and waited to see which suite we were sent to. They knew it must be on the same floor as the Prince's suite, so they posted their firearms team on the roof garden."

Zahir's large, shrewd eyes studied Harry. After an interval he conceded, "You could be speaking sense now. So if you are not the informer, who is?"

"How would I know?" Harry said. "I didn't even meet everyone."

"You met us all except one."

"Yes, the inside man, the ex-RAF type on the staff of the hotel." The injustice fired Harry to say more than he'd intended. "I can't think why he gets special treatment. If he's on the team he should be here, ready to face the music like the rest of us."

"Music?"

The phrase had to be explained. Then, as if such details were beneath him, Zahir gestured to Rhadi to enlighten his friend.

"The man at the Dorchester went missing the day after we were there. No one knows where he is. He's lost his job, moved out of his old address and gone."

"Who is he?"

"His name is Dixon-Bligh."

Harry had never heard of him. "The police must be onto him if he quit the next day."

"They're trying to find him, yes, but it's complicated. He's also wanted for questioning in connection with the killing of his former wife."

"He's a killer?" Harry piped up. "How did we get into bed with this monster?"

"I only said they want to interview him."

"We all know what that means."

"It isn't certain."

Harry digested the information. He still felt he hadn't been given all the facts. "He's done a runner, you said? Isn't it obvious he's the one who grassed us up? I don't know why you give me the third degree as if I'm the snitch when you could be looking for this bastard."

No one answered.

"Wait a minute," Harry said, as an ugly thought surfaced. "You haven't already topped him, have you?"

# 28

THE PHOTOCOPIER AT Fulham nick must have been red-hot over the weekend. McGarvie was now in possession of a thick stack of paper: Diamond's entire record of cases with the Met. Three of the most experienced officers in the incident room had combed each page for the crucial mentions of DC Weather's name among the detectives involved.

"One stands out," McGarvie informed Diamond when he turned up on Monday. "This Florida. Protection racketeer. A hard man."

"Can't disagree with that."

"Jacob Blaize headed, right?"

Diamond nodded.

"With you as second in command?"

"Sidekick."

"And Weather was a junior officer on the team, mainly on surveillance duties, but I discovered he also sat in on several interviews Blaize did with Florida."

Tell me something new, Diamond thought.

McGarvie was showing signs of excitement. "And we can assume Weather spent time alone with Florida when Blaize left the room, as he must have."

"Frequently," Diamond confirmed.

"You know that for sure?"

"Blaizy was always being caught short."

The eyes widened, revealing more than anyone would wish to see of the engorged blood vessels. "Was he, by God? That's something I didn't get from the files."

"Well, you wouldn't."

"It meant interruptions, did it?" He was getting as hyper as when he had dug up the gun in the garden.

"Every ten to fifteen minutes."

"Sounds like prostate trouble."

"He was on a waiting list."

Diamond was amused to see McGarvie bring his palms together and rub them as if he was using the drying machine in the gents: the association of ideas. "You see what this means? This was before we had videotaping. An old hand like Florida would have made use of those breaks. He'd get to work on the young officer sitting across the table. He'd try intimidation."

"For what? A smoke?" It was hardly enough to justify the killing of Patsy Weather, Diamond was implying, and McGarvie needed to do better.

But he was way ahead, compounding the plot. "No, he'd twist the facts of the case to make it seem he was being set up by you and Blaize. He'd shake the young man's confidence, doing his damnedest to turn him, you see. He'd think he'd got him as an ally, someone who could testify later that the interview had been improper. When he didn't do it by persuasion, he'd use threats——threats he really meant to carry out. He saw enough of Weather to remember him long after. When a man like Florida has festered in jail for twelve years——"

"Seven," Diamond said. "He was out after seven."

"More than enough to turn his brain."

"His brain didn't need turning. He hated the police. I can see—just about—that he might have wanted revenge on Blaizy and me. We nailed him. But Stormy Weather? I don't think so. He was small beer."

McGarvie was unshakeable. "You and I don't know what

passed between them. Maybe Weather was induced to make a promise he never kept. Maybe Florida thought he could rely on Weather to save his skin."

Maybe . . . Maybe . . . This was futile speculation and both knew it. Nothing would be certain unless Stormy admitted he'd played along, or Florida was induced to tell all. No matter; for the present it suited Diamond if Florida was the prime suspect, leaving him free to pursue Wayne Beach. Just to get a measure of McGarvie's resolve he asked, "Have you given up on Dixon-Bligh, then?"

"No trace. He's holed up somewhere. Arrears of rent. The Met are working on it." He made it sound like their problem.

Joe Florida was firmly in the frame.

Stormy Weather arrived at Bristol Temple Meads just after eleven, and Diamond met him on the platform and remembered to call him Dave. They drove directly to Sion Hill, an elegant, curving street of eighteenth-century houses built on an incline above the Gorge.

"Bit of a change from Latchmere Road," Stormy remarked when they were parked opposite a gracious four-storey terrace with ironwork balconies, tall shutters and striped awnings.

"Envious?"

He eyed the building approvingly. "It isn't bad for a second home. Does he own all of it?"

"That's what I heard from my snout."

"He must have salted some money away between his prison terms."

"More than you and I ever earned, Dave."

They lapsed into silence, brooding on a theme familiar to policemen: the inequity between the law enforcers and the law breakers. "Personally," Stormy said after some time, "I wouldn't choose to live in Bristol. The traffic is a pain. Always was."

"Sounds like the voice of experience."

"Does it? I'm only an occasional visitor."

"Best way."

"As a matter of fact," Stormy said, "I'm interested in Brunel."

Diamond had to think before cottoning on that Stormy was speaking of the Victorian engineer. "Top hat and big cigar?"

A nod. "One of my heroes. I do some model making as a hobby, and his constructions are quite an inspiration. I made an SS *Great Britain* and a Suspension Bridge."

"From kits, you mean?"

"God, no. That's schoolboy stuff. I go there and take photos and draw up plans and build the things from my own materials."

Weird, the things some policemen do with their spare time, Diamond thought. Keith Halliwell bred pigeons for racing and John Wigfull had a telescope and was supposed to use it to study the stars.

Stormy went on, "So I've made quite a number of research trips, you could say. Getting here is the hardest part."

"Ah, the one-way system is our secret weapon in the war against crime. You'd find it easier escaping from a Dunkirk beach than Bristol. If you want to visit the Brunel sites you're better off using the railway he built and walking the rest."

Stormy agreed with that. He glanced at the house again.

"What do we do now? Go in?"

"Let's watch for the time being," Diamond said. "The place is probably stiff with shooters."

"Catch him off the premises? We've tried that once."

"This time I expect a result. So you're an admirer of old Issy Brunel?" he said, pleased to have found a topic unconnected with the tragedies in their lives. "Have you been to Bath?"

"Not since I was a kid."

"You ought to come. He changed the look of the city when the railway came through. The old GWR station is one of his buildings and so is the viaduct behind, but he also cut through Sydney Gardens, one of those parks the Victorians liked to strut around in their finery, and it was a neat job."

"Yes, I'd like to see that."

"You wouldn't."

Stormy blinked and frowned. He may also have blushed, but on his blotchy skin it was impossible to tell. "What do you mean? I know what I like."

"You wouldn't *see* it—that's what I mean—unless you went right up to it. The point is that the railway is hidden from view. Really clever."

The first person to emerge from the house, after about ten minutes, was in a red leather jacket and skirt with matching boots and a hat with a large rim that flopped. She set off down the hill with a slinky walk as if she knew her movement was being appreciated.

"Now I *am* envious," Stormy said.

Diamond gave him a look. The remark was lightly made, the automatic reaction to a pretty woman, but to his still wounded mind it didn't come well from a recently bereaved man. He let it pass.

"I wonder if she comes with the house," Stormy added, oblivious of Diamond's thinking.

"Visitor, I expect."

"That's not the vibes I got."

"You could be right. Maybe he sent her to do the shopping."

"She doesn't look to me as if she's on her way to Tesco's."

They waited ten minutes more.

"I reckon she's his bird," Stormy insisted.

"Daughter, more like," Diamond said.

"He's not that old, surely?"

"You've got to remember Fulham was fifteen years ago, Dave. Hello, we've got action."

A dark green Range Rover had pulled up outside the house and a man in combat trousers and a khaki vest got out. He had the look of a body builder, with heavily tattooed arms.

"That isn't Beach, is it?" Stormy said.

"Not the way I remember him," Diamond said. "I remember a puny guy."

The muscleman pressed the doorbell.

"Just a caller, then."

"Or a customer."

"What—come to buy a gun?"

"Keep your eyes on the door, Dave. Let's see who opens it."

Unfortunately, nobody did. The caller tried the bell twice more, looked at his watch, stood back and looked up to the balcony, and then gave up, returned to his car and drove off.

"We've wasted our time again," Stormy said.

"No, look. Coming round the corner."

The woman in the floppy hat and red leather had started up the hill towards the terrace, this time carrying a folded magazine.

Diamond watched and something made him sure he'd seen her before. He couldn't tell the colour of her hair under the hat, but the face was one he knew. She wasn't Janie Forsyth, the she-cat who had attacked him, and she wasn't Danny Carpenter's wife, Celia. He needed a closer look.

Without a word to Stormy, he opened the door of the car and stepped across the street and stood outside the house.

Ten yards from him, the woman hesitated. Diamond stared, frowned and stared harder. It required a great leap of the imagination to tell that this lady in red leather was not, after all, a lady.

"Wayne?"

Wayne, if it was he, turned and started running back down the hill. Diamond pursued. His overweight, lumbering movement was about as ineffectual as his quarry's, hampered by high heels. But he kept running and managed to reach out and get a hand on a leather sleeve at the street corner and bring the chase to a skidding halt. He swung the person around and when they were face-to-face it was obvious he was right. This was not, after all, a woman. This was a skillfully made-up, smartly groomed, cross-dressed Wayne Beach. Prison life generally leaves its mark on an ex-con, but the result, in this case, had been unusual.

"How long have you been out, Wayne?"

The face tautened, making a mockery of the lipstick and foundation. "What do you want? Who are you? I know you, don't I?" The voice also was at odds with the get-up, all too guttural.

Diamond showed his warrant card and reminded Beach who he was and how they'd met.

"You look different. You've changed," Beach said.

"That's rich. What's all this nonsense, flouncing about in skirts?"

"It's a free country. I can dress how I want."

"Is it a disguise, or what?"

"These are the clothes I choose to wear now. I don't need to justify them to you or anyone else."

"Have you had the operation?"

"No, but I might."

"What are you doing here in Bristol?"

"Visiting."

"Come off it, Wayne. You live here. The house with the yellow door. Are you going to invite us in?"

"Us?" Beach looked across the street and saw Stormy Weather close the car door and step towards them. "Beetroot face, as well? I know him. Once seen, never forgotten. What's going on?"

"Questions, that's all, if you play it right."

"I did my time. You've got no right to persecute me."

Stormy came over and took stock with a hyperthyroid stare. He shook his head and said, "Well, I'll be buggered."

"I wouldn't bank on it," Diamond said. "However, Wayne is going to invite us into his house for a coffee and answer our questions."

"I don't have to," Wayne said.

"I don't have to go to a magistrate for a warrant, but I will if I'm pressed."

The bluff worked. Wayne felt in his shoulder bag for a key and in so doing gave Diamond enough of a glimpse of the magazine he was holding to show it was the *Shooting Times*. They entered a hall with a crimson carpet and striped Regency wallpaper.

"Nice pad."

"Nicer than Latchmere Road," Stormy said.

Wayne turned. "Listen, I only pick up the social to keep my probation officer happy."

"Rest easy, Wayne. We're not here about your fraudulent claims."

Beach removed the hat and hung it on a peg. He wasn't wearing a wig. He'd grown his own brown hair to a thickness any woman would have envied and had it clipped sheer at the back, twenties-style. In the kitchen—a gleaming place of natural wood and silvery appliances—he filled the kettle. They all sat on stools.

"What *do* you want?"

"You were released from the Scrubs when?" Diamond asked.

"Christmas. Just before."

"So when did you move down here?"

"Not long after."

"Not good enough," Stormy said. "We're talking dates, Wayne. You know the day you moved in."

Beach gave a sigh and a toss of the head, playing the harassed female to perfection. He unhooked a spiral diary from the wall and flicked through the months. "February the fifth."

"Let's see that." Diamond was reviewing his mental picture of that February morning in Royal Victoria Park. What if Steph had been approached by someone she supposed was a woman? Might that have been why her killer got so close before firing the shots? And why Wayne Beach got away without being noticed?

He handed the diary across. Diamond studied it. Each day was a narrow strip where appointments could be written in. February the fifth had the pencilled entry "*Bristol. Keys from Homefinders 11:30.*" Various other appointments were filled in throughout the month, some indicated by initial letters. He looked at Tuesday the twenty-third, the day of the murder, and it was blank.

"What about this day here?"

Beach came over to look and treated Diamond to a whiff of some perfume heavy with musk. "It's blank."

"Does that mean you had a free day, or what?"

"No. If you look, you'll see each Tuesday is blank. I keep Tuesdays clear."

Diamond checked the rest of the diary and saw that this was so. "Why?"

"They're not really clear. Every Tuesday is spoken for. That's when I go to London to see Mr. Dawkins."

"Who's he?"

"My probation officer."

"Ah." The sound came from Diamond as if he'd taken a low punch, and that was how he felt. "And you definitely went to London on the twenty-third?"

"I had to. Dawkins thinks I'm living in Clapham."

"What train do you get?"

"The seven twenty. I check in at his office at ten thirty."

This was beginning to look like a solid alibi. "I'll check with him myself."

"You wouldn't let on?" Wayne said in horror.

"What—that you're living the life of Riley here in Bristol flogging guns to any lunatic with cash in hand? Of course I'm going to let on. I'm a copper, Wayne, not your favourite uncle."

In the act of pouring the coffee, Beach spilt some over his immaculate work surface. "Who said anything about guns?"

"Half the criminal fraternity of Bristol. You're well known. It's a change from shooting taxi drivers in the leg. Two sugars, please."

"Do I look like a gun dealer?"

"In your skirt and lipstick? At the risk of being misunderstood, I'd say you've got a very good front. I suppose the weapons are shipped in, up the Channel."

"You're talking through your arse."

"Can we look in your basement?"

Beach sighed and dropped the pretence. "What exactly do you want?"

"I want you to look at that calendar and tell me who bought automatic handguns in the month of February."

"I wasn't dealing then. Honest to God. I'd only just moved in. You can't start a business from nothing."

Diamond reached for the calendar again. "There are letters here I recognise. DC on the twelfth and again on the fifteenth. Would that be Danny Carpenter?"

Wayne passed a hand nervously through the shingled hair. "Listen, you don't move into someone else's manor without a by-your-leave. I had to square it with the local chiefs, or I wouldn't last five minutes. On the days you're talking about, I wasn't dealing. I was making arrangements."

"Dressed like this?"

He glared. "I might be different, but I'm not stupid."

"What brought you to Bristol?"

"I have to make a living. London was too hot to start up again. This is the next best."

"Was there talk of a hitman coming to Bristol or Bath towards the end of February?"

"I wouldn't know. People didn't talk to me then. I was the new kid on the block. What's all this about?"

"You didn't hear? Don't you read the papers?"

Beach shook his head. "Boring."

"Just your gun magazines, eh?"

"That's my job."

Diamond didn't enlighten him about the shootings. He could see nothing of use emerging. The disappointing conclusion was that they'd wasted their time on Wayne Beach. "We're leaving now," he said abruptly. "You've got about twenty minutes before Bristol Police come here with an armed protection unit and knock down the door."

"Did you believe him?" Stormy asked.

"Did you?"

"I did, oddly enough."

"Me, too. If he'd written something in against the day Steph was shot, I'd have been suspicious. He could have done it any time. The fact that it was left blank is more convincing. I'll still check with the probation officer."

"And will you turn him in?"

"Will I? Dave, anyone who trades in guns is scum. Whoever shot my wife and yours acquired their weapon from some flake just like him."

He drove Stormy back to Bath, not to visit the Brunel sites, but to show him the place where Steph was killed. They parked on Royal Avenue, the road that bisected the lawns below the Crescent. Already some of the foliage had a reddish tinge and the ground under the horse chestnuts was littered with husks split by small boys in the quest for the new season's conkers. They crossed the dew-damp grass to where the body was found. He picked an empty crisp packet off the grass and crushed it in his hand.

"What's the park called?" Stormy asked.

"The Victoria. The Royal Victoria to give it its full name. This part is the Crescent Gardens." He pointed out the advantages to the killer, the screen of bushes hiding the car park, the bandstand, the large stone vases. "He must have waited unseen while she walked along the path and then crossed the lawn. He may not even have spoken to her."

"And then he fired the shots and left her?"

A nod from Diamond.

"Didn't try and move her?"

Stormy wasn't being ghoulish asking these questions. He was airing theories, and Diamond was willing to discuss them.

"Too risky. I think it was in his plan to leave her to be found."

"Yet that wasn't the m.o. in Patsy's case."

"I know, Dave, and I have my view on that. It's all supposition, but I think it makes sense. He covered his tracks the second time. He chose an even more secluded place to meet your wife. It could have been that little park above the railway embankment or somewhere miles away. The crucial thing is he tricked her into going to the place, the same as he'd tricked Steph."

"How?"

"Don't know. A phone call most likely. Something he knew would bring them out. The location was written in Steph's diary, so she knew where she was headed. She was easily swayed by any appeal to her good nature—some old friend in trouble. You name it."

"Patsy, too," Stormy said. "She'd drop everything and go if anyone needed her. Well, you remember what she was like, always supporting some good cause."

It was true. Diamond could recall her doing the rounds of the office collecting for this and that. "Mary," as he still remembered her, was always the one who bought the present when someone was leaving. "Well, the killer arranged to meet Patsy on some pretext and shot her. He'd picked his spot and he'd picked the spot where he would take her after the shooting. That's the added dimension. It's one step on from the murder of Steph."

They walked the short distance back to the car park. It was still early and Diamond offered to show his old colleague his present place of work. "We'll call that probation officer, Dawkins, and check Beach's alibi."

"And the Bristol CID, to tip them off about the gun dealing?"

"Specially them."

Bath Police Station was unusually quiet. They learned that McGarvie had gone with other senior detectives to some location in West London after a tip-off from the Met that Joe Florida had been sighted at a pub.

"Our last shot," Stormy said.

"His." In his office, Diamond got on with the business of tipping off Bristol about Wayne Beach. He said truthfully that he'd got the information from one of his snouts. Then he called the probation service in Clapham and spoke to George Dawkins and had it confirmed that Beach had reported there on the morning of February the twenty-third.

"He's not our man," he told Stormy.

"Wayne isn't anybody's man." He gave a half-smile. "True." Stormy looked at his watch. "I'd better get my train."

"Why—have you got a cat to feed, dog to walk?"

"No, but we've finished for today, haven't we?"

"You're staying at my place tonight. Then we can start early tomorrow."

"On what?"

"The real last shot."

## 29

THEY BROUGHT IN fish and chips and a couple of six-packs and spent much of the evening talking over old times at Fulham nick. Stormy had a better recall of those days than Diamond. You never forget your first year of policing, your first arrest, your first raid.

"I had other postings before then," Diamond said to excuse his hazy memory. "I signed on before you, Dave. Turned fifty this year—and don't say you wouldn't know it."

"What did you do?"

"Do?"

"To celebrate the big five-o."

"Oh—nothing."

"Pity."

"Save it, pal. It was after Steph was killed. What's a bloody birthday after something like that?"

"How long were you married?"

"Nineteen years. Why?"

"The way you talk about her, I'd have thought it was less."

"Why? I felt the same about her as the day we met."

Stormy nodded. "I guess you were the kind of couple who hold hands in the street."

A sharp look was exchanged. So far as Diamond could tell no sarcasm was intended. "If we felt like it, we may have done."

"There's the difference. We kept our distance. Doesn't

mean we didn't care about each other. Like I told you, it wasn't rosebuds all the way for Patsy and me. I played away a few times—call me weak-willed, or oversexed—and she usually found out. But we always patched things up. Try and explain that kind of marriage to a sleuth hound like Bowers."

"Did you have to?"

"Not yet, but he'll be onto it soon. Friends of ours know we scrapped sometimes. They'll tell him."

"I'm glad you told me." Diamond appreciated the honesty. No doubt there would be suspicions that one more "scrap" had resulted in violence and Patsy's death. The man was realistic enough to know the pattern any investigation followed. Bowers *would* dissect the relationship.

Some awkwardness remained between them. Stormy, talkative with a tendency to blunder into trouble, wasn't the sort of man Diamond would normally strike up a friendship with, but then who was? He had almost no close companions in the police. It wasn't a job that encouraged confidences. But he was glad he'd made the gesture of welcoming him to his home. With their common cause they would make an effective team.

"Do you want vinegar with that?"

Stormy shook his head. "What I'd really like is to find out if they nicked Joe Florida."

Diamond said it was simple. He'd call the duty sergeant and find out.

A few minutes later he passed on the news that Florida was being questioned by McGarvie at Shepherd's Bush Police Station.

"Will he ask the right questions?"

"Who knows? They sound confident."

"Aren't you?"

"That Florida is the killer?" Diamond looked away at the photo of Steph he'd put in a frame on the wall unit. "He was never top of my list."

"But he's a vicious bastard. You helped send him down."

"Justly. He was bang to rights."

"So what's the problem, Peter? He's well capable of murder."

"I can't see the logic in it. If he hated my guts—and he probably did—then why not murder me? People like Florida live by a simple, brutal code, Dave. They demand and they get. If they don't get, they give, and what they give is violence. We're not dealing with a chess grand master here. I don't see Joe Florida scheming and plotting in jail for years thinking when I get out I'll murder the *wives* of the coppers who banged me up, and that'll really make them suffer."

"He'd rather kill us?"

"Of course—if he still bears a grievance. And I'm not convinced he had a reason to hate you when all you did was sit beside Blaize in the interviews."

"I was alone with him a lot."

"Doing what? You didn't get physical with him?"

Stormy grinned. "Me—with Joe Florida?"

"I meant restrain him."

"I know what you meant. He asked me things, how long I'd been on the force, if I was married, had kids. You know me by now. I can go on a bit."

"He actually asked if you were married?"

"Yes."

"And you told him?"

"I was trying to seem laid-back."

"What was he after—a smoke?"

"I wouldn't have given him one. No, I thought at the time he was softening me up for something. It was scary, to be honest."

"Softening you up for what?"

"He could see I was new in the job. He had this aura of evil. You must have sensed it, same as me."

"What are you saying, Dave? That he psyched you out? That you did something out of order?"

Stormy was quiet for a time. Finally he sighed and said, "I've never mentioned this to anyone."

Diamond waited.

"He asked me to make a phone call for him, letting his girl-friend know he was nicked."

"And did you?"

"Of course not."

"But you promised Florida you'd do it?"

"Kind of."

"Either you did or you didn't."

He shrugged. "I did, then."

"And you think he remembers?" Diamond said in disbe-lief.

"I remember—and I wasn't sitting in the Scrubs staring at the walls. Things can get out of proportion, Peter."

Diamond took a short swig of beer. "Even if you're right, and he held a grudge as long as this, I still say he'd take it out on you, not your wife."

About eleven, they made up an extra bed in the spare room. "What's the agenda tomorrow?" Stormy asked.

"A trip to Guildford."

"What for?"

"My wife's first husband, Dixon-Bligh, used to have a res-taurant there. McGarvie says he's holed up somewhere, and I want to know why."

"He's the one who could have been mentioned in the diary?"

"Right. 'T' for Ted."

"You think he's gone back to Guildford?"

"I wouldn't rule it out, but if he's covered his tracks, as the Met seem to think, we're not going to find him that easily. We've got to go at him by a different route. I want to trace his ex-partner in the business—if possible."

"Who is he?"

"She, actually."

"A woman." Stormy twitched as a dire thought struck him. "What if he killed her?"

Diamond had thought of this a long time before. He remarked as if recalling some ancient mystery, "It would be helpful to know."

Stormy was still grappling with the implications. "But there's no link between Dixon-Bligh and my wife's murder."

"None that we know of—yet."

After some ninety miles of Diamond's ultra-cautious driving they reached Guildford well past coffee time and had to go looking for a place that would serve them. "To settle my shattered nerves," he muttered. "I don't like the motorways."

"You should have told me," Stormy said. "I could have walked in front with a red flag. We'd still have got here in the same time."

"Cheeky sod."

The first place they looked into after the café was a second-hand bookshop. Diamond, better for the intake of caffeine, explained his thinking. There was always a shelf near the door of out-of-date guides, yearbooks and catalogues. He picked off a 1998 restaurant guide and found the address of Dixon-Bligh's former establishment, the Top of the Town. "See if this gets your juices going, Dave. "*The welcome is warm, the cooking classy at this easy-to-miss haven towards the top of the High Street. Edward Dixon-Bligh recently took over after a career of catering for the top brass in Royal Air Force establishments across the world. The menu reflects his international pedigree, with chowders, cassoulets and pestos, terrine of pork knuckle with foie gras, cinnamon-spiced quail with cardomom rice and fine green beans and pan-fried salmon with sarladaise potato and horseradish cappuccino sauce. Desserts include Thai coconut with exotic fruit sorbets. A fine cellar, mainly French and New World, is expertly managed by Dixon-Bligh's partner, Fiona Appleby, who is pleased to advise.*'"

"It's probably a McDonald's now," Stormy said.

"Can't get more international than that."

But it was no longer in business as a restaurant. They found a body-piercing studio where the Top of the Town had been. A window filled with tattoo patterns and pieces of metal designed to be inserted into flesh. The shaven-headed, leather-clad receptionist almost fell off her stool when the two middle-aged detectives walked in. She thought their generation wasn't privy to the charms of pierced nipples and navels.

Diamond confirmed the impression. He explained he was only interested in the former owners.

"Them? They blew out of here ages ago. They split up, didn't they?"

"What do you do with the mail?"

"It stopped coming."

"They must have left a forwarding address."

"The woman has a cottage at Puttenham. We used to send stuff there."

"Is that far?"

"Take the A31 on the Hog's Back. You'll see the sign. It's about three miles."

"Do you have a note of the address?"

"I remember it. Duckpond Cottage."

"And you think she's still there?"

"Don't bank on it, mister. Are they in trouble, then?"

"It's just an enquiry. Why do you ask?"

'Cos you look like the police."

"It's personal."

Stormy said with a beam across his tomato-red face, "You can't tell a book by its cover."

Out at Puttenham they found Duckpond Cottage on its own at the end of a rutted track that Diamond refused to drive along. The place wasn't a picture-postcard cottage. It was built, probably in the nineteen sixties, of reconstituted stone slabs that had acquired patches of green mould. But efforts had been made with the garden and the paintwork was recent. No one answered when they rang the doorbell. "Par for the course," Stormy said.

Through the letter box a few items of mail were visible inside.

Everyone in a village is supposed to know everyone else's business. At the nearest house a small, elderly man in a cap was standing in his doorway before they reached it.

"Who are you, then?" he piped up.

"Enquiring about your neighbour, Miss Appleby. Does she still live at Duckpond Cottage?"

"Why—has she gone missing?" He was more interested in asking questions than answering them.

It seemed she hadn't moved away.

"You're not from the council about the drainage? Shocking, the state of that lane."

"She doesn't appear to be at home."

"Gone away, hasn't she?" Now there was a note of certainty in the voice, even if it ended as yet another question.

"Did she tell you?"

"I may be old, but my eyes are all right. I saw you prowling around, didn't I?"

"You did."

"She hasn't been at home for the past three weeks."

"As long as that?"

"Easily."

Diamond was not entirely convinced. "We looked through the letter box. I wouldn't say there's three weeks' junk mail on the carpet."

"That's because someone comes in."

"Really? Who's that—a cleaner?"

"In Puttenham? We don't have cleaners in Puttenham. Them's for fancy folk in Guildford."

"Who could it be, then—Miss Appleby herself?"

"Nothing like her. This young lady is taller, with a good figure. She comes in a car once a week."

"So it's a young woman we're talking about. Have you seen her yourself?"

"From a distance. I've watched her come and let herself in. Not Miss Appleby— she's different altogether. This one drives up in a fancy sports car, a red one, and leaves it where yours is at the top of the lane. She doesn't stay long. Just goes inside for a couple of minutes and comes out carrying stuff."

"What stuff? The post?"

"I reckon. I've seen her with a couple of bags, them plastic sacks. Pretty well filled up, they was."

"Not just the mail, then?"

"Some of Miss Appleby's property, I expect. Clothes and things."

"Didn't you ask her what was going on?"

The old man looked affronted. "I'm not nosy."

"But you don't even know who she is. Could be pinching the stuff."

He shook his head. "She don't act like a burglar. She lets herself in with a key in broad daylight. Must be family, wouldn't you say?"

"And always at the same time?"

"Once a week, round about two. What's today, Wednesday? If you're willing to wait you could see her for yourselves."

Not much fell into Diamond's lap, so he was disbelieving when it did. "You're expecting this woman to visit the house today?"

"It's her day, isn't it?"

They moved Diamond's car to the old man's driveway. There would be under an hour to wait. Flattered by all the attention, their host offered them some of the chicken soup he was cooking for lunch, but each of them declined when they saw the state of his kitchen. In matters of hygiene the fancy folk in Guildford had the edge.

"You'll get the best view of Duckpond Cottage from my bedroom window," the old man informed them while he dipped chunks of bread into his soup and sucked on them noisily. "Go on up if you want."

His bedroom promised to be no more salubrious than the kitchen and wasn't, but they were policemen, and their work had taken them into more squalid places. They opened the window that looked out along the lane, leaned out and gulped some fresh air.

"If this woman turns up," Diamond said, "I think we should play this cautiously. I don't know what's going on here, but my instinct is to watch and wait and see where she goes."

"Agreed," Stormy said, then, after an interval, "No offence, Peter, but if she drives off, as she probably will, and we get in your car and follow, would you mind if I took the wheel?"

A sniff from Diamond. "Think you can do better?"

"I'm thinking of your faultless driving. We could find ourselves having to ask which way she went."

He shrugged. "All right." Then added, "I'd better warn you. I'm a nervous passenger."

They heard the car's approach a few minutes after two, just as the old man had predicted. It was an Alfa Romeo convertible with a fawn-coloured top, and it halted at the top of the track leading to Duckpond Cottage. The driver, a woman, youngish, with black hair teased into fine loose wisps, stepped out and touched the switch in her hand that locked the doors. She was in a turquoise sweater, black jeans and ankle-length boots.

"See what I mean about the figure?" the old man's voice piped up from behind the watching detectives. He must have finished his lunch and crept upstairs. "Isn't that arse a peach?"

Diamond murmured, "Haven't you got something else to do?"

"This is my time for a nap, but I can't get into bed with you here." A strange fit of modesty.

Meanwhile the focus of all the interest was picking her way between the ruts along the track with the confidence of a regular visitor.

Diamond asked Stormy if he'd taken a note of the car's number. He had not.

"You're no better than he is, watching the floor show."

She took a key from her pocket and entered the cottage. Diamond checked his watch.

Three minutes passed.

"Could be checking the answerphone," he said. "It can't take this long to pick up the mail."

And shortly after, she emerged carrying what looked like letters in her right hand.

"We'd better get to the car," he told Stormy. To the old man, he said, "Siesta time."

As the Alfa Romeo moved off in the direction of the main road to Guildford, they started up, Stormy at the wheel.

"I don't fancy our chances if she steps on the gas in that thing," Stormy said.

"Keep your distance, and she won't have any reason to speed."

"Which way do you reckon?"

"The A3 to London, I guess."

Instead she turned south and immediately accelerated. "Hope your motor is up to this, Peter," Stormy said, putting his foot down.

Diamond braced. "The motor may be, but don't count on the owner."

"Got to keep her in sight. Do you think she spotted us?"

"She doesn't know us or the car. She's burning rubber for the hell of it." He hunched down in the seat with arms folded, trying not to watch the speedometer.

They had some overtaking to do. Fortunately, the Portsmouth Road is as good as a motorway in places. Stormy drove with skill and nice judgement, getting the best out of Diamond's old Cortina, staying within sight of the Alfa Romeo without being too obvious about it. Right up the steep approach to Hindhead and the Devil's Punch Bowl the Cortina had power in reserve. "This old heap handles well, Peter."

"It gets good treatment—usually."

"Who *is* this woman?"

"Never seen her before."

"Heigh-ho, she's turning left at the lights." Stormy jerked the car into the left lane and took the turn tightly, tyres screaming. They were now on a narrow two-way stretch through a wooded area, and she hadn't cut her speed.

"Think she's spotted us yet?" Stormy asked.

"I told you. She won't know who we are."

"It's mutual."

They passed more than one sign to Haslemere. "We're still going south," Diamond said.

"Now she's using a car phone."

"Bloody dangerous at this speed."

"Maybe she noticed us."

In another mile the brake lights of the convertible suddenly blazed for no obvious reason. It happened twice.

"She's looking for somewhere to turn off," Stormy said.

"Don't crowd her, then."

When they crested the next hill the Alfa Romeo was no longer in sight.

"What the fuck . . . ?"

"Slow up, man. There's got to be a turn here," Diamond said.

A narrow lane came up on the right, and Stormy did well to spot it and make the turn. They hadn't travelled more than sixty yards when there was a flash of metal ahead and another vehicle came fast towards them, so fast that they were forced off the hard surface onto a mud path, the wheels skidding and screeching against the wood of a low hedge. A white Mercedes with a woman at the wheel. A mop of dark hair in wisps, pale, staring face, turquoise top.

"She's switched cars."

"Flaming hell."

She was past, heading for the road they'd just left and there was nowhere to turn. Diamond swung around in his seat and watched the Mercedes through the rear window. "Back up. Reverse."

Stormy slammed into reverse and steered them back towards the road whilst Diamond strained to see which direction the Mercedes would take at the top of the lane.

"Right. She's gone right."

"Say your prayers, then. We're going arse-out into the road."

By a miracle nothing was passing when they did. Stormy spun the wheel again and they zoomed off in the direction the woman had taken. Two cars were on the road ahead. Neither was a white Mercedes.

"How did she do that?" Stormy shouted over the acceleration.

"Switch cars? Trying to shake us off, I suppose."

"I didn't say *why*. I said *how*."

"Someone must have had it ready. That phone call from the car?"

"Whatever, she's left us for dead."

They overtook the two cars. Nothing else was in view.

"Have you thought why we're risking our bloody lives?" Diamond said as they hurtled along well in excess of the speed limit. "We're chasing a woman who might or might not lead us to another woman who might or might not be able to tell us the whereabouts of a man who might or might not have committed murder."

"Want to give up?"

"No. Keep going."

And persistence paid off. Around the next bend was a sign for road works and temporary traffic lights. In a few hundred yards they joined the end of a stationary line of traffic held by a red light. Three ahead was the white Mercedes.

Back in touch.

"Is it worth getting out?"

"No. We want to know where she's going."

The lights changed and everyone moved again. It was sedate progress behind a container lorry, which suited Diamond. He was looking at signs.

"The next place of any size is Midhurst."

The driver of the Mercedes was getting impatient, repeatedly edging out into the oncoming lane for a chance to overtake the couple of vans and the truck ahead. Each time something appeared in view.

"She must have a death wish if she goes for it."

"So what do we do then?"

The lorry peeled off into a layby and the vans eased towards the kerb, enabling the Mercedes to cruise past and pick up speed again. Nothing was approaching, so Stormy made the same move. Diamond cautioned him yet again to keep some distance back. They didn't have to be obvious.

Without any indication, the Mercedes left the Midhurst Road at a right turn. About a hundred yards in the rear, the detectives followed along a twisting, bumpy road through a dense wood.

"Pull over," Diamond said suddenly. "She's stopping."

They slid into an overtaking bay with enough foliage around it to hide them from the road ahead.

"Think she saw us?"

"Who knows?"

"Let's get out. Don't slam the door."

Diamond's legs felt as if he had run every yard of the trip

from Puttenham, and he was mightily relieved to get his feet
on the ground again. Dipping low, he trotted across a carpet
of dead leaves to a place among the trees that gave reasonable
cover. Stormy did the same.

They could see the Mercedes standing in a cobbled driveway
in front of a large red-brick house. The woman got out, raked
a hand through her hair, stretched, and stood looking along
the road, probably to check that she'd shaken off her pursuers.
Then she stepped towards the house. They heard a door open
and close.

"So?" Stormy said.

"Let's get closer."

There was a point where the wooded area ended and the
landscaped garden began and it was surrounded by a ring fence
six feet high that looked in good condition.

Diamond felt a nudge from his companion.

"What?"

Stormy was pointing at a video camera mounted on a post
inside the fence and swivelling, scanning the area where they
stood. They dipped out of view.

"Strong on security."

"But you and I know that sometimes these things are just
for show."

Diamond decided on the next move. "Give me ten minutes
to size up the place," he told Stormy. "Better if one of us goes
in first."

Stormy said he would wait in the car.

The only way in was through the front gate, so he used it,
conscious that he was likely to be picked up by a camera. The
surveillance equipment looked state of the art.

He crossed the cobbles to the porch and hesitated. To his
left was a large, low, mullioned window with leaded panes.
It probably gave a view of one of the front rooms. He stepped
closer. Inside were two large sofas and a vast coffee table with a

few magazines arranged symmetrically on it. He was reminded more of a dentist's waiting room than a private home. A door stood open at the far end and he was conscious of a movement and saw someone cross the space behind. Female, he was certain, and he assumed she must be the woman they'd been following. At least she wasn't sitting in front of a CCTV monitor watching his movements.

Feeling bolder, he decided to reconnoitre the place from outside. Keeping close to the wall, he edged around the side of the building.

Straight ahead was a sunroom with metal lounging chairs and pink and green cushions. It had an exterior door that he tried and found locked.

He was totally still when he heard the scrape of a stone close by.

He spun around.

She was right behind him, the woman they'd followed from Puttenham, legs apart, leaning slightly forward, hands in front of her in a martial arts stance. There wasn't time for words. He put up a hand defensively and she grasped it with both of hers and tugged him towards her. Totally unprepared for this, he lurched forward and suddenly she executed a twist, thrust out her left leg and he crashed over her thigh and hit the ground hard.

Fortunately he'd landed on turf, or he would have broken a limb for sure. Winded and shaken, he tried to raise himself. But the combat wasn't over yet. She threw herself on him and straddled him with her thighs, forcing him face down. She grabbed his right arm and yanked it across his back. He felt something cold tighten around the wrist, like wire. Then round the other arm.

He was handcuffed.

# 30

THE LINES ON Joe Florida's face gave the lie to his dark hair. They were deeply etched around his eyes and mouth and no one would mistake them for laugh lines. He was probably past fifty. And the striplight overhead lent that hair an unlikely reddish sheen. Seated opposite Curtis McGarvie and Keith Halliwell in an interview room at Shepherd's Bush Police Station, he was well aware of his rights. The clock was ticking. They could hold him without charge for twenty-four hours and it might be extended to thirty-six by an officer of superintendent rank or above for a "serious arrestable offence," but he was entitled to eight uninterrupted hours of rest in the twenty-four. He'd already been in custody more than eight. There had been delays. His solicitor had not been in any hurry to get there. The police themselves were slow, hampered by being a hundred miles away from their incident room.

Curtis McGarvie had thought seriously about transporting the man to Bath, but that would have added hours, and the solicitor would have raised all kinds of objections. So they were doing it here.

McGarvie wasn't discouraged. He'd watched Florida's body language. The man was uneasy each time the questioning returned to the murder of Stephanie Diamond.

"Once more, what were you doing in Bath on Tuesday, February the twenty-third?"

"Get real, will you?"

"Answer the question."

"It's a stupid question."

"So where were you?"

"February was months back, for Chrissake."

"Have you visited Bath this year?"

"For the tape," Halliwell said, "the witness is shaking his head."

McGarvie tried another ploy. "And if I said we have someone who saw you that morning?"

Joe Florida twitched.

The solicitor was quick to say, "If you do have a witness, kindly inform us. If the question is hypothetical—as I strongly suspect it may be—I'm advising Mr. Florida to ignore it."

McGarvie gave a shrug. "It would save us all a good deal of time if Mr. Florida stated where he was that morning."

"He doesn't remember. I doubt if any of us could remember what we were doing on a precise date seven or eight months ago."

"He does," McGarvie said. "It's obvious from his demeanour."

And Florida twitched again.

She ordered Diamond to stand. Not easy when you're cuffed. Then she frisked him—expertly. She unlocked the sunroom door and prodded the small of his back. Inside, she pressed on the handcuffs and forced him to his knees.

"Face down again."

He had no option.

The cuffs weren't the old-fashioned sort. They were steel wire loops that cut into the flesh, and they hurt. They hurt still more when she grabbed his right foot and bent the leg back and fastened it to the wrists.

"I'm going for the other one," she said, and he realised she wasn't speaking to him. At the edge of his vision he could just make out a movement. A shoe, a trainer. He couldn't see who the wearer was.

A male voice said, "Don't try anything."

Some chance.

The woman was already gone. She knew about Stormy, too. The camera hadn't been for show.

He lay humiliated, in pain and confusion. It was bad enough being a loser, but to lose so pathetically was dire. The speed of the attack, its cold efficiency, had caught him off guard. True, he wasn't in the prime of youth, but he'd always believed he'd give some account of himself in hand-to-hand combat. Joke. He'd raised one hand and been thrown and disabled by a woman half his size.

He still didn't understand why. The attack was over reaction considering all he'd done was stroll around the outside of the house.

*All* he'd done? Being brutally honest, that wasn't all.

He'd tried a door handle, and that had been ill-advised. If you act like a house breaker, you lay yourself open to attack.

Even so.

It wasn't long before he heard the door open and her voice ordering someone to get down beside him. Apparently Stormy hadn't put up much of a fight either.

Stormy started to say, "You don't have to—" Whereupon he was dumped beside Diamond.

"She surprised me," he told Diamond.

The big man was in too much discomfort to answer.

He heard her tell her colleague, "I can handle this now." To Diamond, she said, "I'm going to release your leg. Don't get ideas. I'm armed."

The relief was exquisite. His hands were still bound, but blood returning to the veins was bliss.

"On your feet, both of you. I'm prepared to use this gun."

With difficulty, they obeyed, and a sorry sight they made. Stormy's nose was streaming blood and Diamond's face was heavily smeared with mud. And they were staring into the barrel of an automatic. She was using the two-hand grip rec-ommended on all the weapons training courses.

"Who exactly are you?"

Diamond darted a glance at Stormy, trying to convey that the truth was the best option now. "Police officers investigating a crime."

She almost snorted at that.

"If you look in the back pocket of my trousers, you'll find my warrant card," he told her. "I'm Detective Superintendent Diamond, and I work out of Bath."

"DCI Weather," Stormy chimed in. "Mine's in my inside jacket pocket."

She stepped forward, still holding the gun in her left hand, took the ID from Stormy's pocket and clearly decided it was genuine. "This beats everything. What sort of police work is this, breaking into a private house?"

Playing it straight, Diamond explained that they'd gone to the cottage at Puttenham looking for Fiona Appleby, seeking information about her ex-partner, Edward Dixon-Bligh, who was wanted for questioning in connection with two murders.

"*Murders?*"

"Right."

"My God, you've got some explaining to do."

"Do you want to hear about that, or shall I carry on telling you how we got here?"

"All right. You saw me go into the cottage and thought I was Fiona?"

"No. You're the one who collects the mail."

"You knew this?"

"We found out."

"Who from?"

"The neighbour."

She clicked her tongue at her own carelessness.

Quick to follow up, Diamond asked, "So do you know what's happened to Fiona?"

She ignored that. "Let's get back to this peculiar mission of yours—how two senior detectives come all this way to interview a minor witness. A DCI and a super? What am I missing here?"

One thing was clear: this young woman was well-briefed on police procedure.

"Before I answer that, who do you work for?" Diamond asked.

"That's not for discussion. I asked you to explain yourselves."

"You act as if you're on the side of law and order. Are you?"

She hesitated, then nodded.

"Okay," Diamond went on. "Did you read in the paper about the woman's body found recently beside the railway embankment near Woking?"

She had. "The ex-policewoman?"

"Right. She was Dave's wife, Mrs. Patricia Weather. My own wife was murdered in a public park in Bath last February."

Plainly she was unprepared for this. She said nothing, but her eyes widened.

Diamond explained more, trying to sound reasonable. "Before you ask, we're acting on our own initiative. Unofficial, in other words. We have a common cause as husbands of the victims. The main inquiry is going its own way, and Dave and I are not involved. More to the point, we're not satisfied, so we're following an independent line."

"I've heard of these cases, both of them," she admitted, softening her tone. She actually lowered the gun a fraction. "You're taking a lot on yourselves, aren't you—going out on a limb?"

"Yes. We're out of order. But that's the answer to your question—why two senior detectives are out here trying to see a minor witness."

"And tailing me?"

"Right."

She took time to absorb what she had heard. "You obviously

believe Dixon-Bligh is a serious suspect? On what evidence—
just that he's lying low?"

Diamond explained that Dixon-Bligh had been Steph's first
husband and how they were linking him to the diary entries.

"Why? What's his motive?"

"He's skint. It looks as if he was demanding money from
Steph shortly before she was killed. I interviewed him in
London not long after the murder. I found him unhelpful and
hostile."

She turned to Stormy. "And is the same man linked in some
way to your wife's death?"

"We're not certain," Stormy had to admit. "Like Peter said,
we're helping each other."

"Surely it's up to the SIO on the case to pursue these enquiries?"

"If he had, we wouldn't be here."

She was shaking her head. "All this is so bizarre that it might
just be true. You can sit down, but I'm keeping the cuffs on
you." She waved them towards a couple of wicker armchairs.

"You asked if I have a link with the police, and I do," she told
them. "I'm in SO10, the Witness Protection Unit. I have the
rank of inspector. I'm guarding Fiona Appleby."

"She's alive, then?" Diamond said, encouraged.

"In the next room watching television."

"For her protection?"

"Yes. This is a police house—a safe house."

"Who are you protecting her from?"

"Dixon-Bligh?" Stormy suggested.

She didn't answer.

"I see the answer in your eyes," Stormy pressed her. "You can
trust Peter and me, love. Dixon-Bligh is the enemy, isn't he?"

Diamond cringed at the endearment, but to his mysti-
fication, it worked. The doughty DO10 inspector gave Stormy
a look that was almost a wink.

"And others."

She was clearly reluctant to say more, though all the aggro had disappeared.

Whatever it was that was working for them, Stormy was going to milk it. "Listen, love, what's your first name?"

She balked at that.

"Make one up, then."

"Gina will do."

"Gina—that's nice. And I'm Dave. He used to call me Stormy, but he's more respectful these days." He grinned. "Gina, there's an 'all units' out on Dixon-Bligh. Did you know that? The Met have been looking for him for the past two weeks. If you know this bozo is dangerous, don't you think there might be a tie-in with the two murders?"

She shook her head. "There's no connection I know of."

"Maybe we can put you right on that."

Now Diamond chimed in. "Hold on, Dave. Gina, you just told us Fiona Appleby is under special protection. What's special about her? I thought she was just someone who was living quietly in a Surrey village because her restaurant failed."

"That's true. She's an innocent woman caught up in events outside her control." She stopped speaking, as if reminded she was giving too much away.

Diamond tried gentle persuasion. If it worked for Stormy, why not for him? "If you could see your way, there are things we'd dearly like to ask her."

"No chance."

"She has vital information."

"Do it through official channels."

"We're not official, Gina. We're very unofficial, as I just explained. But you want to stop Dixon-Bligh from harming anyone else and so do we. This is crying out for cooperation."

"In your dreams."

Diamond simply didn't have his companion's charm.

Stormy applied more of it. "Gina, we have something to trade."

The smile returned. "Oh, yes?"

"Information no one else can give you. Think about it—this pain in the arse Dixon-Bligh was once married to Peter's wife. Peter can tell you all about his old haunts, the places he thinks of as safe, the contacts he has. Isn't that right, Peter?"

"Well—"

"Between us, we can find him, but we need to speak to Fiona."

She looked tempted, then adamant. "It can't be done."

"It can, my dear, if she's only in the next room."

"I don't have the authority."

"You want an order from an officer of higher rank?"

She smiled faintly. "Not you. Nor him."

"Your guvnor."

"How would you know who my guvnor is?" She was almost flirting with Stormy.

"Ways and means, darling, ways and means. What if your guvnor gets to hear that two old gits in a clapped-out Cortina followed you all the way from Puttenham to your safe house?"

A muscle flexed at the edge of her mouth.

Stormy said, "You won't forget to report it, will you?"

She didn't answer.

"You don't have to, honey—so long as we keep our mouths shut. But if we boast about it to our friends, you can be sure the one person you don't want to hear the news will get it from the old bush telegraph."

"You're not threatening me, I hope?"

"Far from it." Diamond chipped in and raised the stakes still more. "This is big-time for you. You caught us snooping and overpowered us. Under questioning we admitted we were senior police officers. Then you found we had significant information. Back of the net."

Now the eyes were moving anxiously. "You'd say that?"

"Sure—as a trade-off." He turned to Stormy, who was nodding.

She thought in the silence. There seemed to be deeper impulses at work here, matters outside Diamond's power to persuade. Her voice shook a little as she said, "All right. You can meet her if you wish, since you've gone to such lengths to find her."

"Thanks."

"Trussed up as we are?" Stormy said, pushing the concessions as far as possible.

"I didn't say shake hands with her."

"Gina, look at the state of us. We're a scary sight. Don't you think you should let us clean up first?"

A sigh. "All right. There's a bathroom nearby. But don't get the idea I've caved in. I'm going to have to report all this."

"We'll take our chances."

"I'm the one who's taking chances."

She had keys attached to her belt, and she unlocked the handcuffs and escorted them to the bathroom and watched them clean up.

"Straight through the hall." Still far from comfortable with what they had talked her into, she made sure she didn't turn her back on them. She'd slipped the gun into a holster at her waist. She was well capable of dealing with any aggression. "Last door."

So it was Diamond who opened the door at the end and admitted them to a sitting room where a small woman in a black tracksuit was curled on a sofa watching TV. Fiona Appleby was in her forties probably, with hair streaked with silver. She picked up the remote and switched off the power.

"Everything's OK, Fiona," Gina said at once, and then introduced them as police officers in a way suggesting they had just driven up and called at the front door. "They're trying to trace your ex-partner, and they have a few questions for you."

She had the worry lines of a woman close to breakdown. She turned up her hands in appeal. "But I already told you, I haven't seen him in months. I've no idea where he is."

"Do you mind if we go over familiar ground?" Diamond gently asked. "When did you first meet him?"

"That isn't familiar ground. Nobody's asked me yet." She closed her eyes, remembering. "It would have been ninety-five. December."

"Where?"

"A Christmas party at one of the City Livery companies. Mercers' Hall, I think. I was in advertising at the time and hating it. Ted was doing the catering. He's a brilliant cook." Launched into this, she spoke with intensity, recalling the details. "The canapes were like nothing I'd seen before. Delicious and wonderful to look at. One little pastry concoction with duck pate and cranberry was such a gorgeous bite that I made up my mind to ask the caterer how it was done. I'm passionate about cooking. I went into the kitchen and of course Ted was charming and good-looking and promised to give me the recipe if I went out for a drink with him the next evening. I was flattered. I really hadn't thought it would lead to anything. And we clicked at once because I've always loved to cook and we spent the evening discussing all the television cooks we would shoot on sight and the cookbooks we'd throw into their coffins. He was terrific fun to be with. That was the start of our relationship."

"You teamed up right away?"

"Not immediately. It was more gradual. We had this dream of starting our own restaurant. It was just lovers' talk at first, and yet we began to believe it. The green and white colour scheme and the two little bay trees in tubs outside the door. We talked about where it should be—somewhere just outside London in the southern commuter belt. And before the end of the year we were looking at shop premises. The place at Guildford came onto the market—to rent, that is. The flat upstairs went with it. I had some savings to equip the shop, and I can tell you we did it beautifully. The crockery, the table linen, candles—it was our dream realised. And we got in all the top restaurant guides."

"We've seen one. They rated you."

"So did the public. We were fully booked most evenings, and people came back. They drove in from miles around. It should have been a tremendous success."

"So what went wrong?"

Fiona's expression switched suddenly to a penetrating frown. "Well you know, don't you?"

"We'd rather hear it from you," Diamond improvised.

"His habit."

He gave a nod that was meant to be knowing, encouraging her to say more, while he reeled from the mental jolt she'd just given him.

"I didn't suspect anything when we first met," she went on. "He was nothing like my idea of an addict. Not that I knew the first thing about drugs. I was incredibly naive. Ted handled the accounts, banked the takings. I trusted him. I had no idea he'd run through my savings and was putting nothing back. The money was all going to drug dealers. And all this time he looked perfectly healthy, cooked beautifully, treated me like a goddess."

"What was he on?"

"H," Gina murmured.

Diamond's face registered nothing of this bombshell. Inwardly he cursed his sluggish brain for failing to think of drugs. What else could have brought a successful, articulate man to the squalor of that terrace behind Paddington Station?

"But you know all about him," Fiona said.

"Hearing it just as you tell it is so much more helpful," he said with all the calm he could drag up from his plunging self-esteem. The case against Dixon-Bligh was red-hot now. He wanted to run through it in his head, item by item, but he had to listen. There could be more.

Fiona said, "It came to the point where even I found out

what was going on—that we had a huge overdraft and a mass of unpaid bills. It was heartbreaking. Such deceit. I found a syringe and needles hidden in a casserole dish high up in a cupboard in the kitchen. He was full of repentance. Drug users are when they're found out. I was stupid enough to trust him and expect him to stop. We went on for a few weeks more and the bills just mounted up. He was still buying the stuff, still injecting. We closed the restaurant and I used the rest of my savings to clear some of our debts. Ted went off to live in London and I didn't want or expect to hear from him ever again."

"But you did?"

"Earlier this year. He knocked on my door one afternoon. I suppose it wasn't difficult to track me down. Everyone knows I live in Puttenham. Can you believe he was asking for money again? Addicts have no shame at all. He wanted a thousand pounds. Said it would be a loan and he'd pay me back at ten per cent interest. I told him in no uncertain terms that I was disgusted he had the gall to come back to me wanting more of my money. He went on arguing, saying he now had a very good job at the Dorchester Hotel."

"The *Dorchester?*"

"Assistant chef or something. I didn't believe him, and then he fished in his pocket for some letter on headed notepaper confirming the appointment. I still said it made no difference and I didn't have money to lend him. But he's so crafty, nosing around the cottage, spotting nice bits of furniture he'd never seen before. He soon cottoned on to the fact that my father had died the December before last and I was the main beneficiary. Once he'd got the scent of the money, he said he'd take me into his confidence because he was on the verge of making so much that he'd soon be in a position to pay me back at twenty per cent if I wanted, and he'd still have so much left he'd never bother me again. I thought he was talking about the lottery or something and I treated it all with contempt, and I suppose that just fired him up. Next thing he was telling me about these Arabs he'd met."

Gina said quickly, "I think you should stop there, Fiona."

"Why?"

"They've heard enough."

"But we haven't. We need to hear it all," Diamond said at once. "We know what Dixon-Bligh is like, and we're keen to stop him ruining more people's lives." He ignored the foul look he got from Gina and said, "Together, we'll do it."

Fiona turned to Gina. "You told me they were the police."

"We are," Stormy said.

"I can trust them, can't I? I'd like to tell it."

Gina, outgunned, sighed and said nothing.

Fiona took up her thread again. "Ted told me these Arabs made a deal with him. They'd offered him twenty thousand in return for inside information from the Dorchester. All he had to do was find out in advance when some prince from Kuwait was due to stay. Apparently it's all done secretly for security reasons. Nobody is supposed to know until they arrive, but of course certain people have to be told, and Ted knew who to ask. As simple as that, he said."

"And he'd tip off the Arabs?"

"And get paid. He was ready to write me an IOU on the strength of it. He needed money now for his drugs. He couldn't wait for this payday, as he called it."

"Did you give him any?"

"No. I wouldn't be so daft. You know that old saying? He that deceives me once, shame fall him; if he deceives me twice, shame fall me." Fiona Appleby obviously didn't think she'd put her life at risk to preserve her self-respect. "However, I've got to say this in Ted's favour. He wasn't lying this time. There really was some underhand arrangement going on. Whether these mysterious Arabs would pay him all that money I had no idea, but he believed it. He was going through with it, I'm positive."

"How did you get rid of him?"

"By holding out."

"Didn't he get violent?"

Diamond had struck a wrong note. Fiona stared at him with her large brown eyes. "No. He's never laid a hand on me. He wouldn't."

"Don't count on it," he warned.

Gina murmured, "We don't. Which is why she's here."

"So there's more to this?"

"You can tell them," Gina said. She was now resigned to everything being in the open.

Fiona had her hands across her stomach inside the track-suit top. She curled her legs more tightly. "After he'd gone, I thought about what he'd told me. All that money he was counting on. There had to be something criminal going on and something very big. People don't pay vast sums without due cause. It troubled me. That night I couldn't sleep. All kinds of horrible ideas crept into my head. I thought of the Gulf War. It was never really resolved, was it? Suppose these Arabs he'd met were Iraqi agents planning to assassinate one of the Kuwaiti royal family? If that happened, and I knew in advance and did nothing about it, I'd have to live with the knowledge that I could have prevented a tragedy. Ted was hopelessly dependent. He wouldn't have a conscience. He didn't think past his next fix. It was up to me to do something about it. So I phoned the Foreign Office. And they took it seriously. They sent someone to see me the same day."

Gina cut in. "Fiona's information prevented a serious crime. Not an assassination attempt as it turned out but a huge scam involving diamonds. Our people laid on a stake out at very short notice and stopped the handover, but through a combination of problems the perpetrators got away."

"Not much of a stake out," Stormy commented.

"These are international terrorists. They're highly organised."

"Unlike you and me, Stormy," Diamond said to take the heat out of the exchange. "So who do they work for?"

"That's secure information."

"In short, then, Fiona needs protection now, not just from Dixon-Bligh, but these Arab bandits as well. Do you know their names?"

"It's under investigation."

"Meaning 'no,'" Stormy said.

"Do you know where Dixon-Bligh is?"

"He's in the process of being traced."

"Another 'no,'" Stormy said, all too ready with the slick comment.

Diamond gave him a murderous glare. They didn't want to provoke Gina at this stage. "Leave it out," he said more for Gina's ears than Stormy's. "We're as much in the dark as anyone else."

"Sorry. I'm always shooting off at the mouth," Stormy said, sounding genuine, and it was a pity his face wouldn't register a blush because one was probably lurking there.

Diamond hesitated, uncertain if there was anything more of importance to be learned.

There was, and it came from the least likely source—Stormy.

"Peter, I can't clam up now. I've been listening to all this and getting more and more steamed up. My wife, my Patsy, worked with the District Drugs Unit for two or three years before she retired. It was part of her job to visit the drop-in centres in Hammersmith Road and Earls Court Road. She knew all the heroin users in West London. That's the link, Peter. Dixon-Bligh was on her patch. She must have known him when he was living in Blyth Road, and I didn't think of it."

# 31

ALL THIS CAME like a wake-up call to Diamond. He now remembered Stormy mentioning how Patsy Weather worked with junkies at some stage. Like much else, it had been squirreled away in his memory, unlikely to have been recovered but for this.

Gina was just as fired up as the two detectives. "Can you be certain she knew Dixon-Bligh?"

"If he was on her patch using drugs, you can almost bank on it," Stormy told her, eyes dilated enough to have you believe he, too, was high on something.

"Why would he want to murder her? She'd retired from the police, you said."

"He wasn't to know that, was he? I don't know how they met again. Pure chance, I guess. Patsy was always ready to talk to someone she knew. He'd assume she was still on the strength."

"So he put a gun to her head and shot her?" she said in a rising tone of disbelief. "What for?"

"Fear of arrest. He thought he was nicked."

"For petty thieving to fund his habit?"

"No, no, no," Stormy cut in. "He was on the run. He faced a murder rap. He'd already shot Peter's wife."

"Ah." She raised her hand like a tennis player who has just been served an ace. Then turned to Diamond. "I'm not thinking straight today. When was your wife murdered?"

"February the twenty-third."

"And your wife?" she asked Stormy.

"Disappeared on March the twelfth."

"Two weeks after."

"Just over."

She was checking alternately between the two. "Your wife was shot in a park in Bath?"

Diamond nodded. He'd cross-checked everything in his own mind, and he was as sure of the facts as Stormy, though he tried to appear calm.

"And Dixon-Bligh was once married to your wife? Why would he want to kill her?" Gina asked.

"For money, for his drugs." Put bluntly like that, it was chilling. But every explanation he'd ever imagined was guaranteed to chill.

She kept her bright, shrewd eyes on him, inviting him to say more.

Patiently, he took her through the crucial details. "I told you there were entries in her diary about phoning someone she knew as 'T.' Dixon-Bligh's name is Edward. Ted, right? That's the name you've been using yourself, I notice."

"Right."

He switched to a more immediate way of telling it. "She reminds herself when I'm coming in late: 'P' out. Must call 'T.' He says he needs to see her, and she promises to think it over. She gets her hair done—and that's typical of Steph, wanting to look right, even for a meeting with that berk. She calls him again—from a public phone, so the calls won't appear on our statement—and arranges this meeting in the park on the Tuesday. She says nothing to me about any of this, and Steph wasn't like that. Since reading what she wrote, I've driven myself nuts trying to understand why she set up those phone calls and meetings and kept me out of it. But now I learn he was a drug addict, it's all much clearer. This is the setup. He's pestering her for money, and she doesn't want me to know about it. Steph is confident of handling him herself. He's her ex, and she thinks she knows him. She may well have been sending him small amounts of cash for some time. She'd know my reaction."

"Unsympathetic?"

"To put it mildly."

"Does he possess a gun?"

Unexpectedly, Fiona Appleby spoke up. "Yes."

All eyes were on her.

"What sort?" Diamond asked.

"Pistol."

"Revolver?"

"Yes. He did some shooting in the Air Force. He was on the command team at Bisley. The gun was his own. He kept it in the drawer beside the till. Said he'd produce it if ever anyone tried to hold up the restaurant."

Stormy turned up his palms as if no more needed saying.

But Gina still required convincing. "Why shoot her when all he wanted was money for drugs?"

Diamond answered in a measured tone, drained of emotion. "He brings the gun with him intending to force her to hand over more money than she intends, or credit cards, maybe, instead of the small handout she offers. She refuses. Steph was very strong-willed. He points the gun at her head. She tries to push him away or says something that angers him and he squeezes the trigger."

This had directness, the simplicity of cause and effect that carried conviction.

Gina had listened impassively. She pointed a finger at him. "Okay. It's payback time. You said just now you knew of places he might be hiding in. Were you bullshitting, or can you deliver?"

In point of fact, all the bullshitting had come from Stormy, but sometimes when your bluff is called, the brain goes into overdrive. Without hesitation Diamond launched into the story Steph had once told him about the beach hut. "At one time when he was in the Air Force and married to Steph, they were based at Tangmere, in Sussex. They lived in married quarters, I think, and didn't like it much. The one good thing about it was that they were close to the sea, and on his days off they'd escape to some local beach with a peculiar name; I'm trying to remember. Wittlesham?"

"Wittering?" Gina said, following this acutely. "West Wittering isn't far from Tangmere."

"You've got it. West Wittering. Steph told me they rented a beach hut one summer. They'd use it to change into swimming things, and brew up tea on an oil stove and so on. The point about this is that even after the rental ended, he kept a spare key, and for years he used to go back and open up the hut and use it."

Gina was frowning. "After it was rented to someone else?"

"People only use them a fraction of the time."

"Sneaky."

"That was Steph's reaction. She wouldn't join him."

Gina was ahead of him now. "You're thinking he might be holed up at the beach?"

"It wouldn't be a bad place to hide."

"Out of season, too," Stormy added support. "Nice and quiet. You could survive pretty well in a beach hut."

Diamond put in a note of caution. "I don't even know if the huts are still there. Do they still have them at West Wittering?"

"All the way along," Gina said. "I'm going to call my guvnor."

Eleven hours in, Curtis McGarvie tried another tactic on Joe Florida. Strictly speaking, the murder of Patricia Weather was being handled by DCI Billy Bowers. He'd informed Bowers of the arrest and invited him to join in the questioning, but up to now he hadn't appeared.

"Where were you on Friday, March the twelfth?"

Florida answered casually, "Who knows?"

"London?"

"Maybe."

"Southwest London? Your own manor?"

"What's this about?"

"A woman went missing that day."

"Hold on, will you?" Florida said. "Are you trying to stick something else on me?"

"Her body wasn't found until a few days ago on a railway embankment in Surrey."

"Jesus, I don't believe this," Florida said, turning to his brief. "These assholes want to fit me up with a double murder."

The solicitor said, "My client wasn't informed of this at the time of his arrest."

"Correct," McGarvie told him without apologising. "I was getting ahead of myself. At this stage we're questioning him about the murder of Stephanie Diamond."

"What does he mean—'at this stage'?" Florida demanded. "They can't do this to me."

"We'll take a break," McGarvie said. "We've got a long session ahead of us."

West Wittering was less than an hour's drive from the safe house. The long stretch of coast on the Selsey peninsula is girdled by salt marsh, sand dunes and fields where geese congregate in hundreds. On summer weekends the beach attracts large crowds, but in October is left to a few dog walkers, windsurfers and the occasional scavenger with a metal detector. The land above the beach is owned by the West Wittering Estate and you enter through a coin-operated barrier. When the tide is out, as it was when the armed response team arrived, the stretch of sand is vast.

Officers in helmets and black body armour and carrying Heckler & Koch MP5s were already checking the beach huts with dogs when Diamond and Stormy Weather drove up.

There was an air of confidence about the search. Apparently a local shopkeeper had been shown a picture of Dixon-Bligh and was certain he had bought food a number of times in the past two weeks.

Stormy looked at Diamond as if he was Nostradamus.

The wooden huts, about a hundred and fifty on a turf promenade above the beach, were a testimony to people's individuality. They had obviously been there long enough for some to have been replaced and others given a facelift, so the doors and walls were decorated in a host of different styles and colours. Shuttered windows, verandahs and paved fronts were desirable extras. The majority were padlocked. A few of the oldest had conventional mortice locks built into the doors. It would be one of these Dixon-Bligh had illicitly used.

Diamond eyed the line of pitched roofs stretching almost to the sand dunes on the skyline at East Head and asked the senior man how long the search would take.

"Not long, sir. The dogs will know if he's inside."

This confident prediction was followed shortly by a result. The two springer spaniels started yelping and scratching at the door of one shabby hut towards the near end of the row. Their handlers had to haul them away.

"Game on," the man in charge said.

Everyone took up strategic positions. Officers with sub-machine guns crouched and took aim in the shingle below the level of the huts, watched from behind a stout wooden groyne by the others, including Diamond and Weather.

Diamond told a senior man they didn't want the suspect killed and was informed they were using soft-point rounds.

Through a loudhailer the occupant of the hut was told that armed police were outside. He was instructed to come out, hands on head.

There was no response.

Two more warnings were given. Then the order came to force

an entry. A distraction device, some kind of thunderflash, was lobbed behind the hut and went off with a terrific report.

Instantly four men armed with submachine guns dashed to the hut from either side. The only way in was through the front and it wouldn't take much. The wooden door was half-rotten through years of exposure to salt spray. A burst of gunfire shot away the hinges.

The door fell outwards and hit the paving stones. It had not been locked.

But no one was inside.

The anticlimax silenced everyone. There was that feeling of sheepishness—not unknown to Diamond—when the long arm of the law has reached out and missed.

Finally the man in charge said, "Stupid bloody dogs."

"Back to it, lads," some other officer said. "There's a million more fucking huts."

The man at Diamond's side said, "Which genius gave us this tip-off?"

Diamond said nothing, and Stormy stayed silent as well.

Interestingly the dogs were still straining at their leashes to return to the empty hut. The handlers had a problem getting them back to work.

"I know it's obvious no one is in there," Diamond told Stormy, "but I want a closer look."

They stepped up to the hut and over the bits of timber that had been the door. There were definite signs of recent occupation. Just inside the doorway was a folded sleeping bag. Also a torch, a cut loaf and a carton containing canned food and beer. An *A to Z* of West Sussex and a copy of the *Sunday Express*—last week's edition. He picked up the torch and switched it on. "What do you make of that, Dave?"

Stormy bent closer to the area of flooring caught in the beam of light.

Diamond told him, "That's what excited the dogs."

"Stormy wetted his finger and touched the dark patch. "You're right. It's blood."

After the forensic team and SOCOs arrived there was the usual hiatus. Clearly someone or some animal had shed blood in the beach hut, but it was a mystery where they had gone. The sniffer dogs took no interest in any of the other huts, or the changing rooms, toilets or cafe higher up the beach. With nothing else to detain them, the armed response team packed up and drove away.

"Looks like the Arabs got to him first," Stormy said.

"Killed him, you mean? For blabbing?"

He nodded. "Those guys don't take prisoners. Did you ever see *Lawrence of Arabia?*"

"If he's dead, I don't know where they left him."

"Buried him on the beach, I expect. It wouldn't take long."

"Wouldn't be long before he was found, either. Plenty of people come along here walking their dogs, even at this time of year, and when a dog gets a whiff of blood . . . And how would the Arabs have found him here?"

"They're smart operators, Peter. They escaped from the Dorchester under the noses of one of these hotshot teams of ninjas, so it's not beyond them to track Dixon-Bligh to his hideout."

"Unless."

"Unless what?"

"Unless this is a totally unrelated incident. Remember it was a hunch that brought us here."

"Let's say a brainwave."

Diamond sniffed. "We can hope so."

They sat on a wooden beam facing the band of grey sea and the misty outline of the Isle of Wight. Nearer to them, gulls and sandpipers in their hundreds had colonised the wet sand.

"I hope this smackhead isn't dead," Stormy said. "I want him put on trial."

"Be better off dead when I catch up with him," Diamond muttered.

"You don't want to foul up your career for a scumbag like that."

"Watch me."

"That's precisely why you and I are sidelined."

From behind them a uniformed PC called Diamond over to where the incident tapes kept any onlookers out of the sterile area. "Gentleman here wants a word, sir. He appears to know something."

The informant was a tall, elderly man with a white moustache. He was wearing a windcheater and brown corduroys tucked into green Wellingtons. His red setter started forward and licked the back of Diamond's hand.

"Something to tell me, sir?"

"Seeing all the activity here I wondered if it's anything to do with that fellow they found on the beach yesterday."

"What fellow?"

"Couldn't tell you who he was. I was walking the dog as usual and saw what happened. Some windsurfers spotted him half in, half out of the water at damned near high tide. Blood all over his shirt, but no wound that I could see. He was obviously in a bad way. Out to the world. They took him off in an ambulance."

"Where would they have taken him?"

"Casualty, I expect. Chichester has the nearest A & E Department."

"If my client were to make a voluntary statement about his movements on the day in question," Joe Florida's solicitor said, "and if he proved to your satisfaction that he had no part in the matter under investigation, would you be willing to set aside any possible prosecution on matters of a lower tariff?"

"No deals," McGarvie told him.

"In that case, he has nothing else to say."

Keith Halliwell leaned towards his SIO and whispered something.

McGarvie gave a petulant click of the tongue and sat back in his chair, raking both hands through his hair. Finally he said, "If you were talking about something that happened outside our jurisdiction—we're from another force, Avon and Somerset, you understand—my colleague and I wouldn't"—he sighed, hating this—"wouldn't necessarily be under an obligation to investigate."

"He needs a stronger assurance than that."

"Are you saying that after all this he remembers what he was doing on February the twenty-third?"

Joe Florida pointed to the tape recorder mounted on the wall. "Turn that fucker off, and I'll tell you."

"Typical breakdown in communications," Diamond grumbled on the drive to Chichester. "If someone is brought into hospital with blood all over him and no explanation, it's a police matter. The local CID must have been out at that beach looking for evidence. Why didn't we hear about it?"

"Because we were with Gina's lot," Stormy pointed out. "They're not exactly the local plod."

Thanks to Stormy's driving they reached St Richard's Hospital inside half an hour. The doctor in Accident & Emergency took them into an office at once. A stethoscope hung from his neck and he fingered the sound receiver as he spoke. "Yes, I was on duty yesterday when the man was brought in from West Wittering. From the contents of his pocket he was called Edward Dixon-Bligh, but he hasn't been formally identified yet."

"So he's dead?"

"On arrival."

"Do you know the cause?"

"Loss of blood."

"But where from?"

"His mouth. This is hard to believe, but someone cut out his tongue."

# 32

THE NEXT AFTERNOON Diamond, back in Bath, was summoned to the top-floor suite known as the Eagle's Nest. Curtis McGarvie was there already, seated in the armchair closest to Georgina's desk. He had a half-empty mug of coffee in his fist, revealing he'd been there some time. And he was sitting at an uncomfortable angle with his knees pointing at Diamond presumably to line himself up with the inquisition.

Georgina cleared her throat. "Thank you for coming, Peter." The greeting had a faintly pejorative edge, and the follow-up confirmed it. "If you were expecting a pat on the back, think again. Just because the Yard are treating you like some footballer who scored the winning goal, it doesn't excuse your conduct here. You defied my explicit instruction to stay out of the investigation into your wife's death."

"I did stay out, ma'am."

"What?"

"Ask DCI McGarvie. I haven't troubled him at all. When did we last speak?"

McGarvie glared and said, "That isn't the point."

"You ran what amounted to a parallel investigation," Georgina steamed on. "You visited the crime scenes and interviewed witnesses. What's that, if it isn't interference?"

"Am I prohibited from visiting the place where my wife was murdered? No one made that clear to me."

McGarvie said, "You also turned up at the scene of the Patricia Weather murder—even before I did."

"Nobody barred me from other cases."

"Come off it, Peter. We all know it was a carbon copy of your wife's shooting."

"We didn't know at the time. Stormy Weather is an old colleague. I was with him at Fulham. I'm allowed to have some sympathy for an old mate who goes through a similar experience, aren't I?"

Georgina said, "This is evasion. You teamed up with DCI Weather and drove all over the south of England like . . ." She turned to McGarvie for help, and got none. ". . . like a rerun of *Starsky and Hutch*."

"If you knew my driving, ma'am, you wouldn't make that comparison."

"Don't mess with me. You go off on your own without any consultation, riding roughshod over sensitive lines of enquiry, blundering into this safe house where the witness was being kept."

"That was to enquire about Ted Dixon-Bligh, ma'am."

"And you're going to justify it on the grounds that he was the killer."

"No, ma'am. He was family."

"I beg your pardon?"

"My wife's ex-husband. I wanted to see him on a family matter."

Georgina made a puffing sound of irritation.

Diamond explained, unfazed, "DCI McGarvie told me he was holed up somewhere, and the Met couldn't find him. You'll confirm those were your words, Curtis?"

McGarvie wasn't willing to confirm anything. He stared straight ahead.

"You don't seem to remember. You'd lost all interest in Dixon-Bligh, or so it appeared to me at the time. You were getting very interested in Joe Florida. What happened about Florida?"

"Released without charge," McGarvie said after a pained pause. "After eleven hours, he finally decided to tell us he had an alibi."

"What was that?"

"He was having his car tyres replaced at a garage in Hammersmith."

"True?"

"Confirmed, yes."

"It took eleven hours to get that out of him?"

"The old tyres left a set of prints outside a betting shop that was torched the previous evening."

"Back on the protection game?"

"Apparently."

Diamond gave a sigh that was almost sympathetic. "We can't win 'em all, can we? I helped trace Dixon-Bligh, as you know, but it was too late."

Now McGarvie waded in. "You knew he was wanted for questioning. If you'd informed me about this beach hut at West Wittering, I would have collared him."

"I honestly didn't think about the beach hut until I was at the safe house."

"You're trickier than a cage of monkeys."

Georgina continued with the tongue-lashing. "The whole point is that your actions would have undermined a prosecution against this man. It's lucky for you he's dead."

This time he was silent. He'd made all the points he wanted.

Georgina banged on for a few minutes more, saying she'd considered formally disciplining him and it was only because of the tragedy of Steph's murder that she chose to be compassionate.

He didn't thank her.

He was on the point of leaving when she seemed to relent

a little, maybe deciding she'd taken too strong a line. "It's brought closure, anyway, Peter."

"What do you mean?"

"The man is dead."

"That's closure?" he said in a flat voice.

"In the sense that we can draw a line under the investigation. I realise it doesn't put an end to your personal grief."

He was silent.

Georgina asked, "Did you have any suspicion Dixon-Bligh was involved with this Arab group?"

"Not till I was told, ma'am."

"The manner of his death—removing his tongue—seems particularly brutal. I'm told it's considered a just punishment for an informer. In their society a thief has his hand cut off."

"I've heard."

"There's no question that it was an act of revenge by the diamond robbers?"

"That's the strong assumption."

"They'll be out of the country by now."

"I expect so."

"Difficult, bringing international criminals to justice. Still, it's the Yard's problem, not ours. We're left with some tidying up of our own. It's time for some co-operation between you two. Curtis will need chapter and verse from you, every bit of evidence that seals Dixon-Bligh's guilt. It has to be written up before we can close the file. I rely on you, Peter, to pass on your findings. It will be hard for you, I appreciate, but a necessary duty."

"Bit of a turnaround," he commented.

"What?"

"You warn me off, tell me not to show my face in the incident room, and now you want me to tell him how it was done. Cool."

Not merely cool. In that atmosphere you could have preserved a mammoth for a million years.

"Well, I've got good news for you, Curtis," Diamond filled the silence. "You won't have to put up with those findings of mine because they don't exist."

"Just what do you mean by that?" Georgina asked.

"Dixon-Bligh didn't murder my wife."

"For God's sake, Peter."

"Will you hear me out?"

She sighed and leaned back in her chair.

Diamond said, "I almost convinced myself he was the killer when I heard he was a junkie. It provided the selfish, blinkered, crazed motive I was looking for. But something didn't fit. I also learned yesterday that he was a chef at the Dorchester."

Georgina took a deep, audible breath. "We know about that."

He nodded. "But you didn't follow it up."

"What do you mean—'follow it up'?"

"I did. This morning I phoned the Dorchester and asked if they happened to know if he reported for duty on February the twenty-third, the morning Steph was murdered. Yes, they said, he was in the kitchen, cooking."

"This I refuse to believe," McGarvie said to Georgina as if Diamond had finally flipped. "How would anyone remember one day in February?"

"Because it was Shrove Tuesday—Pancake Day."

"So?"

"People in the catering business remember Pancake Day. The Dorchester put on a big charity lunch hosted by the Variety Club of Great Britain. All the catering staff were there from early in the morning. It was one of the biggest lunches of the year."

"Is this certain?"

"Dixon-Bligh was in the kitchen at the Dorchester cooking three hundred pancakes."

"So he was definitely innocent?"

"Of murdering Steph? Yes. And almost certainly of murdering Patsy Weather. But there's no question he was involved in the diamond heist that went wrong. His fatal mistake was blabbing to his girlfriend."

For some minutes after Diamond left Georgina's office, nothing was said. McGarvie sat in the armchair shaking his head at intervals.

Eventually, Georgina said, "He's a loose cannon with a habit of hitting the target. A good detective. The best. I only said the things I did because I thought he'd cracked this, gone off and cracked it, and hung you out to dry."

"I know, ma'am."

"But he failed. We all failed. This was one of those wretched cases that beat everyone."

# 33

ON THE FIRST day of November, Curtis McGarvie's overtime budget was cancelled by Headquarters. Inevitably, the Stephanie Diamond inquiry was scaled down drastically, and the decision came almost as a relief to the team. They'd run through their options. Nothing new had come up. McGarvie remained in charge, with Halliwell as his deputy, assisted by three CID officers and two civilian computer operators. These days they rarely stepped outside the incident room.

Peter Diamond observed this with detachment. He'd long since lost any confidence in the murder team. He, too, was becalmed, but he promised himself it was temporary. He would never give up. He still lay awake for long stretches of the night wrestling with the big questions: why had Steph never mentioned her appointment in the park? Who was "T"? What was the link—if any—with the shooting of Patsy Weather?

One rainy afternoon he phoned Louis Voss at Fulham. This wasn't in any way inspired or clever. He just felt the need to talk to someone he trusted.

After they'd got through the small talk he said, "You saw the stuff in the papers about Dixon-Bligh, I'm sure."

"Poor sod, yes," Louis said. "He wasn't your man after all, then?"

"Someone else's. It gives fresh meaning to that old phrase about guarding your tongue."

"Ho-ho. So where are you now on this investigation?"

"Nowhere."

"I can't believe that, Peter."

"None of the suspects measured up."

"Square one, then?"

"Square one—which has to be Fulham nick when you and I and Stormy and Patsy were keeping crime off the streets of West London, or trying to."

"Patsy?"

"Mary Poppins if you prefer—though I thought we'd all moved on since then."

"You're speaking of Stormy's wife?" Louis said.

"Or wife-to-be, in those days. I'm still wondering why those two got hitched."

"She was a good-looking woman, a knockout when she was young."

"That's what I mean. He's a likeable guy, but let's be frank, his looks are against him."

Louis laughed. "Who told you that? Stormy pulled the girls like a tug-of-war team."

Unlikely, he thought. He'd heard Stormy admit to playing away but hadn't pictured him as quite so active. "I can't say I noticed at the time."

"You were a boss man. The guys at the workface knew the score, and Stormy scored more than most. Don't ask me his secret."

Louis had no reason to exaggerate, Diamond reflected. He heard himself say something rather profound. "Maybe women feel more confident with an ugly man. Or more confident of keeping him."

Profound, yet hard to prove. Still, he'd watched a trained protection officer, Gina, mellowing under Stormy's charm offensive even though it had all the subtlety of a Sherman tank. "So did he change his ways after she married him?"

"Did he hell!"

"She put up with it?"

"At a price, no doubt." Now it was Louis who ventured an opinion on the ways of women. "A smart wife has her terms. Read the tabloids. There are plenty of examples."

"Of big divorce settlements?"

"No, of wives who stay married and appear to put up with all the philandering—at a price. They come out the winners."

"So you think she had Stormy's number?"

"Oh, yes," Louis said. "I watched it happen over the years. He had flings, but none of them lasted. She always reined him in."

"Did she play around herself?"

"You're joking. She was more interested in nannying than nooky. She put her energies into chivvying us into being nice to each other—which isn't easy in our job. Well, you know what she was like. A cheery word for everyone."

"I remember."

"No one was better at organising a leaving party. She put on a terrific do for me when I retired. It was such a send-off I felt embarrassed coming back to the civilian job a couple of years later."

"Yes," Diamond said. "She laid on a good party when I left Fulham."

"I remember. And even after her retirement she was always coming back reminding us to organise some do or other that couldn't be ignored. We thought the world of Trish—which made it all the harder to understand why she was murdered."

"Did you just call her Trish?" Diamond asked.

"For Patricia."

"Is that what she was known as?"

"After the Mary Poppins joke was played out, yes."

"Stormy calls her Patsy."

"His privilege. She was Trish to the rest of us. Is this important?"

"I don't know," Diamond said, but he could hear blood pumping through his head like a swan in flight. "I'd better go, Louis. I'll talk to you again."

He put down the phone.

The monstrous thought bombarded his brain. Could "T" have been Trish—a woman? In the weeks immediately after the shooting he'd done his utmost to keep an open mind about the sex of Steph's murderer. But as the main suspects had lined up, all of them male, he'd drifted into thinking only a man could be the killer.

It needed a huge leap of the imagination to cast Patricia Weather as a killer. Nobody ever spoke badly of her. He remembered her as a warm, outgoing personality. She and Steph had probably met once or twice at social events, but they were never close friends. He could think of no reason for them to fix a meeting so many years after he and Steph had left Fulham and gone to live in Bath. And he knew of nothing that could have driven her to murder.

Besides, someone had murdered *her,* for God's sake.

Out of the question, then?

Not when he came at it from another direction. All along, he'd been at a loss to explain why Steph had gone to the park that morning to meet her killer. But if "T" were Trish, sweet, caring Trish, the woman everyone regarded as Mary Poppins, and she suddenly made contact and suggested a meeting, it was possible Steph would have gone along.

Trish, being so efficient, would almost certainly have done the weapons training course in the underground range at Holborn nick. It was on offer in the eighties, and she would have wanted to prove herself as good as the men.

But that was a world away from murdering Steph.

For the millionth time, he came up against this barrier. Why should *anyone* have wanted to kill his gentle, trusting, unthreatening wife?

He reached for a pen and paper and forced himself to jot down her possible motives.

1. *She had a grudge against me.*
2. *She had a grudge against Steph.*
3. *She feared Steph knew some secret about her.*
4. *She was out of her mind.*

None of them stood out. Number one seemed unlikely; she was one of the few colleagues he'd never had a spat with. Two and three were doubtful, considering Steph had never actually worked with the woman and scarcely knew her. And he'd heard nothing about a mental illness.

*Maybe I'm wrong,* he thought. *Maybe they* did *know each other, and I didn't get to hear of it because Steph didn't think it important.*

He picked up the phone and pressed *redial.*

"Louis? Me again. This is a long shot, but do you know anything about Trish Weather's life before she arrived at Fulham?"

"Can't say I do."

"Could you find out?"

"That's personal data, Peter."

"Yes, family, education, previous employment, all that stuff. Should be on her application to join the police, if that's still on file."

"You're not listening," Louis said. "I can't access people's personal files."

"But she's dead, Louis."

The line went silent for a time.

Then Louis said, "Couldn't you get this from Stormy?"

"I'd rather leave him out of it at this stage."

Louis sighed.

He heard nothing back the next day. No bad thing to mark time, he told himself. He'd leapt at the possibility that Trish might be the "I" in Steph's diary. Now he needed to ponder it calmly.

And the more he pondered, the more he feared it was another blind alley.

He'd almost abandoned the idea when Louis phoned back.

"There isn't much, Peter. She applied for the police straight after leaving school. Did her basic at Peel Centre—Hendon, to you and me—and spent a year at West End Central before she started at Fulham. It's a clean record."

"Any firearms experience?"

"She was an AFO from nineteen eighty-seven."

"Was she, indeed!"

"Also did courses on juveniles, driving, race relations and drugs."

"Is there anything on her early life?"

"Not a lot, but this might interest you. She was born and brought up in Bath. She did her schooling at the Royal High School. The family lived in Brock Street."

Brock Street led to the Royal Crescent and Royal Victoria Park. He gave a whistle that must have been painful to hear down a phone line. "Spot on, Louis."

"Does that help?"

"It's not what I was rooting for, exactly, but it may answer one question I've sweated blood over—why they met where they did. You see, the park where Steph was murdered wasn't a place she would have chosen. She had her favourite parks, but the Victoria wasn't one of them. I've always believed her murderer suggested meeting there."

After a pause, Louis said, "Peter, you're not seriously putting Trish in the frame for your wife's murder?"

"Things are falling into place."

"But she's dead. She was the second victim."

Diamond didn't answer. His thoughts were galloping ahead.

Louis waited. "Peter?"

"Yes?"

"I can see problems here. You want to be careful."

"Why?"

"You know what McGarvie and Billy Bowers will think if they get wind of this theory? They'll think you went out and shot Trish Weather yourself." After another long pause he said, "God, I hope you didn't."

## 34

A Mr. and Mrs. Gordon Jessel still lived in Brock Street, Bath, according to the phone directory. A check of the birth registers confirmed that they were the parents of Patricia.

Seized by the need to share the news with someone else, Diamond called Julie Hargreaves that evening and told her he had a new theory that "F" was Patricia—or Trish—Weather. At first she refused to entertain it. But so had he, at first. Julie caught her breath when he mentioned that Trish had been an Authorised Firearms Officer.

"So what do you have here?" she said, assessing the information with the precision he valued so much. "The name beginning with 'T.' The link with Fulham and the police. Experience with guns. The fact that she was brought up in Bath, so she knew where to set up the meeting with Steph. Anything else?"

"Something pretty important. Steph wouldn't have thought of Trish as threatening. She had this friendly personality everyone warmed to."

"Then why?" Julie asked. "What had this charming woman got against Steph?"

"Before I come to that, there's a different 'why.'"

"Yes?"

"Why did Steph go to the park at all?"

"It was fixed. It was in her diary."

"Yes, but what was their reason for meeting? It's not as if they were the best of friends. They met a couple of times when I was serving at Fulham in the eighties, but they didn't know each other well."

"You've worked it out, haven't you?"

"It's preyed on my mind all these months, Julie, and the explanation is so bloody obvious I'm ashamed of myself. Steph gave it to me the night before she was killed and I didn't see it until today."

"Share it, then. I want to hear it, guv."

"You have to know the kind of person Trish Weather was. We called her Mary Poppins in the old days. She was forever chivvying us into behaving properly, doing the right thing, giving presents to anyone who left. She was the mother hen of the place."

"There's usually one."

"Right. I've been told that even after she quit the police to set up her temping agency, she kept dropping in at Fulham nick to look up old friends. It was as if she couldn't bear to leave."

"It happens."

"Now listen, Julie. On the last evening I spent with Steph she reminded me my fiftieth birthday was coming up. What's more she told me some friends had seen an article in the paper that mentioned my age and they were talking about giving me a surprise party. She wouldn't say who. You don't, do you, if it's meant to be a surprise? She was just sounding me out, confirming what she'd guessed already—"

"That you couldn't think of anything worse?"

"You know me and parties, Julie."

"You think Trish was behind the surprise party?"

"I'd put money on it." Immediately he was hit by a doubt. "Don't tell me it was you."

"I didn't even realise you had a special birthday this year."

Relieved, he let his excitement bubble over. "Everything

points to Trish. In the diary Steph actually notes which evenings I'm out, so she can call her and discuss it. She knew very well what my reaction would be."

"You think Steph squashed the idea?"

"No, that wasn't her style. Softly, softly. As I say, she spoke to me first, just to be certain of my reaction. The next day—if I'm right—she meant to break the news to Trish that it wasn't such a good plan. Knowing Steph, she'd want to do it without hurting the woman's feelings."

"She could tell her on the phone."

"No, they fixed to meet. She'd prefer to tell her face-to-face."

"Who suggested the meeting, then? Trish?"

"I think so. She'd have said it would be nice to meet anyway and she came to Bath sometimes to visit her parents. Steph was friendly, as you know. She'd have fallen in with the idea. They picked the park because that was really close to where Trish's people live. Does that sound plausible?"

Julie sidestepped. "But why did Trish bring a gun with her?"

"She had a different agenda."

"Obviously."

"The surprise party was just a blind."

"Okay," she said with a huge note of doubt. "So what turned her into a killer?"

"Julie, that's the big question only one person can answer now."

"Stormy Weather."

He didn't need to confirm it.

Julie said without prompting, "You think Stormy shot his own wife, don't you? He found out she'd killed Steph and he put her down like a dangerous dog."

"He's been a strong support to me," was all he would answer.

"I haven't met the man," she said. "I'm just looking at it coldly. He's a Chief Inspector. You and I know what he'd face if his wife was convicted of the murder of another officer's wife. He'd be finished."

He said indifferently, "I'm not going to shop him."

Julie latched on immediately. "Exactly. What's done is done. If Stormy shot his wife, leave it to Billy Bowers to work it out."

He started to say, "But I have to know why—"

Julie cut in, "Guv, I know how your mind is working. Stay away from Stormy. Don't have any more to do with him. You can only panic him."

Speaking more to himself than Julie, he started the statement a second time and completed it, "I have to know why Steph was murdered and I will."

A November storm hit the West Country that night, uprooting trees and bringing down fences. Roads right across Somerset and Wiltshire were closed by flooding. Diamond decided not to drive. He took the InterCity to Paddington, crossed London on the Bakerloo Line and completed the journey to Raynes Park by a suburban train. And at intervals, resonating with the rhythm of the wheels, he fancied he heard Julie's voice urging him to stay away from Stormy.

Fat chance.

Before doing anything else at Raynes Park, he needed to relieve himself. He found the "Gentlemen" sign on the station platform and discovered from a smaller notice on the door that not every man in Raynes Park was gentle. "*Due to continued vandalism these toilets are locked. If you need to use the facilities please ask a member of staff for the key.*" "I should be so lucky," he said grimly, looking along the deserted platform. There was a similar notice on the ladies' door. He went down the steps and into the street.

A sheet of rain and a buffeting wind hit him when he stepped out of the station. In the street, umbrellas were being blown inside out. He never carried one. He put up the collar of his old fawn trench coat, jammed on his trilby more tightly and set off for Stormy's local shops. They began almost at once, along one

side of Approach Road, and they were about as accommodating
as the station facilities. The pharmacy had ceased trading.
The fish and chip shop wasn't frying. There were a couple of
others with shutters up, covered in graffiti. There *was* a public
convenience. The sign on the door read: THESE TOILETS ARE
PERMANENTLY CLOSED. Driven desperate by the sound and
sight of the rain, he stepped around the back.

Feeling better, he applied his mind to other matters. He
looked for the hairdressing salon. If you want to find out
about a woman without speaking to her husband, try her
hairdresser. A shop on the corner called Streakers had an
art nouveau design, tastefully done, of running nudes with
their hair in curlers. He went in with a gust that blew the
showcards off the counter.

One of the stylists put down her scissors and came over. She
was the manager, he discovered.

"I was wondering," he began when he'd shown his warrant
card, "if by any chance you cut the hair of Mrs. Weather, the
local woman who was shot and found dead by the railway at
Woking." His voice was calm, but he hoped to God he'd struck
lucky. There simply wasn't time to do the rounds of all the
salons in the area.

"Trish was a client of mine, yes," the bright-eyed, thirtyish
manager told him—and it didn't escape him that she used the
"T" word unprompted. She took him into the staffroom and
sent the junior there to sweep the salon floor. "We couldn't
believe it when we heard. She was such a sweet person."

"You said she was your client. You personally did her hair?"

"I did."

"For how long?"

"More than a year, once a week. After she left her job in
the police she had a regular Friday morning appointment.
Personal grooming was important to Trish." She was eyeing
his saturated old mac.

"You got to know the lady well, then? Did she talk about her life?"

She had, quite a bit, he learned. She had been struggling to build up the temping agency. Just when it was starting to take off, a big agency with a chain of branches opened right across the street. They spent a lot in advertising and offered better terms, so her business was hit hard.

The agency didn't interest him at all. "Did her police work ever come up?"

"Not much."

"It was a big part of her life. Didn't she talk about the people she worked with?"

She shook her head.

"Did she ever mention someone called Steph or Stephanie?"

"No."

Some of the gloss was knocked off his theory.

She told him, "I got the impression the work was high pressure but quite satisfying. She missed it after she left. Things got more difficult generally."

"Not just the business, then?" He was alert to each nuance. "Her personal life?"

She smoothed her hands down her white tabard. "If you don't mind, I'd rather not go into that."

"Why not? She's gone."

"But Mr. Weather hasn't."

He told her sharply, "This isn't about being good neighbours, ma'am. It's a murder inquiry. Did she complain about him?"

"No more than other clients do about their husbands. We hear it all. You get them in the chair and they tell you all kinds of confidences."

He waited, and getting nothing, said, "So the marriage was under some pressure?"

"I think being at home Trish had more time in the house and got rather, well, possessive."

"And?"

"I felt sorry for Mr. Weather, to tell you the truth. You know he slept outside in the van? If you went past in the evening, there was often a light on inside."

"I didn't know he has a van."

"When I say 'van,' I mean a caravan thing, except it wasn't a caravan. You could drive it."

"A motor home?"

"Yes. That's what I mean. Big enough to live in. It used to be on their drive."

"It wasn't when I visited. Perhaps he moved it."

"After Trish disappeared he moved back into the house. He must have parked the motor home in some other place. Or sold it."

"You were saying you felt sorry for him," he prompted.

"There was one time when she hurt her leg and couldn't come here, so I went to the house to give her the shampoo and blow-dry and I was really surprised to find how feminine everything was, beautifully clean and tidy and all pink and white with swathed curtains and ballerina pictures on the walls. Dolls and soft toys. A little figure in a crinoline covering the spare toilet roll in the bathroom. There was nothing of him anywhere to be seen."

"Except in the motor home outside?"

"I didn't go in there. I suppose her feminine side had been cramped by the police job. When she got the opportunity, she went a bit overboard."

This made sense to him, and he was glad of the insight into Stormy's marriage. It compensated a little for his disappointment at learning nothing of Trish's feelings towards Steph.

"One more favour, and I'll let you get back to your client. Could I see your appointments book for February and March— or are you computerised?"

"No. We're far too busy to learn. Stay here and I'll send in the junior with it."

With the book in his hands, he flicked back the pages to the months he was interested in. There was obviously a system. Regular bookings were entered by someone in a clear, neat script. The others, arranged a short time ahead, or on the day, bore the signs of being hastily inserted in a variety of styles. He soon located *Mrs. P. Weather* in the tidy hand, each Friday at eleven thirty. She'd booked for the whole of February and March.

There was something else about the system. As clients arrived for their appointments, a tick was placed beside their names. There were ticks for Trish Weather up to Friday, February the twelfth. For the nineteenth and subsequent Fridays her name was crossed through and other names had been squeezed in above.

He took the book out to the manager and showed her. "Does this mean she didn't come in after February the twelfth?"

"That's right."

"Did she cancel?"

"She must have done—or we wouldn't have slotted another client in."

"In person?"

"I really can't remember that far back."

"You must have thought about it when you heard she was murdered."

"They didn't find her for six months. No, I didn't think it mattered. Is it important, then?"

*Is it important?* he thought. For crying out loud, *is it important?*

"If she cancelled, would she have called you personally?"

"Any of the staff could have taken the message. It's a matter of who's free to pick up the phone."

Clearly, she had no memory of speaking to Trish.

"If someone cancels, don't they normally make another appointment?"

"Unless they say they'll get in touch later. If they're ill, somebody might cancel for them."

"The husband?"

"Anyone."

"And if you don't hear from the client after that?"

"We don't chase them up, if that's what you mean. If they don't get in touch again, that's the end of it."

And it was for Trish Weather, he thought.

He left the salon to walk to the Forester, the local he'd visited before. There was a fair chance that by this time, eleven thirty, Stormy would be installed there.

The downpour was so heavy by now that everyone else was sheltering in shopfronts and under awnings. Peter Diamond strode through the rain without caring, his thoughts ten months in the past and a hundred miles away, picturing Steph's meeting with the person who was armed and ready to execute her.

From that day to this the question uppermost in Diamond's mind had been "Why?" Elusive, maddening, paining, it had always been the key. He'd been certain he would find Steph's killer when he understood. He'd not wavered, tortuous as the route had been.

Finally, he knew.

The motive wasn't rage or passion or revenge or greed. It wasn't malice. It was more appalling than any of those: a decision made in cold blood and carried out impassively. Steph had died for no better reason than that she had made a phone call that—unknown to her—undermined a killer's alibi.

He understood enough about the tunnel vision of the murdering mind to know that her life, her individuality, the precious, warm, vital person she was, had not come into the reckoning. She was a risk, so she was eliminated.

Sheer, bloody-minded persistence had gotten him to the truth. No inspiration, no shaft of light, just his refusal to give in.

The saloon bar of the Forester was almost empty. Stormy was in there seated at a table with his back to the door. Inconveniently, someone else was with him, a woman. Dark-haired, well made-up, probably around forty, she was in a backless peacock blue dress you wouldn't have expected to see outside a nightclub.

Diamond marched up to the table and said, "Can we have words?"

Stormy turned in his seat. "Peter?" He tried to make it sound like a greeting and didn't convince. "What brings you out here? You're drenched, man. Get that coat off and let's line up a drink for you."

"Don't bother."

A frown threatened Stormy's face momentarily, and then he recovered to say, "This is Norma—as charming a lady as you'd meet anywhere. Norma, say hello one of my old workmates, Peter Diamond."

Diamond said to the woman, "Leave us alone, would you? We have things to discuss."

She looked to Stormy—who leaned towards her and whispered in her ear. She picked up her coat and walked out of the bar, leaving her drink half-finished.

"What's up?" Stormy asked when Diamond was seated opposite him.

"You want to know what's up?" Diamond said in a hard, tight voice. "Everything's up—for you. I came here not wanting to believe you murdered your wife."

He stared back. "You're not making sense, Peter."

"Did you ever love her?"

"Patsy?"

"Trish. She liked to be known as Trish."

Stormy gripped the tankard in front of him with both hands. "Of course I loved her. Haven't I made that clear?"

"The story I got is that she wouldn't let you in the house."

"I told you we had arguments sometimes. I made no secret of that."

"You slept outside in a motor home."

"Have you been talking to my neighbours?"

"Is it true, then?"

"Sometimes," Stormy admitted. "Model-making is my hobby. We spoke of this, didn't we? I keep my materials in the motor home. I can make a mess in there and nobody bothers, and if I want to work late I can."

"So that's all it was?" Diamond said without irony, as if he was reassured. "Your marriage was okay?"

"Absolutely."

"And you got on all right with the in-laws?"

"I got on fine. I still do."

"Visited them from time to time?"

"Often."

"Strange," Diamond said in a voice as dry as last week's bread, "because when we were sitting in the car on Sion Hill in Bristol you told me you didn't know Bath at all—and it turns out Trish's people live in Brock Street."

For a moment it seemed Stormy Weather hadn't taken in the point. He was still coming to terms with the realisation that his background had been investigated. "In the car we were talking about the Brunel sites. All I said was I haven't seen them."

"No. I asked if you'd been to Bath and you said not since you were a kid. That was a lie."

Stormy didn't deny it.

For Diamond, these were pivotal admissions. The molten rage inside him threatened to erupt any second, yet he had to contain it to get the truth. "What was the problem in your marriage? Was it the fact that you had no children?"

"Plenty of people don't have kids," Stormy pointed out, rashly adding, "You don't."

Don't rise to it, Diamond told himself, don't rise to it. Keep the focus on him. "You admitted to having affairs. Had Trish given up on sex?"

"I don't see where this is leading."

"This Norma I just met. How long have you known her?"

"Leave Norma out of it."

"I can ask the barman or anyone else. I get the impression you're regulars here. Does she want to marry you?"

His silence was as good as a nod.

"But Trish wouldn't let you go, would she?" Diamond pressed on. "She had things sorted as neat as a knitting pattern. The house to herself, all frills and pink wallpaper and nothing out of place. A good pension. A nice welcome any time she wanted to look up old friends at the nick. And this Mary Poppins image of a perfectly managed existence. No, she didn't want a divorce fouling up her tidy life."

Stormy took a long sip of beer, transparently trying to appear calm.

"Your life was bleak, sleeping in the motor home and only allowed into your own house on sufferance. She wouldn't let go, and Norma wanted something more permanent. The pressure got to you."

The calm was ebbing away.

"Like me, you knocked off a police weapon in those Fulham days when old Robbo was mismanaging the armoury. Piece of cake. No big deal. Like me, you tucked the shooter away and almost forgot about it, right?"

"Who told you this?"

"You planned it well. Some time between February the twelfth and the nineteenth you took out your gun and put two bullets into Trish's head."

Now Stormy decided a show of outrage was wanted. "I don't have to listen to this crap."

"You do. You don't know who's waiting outside," Diamond bluffed.

Stormy glanced at the door.

"The timing of the murder is absolutely crucial—because she wasn't killed a couple of weeks after Steph was shot, but *before*."

He swayed back, squeezing his eyes shut as if it were a physical blow. "You can't say that."

"I know it. Trish missed her appointment on the nineteenth."

The eyes shot open and real panic flashed in them. "What appointment?"

"The hairdo."

He stared blankly back.

"The shampoo and blow-dry. You were so cut off from her life you didn't know she went to Streakers every Friday. I've been to the shop and seen the book. She missed the next appointment on the twenty-sixth as well, when she was still alive according to you. And the one after." They were hammer blows and Stormy was reeling from them.

Like any good fighter sensing the end, Diamond didn't relent. "You're a detective. You've seen plenty of killers fail because someone discovered the body. You thought of a very good place where nobody walked their dogs. After shooting her, you drove the body to Woking and dumped it on the railway embankment where it wouldn't be found for months, if not years. Went home with the idea of waiting a couple of weeks before you reported her missing. Devious, that was—to confuse everyone over the date she disappeared, just in case they investigated your movements on the day of the murder."

Stormy grasped the arms of his chair to get up, but Diamond grabbed his shirt-front and held him where he was. "Don't even think about it."

"Free country," he said in a rasp.

"Not any more it isn't—not for you. You thought you'd got it all sussed after you disposed of Trish. You were sitting at home—back in the house you owned—when the phone rang and it was Steph, my wife, expecting to speak to Trish. Awkward. You said she was out and offered to take a message and it soon became obvious they'd arranged to meet in Bath to discuss the surprise party Trish wanted to arrange for my fiftieth. Man, oh man, that threw you, didn't it? Your plan was in ruins. You'd meant to wait another two weeks before doing your worried husband act and reporting your wife missing. But Steph would kibosh that. She'd say it was you she spoke to on the phone, not Trish. She'd say Trish didn't turn up for their meeting. She was trouble."

A strange thing was happening to Stormy's face. The red blotches were standing out like a leopard's spots, separated by patches of dead white skin. His lips, too, were drained of blood. They didn't move.

Diamond leaned closer, still holding him by the shirt, his voice cracking with emotion. "You decided to kill my wife, you sick fuck, simply because she got in the way of your plan. You'd killed once and it was easy, so you'd do it again. Am I right?"

Not a flicker.

"This wasn't done in the heat of the moment. This was premeditated, cold-blooded murder. You thought it through. When you'd worked out what to say you phoned back and told her you'd spoken to Trish and she'd asked you to confirm the time and place of their meeting. It was to be the Crescent Gardens, opposite the old bandstand, at ten. You drove to Bath and waited in the park. When Steph arrived, expecting to meet Trish, you walked up to her and took out the gun and shot her twice in the head. Then you got in your car and drove home."

The eyes confirmed it, even if the voice was silent.

"By killing her, you kept your trump card, the chance to mislead everyone about the date of your own wife's death. You waited another two weeks before reporting that Trish was missing. And ever since, you've been doing your damnedest to lay false trails, insisting on calling her Patsy, putting in the frame every villain we ever crossed, sending me every bloody way but here. I took you for a friend and you're a bloody Judas, the worst enemy I could have had."

The man had nothing to say. His eyes were opaque. He seemed indifferent, passive. But it was a trick.

Abruptly his two hands reached up and smashed down on Diamond's wrist, wrenching it away from the shirt. He stood, wheeled around and made a dash for a door at the back.

Diamond's reaction was slower than it should have been, partly because of where he was seated. The table tipped over and the glasses crashed as he shoved them aside and stepped out. Unfortunately he blundered into a bar stool and stumbled to his knees. The door had slammed before he was on his feet again.

He charged across and yanked it open. He was looking out at the car park, and Stormy Weather was already climbing into the passenger seat of a white motor home driven by the woman in the blue dress. He must have given her the order to wait with the engine running.

Diamond sprinted.

The vehicle had revved and powered away before he made a grab for the door. He grasped the handle and had his right arm tugged almost out of its socket. Acting on impulse and anger alone, he held on, taking huge strides beside the cab, and jerked the door fully open.

A mistake.

He was staring at imminent death, into the muzzle of a gun. Stormy Weather, eyes wild with panic, took aim.

The bullet hit Diamond like a sledgehammer and he fell backwards and knew no more.

## 35

"PETER."

"Mm?"

"How are you doing?"

"Steph?" He tried to rise and felt a searing pain in his chest.

"Stay still, love. Don't fight it."

"Fight what?"

"You can relax. The job's done. You're a brave man."

"Is it really you, Steph?"

No answer.

"Am I dead?"

"Not dead. You'll survive this time, lucky you."

"Love you, too."

"You, too . . . You, too . . . You, too . . ."

She was fading and another voice, not Steph's, was saying, "He's coming round, I think."

He succeeded in opening his eyes and was conscious of someone above him. Devastated, he saw she was not Steph, but a much younger woman in nurse's uniform. He asked, "Where did she go?"

"Who do you mean?"

"Steph was here."

"You must have heard Sister speaking."

"Her sister went back to Liverpool. Where am I?"

"Kingston Hospital. Listen, you're a little woozy from the

injection, and you will be for some time to come, but you're going to be all right, as Sister was trying to tell you."

"Hospital?"

"You were shot in the shoulder. Don't try to move it. The back of your head hit the ground hard, but there doesn't seem to be any damage to the skull. You've got visitors, by the way."

"Steph?"

"Who's this Steph you keep on about?" She spoke to someone else. "He's still bosky, poor bloke. Maybe it's better if he rests for a while."

When he came round again, he was clearer in the head and sadder. The visitors were seated by the bed. They were a youngish man whose face he couldn't put a name to and another he'd never seen in his life.

"Bowers. Billy Bowers," the first man said when it was obvious Diamond was at a loss. "Woking CID, investigating the death of Patricia Weather. Remember?"

"Now I do."

"And this is Sergeant Sims. He was on the search party, but I don't think you met him that day. How are you feeling?"

"Sore."

"Clear-headed?"

"Better than I was. I expect you want to know who shot me."

"Dave Weather. He's in custody."

He flexed and gave himself a stab of pain. "You nicked him? Brilliant!"

"Thanks to the tip-off we got from your friend DI Hargreaves."

He was talking about Julie. What did Julie know about it? With an effort, Diamond recollected his last conversation with her. He'd told her on the phone he was going after Stormy.

"Pity we didn't collar him before he shot you. If only you'd told us—"

"If I'd told you, I wouldn't have been allowed within a mile of him."

"You've got a point there," Bowers admitted with a grin. "We had the tactical firearms unit waiting outside the house. When the shot was fired in the pub car park, they got round fast. Those motor homes aren't built for easy getaways."

"Was there a shoot-out?"

"No, they gave themselves up. We'll release the woman without charge later on, but Weather won't be joining her. He thinks we know the lot, and of course we don't—yet. What I need is your account of what happened."

Later in the day, he was seen by a doctor who told him the bullet had ripped through the deltoid muscle and pierced the scapula. There was some splintering of the bone and he would be kept overnight for some more "hoovering" under anaesthetic. Apart from the scar, there would be no permanent damage.

"You're lucky."

"Oh, yes?"

"Or were you looking for early retirement?"

"A living death? No thanks."

Keith Halliwell came to visit later in the day, a call Diamond appreciated. He brought with him a bottle of malt whisky and a get well card signed by everyone on the Bath murder squad.

"You should have been in the incident room when the news came through, guv. Mr. McGarvie's face had to be seen to be believed. Not only did he screw up, but you got your man and Bill Bowers gets the collar. He's not a happy bunny."

"If I could move my arm I'd wipe away a tear, Keith."

"All I can say is it's lucky for Weather he isn't in our nick. What a weasel, cozying up to you when he'd murdered your wife. How could he do that?"

"It suited him nicely, Keith. When I first offered to work with him he backpedalled a little, but after he thought about it, being with me he was beautifully placed to foul up the works. Any time another suspect was in the frame, whether it was Joe Florida or Wayne Beach or Dixon-Bligh, he said just enough to point the finger their way."

"You must hate the man."

"Hate is too good a word."

"At least you got satisfaction."

Later, after Halliwell was gone, he thought about that word "satisfaction." In earlier times a duellist was said to demand satisfaction for some offence. There had been none in catching Weather nor would there be when he was sent down for life. It had mattered that he was caught. The law of the land would be upheld.

Satisfaction?

No.

Yet he felt less gloomy than he had at the lowest point. He would never admit to anyone that he believed in the supernatural. The words he'd attributed to Steph when he was lying in the hospital bed must have been spoken by one of the nursing staff. Must have. He'd been drowsy from some pain killer, hadn't he?

At the time, he'd believed every word.

Well, someone sounding very like Steph had said the job was done. He was comforted by that, whatever the explanation. In this savage world any comfort is worth holding onto.

# About the Author

PETER LOVESEY WRITES in a garden office he calls his shed, but in reality it's a handsome white shingle-tiled building in the American colonial style. Carpeted, double-glazed and heated, it contains a collection of books on the history of track and field, his other strong interest. As a child in 1948, he was taken to the London Olympic Games and a lifelong enthusiasm was sparked. When, years later, he came across a picture of a Native American named Deerfoot who visited Britain in 1861 and amazed everyone with his running, Peter began a quest to find out more. From this ultimately came his first book, a history of the sport called *The Kings of Distance*.

Encouraged, he entered the 1970 First Crime Novel contest with *Wobble to Death*, based on a Victorian long distance race, and won the £1000 first prize. This launched him as a mystery writer, but he continues his sports research and writing and is a mainstay of the International Society of Olympic Historians.

The Victorian mysteries developed into the Sergeant Cribb series, which really took off when they were televised (leading in UK ratings in the 1980s) and were chosen to launch the PBS *Mystery!* series. One of the Cribb novels, *Waxwork*, was awarded the Silver Dagger of the Crime Writers Association. Peter now has a small armory of such weapons, including the 2000 Cartier Diamond Dagger in recognition of his career. For some twenty years he has been writing the Peter Diamond series, so the honor had an extra cachet.

Peter married Jax, a psychologist he met at university, and she encouraged him to give up his lecturing job and become a full-time writer. As proof of her support, she co-wrote many of the TV episodes, but really she prefers painting and learning foreign languages to writing. While Peter was working on his novels, Jax embarked on a London University degree in Mandarin Chinese. They have a son, Phil, and a daughter, Kathy. Phil is a suspense writer who recently picked up his first Dagger Award for the best short story of the year. Kathy took a different route, moved to America and became a Vice-President at JP Morgan Chase.

Continue reading for a sneak preview of the next
Peter Diamond Investigation

# The House Sitter

After lunch Georgina Dallymore, the Assistant Chief Constable at Bath, took an hour off work and drove out to the cattery at Monkton Combe. She'd decided to board Sultan while she was away on holiday. She needed to be sure it was a place where he would be treated kindly. He wouldn't get the devoted attention he got at home, but he was entitled to some comfort, and she was willing to pay. She'd brought along the framed photo she kept on her desk, just to make clear how special he was.

She expected a better response than she got.

"He's a long-hair, then," Mrs. O'Leary, the cattery owner noted without a word about his good looks. "He'll need grooming."

"Every morning."

"Getting down to basics . . ."

"Yes?"

"Getting down to basics, has he been done?"

Georgina frowned. Even an officer of her rank didn't always catch on immediately. "I don't follow you."

Mrs. O'Leary gave a wink, raised two fingers and mimed the action of scissors. "I won't have rampant males making nuisances of themselves in Purradise."

This was the moment Georgina decided there was no way Sultan would be happy in Purradise. "He was neutered as a kitten, if that's what you mean."

"I should have known, looking at the picture. He's too dopey-looking for a stud. Is he up to date with his injections?"

"Fully."

"Any problems I should know about? Parasites?"

"I don't think I need take up any more of your time," Georgina said, putting the photo away. "I've several other addresses to visit."

"Please yourself. You won't find one better than this."

"I'll make up my own mind, thank you."

"Where are you off to, anyway?"

"That's really no concern of yours."

"I'm not asking which catteries you're trying. I'm talking about your holiday."

Georgina couldn't resist telling Mrs. O'Leary, "Egypt. The Nile Cruise, as a matter of fact."

"Not bad. I thought you police were underpaid."

"It's my first overseas trip in ten years."

"They treated their cats like gods, the Ancient Egyptians. They were more important than people. Did you know that?"

"Yes, and I applaud it. Good afternoon." Georgina turned and walked with dignity towards her car.

"Stuck-up cow," Mrs. O'Leary said. "You'll end up paying through the nose for some house sitter who runs up enormous phone bills and burns holes in your carpet."

But she wasn't heard.

# 1

IF YOU WERE planning a murder and wanted a place to carry it out, a beach would do nicely.

Think about it. People lie about on towels with no more protection than a coating of sunscreen. For weapons, there are stones of all weights and sizes, pieces of driftwood, rope and cable. When it comes to disposing of the body, you're laughing. If a hole in the sand doesn't suit, then with a bit more effort you can cover the victim with stones. After the deed is done, the tide comes in and washes everything clean. Your footprints, fingerprints, traces of DNA, all disappear. Scenes of crime officers, eat your hearts out.

Every half-decent weekend in summer, the shoreline at Wightview Sands on the Sussex coast is lined with glistening (and breathing) bodies. This stretch of beach is estate-owned and spared from the usual seaside line-up of amusement arcades and food outlets. The sand is clean and there is plenty of it, in sections tidily divided by wooden groynes. Lifeguards keep watch from a raised platform. There are no cliffs, no hidden rocks, no sharks.

This Sunday morning in June, the Smith family, Mike, Olga and their five-year-old daughter, Haley, arrived shortly before eleven after an uncomfortable drive from Crawley, paid their dues at the gate, and got a first sight of the hundreds of parked cars on either side of the narrow road that runs beside the beach.

"Should have started earlier," Mike said. The heat had really got to him.

"We'll have plenty of time to enjoy ourselves," Olga said.

"If we can park this thing."

They cruised around for a bit before slotting into a space on the left, sixty yards past the beach café. Outside the car, the breeze off the sea helped revive them. They took their towels and beachbags from the boot. Mike suggested a coffee, but young Haley wanted to get on the beach right away and Olga agreed. "Let's pick our spot first."

Picking the spot was important. They didn't want to sit too close to the lads with shaven heads and tattoos who had several six-packs of lager lined up beside them. Or the howling baby. Or the couple enjoying what looked like a bout of foreplay. They found a space between three teenage girls on sunloungers and a bronzed family of five who were speaking French. Mike unfolded the chairs while Olga helped Haley out of her clothes. The child wanted to run down to the sea with her bucket and spade. The tide was well out.

"Remember where we are," Olga told her. "Just to the right of the lifeguards. Look for the flags."

"You're fussing," Mike said.

"Stay where we can see you. Don't go in the water without us."

"Lighten up, Olg," Mike said. "This is a day out. We're supposed to relax."

Haley ran off.

"If I don't get my fix of coffee soon, I'll die." Mike went in the other direction.

Olga sat forward in her chair and watched every step Haley took. Whatever Mike said, she didn't fuss for fussing's sake. She knew how easily things could go wrong because she'd worked as a nurse in an A & E department before she got married. The beach was new territory. Until the child had been to the water and found her way back at least once, it was impossible to relax.

Briefly Olga's line of sight was blocked by a woman doing exactly what Olga and Mike were doing a few minutes before, choosing the best place to sit down. She was hesitating, taking a good look around her. Olga couldn't see past her. The woman took a few steps down the beach, spread a large blue towel on the sand, unfurled a windbreak and pushed the posts into the sand to screen herself on three sides. To Olga's relief, she could now pick out the tiny figure of Haley again, jumping in the shallows.

The woman took time to get settled. She took off her head-band and shook her hair loose. It was copper-coloured and looked natural too, right for the pale, freckled skin. She was some years older than the giggly girls on sun loungers. Around thirty, Olga reckoned, watching her delve in her beachbag and take out a tube of sunscreen and a pair of sunglasses. Finally she sank out of sight behind the windbreak.

Sunscreen was indispensable today unless you wanted to suffer later. The light was so clear you could see the green fields of the Isle of Wight ten miles across the Solent.

Mike returned with his hands full. "Where's the kid? I got her an ice cream."

Olga pointed Haley out. "You'd better take it down to her."

"My coffee's going to get cold."

She laughed. "Should have thought of that when you bought the ice. All right. Give it to me." Her own coffee was just as certain as his to lose its heat, and she was not one of those submissive women, but she didn't want another argument to ruin the day, so she took the ice cream down the beach, threading a route through the sunbathers, feeling cool drips on her hand and trying not to sprinkle them on other people's warm, exposed flesh. Grateful to reach the damp sand where no one was lying, she kicked off her flip-flops and enjoyed the sensation of the firm surface against the soles of her feet. She felt like a child again.

Haley had found two other girls about her own age and was helping them dig a canal. She didn't want the ice cream, or, more likely, didn't want to eat it in front of her new-found friends.

"Shall I eat it for you?" Olga offered.

Haley nodded.

"You remember where we are? Near the lifeguards. The flags. Remember?"

Another nod.

Olga turned and made her way back more slowly, licking the sides of the ice cream. The beach looked entirely different from this direction. The people, too, when you saw them feet first. She was surprised at where she'd left the flip-flops, much further to the right than she thought. She set a course for the flags above the lifeguard post, beginning to doubt if Haley would have the sense to do the same. Before spotting Mike, she passed the woman with the copper hair, now down to a white two-piece and spreading sunscreen on her middle. Their eyes met briefly. She had a nice smile.

"She all right?" Mike asked, propping himself on an elbow.

"She's with some other girls, digging in the sand. Can you see?"

"What's she wearing?"

Typical Mike, she thought. "Navy and white."

"Right. I can see." He lay back on the sand and closed his eyes.

Typical Mike.

Olga lifted the lid off her less-than-hot coffee, still watching her child. Bits of conversation were going on all around. A beach may be restful, but it's not quiet.

"I didn't fancy him," one of the teenagers was saying. "He's scary."

"What do you mean—'scary'? Just 'cos he didn't have nothing to say to you. That's not scary."

"His eyes are. The way he looked at me, like he was stripping off my clothes."

"You wish!"

The giggles broke out again.

Just ahead, a man in a black T-shirt crossed Olga's line of vision. She could see his top half above the windbreak. He was talking to the copper-haired woman. From the tone of the conversation, they knew each other and he was laying on the charm and not getting the response he was trying for. To Olga's eye, he wasn't an out-and-out no-no. In fact, he was rather good-looking, broad-shouldered, with black, curly hair and the cast of face she thought of as rugged—that is to say strong-featured, with a confident personality defined by the creases a man in his thirties begins to acquire. He was saying something about coincidence. His voice was more audible than hers. "How does it go? Of all the gin joints in all the towns in all the world. . . . For that read "beaches." What are you doing here?" She made some reply (probably "What does it look as if I'm doing?') and he said, "OK, that was pretty dumb. It's a nice surprise, that's all. Can I get you an ice cream or something? Cold drink?" Obviously not, because he then said, "Later, then? You don't mind if I join you for a bit?" Then, "Fair enough. Suit yourself. If that's how you feel, I'll leave you to it. I just thought—oh, what the fuck!" And he moved off, the smile gone, and didn't look back.

Olga glanced towards Mike to see if he'd been listening. His eyes were still closed.

In another twenty minutes the tide was going out amazingly fast across the flats, transforming the scene. Haley hadn't moved, but she was no longer at the place where the waves broke. She was at the edge of a broad, shallow pool of still water. A bar of sand had surfaced further out, and the waves were lapping at the far side. A child could easily become disorientated. The other girls were no longer with her.

"I think I'll go and talk to her," Olga said.

Mike murmured something about fussing.

She made the journey down the beach again, marvelling at the huge expanse now opened up. Men on skateboards were skimming along the wet sand, powered by kites as big as mattresses. A game of beach cricket was under way.

Haley looked up this time and waved.

After admiring the excavations in the sand, Olga asked if she was ready for some lunch. Hand in hand they started back. "I like it here," Haley said.

"Isn't it great? But it's lunchtime. Now let's see if we can find our way back to Daddy."

"There." The child pointed in precisely the right direction. Kids have more sense than adults think.

"Race you, then." Enjoying the sight of her loose-limbed, agile child, she let Haley dash ahead and then jogged after her to make it seem like pursuit, until the risk of tripping over a sunbather forced her to slow to a walk. Already Haley had reached Mike and given him a shock by throwing herself on his back. Laughing, Olga picked her way through the maze of legs, towels and beachbags. The copper-haired woman, comfortable behind her windbreak, looked over her sunglasses, smiled again and spoke. "You're a poor second."

"Pathetic is a better word."

"Wish I had her energy."

"Me, too."

Olga flopped down beside Mike and reached for the lunch bag.

Mike revived with some food inside him and actually began a conversation. "Amazing, really, all this free entertainment. Years ago, people would queue up and buy tickets to see a tattooed man. One walked by just now with hardly a patch of plain skin left on him. No one paid him any attention."

"I wouldn't call that entertainment."

"Then there are the topless girls."

"I haven't noticed any," Olga said.

"Over there, on the inflatable sunbeds."

She took a quick glance. "Girls? They look middle-aged to me. Trust you to spot them."

"I was talking about the way things have changed. Your dad and mine would have paid good money to watch a strip show."

"Not mine."

"Don't you believe it. He was no saint, your old man. I could tell you things he said to me after a few beers."

Olga said, "Let's talk about something else. When are we going for a swim?"

"Not now, for Christ's sake. It's miles out."

Unexpectedly, Haley asked, "Can I bury you, Daddy?"

"What?"

"I want to bury you in the sand."

"No chance."

"Please. The girls I was playing with buried their daddy and it was really funny. All you could see was his head."

"No, thanks."

"You can bury me, then."

"I'm not going to bury anyone."

"Please."

"Later, maybe."

Haley sighed and went down the beach to look for her new friends. Olga, reassured that the child wouldn't get lost, opened a paperback. Mike lit a cigarette and took a leisurely look around him to see if there was more entertainment on view.

The afternoon passed agreeably, more agreeably for Olga when the topless women turned on their fronts.

"A bit creepy, I thought, the kid wanting to bury me," Mike said after a long silence.

"There's nothing creepy about it. It's something children like to do. It's comical, seeing someone's head above the sand and nothing else, specially if it's their own dad."

"If you say so."

"Well, you've got to have a sense of humour."

"There's enough death on a beach without having your own child wanting to bury you."

"I don't know what you're on about."

"You only have to take a walk along the shoreline. You'll see fish half-eaten by gulls, bits of crabs, smashed shells. Nothing is growing. It's a desert, just stones and sand."

"Cheerful!"

"You asked."

Olga may have slept for a while after that. She felt a prod in her back and seemed to snap out of a dream of some sort. The paperback lay closed beside her.

"Time to face it," Mike said. "The tide's turned."

Olga heaved herself onto her elbows and saw what he meant. That big expanse of sand had disappeared. "Oh, my God. Where's—"

"She's OK. Over to the right."

Haley and the others were playing with a Frisbee.

"We must tell her if we go for a swim. I don't want her coming back and finding us gone."

"We'll do it, then."

On the way down, Olga interrupted the Frisbee throwing to tell Haley they wouldn't be long. The child was so involved in the game that the words hardly registered.

The conditions were ideal. The waves had reached the stretch of beach that shelved, so getting in was a quick process, and the water coming in over the warm sand wasn't so cold as she expected. After the first plunge, the two of them held hands and jumped the waves and it was by far the best part of the day. Once when a large wave swept them inwards, Mike lifted her and carried her back to the deeper water. There, they embraced and kissed. The tensions rolled off them like the beads of water.

They stayed in longer than they realised. The people closest to the incoming tide were gathering their belongings and moving higher up.

"Where's Haley?"

Mike didn't answer. He took a few quick steps higher up and looked around.

"Mike, can you see her?"

He said with his irritating, offhand manner, "She'll be somewhere around."

"I can't see the girls she was with. Oh, God. Mike, where is she?"

"She won't be far away."

"We've got to find her."

"You told her we were going for a swim. She saw us."

"But she isn't here."

He began to take it seriously. "If she's lost, someone will have taken her up to the lifeguards. I'll check with them. You ask the people who were sitting near us."

She dashed back to their spot. No sign of Haley. The woman with copper hair was lying on her side as if she'd been asleep for hours, so Olga spoke to the teenagers.

"No, I'd have noticed," one of them said. "She hasn't been back since you ate your sandwiches. Pretty little kid with dark hair in bunches, isn't she?"

"You're sure you haven't seen her?"

"We've been here all the time. She went the wrong way, I expect. Not surprising, is it, with all these people?"

Olga asked the French family. They seemed to understand what she was saying and let her know with shrugs and shakes of the head that they hadn't seen Haley either. She looked up to where the lifeguards had their post, a raised deck with a wide view of the beach. Mike was returning, looking about him anxiously.

She felt the pounding of her heart.

"They're going to help us find her," he said when he reached her. "It happens all the time, they told me. All these sections between the groynes look the same. They say she's probably come up the beach and wandered into the wrong bit."

"Mike, I don't see how. I told her several times to look for the flags."

"Maybe there's another flag further along."

"She'll be panicking by now."

"Yes, but it's up to us not to panic, right?"

Easy to say.

"You stay here. This is the place she'll come back to. One of us must be here," he said. "I'll check the next section."

She remained standing, so as to be more obvious when Haley came back—if she came back. Appalling fears had gripped her. A beach was an ideal hunting ground for some paedophile. Her Haley, her child, could already be inside a car being driven away.

"She'll be all right," one of the teenagers said. "Little kids are always getting lost on beaches. It happened to me once."

Olga didn't answer. She was shivering, more from shock than cold. Supposedly a non-believer, she started saying and repeating, "Please God, help us find her," out there on the beach. All around her, people continued with their beach activities, unaware of her desperation.

Mike came quickly around the edge of the groyne shaking his head. He wasn't close enough to be heard, but it was obvious there was nothing to report. The worry lines were etched deep. He pointed as he ran, to let Olga know he would search the section on the other side. She folded her arms across her front. Her teeth were chattering.

"Why don't you cover up your shoulders?" one of the

teenagers suggested. "There's a wicked breeze since the tide turned." She got up and brought a towel to Olga. "Try not to worry, love," she said, wrapping it around her and sounding twice her age. "Someone will bring her back."

Olga couldn't speak. She wanted to be doing something active towards finding Haley, organising search parties, alerting the police. Instead, she had to stand here, gripped by fear and guilt. How selfish and irresponsible she had been to go for that bathe and stay so long in the sea. She'd put Haley completely out of her mind while she and Mike enjoyed that stupid romp in the waves.

"Isn't that your little girl?"

"What?" She snapped out of her stupor.

The teenage girl who had brought her the towel was still beside her. "With the man in the red shorts on the bit above the beach."

"Oh, my God!" Haley, for sure. She was holding the hand of a strange man, the pair of them standing quite still. Olga screamed Haley's name and started running up the beach towards them. "She's mine! That's my child! Haley!"

Haley shouted, "Mummy!" and waved her free hand. The other was still gripped by the man, a shaven-headed, muscled figure in tight fitting red shorts that reached to his knees. He didn't attempt to leave.

Continuing to shriek, "He's got my child! That's my child!" Olga scrambled up the steep bank of pebbles, nightmarishly slipping back with each step yet oblivious of the pain to her bare feet.

As soon as she was close enough she shouted, "What are you doing with my child?"

He called something back. It sounded like, "Easy, lady."

"Let go of her!"

She stumbled the last steps towards them and heard him say, "I just found her. I'm the lifeguard."

She had to play over in her brain what he had said because it was so clear in her mind that he was evil, a child snatcher.

But when she reached the stone embankment above the pebbles, the man released Haley, who flung herself at her mother with arms outstretched.

"Oh, Mummy—I was lost."

"What happened? Are you all right, darling?"

"This man found me."

He said, "Did you hear me, Mrs? I'm the lifeguard. She was in our hut. One of her friends went there for first aid."

"One of those girls I was playing with was hit in the face by the Frisbee," Haley said. "It wasn't me that threw it. Her eye was hurt, so we all went up to get some help. She's all right now. Her mummy came and took her and her sister away. I was left. I couldn't see you anywhere."

Olga felt tears streaming from her eyes. She apologised to the lifeguard, and thanked him all in the same sentence. Haley was still in her arms, gripping her possessively. She'd had a big fright. Olga carried her back to their spot on the beach. Mike hadn't returned, but the people around smiled and asked if Haley was all right.

Olga explained what had happened. She looked in the picnic bag and found a can of drink for Haley. "We'll be leaving as soon as Daddy gets back," she said. "The tide's coming in, anyway."

People were packing up all around them. The French family dismantled their windbreak and folded their towels. The teenagers said goodbye and carried the loungers back to the store. Of those around them, only the copper-haired woman appeared intent on staying until the tide forced her to move. It was practically at her heels.

"Where's Daddy?"

"He went looking for you. He'll be back soon."

"We'll have to get up soon, or we'll get wet."

"I know. We can give him a few minutes more. We might have to meet him at the car."

"Is he cross with me?"

"I'm sure he isn't. We'll tell him what happened."

Olga used the time to fold the towels and fill the bags.

Presently Haley asked, "Why isn't that lady packing up? Her feet must be getting wet."

The child was right. The woman hadn't made any attempt to move yet.

Olga couldn't see her properly. The windbreak was around her head and shoulders. Probably if Olga hadn't already made such an exhibition of herself she would have popped her head over the canvas and said, You'd better move now, sweetie, or you'll get a wave over you any minute. The experience with Haley had temporarily taken away her confidence.

A little further along, the lager lads with their empties heaped in front of them were watching with obvious amusement the progress of the tide towards the woman's outstretched feet.

Olga looked round for Mike, and there he was at last, striding towards them.

"Brilliant! She came back, then. Are you OK, Hale?"

Haley nodded.

Mike kissed her forehead. "Thank God for that."

Olga started to explain what had happened but was interrupted by Haley.

"Mummy, don't you think we ought to wake the lady up? She's going to drown."

"What are you saying?" Full of her own drama, she'd shut everything else out of her mind. Now she saw what Haley was on about. "God, yes. Mike, you'd better go to her. She's out to the world. I don't know what's the matter with her."

He said, "It's none of our business, love."

"There's something wrong."

With a sigh that vented all the day's frustration, he stepped the few paces down the beach to where the water was already lapping right around the windbreak. He bent towards the woman. Abruptly he straightened up. "Bloody hell—she's dead.'